Bernardine Kennedy was born in London but spent most of her childhood in Singapore and Nigeria before settling in Essex, where she still lives with her partner Ian and teenage daughter Kate. She also has an adult son, Stephen. Her varied working life has included careers as an air hostess, a swimming instructor and a social worker. She has been a freelance writer for the past thirteen years, specialising in popular travel features for magazines. Her other novels, EVERYTHING IS NOT ENOUGH and MY SISTERS' KEEPER, are also available from Headline.

Bernardine Kennedy's website address is
www.bernardinekennedy.com

Chain of Deception

Bernardine Kennedy

headline

First published in 2003
by HEADLINE BOOK PUBLISHING

First published in paperback in 2003
by HEADLINE BOOK PUBLISHING

A HEADLINE paperback

10 9 8 7 6 5 4 3 2 1

Cataloguing in Publication Data is
available from the British Library

ISBN 0 7553 0090 4

Typeset in Plantin by
Letterpart Limited, Reigate, Surrey

Printed and bound in Great Britain by
Mackays of Chatham plc, Chatham, Kent

Papers and cover board used by Headline are natural,
recyclable products made from wood grown in sustainable
forests. The manufacturing processes conform to the
environmental regulations of the country of origin.

HEADLINE BOOK PUBLISHING
A division of Hodder Headline
338 Euston Road
LONDON NW1 3BH

www.headline.co.uk
www.hodderheadline.com

For All My Family,
Especially Ian, Steve, Kate, Amy
and Nadine

Prologue

As the smiling couple strolled from the church porch into the July sunshine, the gathering of passers-by who had stopped for a curious look at the bride and groom all gasped in unison and then slowly a gentle ripple of applause spread down the street.

The groom, tall and fair with well-formed muscles visible through his morning suit, gazed proudly down at his new wife who, despite the broad smile, blushed and lowered her head slightly at the spontaneous acknowledgement from the unknown crowd.

'Who are they?' the groom whispered out of the side of his mouth, the smile still firmly in place.

'Not a clue, they're all just passing, I think, and stopped to look, the way we all do when there's a wedding.'

Arm in arm the couple carried on walking and as they made their way down the small flight of steps, the guests from inside suddenly spread out all around them, engulfing the newlyweds in a sea of smiling faces and elaborate hats.

A woman stepped forward quickly, noticeably marking out her territory as mother of the bride. The similarity between mother and daughter was eye-catching and the only thing that separated the two was the natural ageing process, although as far as the mother was concerned that looked as if it had been halted ten years previously.

'Oh Lucy, Daddy and I are so proud of you, you look absolutely stunning, and of course you too, Don, just too handsome for words . . .'

The perfectly enunciated words carried over the guests who all murmured agreement.

'And of course the bridesmaids, and the best man – oh, this is all so exciting. Our little girl, a grown-up married woman.'

'Calm down, my darling, you'll be in tears again and that will start us all off.' The father of the bride, his arm sliding protectively round his wife's waist as he spoke, smiled conspiratorially at his daughter.

Lucy looked from one to the other, smiling happily; she couldn't imagine how she could ever feel happier than she did at this moment. She had just married a man she was totally besotted with, her best friend Sadie was chief bridesmaid and her parents had, with absolutely no expense spared, put together the perfect wedding. In fact, everything was perfect.

Well, almost perfect, Lucy thought as she looked around her. Standing slightly apart from the other guests, was her new mother-in-law, looking angrily in their direction with the usual pinched and pained expression on her skeletal features. Beside her slouched her other son who looked to Lucy as if he had actually dressed down for the occasion –

2

his tie was loosened already, his jacket slung carelessly over his arm, his shirt sleeves rolled up almost to his elbows. Quite openly he glared across at Don and Lucy.

'Right, everyone, it's time for the photographs, so on your marks . . .' As the father's voice rose humorously above the crowd, it was impossible not to notice the mother of the groom's face almost sink in on itself with dislike as her gaze swept the scene in front of her. Everyone in the immediate family noticed the woman grab her other son by his sleeve and drag him away. That was the last they saw of either of them.

A shadow passed over Donovan Cooper's face as he watched his mother do her best to humiliate him and spoil his day. Lucy gripped his arm reassuringly; although upset for her new husband, she was also relieved. It was the first time she had seen Don's estranged mother and brother and she could not stop herself hoping that it would be the last.

Don wasn't relieved to see them go, he was furious although desperately trying not to show it. He had wanted both of them to stay for the whole event. For weeks he had been anticipating the gnashing of jealous teeth from the pair of them when they realised the full extent of his social and financial rise via his new bride. In fact the whole elaborate wedding, with no expense spared, had been arranged with that in mind, as far as he was concerned.

The rest of the day passed without a hitch and in a flash, or so it seemed to Lucy, they were upstairs in the hotel room getting ready to leave for their honeymoon cruise around the Caribbean.

'Well, Mrs Cooper, how does it feel to be my wife?' Don was watching Lucy as she touched up her make-up ready for the big departure.

'Really strange actually. Me, a married woman! Though I'm sure I'll get used to it. Mrs Cooper.' Lucy rolled the name around thoughtfully. 'That sounds really odd, I can't imagine myself as Mrs Cooper. Mind you, I'll have to carry on using my maiden name at work, everyone knows me now and my clients—'

'Like hell you will', Don interrupted sharply, a little too sharply. 'You're Mrs Cooper now, my wife, married to me and that's how I want you to be known. Stuff your clients.'

Lucy blinked. For a second or two she wondered if he was joking but the intense expression that darkened his face told her that Don was deadly serious.

'I want everyone to know that we're married, that you're mine. My bitch of a mother would love it if you didn't take my name, she'd see it as you putting one over on me. I'd never hear the end of it.' Suddenly he smiled. The broad, gleaming smile that lit up his handsome face and made Lucy go weak at the knees. 'Come on, Mrs Cooper, let's go and face the crowd again. It won't be long before we'll be relaxing in the sun, topping up the tan and sipping ice-cool cocktails under the Caribbean sky.'

Lucy smiled and put her arms round his neck. 'I love you, Don, and of course I'll be Mrs Cooper. I'll be whatever you like, just so long as we're together for ever.'

Because her face was buried in his neck, Lucy didn't see the smile of victory that lit up Don's face. Lucy, and everything she owned, now belonged to him and the ground rules were laid down in that defining moment. Lucy had deferred to him, her husband. And he knew she would continue to do so.

Donovan Cooper's ship had come in.

Chapter One

Standing by the wide plate-glass window with her back to the open-plan office, Lucy looked at her slightly blurred reflection. Tall, blonde and immaculately turned out, she appeared every inch the successful career woman with the world at her feet. The woman that everyone thought she was.

If only, she thought wryly.

Trying to look nonchalant, she quickly punched a number into her mobile phone while at the same time tapping her foot impatiently, her hand cupped over her mouth in an attempt to shield her voice.

'Oh, sod it, sod it.' The words came out louder than she intended as she snapped the phone shut sharply in frustration and stuffed it into her skirt pocket. Her eyes looked out over the bustling London street four storeys down but she saw nothing. Her mind was far away from Pettit's PR Consultancy.

'What's up, Lucy? Talking to yourself again?' Paul looked over at her and grinned with one dark eyebrow quizzically raised. 'One of the first signs of madness, that. Job must be getting to you. I don't know, women. They really can't hack it in the workplace. Back to the kitchen for you all, I say, barefoot and pregnant with a sprog on each hip!'

Lucy slowly and deliberately looked him up and down dismissively. Paul had the eyes and ears of a bird of prey, absolutely nothing got past him and she mentally kicked herself for dropping her guard but she also knew she couldn't keep disappearing out of the office to make phone calls, even short, sharp non-productive ones.

Lucy and Paul had both started at the firm at about the same time and were more competitive with each other than with anyone else. Both were good at their jobs, both were young and ambitious and both of them wanted to be the best.

'I was just trying to get through to my accountant, is that a problem? This is my personal mobile. Mine, not yours,' she snapped. 'Not that it's any of your business.'

Trying to look cool and calm she walked back to her desk but she was concerned and having problems hiding it. Fergus had been incommunicado for over a week and it worried her. Usually they spoke at least twice a day and exchanged regular nonsensical text messages, so either something dire had happened or he was avoiding her.

Swiftly dismissing the unwanted thought that maybe he had had enough of her, enough of the subterfuge, she started fiddling with the wad of post that had appeared in her tray. She heard Paul talking and caught the words, 'Accountant my arse. The ice maiden wouldn't get that stressed about an accountant, she's found herself a shot of a de-icer on the side. I recognise the signs.' His laugh drifted over towards her. 'Never employ women in men's jobs, I say. Their hormones always let them down eventually. They're all just so predictable. Present company excluded, of course.'

The accompanying giggle told her that Paul's audience was again the silly young temp who spent nearly all her time hanging on his every word and twittering like a hungry baby sparrow at his every joke, funny or not.

Eighteen, slender as a reed with a thick mane of auburn hair and a short leather skirt that barely skimmed the top of her tights, Daniella Schwarz had gravitated towards a receptive Paul from day one. Charming and confident, Paul always had a fan club on the go, they all loved him and he could charm anyone from eight to eighty with his ready smile and jovial flattery. Lucy was only too aware of Paul's agenda with women. It was always the thrill of the chase with him. Charm them, hopefully bed them, dump them and then make it impossible for them to stay with the company. More temps had passed through Pettit's, it seemed, than the local employment agency itself.

'Paul?' Lucy smiled sweetly in his direction. He swivelled round on his chair to face her, the expectant grin hovering as always.

'What would you like, oh precious one? My body? Have you finally succumbed to the inevitable?' Opening his brilliant blue eyes wide, Paul looked at her. The slight smirk on the edge of his lips annoyed Lucy out of all proportion.

'Watch my lips – piss off back to the school playground, little boy, and take your schoolgirl friend with you! You are just so bloody arrogant and sexist, one day someone, somewhere, will take you seriously and you'll end up in court. What you really need is a good castrating. Could my cat recommend an excellent vet?'

The twittering got even louder but she tried to ignore it, silently cursing herself for letting the stereotypical office flirt get to her, especially as it wasn't really him she was annoyed with. Now they would have a field day in the office and Paul would be even more determined to make her life difficult. She tried to concentrate on the work piled up in front of her but the words and figures danced before her eyes.

Why was Fergus's phone permanently switched off? Why hadn't he called? Why hadn't he been seen around the office? As a motorbike courier he often came into the building and found an excuse to ask for her but lately . . . nothing.

'Lucy, do you still want your calls fielded? Only I've got your Don on the line, says it's urgent he speaks to you now.'

Lucy felt her heart start banging away; the last person she wanted to talk to was her husband Donovan but she knew she would have to. He was so unpredictable, he could easily start hurling abuse at the voice on the other end of the phone, regardless of who it was.

'It's OK, Sal, I'll take it.'

She couldn't resist a glance at Paul to see if he was still monitoring her every movement. It was an open secret that Paul Gower would love to put one over on Lucy and snatch her potential promotion. She was well into paranoia about it, but Lucy knew that whether Paul was listening or not she had to take the call, to check that nothing was amiss.

'Hello, is that you, Don?'

'Yes of course it's *me Don*, you daft bitch,' he snarled down the line.

'What's so important? You know the company's line on personal calls.' Just the sound of her husband's voice depressed her and she found it hard to disguise her impatience.

'So nice to know you're pleased to speak to me, my darling wife,' the sarcasm dripped down the phone line, 'but I thought you'd like to know that that stupid plumber hasn't turned up and your mobile was busy – it's really strange how you used to be able to talk to me from work but now all of a sudden, since you've frozen me out, the policy has changed.'

A surge of anger swept over her. She was the one working and supporting both of them but still he expected her to deal with everything while he divided his time equally between his bed, the gym and the trendy wine bar on the corner, full of gullible young girls who readily fell for his chat-up lines. Lines that didn't include 'I'm married'. Don liked to pretend he actually worked – he told everyone that he worked and Lucy knew that he really did see it as a job. But it wasn't real. The only reimbursement he received from the exclusive London gym was cash-in-hand pocket money and a few perks. None of this was any help to Lucy.

'Don, surely even you can manage to pick up the phone to a plumber and find out why. The number's on the pad beside the phone. Now I have to go. I've told you before, all our calls are being monitored. I cannot make or take private calls. I'll see you tonight.' Before he had a chance to respond she replaced the receiver and opened a file.

Her apprehension made it easy for her to lie about calls being monitored. She would have said anything to get Donovan off the phone before she had to listen to a tirade of abuse within earshot of Paul.

Unable to concentrate any longer, she stood up purposefully and picked a couple of imaginary bits of fluff off her skirt before grabbing her jacket from the back of her chair. She slipped it on and slid a few files into her briefcase.

'Anyone wants me I'm lunching with a client. I'm on the mobile and I'll be back about two thirty.'

As she expected, Paul's antennae starting twitching. Sometimes she felt he spent his working day watching her, waiting to catch her out.

'Might I ask which client? Not that I personally give a toss, it's just in case Caroline asks. I assume you're answerable like the rest of us?' She opened her mouth to answer but he continued, 'And what's all that crap about calls being monitored? Taken to lying to the old man, have you?'

'Get a life, Paul, and stay out of mine,' Lucy snapped at him. 'If Caroline wants to know where I am and who I'm with, I'll tell her, but you can just mind your own goddamned business.'

In the washroom, Lucy checked herself in the full-length mirror. The classic and beautifully cut black designer suit and dateless patent Gucci shoes, the uniform of PR girls all over the capital, were businesslike and spotless but the cold efficiency of the outfit was softened by a pale pink cashmere roll-neck and a pair of delicate diamond studs in her ears.

As she ran a brush through her natural blonde bob she wondered vaguely if it was time for a trip to the hairdresser. Normally shiny and sharply trimmed, it was looking a little lank, and although her make-up was perfect, nothing could completely disguise the black rings under her eyes and the pallid complexion that reflected too much worry and not enough sleep. She carefully touched up her lipstick and blusher to add some colour. Soon, something would have to give or she would go mad. Despite the circumstances, the guilt Lucy felt at deceiving her husband was overwhelming and it was starting to show. She was also being economical with the truth to Paul, and Lucy felt another twinge of conscience. She never usually sneaked off during office hours, in fact she was often the only one working overtime, but she had to get out of there and away from Paul before she said something she knew she would regret.

The meeting with her client wasn't scheduled for another two hours but she wanted, needed, to go and have a strong caffeine hit and a cigarette in peace beforehand. No Paul aggravating her, no Don on the phone harassing her, just a little time alone to think about Fergus. Where was he?

The open-plan coffee shop tucked away up a side street was bustling with early lunchers but she found an armchair in the corner. Opening her folder of notes to look busy, too busy for conversation if anyone tried, she let her thoughts drift. Fergus. Why hadn't she heard from him? Gentle, laid-back Fergus who had lately made her life worth living despite the horrors of a crumbling marriage to macho man Donovan Cooper.

On the dot of seven thirty, Lucy put her key in the lock of the communal front door of her block of flats. She prayed Don would be out. The lunch hadn't gone well and she had had to pull out all the stops to hang on to the account. She hated being flirty and pandering to the ego of her detestable but nonetheless important client, but she was very aware that if she had lost the profitable account, been unable to persuade the lecherous bastard from the up-and-coming travel company to stay with Pettit's, then without doubt the promotion to senior executive would go to Paul. Caroline was a fair boss, but also a shrewd and successful businesswoman with no time for losers.

To cap it all, Paul had deliberately set out to rile her when she got back, her punishment, she knew, for putting him down in front of Daniella the temp. It had taken all her willpower not to smash him on the chin and walk out for good. Deep down she knew he was only teasing her, showing off in front of an audience, but at that moment the last thing she needed was someone else going on at her. Her husband was more than enough.

Feeling more like forty-seven than twenty-seven, she took a deep breath before trudging up two flights of stairs, an overflowing M & S carrier bag of groceries in each hand and a heavy briefcase weighing down her shoulder. Pausing at the door to the flat, she listened carefully and her heart sank as she heard the sound of the television drifting out into the hallway.

He was in.

Dumping the heavy, over-filled bags down, she switched her mobile to a silent ring and despondently let herself into the flat that had once been her pride and joy but which was now more like a battle zone. Every day it became harder to make the journey home.

Forcing herself to be civil, she smiled. 'Hi there, I'm back. God, what a day I've had . . .'

Before she could continue he started.

'Decided to come home at last, have you? I wondered if you'd managed to find yet another business dinner to go to, more friends to see, more fun to be had. Without me, of course, as usual.'

Don didn't bother to look at her but, from the petulant tone of his voice and the pout of his lips, she knew he was all geared up for a row. It always followed the same route. Dinner that allegedly wasn't up to his standards, a blazing row and then he could sanctimoniously justify storming off to pose in the bar for the night, lapping up all the admiring glances that he invariably attracted. The scenario was all too familiar to Lucy, it happened far more often than not.

'I had to stop on the way for the shopping, I told you this morning. Now I've really had a lousy day at work, and I'm tired, so please don't start, I haven't got the energy. I've had Paul Gower on my back and I had to deal with a difficult client. I'm completely knackered, Don.'

She glanced at the muscular, almost naked man lounging full length on the cream leather sofa, a large glass of whisky in one hand and the remote control in the other. Once again she wondered how someone so obsessed with fitness and physique could happily slob around indoors in minuscule underpants, little bigger than a posing pouch, doing nothing. His life was one long holiday centred around the gym, Body Beautiful Inc., where they had met. The gym where he had romanced her with a determination that she could now see was fired by her ability to provide for him and his hobby. In the beginning she had fallen for his story about training to be an instructor, whereas of course he was really only a part-time assistant who was paid a small salary plus free use of the equipment when the gym wasn't busy. It wasn't even enough for his day-to-day spending, let alone contributing anything to their sky-high London living costs and his luxurious needs and wants.

Although Donovan still physically resembled the muscular, handsome man she had met, fallen in love with and married, he certainly wasn't the man she had thought he was. His true character had slowly but surely emerged, turning him into someone she no longer recognised, someone she disliked intensely and was now frightened of. With hindsight she could see that the signposts had been there all along but, carried along by the romance of it all, she had not picked up on them until it was too late.

It had started shortly after they were married with almost childlike demands on her time, followed by continuous demands on her bank account. Lucy had eventually agreed to a joint account, convincing herself that it wasn't Don's fault she earned so much more than he did, but Don had viewed the account as a bottomless pit and the more he spent the more he wanted. Every time Lucy capitulated, the demands had increased. Towering over her and standing suffocatingly close, he would use his obviously superior strength as an unspoken threat. If she tried to stand her ground, Don would keep on and on, sometimes for hours, until she could stand it no longer and gave in.

The final straw had been a few short weeks earlier when Don had demanded that she increased the limit on her credit card to what Lucy thought was a completely unrealistic amount. When she had tried to reason with him, he had erupted into a fearsome rage, far worse than she had ever seen before, that had culminated in physical violence.

Don still didn't look up as she walked through to the kitchen to unpack the shopping. She glared at the dirty dishes spread all over her carefully chosen granite worktops and the congealed mess on the stainless steel hob. She heard Don calling through to her but chose to ignore him. He raised his voice a notch.

'I said, what's for dinner? I'm starving, not had anything since that poxy little sandwich at lunchtime that you left in the fridge. I need my bloody meals on time if I'm going to be able to compete in these competitions. Nutrition is important to me as you well know. Not that you give a toss about my career, you selfish bitch. It's all me, me, me, with you, isn't it?'

Despite the edge in his voice she still ignored him and continued unpacking the groceries. The mountain of dirty dishes that he hadn't even bothered to put in the dishwasher told a different story. Donovan Cooper always ate like a horse, one sandwich at lunchtime was simply not on his menu.

Suddenly the volume of the television increased and Lucy could hear him channel hopping through the state-of-the-art satellite system that she never had time to watch but had to pay for each month, along with every other expense associated with married life. Since the day they had got married Don had contributed nothing either financially or emotionally.

The television boomed and the pressure built inside her until she couldn't stand it any longer, and without thinking of the consequences she picked up the remaining full bag of shopping, stormed into the lounge and dropped it straight into his lap.

'What the fuck . . .'

'You wanted your dinner, well, here it is. First you unpack it, then you cook it and then you get to eat it. That's how you get a meal on the table, just in case you hadn't noticed, and after that, surprise, surprise, you clear up. That's the process that I go through every night after a full day's work. Not that you understand the meaning of the word work.'

Don leapt to his feet, throwing the bag to the floor. Tins and packets flew across the room as he scrambled towards her, spilling his drink over the fluffy off-white carpet in the process. Standing her ground, Lucy folded her arms and stared.

'Yes, Don? What are you going to do? Hit me again? Go on then, do it, get it over with and then you can get out of my life and my home for good. I've had enough!'

He stood in front of her, a good head taller and considerably broader than his wife, clenching and unclenching his fists as he tried to control himself, his handsome face distorted with the fury he was trying to contain.

'Oh, no way, Lucy-Lou, you'll never provoke me into

that again, no way. I'm not going anywhere, this is my home whether you like it or not.'

The steely blue eyes looked straight into hers and again she felt the cloud of fear that he always invoked in her when he was angry, and lately he was always angry. Angry with everything, including his wife. Especially his wife.

'We're married and what's yours is mine so I'm certainly not going anywhere. Not heard of communal property?' His voice was venomous as he glared directly into her eyes. 'If you don't like it why don't you piss off? Go on, run back to Mummy and Daddy, I'm sure they'll set you up again at the drop of a hat. Anything for their precious little princess.' He reached out and tried to grab her arm but she stood rigid, both arms defiantly glued across her midriff, matching his glare.

His face was so close she had no choice but to inhale his alcohol-fuelled breath and it nearly made her gag. His mouth stretched in the semblance of a smile as he looked down at her. The muscles in his arms flexed and the distended veins in his neck bulged dangerously.

'Have you forgotten the immortal words you lovingly declared to me? In a church, no less?' His brittle smile widened. ' "Till death us do part" was one bit, and how about "all my worldly goods I thee endow"?'

Lucy smiled back with her mouth but her eyes glistened with unshed tears. 'I didn't realise then that you were nothing but a lazy slob with no scruples about living off his wife. Sorry, Don, but I'm not your meal ticket and neither are Mummy and Daddy.' Turning swiftly, Lucy walked out of the lounge. She was terrified he would grab her from behind.

The last time he had stood nose to nose with her like that he had grabbed her upper arms so tightly that the bruises took days to fade. The accompanying head butt had left a scar that was still livid pink but camouflaged now by a newly cut fringe. She had screamed and cried and then afterwards vowed never again to let him see her hurting in any way, either mentally or physically.

This time he let her go but she could hear the bitter laugh as he mimicked her. 'Mummy and Daddy, Mummy and Daddy. How old are you? You sound like a fucking five-year-old.'

Behind the safety of the locked bathroom door she undressed and wrapped herself in the comforting fluffy bathrobe her parents had sent her for her birthday. She perched on the step of the corner bath and watched the swirl hypnotically for several minutes before looking critically at her reflection in the wall-to-ceiling pink-tinted mirrors.

The tear-stained face that looked back at her bore little resemblance to the smiling, happy face on her wedding day. Just as the sneering and vicious man sprawled in front of the television was nothing like the one she had married just a few years before. She wondered again how someone she had been totally in love with could have changed so much. Donovan Cooper, the gentle giant she had fallen for, had somehow changed into an unpredictable and unreliable King Kong of a man with a paranoia that was making her life frighteningly unbearable.

Checking her jacket pocket, she was relieved to find her phone. She clicked it open and dialled.

'Sadie?' she whispered. 'It's me. Can I come round this

evening? I really need someone to talk to.'

After a long soak in the bath she cautiously unlocked the door. A look round reassured her that Don must have gone out. She darted into the bedroom and, hair still damp, pulled on a pair of Lycra leggings, T-shirt and trainers. Sadie didn't live far away so Lucy was intending to jog there and clear her head en route.

But as she left the flat she was confronted by Don. He was waiting for her at the top of the stairway, leaning casually against the banister. She noticed that he was dressed top to toe in new clothes. The most expensive designer sportswear that her salary and credit card could provide, she thought wryly.

'I wondered how long it would be before you came out.' He looked her up and down in fake appreciation. 'Not bad! Who's the lucky fella then?'

'I'm going for a jog, Don, isn't that obvious? Even someone as intellectually challenged as yourself should realise that.'

'Oh, I do realise, I'm not as stupid as you like to think, but it's where you're jogging to that's important. Maybe I ought to join you.' Two steps and he was in front of her, using his massive shoulders to block her way.

Lucy sighed and gave in. 'If you must know I'm going to see Sadie. I promised I'd drop in after dinner but as you seem to have lost your appetite I'm not going to bother to cook.'

'Yeah, right, so you're going to Sadie's, are you?'

'Yes, I am, but what about you? You've brushed yourself up quickly. Which poor little bimbo is going to be on the receiving end of your charms tonight?' Lucy laughed drily. 'It's OK, I don't really want to know. Now excuse me, I'm going to be late.'

She pushed past him and jogged down the stairs, aware all the time of his presence behind her, but he didn't say another word and, once on the street, walked off in the opposite direction.

Ten minutes later, sweating and breathing heavily, Lucy pressed the bell to Sadie's flat. Lucy was all too aware that her relationship with her best friend was being tested to the limit, it was becoming very one-sided, with Lucy always talking and Sadie listening while noticeably not saying 'I told you so'. But there was no one else Lucy could turn to, no one else she could trust.

'I don't know what to do, Sadie, Don is just so . . . he scares me now, he really scares me. The violence is there all the time, under the surface.'

Sadie tried to be tactful. 'I know what you're saying, Lucy, and I can understand how hard it is, but to me Don is what he's always been, one huge bloke, who doesn't think twice about using his bulk to intimidate people. I think you've just discovered the real person. I mean, you were completely besotted with Don and oblivious to his faults, waiting on him hand, foot and finger. But now your mind is on Fergus. That must affect the way you are with Don, he must notice you're distracted.' Sadie looked at the floor, taking refuge behind her thick black hair which hung heavily over her face. She didn't want to make eye contact as she spoke the words she knew Lucy would not want to hear. 'Don is ultimately one hundred per cent self-obsessed. If your life doesn't revolve around him, which it doesn't at the moment, then he's going to hate it – and you.'

'No!' Lucy fired the word at Sadie like a bullet. 'It's not like that, it's not my fault he's the way he is. I've told you before, it's only because of the way Don is that I even got involved with Fergus. I was so down and he was just . . .' She paused, searching for the right words. 'Oh, I don't know, just sort of there.'

Sadie shrugged her shoulders and sighed. 'I can't tell you what to do but I can cheer you up with a bottle of wine. Dry white do you?' She smiled apologetically.

Lucy had always thought that Sadie's most attractive feature was her smile. Wide and warm and framing perfectly white teeth, it drew people to her and despite being much shorter and plumper than the svelte Lucy, Sadie attracted men to her like moths the moment she smiled.

Lucy felt herself relax. 'Dry white will do fine, thanks.'

'That's lucky 'cos it's that or nothing. Nearly a week to go to payday unfortunately. Still, I'm getting a bit better at money management, only one week skint out of four now.'

Lucy looked affectionately at her friend. 'I should have brought some with me, I didn't think.'

'Your turn next time!'

Lucy smiled to herself. At least Sadie was still exactly the same as ever. Always there for her and always supportive, whatever happened.

Lucy and Sadie were unlikely friends, but despite their obvious differences the two girls had bonded almost as soon as they had met at the start of their first term at university. Everything about them was opposites. Their looks, their backgrounds, their ambitions, but something clicked and they became inseparable.

Lucy's ambition was to live and work in London, to have a successful career and the accompanying high salary. Sadie wanted to change society and to work with the disadvantaged. 'The capitalist and the socialist, who'd have thought?' Sadie would laugh when they disagreed.

Sadie's father was a GP in a small but busy surgery and her mother ran it the same way she had always run the family home, efficiently and with a rod of iron. Despite working her way through university, Sadie had still ended up in debt and was working all hours to try to pay it off. It would never have occurred to her to be financially supported by her parents, or anyone else for that matter. She had always found Lucy's dependence on her parents a little strange.

Although never short of would-be boyfriends, Sadie had never had a long-term relationship. She preferred to play the field and have fun. Her upbringing crossed the cultural divide so although she was a party girl who enjoyed a drink and a flirt along with the odd date here and there, she firmly believed that marriage was a commitment for life. She had never understood Lucy's relationship with Don, especially the way they had rushed into it without really knowing anything about each other.

Padding out to the tiny kitchen that was not a lot bigger than a cupboard, Sadie pulled a cold bottle of cheap wine out of the almost empty fridge and took it back to Lucy, waving it victoriously.

'Dadaa! Now, let's have a drink and a bit of light-hearted goss! You can start by telling me all about work and that gorgeous Paul Gower. God, I could do things with him that would make even you blush.'

'Sadie! How could you? I've told you what a little shit he is.'

'I know, I know.' Sadie laughed. 'But he is just so cute with it, and he earns well, maybe he could keep me in the manner I would love to become accustomed to!'

Lucy looked at her friend. Her best friend. She knew Sadie wanted to get her off the subject, but it wasn't working.

'Sadie, what am I going to do? Don treats me like shit and now it looks like Fergus is avoiding me. What is it about me? What's wrong with me?'

Sadie took a deep breath. 'Lucy, you know we've been friends for a long time and I love you dearly, but you're going to have to take a step back and decide for yourself where you're going. If Don finds out about Fergus he'll likely kill the pair of you. Can't you go and stay with your parents for a couple of weeks? Have some time away to clear your head?'

'But Fergus—'

'Fergus nothing,' Sadie interrupted sharply. 'You have to resolve the Don issue first. A couple of years ago you wouldn't have given someone like Fergus a second glance. Just because he's gentle and laid-back and the opposite of Don . . . You're on the rebound but without even dealing with your marriage first.'

Lucy frowned and stared at Sadie. 'How can you say that?'

'Because you asked me what to do and because I'm your friend. Think about it at least and at the same time give a bit of thought to the fact that, with his mobile out of action for whatever reason, you have no way of contacting Fergus. Doesn't that suggest he may have secrets you don't know about?'

'I know everything about Fergus, everything. You don't know him, you haven't even met him.' Lucy's eyes were wide but the tears were there, ready to fall at any second.

Sadie went over to her friend and hugged her tightly. 'You thought you knew everything about Don. Come on, have another glass of wine and we'll figure something out between us. All is not lost, you just need a little bit of TLC and a lot of wine.'

Lucy got a taxi home, worried about jogging through London streets in the dark, especially as she could feel the effect of the cheap wine working its way through her veins. Deep down she knew Sadie was right but it didn't stop her trying to ring Fergus en route.

His mobile was still turned off.

From the street she could see the flat was in darkness so either Don was already in bed or, more likely, still out.

Creeping in quietly, she looked around and heaved a sigh of relief to find him still out. Quickly, not even bothering to wipe a flannel over her face, she changed into her nightie and jumped into bed, ready to feign sleep if Don came in.

Suddenly her head started throbbing and she felt quite sick. Lucy knew it couldn't be the wine, she had only had a couple of glasses and she and Sadie easily sank a couple of bottles on occasions.

'You look a bit bleary-eyed this morning, Mrs Cooper.

Not been out on the tiles all night, have you?' Paul Gower was already at his desk, looking bright and alert, whereas Lucy felt like death warmed up. The cheap wine probably hadn't helped but Lucy knew it was more than that. She wondered if she was sickening for something.

'Don't be so stupid, Paul. I feel awful, I think it must be a virus of some sort. I actually feel quite nauseous.'

'You do look awful. Go and sit down and I'll get you a coffee.'

Lucy looked at Paul suspiciously, he seemed genuinely concerned. 'What's up with you? Why are you being nice to me?'

Paul grinned. 'I just like to keep you on your toes. Black or white?'

'White, no sugar, thanks.'

As Paul disappeared over to the small kitchen in the corner of the office, Lucy was aware of Daniella glaring at her. The girl was captive at the semi-circular reception desk by the main door but had obviously heard the conversation. Despite her thumping head and clammy hands, Lucy couldn't help smiling to herself. Just because Paul was being nice to her instead of sniping, the silly girl was jealous!

'Here you are, white no sugar as requested, plus a couple of paracetamol to tide you over. If they don't work, you ought to get off home. We don't want all your germs around here.'

'No, I'm sure you don't, Paul, same as I'm sure you'd love me to go home and leave you to your own devices with all my clients.'

'Oh, wow, that was a bit sharp, even for you. Been

sleeping in the knife drawer?' Paul laughed, a deep, genuine laugh that echoed round the room. 'Do you really think I'd do that?'

'Yep. I do. But thanks for the coffee and pills. I'm sure they'll do the trick.'

Lucy lasted another hour before finally succumbing and heading for Caroline Pettit's office.

'Sorry, Caroline, but I'm going to have to go home. I think I've got flu or something similar. I feel really shitty.'

Although nothing was said directly to indicate a lack of sympathy, Lucy could sense it. Caroline could be impatient at the best of times if she felt her employees weren't giving one hundred and ten per cent and Lucy knew Caroline viewed sickness as weakness. Almost a lack of commitment. At that moment Lucy also realised that her intention to take a couple of weeks off as Sadie had suggested wouldn't go down at all well.

'Well, if you feel that bad then you must but I'll need a full update on where everything is at with your client list. If necessary I'll ask Paul to cover anything urgent.' Caroline Pettit leaned back in her vast leather chair and crossed her legs daintily. Lucy had never met anyone else who could make such a simple movement look threatening.

'It's all right, Caroline, there's nothing that can't wait a couple of days and it is nearly the end of the week. I'll be back on Monday.'

'I'll give it until then, Lucy, but if you're not well enough to come back in on Monday, then you have to liaise with Paul. The firm must come first, as you well know.'

Lucy could feel herself blushing. She almost felt naughty. It was like being back at school in the head's office. Caroline stood up sharply and moved round to the front of the desk. Looking down at the apologetic Lucy perched uncomfortably on the edge of a hard chair, she raised her perfectly plucked eyebrows in a gesture that spoke volumes. Caroline Pettit's drive and ambition were well known in the cut-throat business of public relations and although not exactly popular, she commanded a healthy respect from all her staff who were well aware that the high salaries they were all paid came with a price. Caroline never had any qualms about cutting adrift anyone who didn't come up to scratch.

'I'll be in first thing on Monday, Caroline, I guarantee, and I'll work late to catch up. I'm sorry, but I really do feel rough and I rarely have any time off.'

'I know that, Lucy, but I'm certainly not going to congratulate you, it's no more than I expect. Now is there anything else?'

Lucy knew she was dismissed. Once outside the glass office that protected Caroline from noise but not from view, Lucy looked round to see her boss back behind her desk, fingers poised over her keyboard, looking thoughtfully into the middle distance. As always, not a hair was out of place and not a single crease dared mar her designer suit. With her small delicate features and flawless skin she reminded Lucy of an exquisite china doll, one that should be put up on a shelf and admired rather than played with.

Lucy guessed Caroline was mentally adding a black mark to her name.

'Everything all right, Lucy?' Paul had padded over so quietly he made her jump. 'Going home, are you? Anything you want me to cover?'

'No thanks. I'll be back on Monday and Caroline has agreed there's nothing that can't wait.' Lucy shrugged her shoulders and smiled. 'Sorry, Paul, no chance to jump on my grave just yet!'

Paul laughed and put a comforting arm round her shoulder. 'As if, Lucy. As if! Come on, I'll call a cab and drop you off. You should be tucked up with a bowl of chicken soup for company.'

'I'm not that bad, for God's sake, I can manage to drag my weary body home.' Looking at his concerned face she suddenly felt mean. 'But thanks anyway, I appreciate the thought.'

Knowing that Don would most likely still be in bed, the last thing Lucy wanted to do was go back to the flat but she knew she had to. Caroline had been known to phone and check up on sick staff, just to reassure herself that they weren't playing hookey at her expense.

As silently as she could, Lucy let herself into the flat and without bothering even to get undressed she grabbed the spare duvet from the depths of the airing cupboard and curled up on the sofa. She fell asleep instantly.

She woke with a start to feel a sudden wave of nausea sweeping over her. She stumbled into the kitchen for a drink of water, leaning her head on the edge of the cool ceramic sink while she waited for the tap to run really cold. As the dizziness passed, she looked at the wall clock and was surprised to find it was still only 11 a.m. She felt as if she had been asleep for hours. She wondered if Don had left the flat without disturbing her. It seemed unlikely but she tiptoed silently down the hallway to the bedroom to check. She opened the door a fraction, hoping that both the room and the bed would be empty and she would be able to crash out alone.

The last thing Lucy saw before she passed out clean on the floor was her husband sitting on the edge of the bed with a hypodermic syringe in hand, ready to inject himself. Concentrating hard on the needle while firmly gripping his thigh in his other hand, he was completely oblivious to her. In fact as he held the syringe aloft, his eyes fixed, he was completely oblivious to everything.

'Lucy, wake up, Lucy, what's the matter? Come on, you daft cow, wake up.'

As the red mist cleared from her eyes and Lucy came round, her mind was confused, she couldn't remember what had happened. All she could get her befuddled head around was that she was lying on top of the bed fully clothed and Don, with an expression of panic written all over his face, was leaning over her, shaking her shoulder.

'What happened?' She tried to focus on his face.

'I don't know, you fainted or something. What are you doing here? Why aren't you at work?'

'I didn't feel well, I think I've got flu . . . Don't worry, I'll be OK.' Lucy looked at her husband and for a split second felt moved by his concern, he really looked worried about her.

And then she remembered.

Despite her spinning head, Lucy forced herself to sit up.

She wondered if she had imagined the scene that had confronted her minutes earlier. She pushed her hair away from her face and looked directly at him.

'Could I have a drink of water please, Don? I feel dizzy again.'

As he scuttled off, she quickly looked around but there was no sign of anything out of the ordinary. He came back with a tall glass of cold water straight from the fridge.

'Here.' Smiling slightly, he handed it to her. 'Sip this slowly. Are you feeling better?'

Again Lucy looked at him, trying to piece the situation together but the nausea made concentration difficult.

'Don, what were you doing when I came into the bedroom?'

'What do you mean, what was I doing? I was getting some clothes on, that's what I was going.' Don lowered his eyes and walked over to the window, feigning interest in the flickering neon sign on the building opposite. 'I heard a noise and wondered what was going on. You should have told me you were home, I thought we'd got burglars.' Don laughed nervously and turned back round. Reaching out, he grabbed one of her hands and started to pull her forward. 'Now why don't you get undressed and get into bed. I'll head off to the chemist and get you some flu-type tablets.'

As the door closed, Lucy tried to figure out what had happened. Was it the sight of Don with a syringe in his hand that had made her faint or was it because she fainted that she imagined it all? As the dizziness washed over her again she lay back, not really able to concentrate on anything very much.

She would think about it all later, she decided, when she felt better. She closed her eyes and tried to let sleep waft over her but her mind remained active. She found she couldn't switch her brain off, no matter how hard she tried.

Chapter Two

'So you're going to work today then.'

Lucy was quietly getting dressed, trying not to disturb Don who was still hibernating in the depths of the over-sized wrought-iron bed that dwarfed the bedroom.

'Yes, I have to.' She didn't look at him as she spoke, just continued pulling her shiny black tights on. 'If I don't get back today then Paul will take over some of my accounts. What are you going today?'

'Going to the gym of course, what a stupid question.'

Lucy turned round. 'Why is that stupid? You're still in bed, for God's sake. What is it with you? Why can't you just be civil at least . . .' Lucy stopped, aware that the tears were about to start again.

She still didn't feel one hundred per cent. All weekend she'd felt washed out and depressed, permanently on the verge of tears. For the first couple of hours after she had passed out Donovan had been solicitously caring, bringing hot drinks and tucking her up, but after that he had gone out and not returned until the early hours. The rest of the weekend she might just as well have been alone, for all the use he was to her. And he had been through her handbag and taken all her cash – again.

'Oh, for God's sake,' he said now, 'don't start grizzling again, I had enough of that yesterday. Just go to work and let them look after you. I'm sure *Paul* will be more than willing, he did so well last time, as you keep reminding me. Much more up your street, he is, smart-arse little tart. Go on, just piss off.'

'Don, what are you going on about? I can't stand Paul, you know that, he's not even a friend – in fact, given half a chance, he'd have my job out from under me. I really don't understand you sometimes.'

He pulled the covers up over his head and ignored her. Lucy knew he had no intention of going to the gym.

She didn't bother to say goodbye to him. He wouldn't acknowledge her anyway. Not now, not in that mood.

She poured herself a cup of coffee and perched on the kitchen stool to put on her make-up. With hindsight and a clear head she knew exactly what she had seen on Friday. Don had been injecting something, she had seen it with her own eyes, and he had seen her see him. Yet he had nonchalantly carried on as normal over the weekend.

But what was it? Lucy guessed it was probably steroids of some sort but it didn't make sense. Don had always been a fitness freak but he was strongly against any artificial enhancement; as far as she knew he had never even taken pills, let alone anything else. Why on earth would he start doing something so dumb, and also dangerous?

After a quick check in the mirror, Lucy left for work.

She soon regretted her decision to take a bus instead of the underground. The wind howled around her ankles at the bus stop and her hair was in danger of taking off from her head. She was pulling the full-length beige raincoat tightly to her with one hand and trying to erect her umbrella with the other when her phone started trilling in the depths of her briefcase. Cursing loudly she dug deep.

'Hello, you. How's things?'

'Fergus! Where the hell have you been? I've been worried sick, what's been going on?'

The voice on the other end of the line sounded bemused. 'Hey, hey. Stay cool. I had an accident on my bike, broke my arm and my bike. No big deal but my phone got kinda beat up as well, not to mention my head.'

'Are you OK? There are other phones besides mobiles, you could have let me know somehow.'

'Girl, I'm sorry, things just got a bit out of hand. I've really missed you. Meet me for lunch? One o'clock at the deli? I'll give you all the news then. Got to go. See ya lunchtime.'

Before she could respond, the line went dead. She checked the number. Withheld. Dammit, she thought. Without knowing what had happened at work after she left on Friday she had no idea of what appointments were now in her office diary. No idea whether or not she would be able to meet Fergus and no way, once again, of contacting him.

As the overcrowded bus wove its way through the busy London streets, Lucy found herself standing at the back crushed tightly between too many passengers, each clasping their bulging briefcases, handbags and soggy umbrellas. Half-heartedly her eyes wandered over the cross-section of London life that was being jostled by the movement of the rush-hour bus. It was all there, a melting pot of age, race and finance. A snapshot in time, her PR brain told her.

But then her eyes settled on a young couple who were standing together, so close that even a cigarette paper couldn't have passed between them. He had one arm round her waist and she had her free hand on his shoulder as they gazed silently at each other, completely oblivious of everyone and everything. Lucy could almost feel the sexual tension between them and it started her thinking about, and analysing, her dying marriage to Don and comparing it to what she maybe had with Fergus.

Fergus had appeared in Lucy's life a few months before when she was most vulnerable and about to hit rock bottom. On her office desk she had a postcard that said, *'When you reach the end of your rope, tie a knot in it and hang on.'* Lucy would look at it and wonder how long she would be able to hang on. Don was battering her mentally whenever they were together and, much as she loved her job, it was all she could do to get up in the mornings. And then along came Fergus with his big, gentle eyes and soft, slightly anglicised Irish lilt. Fergus who, from their very first meeting, had looked at her admiringly every time they came face to face. Slowly she had started to look forward to delivery time and eventually her resolve had flown out of the window and she had gone for a drink with him. Nothing else, just a swift glass of wine in the pub opposite, but from that moment they had both known it was going to be much more.

Against her better judgement, Lucy became caught up in a full-blown affair but their times together were few and far between, so few and far between that Lucy sometimes wondered how they managed to have a relationship at all. How, she wondered, could someone who was supposedly a high-flyer, a bright, intelligent and attractive young woman with the world at her feet, get herself into such a mess over men? Never in a million years could she have imagined herself as a married woman falling in love with someone else.

She thought back to how they had all reacted at university when one of the lecturers had had to make a quick exit from her career. Her irate husband had plastered one of the main external walls with all the details of her affair, in beautifully presented and very graphic graffiti. Everyone had thoroughly enjoyed it and the general consensus was that it served the woman right. Only now did Lucy think there was probably another side to the story. Suddenly she felt sorry for the woman and wondered where she was and what she was doing. How could she ever have got over the humiliation?

Lucy couldn't bear to think of the reaction at Pettit's if they found out that, firstly, she was having an affair and, secondly, that it was with a lowly motorcycle courier, deemed one of the necessary evils of life in London. Lucy knew it wasn't the job of his choice. Fergus had come to London to attend drama school, to follow his dream of becoming an actor, but circumstances had taken that away from him and now he drove around London all day taking his life in his hands delivering packages.

Lucy's mind had wandered so far she nearly missed her

stop. She wondered what would happen if Don ever found out. She knew that the kindly and gentle Fergus wouldn't stand a chance against raging bull Don. She also knew with certainty that her job wouldn't survive, Don would see to that. Just the thought of it all made her palpitate. By the time she actually walked into the office she was already worn out.

The morning was predictable. Caroline was on her case making sure she was up to scratch on her workload after her unscheduled day off and Paul was being as irritating as always. The good thing was that lunchtime was free in her diary. Deep down she knew she needed the brownie points of working through but she couldn't bring herself to, she desperately wanted to see Fergus, to reassure herself that she wasn't making a complete fool of herself with him.

Just after one o'clock she walked into the small deli that was only one street away from the office. With its long and narrow layout it was easy to hide behind a pillar at the back, far away from the takeout counter. Fergus was already there, a cup of black coffee in front of him and a hand-rolled cigarette between the fingers of his heavily plastered arm. She ordered a coffee and made her way through to him.

Waving a greeting to her with his good arm he smiled broadly, a wide smile that showed his slightly crooked teeth, a smile that reached his eyes and lit up his face. He genuinely looked happy to see her and that alone cheered her up.

'You made it then. See my war wounds? I am actually legitimately plastered for once.'

Although Lucy had been angry at his almost casual

attitude to her on the phone earlier, it faded instantly when he spoke. His gentle voice always soothed her and seeing him lounging sideways on the straight-backed chair, leaning against the wall, looking so calm and relaxed just reinforced her feelings for him.

'Oh, Fergus, whatever happened to you? No one at the office knew anything about it, or if they did, no one told me. The relief rider just shrugged his shoulders and looked at me as if I was mad when I cornered him in the stairwell. Are you really OK?' Instinctively Lucy glanced around before reaching out and touching his shoulder.

'Fine, Luce, just fine. One night in hospital with concussion and a couple of days feeling sorry for myself. Got four stitches in my head as well and a few cuts and bruises. A black cab decided to take me on at Hyde Park Corner. He won but at least I escaped with my legs intact. They're usually the first to go. I've seen so many ex-riders with wonky legs, even no legs. You can spot them a mile off!' His face creased with amusement and Lucy couldn't help but think that if the same had happened to Don he would have been screaming death and destruction to the taxi driver.

'You really should have called, I was worried sick. I didn't know whether to consider myself dumped or what.'

'Sorry.' He looked at her sheepishly, an expression of contrition on his face. 'It was just, well, you know how it is. I was a tad incapacitated for a few days and then time passed, family commitments and all that. Still, I'm getting back to normal now. What about you? How are you coping? How are things at home with Mister Universe? Still pumping iron and topping up his veins with alcohol?'

'Not just alcohol, Fergus. I think he's into something much heavier than alcohol.'

'Such as?'

'Oh, at a guess, steroids. I've seen it before at the gym. They all seem to think a piddly little gold-painted cup on the shelf is worth wrecking their health for.' Lucy smiled weakly; it was hard trying to find humour in the situation. 'Still, at this moment in time I don't really care that much, although no doubt I'm funding it. Right now I don't want to talk about Don, I haven't got long before I have to be back. Any chance of a quiet drink one evening this week? Can you get away? I'm sure I could, for a couple of hours at least. I've missed you.' Lucy smiled nervously, unsure if she had overstepped the mark, but he put his hand on top of hers and patted it gently.

'Me too, girl, me too. I've missed you. How about Friday? There's a wicked gig at the Castle, Denny's playing and I promised to go and show some support. You can come as well, you enjoyed it last time.'

Disappointment swept over Lucy as her vision of a romantic evening faded. Although besotted with Fergus she didn't like his friends at all and she hated going onto his territory. She knew they called her 'Fergie's posh totty' behind her back but when she had mentioned it he just laughed and said it was only harmless fun, that they were only jealous.

'Oh, Fergus, you know I can't make Fridays, it's my gym night and Don's always there. I can't.'

'Come on, girl, be adventurous, take a chance for once in your life. Throw off the shackles, loosen up and have some fun. I'm sure you can think of something.'

Lucy looked at him across the table, as thin and rangy as Don was muscular. She wondered if she was with Fergus because he was the complete opposite of the husband she had come to despise and dislike in equal proportions. Sadie thought so. But then again, Sadie had never liked anyone that Lucy was involved with, at university, during the holidays, Don, now Fergus. No, Lucy thought, Sadie was too biased to be taken notice of. That Fergus had a way with women was indisputable. His Irish-West Indian parentage had given him the best of both sets of genes. Small, delicate features from his Irish mother, skin the shade of antique pine from his half-Jamaican father; they were a winning combination. Add to that the gentle mellowed accent and, as a rule, females of all ages fell at his feet. Just like Lucy had done the first time he had delivered a package to her at Pettit's three months previously, dressed from top to toe in black biker's leathers, smiling his crooked smile and looking straight into her eyes.

At thirty-seven he was ten years older than Lucy but he could easily have passed for a lot less. All the females in the office enjoyed a gentle flirt with him whenever he was in the office but it was Lucy who had caught his eye. It had been a while before Fergus had admitted to her how much he hated his job. How it was only a job to pay the bills. Fergus Pearson, it emerged, was a budding actor who had given it all up and gone to work as a courier fifteen years previously when his girlfriend had unexpectedly become pregnant.

'Lucy? Are you still with me, girl? How about it? Think you can make it?'

'I'll try. I'll ring you as soon as I can figure something out . . . maybe I can say I have to work. I'll ring—'

'Sorry, you can't ring this number,' he cut in apologetically. 'It's . . .' He picked up the phone which was on the table and waved it at her. 'Well, it's not actually my phone. I've borrowed it. I'll have to ring you.'

'That's OK. I guessed that.' Lucy smiled as she handed over a gift bag. 'I've got you another, I got it on the way here. I've hated not being in touch with you.'

He took the bag and opened it. 'Cool! I'll have to keep this well out of sight. Where I live it would be robbed within seconds and sold on in minutes.' Soon he was engrossed in the top-of-the-range model Lucy had presented him with. She stood up, again unsure whether she had gone too far.

'I have to get back. I was ill last week, I had a virus of some sort, so I have to look doubly busy for a while. Caroline is OK but she certainly expects a lot and the pressure is on. How long are you going to be off work? And what about the bike?' Lucy knew she was babbling.

'Dunno, girl. Bike's a write-off and the plasters on for six weeks. Gotta sort out the insurance as well. Bit of a bummer really, I'm lost without the bike. One of the problems of using your own for work, it's fine when all's well, but just one accident throws everything into chaos. No wages, no transport and broken bones to boot.'

Again Lucy looked around to check there was no one she knew in the deli before leaning over and lightly kissing his forehead. 'Ring me. I've programmed my number in already for you.'

'Cool.' Fergus looked up. 'Thanks for this, it's a good

thought. We'll sort something out, girl, you just hang on in there. Maybe we could get away for a whole day out now I'm off work. Maybe the seaside? Ice cream and candy-floss, then if you're good maybe some popcorn and a ride on the Big Wheel.' His smile stretched wide and his whole face creased with humour.

If anyone else had called her 'girl' she would have been up in arms and screaming sexism but when Fergus said it, it just rolled off the tongue affectionately and Lucy loved it.

'Sounds great and I'll try for Friday anyway. Now you take care.'

'My stitches are coming out in a couple of days. You can come and watch if you like.'

Lucy laughed. 'I don't think so. The way I've been feeling lately I'd be out like a light before they did anything.' Lucy paused; she didn't want to ask but she had to know. 'Won't Margot be going to the hospital with you?' She tried to ask the question lightly but the thought of Margot, Fergus's partner and the mother of his daughter, being with him made her feel quite jealous. She hated herself for feeling like it, she knew she had no right to.

Fergus raised his eyebrows and grimaced. 'You're joking, right? Margi thinks I should be back on the road already on a hired bike, broken arm an' all. Sympathy was never her strong point. So long as she gets the wages on demand she doesn't give a toss about anything or anyone else.' Sucking in air through his teeth, Fergus tutted gently. 'No, we can safely say Margot will not be with me.'

Relieved, Lucy smiled again. 'Must go. Speak to you later now you've got another phone.'

Weaving her way gracefully in and out of the crush of tables she was aware of admiring stares. A strikingly attractive natural blonde with fair skin that tanned at a glimpse of the sun, and long shapely legs, she was often mistaken for being Scandinavian. Her private education and privileged childhood spent travelling all around the world had instilled a confidence in her that was evident in the way she walked, the way she talked, even the way she drank a cup of coffee. It wasn't a conscious thing, it was just part and parcel of Lucy Cooper. But Donovan Cooper was slowly but surely eroding that confidence and it was this new experience of insecurity that had led Lucy into the arms of Fergus against all her principles and better judgement. From being happy and sure of herself, Lucy was now full of self-doubt.

She tried to concentrate and get on with her work during the afternoon. She loved her job and usually thrived on the pressure that went with it. It was the pressure of her personal life that was getting to her. Normally she could separate the two but that afternoon her mind kept drifting back to Don, trying to figure out whether there was anything she could have done to stop the downward spiral of their relationship. Even when Don behaved abominably he had the uncanny knack of making Lucy feel that it really was all her fault. That maybe there was something lacking in her, and if she had behaved differently then everything could have been OK. It often led Lucy into desperately trying to analyse herself and her past.

If any childhood could realistically be described as idyllic then Lucy knew without a shadow of a doubt that was what she had had. Aside from the normal ups and downs that beset every young girl, Lucy had sailed happily through her childhood and adolescence, loving every minute of boarding school, but even more she had loved the jetting around the world that went with her father's high-flying career in the oil industry. She adored her parents and they indulged their only child. Money was no object and Lucy had never wanted for anything. Also, her parents had given her complete freedom and trust and Lucy had always respected that. As far as she could tell she had never been unhappy or unsettled with any aspect of her life or herself.

Until, that is, Donovan Cooper came into her life.

Realistically, Lucy could see, looking back, that everything had been great up until she met him. Or rather, until she ignored everyone's reservations and made the biggest mistake of her life. She married him.

Five years before, fresh from university and with a good career offer from Pettit's PR Consultancy dangling in front of her at the end of the holidays, Lucy had decided she needed to get fit. Several years of too much junk food and alcohol and too little exercise had added an extra fourteen pounds and she was determined to lose it so she would look the part of a successful PR executive.

After a quick glance around the area where she and Sadie were going to share a flat she had settled for the rather pretentiously named Body Beautiful Inc. The fashionable and upmarket gym was only a stone's throw from her new flat. It seemed the perfect choice; all glass partitions and state-of-the-art equipment. Lucy justified the huge expense by telling herself that just the thought of the exorbitant subscription she had splashed out on would motivate her to go regularly.

'Please, Sadie,' wide-eyed and pleading, Lucy had looked at her best friend and clasped her hands as they stood side by side trying to look inside without being obvious. 'I'm begging you, please come with me, I can't possibly go in there on my own. If you won't come in there with me I may just have to kill you very soon. Pleeeeease.'

Sadie had peered in and snorted. 'In your dreams. Just look at them. If I wore Lycra up my fat bum like that it would disappear, never to be seen again. Sorry, Luce, I could manage a gentle little keep fit class as a special favour to you, my best friend, but that – no, no, no. Imagine paying out all that money just to torture yourself. Borders on masochism if you ask me. It's not normal.'

Sadie had no hang-ups at all about her shape. She bounced happily through life leaving a trail of besotted admirers in her wake, along with a selection of bemused model-shaped females who couldn't quite figure it out.

'Oh, come on, you don't have to do much and just look at all those men – where else would we find such a selection of testosterone on legs. I tell you what, I'll pay for your introductory sessions and if you really, really hate it then I won't mention it again, promise. And look at that notice,' Lucy pointed at the window, 'half price for the first year, a bargain!'

Sensing Sadie was wavering, Lucy had edged her closer to the pristine smoky glass doors. Just at the moment they pressed their noses against the doors they swung open and a couple of muscular young men in jogging suits emerged, carrying sports bags the size of suitcases. Looking the two girls up and down, they smiled appreciatively before disappearing off down the road.

'OK,' Sadie grinned, 'you've convinced me. I'll give it a go but I'm not promising anything longlasting. Taut, muscular buttocks aren't high on my list of priorities.' Sadie paused and rolled her eyes at the two men. 'Unless of course they're on someone else!'

Before she could change her mind, Lucy had her by the arm and was propelling her through the doors.

The first visit had been quite an eye-opener and despite the gentle introductory session, neither of them had been able to walk easily for three days, but the facilities were wonderful and before long Lucy and Sadie were regulars.

A whole new social life accompanied the actual boring business of getting fit. There were several like-minded souls there who, like Lucy and Sadie, had no qualms about working out wildly and then heading off for a snack and a glass or two of wine.

One evening, after they had been going for a few weeks, Lucy was jogging away furiously, head down, on the enormous and hugely complex running machine when she became aware of someone in front of her. Still keeping going, she looked up.

'Hi there. How's it going?' The well-built young man in tight shorts and cutaway T-shirt whom she had been eyeing up surreptitiously for weeks was suddenly standing in front of her, a wide smile stretched across his tanned face.

'Not too bad I suppose,' she said, conscious of her sweaty T-shirt and sodden hair stuck to her forehead. 'Bit too much like hard work though, I'm naturally slothlike.'

'It'll get better as time goes on and you build up your stamina.' The wide smile remained. 'I'm Donovan, by the way, but my friends call me Don. I've been watching you for ages, you've settled in so well, you're starting to look like a real pro already, really toned. I'm training to be an instructor so I have to keep an eye on all the novices. Part of the job.' The perfect smile widened even more, revealing dentally enhanced, gleaming white teeth. 'I've noticed you're sweated out, maybe even a little dehydrated, you look like you need some liquid right now. Fancy a juice upstairs with me? I'm due a break.'

Lucy heard a smothered giggle from Sadie and glared in her direction before stopping the machine and switching her own best smile on Donovan.

Standing with his legs apart and his hands on his hips, Lucy thought he was the most perfect specimen she had ever seen. A soft layer of perspiration emphasised his bulging muscles which were deeply tanned, and tight black Lycra clung where it touched.

'OK, I'd like that. I'll grab a shower and get changed and meet you up there.'

As he walked away Sadie jumped off her machine.

'Lucy, Lucy, I despair of you. Have you lost it com-pletely? You were simpering and blushing like a silly little schoolgirl. I'm surprised you didn't go the whole way and kiss his feet. What on earth's got into you?'

'What do you mean?' Lucy's tone was defensive, she knew what Sadie was thinking. 'He invited me for a drink and I said yes, what's wrong with that? He's cute.'

Sadie rolled her huge dark-brown eyes. 'Cute? Did I hear you say cute? Cute as in Godzilla? Come on, Lucy, it's not like you to go all girlie over a big blond dipstick who sashays around here all day like he's a catwalk model. Never mind superman, he's the original plastic-man, all muscles and teeth, with his tanned head up his arse and his brains down his Lycra.'

'That's a bit over the top, Sadie, even for you.' Lucy felt a hint of irritation with her friend. 'I'm not being girlie, I just think he looks great and I quite fancy him, if you must know. You're just being bitchy and socially judgemental. Do I detect a hint of jealously there, Miss Khan? Do you fancy him yourself?'

Sadie's infectious giggle echoed around the room as she walked back over to her machine, doing a passable imitation of the muscular Donovan en route.

'I'm sorry, Lucy,' she smiled over her shoulder, 'you go and have your drink. I'll meet you up there after a suitably polite interval. Meanwhile, I'm going to cast my eyes over the real men in here – there are one or two, you know.'

'Bitch.' Lucy smiled reluctantly.

'Girlie girl,' Sadie shot back as Lucy headed for the locker rooms.

Lucy did the best she could after a quick shower, quickly blow-drying her hair and applying just enough make-up to look casual. Then she headed up the stairs to the juice bar.

Don was already sitting up at the counter on a high stool with a tall mud-coloured drink in front of him. The high-tech stainless steel and perspex design of the room, with a vast mirrored backdrop, made it look larger and more crowded than it actually was.

'What can I get you?' Don slid off his stool as she approached; he held out a welcoming arm and guided her to an adjoining stool. Before she could answer he carried on assertively, 'At a guess something iced and thirst-quenching. I've been watching you work, you take it far more seriously than your friend. She's only really playing at it, she's a lousy advert for the gym, but you . . .' He paused and looked Lucy up and down appreciatively. 'You've taken to it like a duck to water, you could so easily be a fitness trainer, you know. You've got the motivation and the looks. Blonde and toned, just what the job needs, and I love the tan. Do you use the sunbeds?' His eyes rested on her face and she laughed lightly at him, hoping she was hiding her embarrassment.

'No. I've just come back from holiday. My parents are living in the Middle East at the moment so I've been with them for a few weeks. I just wanted to get fitter and thinner before starting my new job.'

'Sounds interesting, what are you going to do?' Don's eyes never left hers; he appeared completely absorbed in what she was saying.

'Public relations. I'm getting ready for the real world of work for the first time. I've been a student for so long it's going to be a bit of a culture shock entering the realms of nine to five. Tomorrow's my first day. I'm dreading it but looking forward to it at the same time.'

'Tell me about it. Ever since I started here I don't have a minute to myself, it's nonstop, but there you go, we all have to earn a crust although here the crusts are minimal. Still, money isn't everything and I'm committed to health and fitness. It's so much more attractive, more appealing than being fat and unkempt. Your friend has that couldn't care less attitude about herself and I really hate it. You can almost see the outline of all those burgers and chips on her hips!'

Lucy was taken aback by the ferocity of his remarks although she guessed that was the trainer talking.

'Really? I think Sadie is lovely, she's fun and bubbly and happy with herself. That's important as well, don't you think?'

'I don't see how you can be happy with yourself if you're not in peak condition.'

'Mmmm,' Lucy mumbled, unsure where the conversation was going and keen to redirect it. 'Tell me about yourself.'

The conversation batted back and forth gently for a few minutes and Lucy was really starting to enjoy herself. He had a way of locking eyes and smiling intimately, making her feel as if she was the only person in the room.

Suddenly the Tannoy sprung into life.

'Would Donovan Cooper please report to the reception desk right away, Donovan Cooper to reception please.'

Don shrugged his wide shoulders in apology. 'Sorry, Lucy, duty calls. Give me your number and I'll ring you. We could maybe have a drink together, away from here.'

Lucy scrabbled in her handbag for pen and paper. 'Sounds good to me. Make it an evening call though, I'll be hard at work during the day from now on.'

Just as she was handing over the piece of paper, Sadie bounced up to them both.

'Not interrupting anything, am I?'

'No, of course not. Don's got to go now anyway.'

Sadie looked at the mountain of a man in front of her. 'Oh, that's a shame. Still, never mind. I'm sure we'll get the chance to meet each other again, judging from the look on your faces and the number changing hands!'

The expression on Don's face changed slightly as he gave Sadie an appraising look without answering.

Lucy looked from one to the other, disconcerted by the sudden change in atmosphere. She reached over and touched his arm. 'Give me a call, huh?'

The smile was quickly restored. 'I will, soon!'

As he strutted over to the stairs, taking long steps and casually swinging his arms, Sadie snorted behind her hand. 'You're not really going to go out with Godzilla, are you, Lucy? Tell me you're just leading him on for a laugh.'

'Actually I'm not. I like him and I might just go out with him. So there!'

Sadie held both her hands up in front of her in mock surrender. 'OK, I'm saying nothing else. I'm going to have a drink and de-stress. I'm out to dinner tonight. That new Thai restaurant in the town has got a special two for the price of one offer on so Carla and I are off to pig out. Wanna come?'

Lucy creased up with laughter. 'No way, not after all that work. You are just so mad, Sadie. After all that jogging you're off to pig out at a Thai restaurant? Barking mad, you are, absolutely barking.'

Sadie smiled wryly. 'Has plastic-man got to you already? This time last week you'd have been up for it as well.'

'Yes, I know, but my new, far too expensive, size ten little black suit is hanging on the wardrobe mocking me. I have to get in it tomorrow.'

They linked arms and were still teasing each other as they left the building, both unaware of Donovan Cooper watching them through the glass. Both unaware of the look of dislike that swept across his face as he looked at Sadie.

Later that evening as Lucy was busy throwing shoes all over the bedroom and panicking at the thought of which pair to wear for her first day at Pettit's, the phone rang.

'Hi, is that Lucy? It's Don Cooper here, from the gym? I thought I'd take the bull by the horns right away and see if you fancied that drink tonight? I'm finished at work now.'

Relieved he couldn't see her, Lucy could feel a soppy grin stretching across her mouth. 'Don, hi. I would like that but tonight I can't. I'm having an evening of indecision and nerves as I try to figure out just what look I need for my new job tomorrow and I also want an early night to prepare. It's nine o'clock already. How about Friday? By then I'll have got the first week over with and will probably really need a drink.'

'No problem. I look forward to it. Is your little fat friend still with you or has she lumbered off to pig out as usual?'

'Sorry?' Lucy wasn't sure if she had heard correctly. 'What did you say?'

'Just a joke. But she needs to shift at least three stone and she just doesn't seem to care. I don't know why she wastes her money at the gym if she's not going to bother doing what she's told.'

Lucy hesitated. She felt annoyed but at the same time she could see that from a professional point of view Don had a point.

'Actually, Sadie is my flatmate, and maybe you're right, she doesn't take it too seriously, but she came along to the gym to keep me company and she's also my best friend so criticism is off limits. We're like sisters and I love her dearly.'

There was a slight pause before Don responded. 'Oops, I take that as a slapped wrist. I won't say another word about her. So I'll see you on Friday then. Give me your address and I'll pick you up in the four-by-four.'

Lucy was glad that Sadie hadn't been around to hear that. She could just picture her friend doing the walk and taking the piss.

'Don, why on earth have you got an off-road car in central London? It must be a nightmare to park.'

'Oh, no problem for me. I get free use of the underground car park at the gym twenty-four seven. I need something big and powerful to get me into town quick. We can't all afford to live in the city epicentre, I have to drive in from the boring old suburbs. Anyway, what's your address?'

A flicker of caution entered Lucy's mind, just a slight wariness about giving her address to him. She could imagine Sadie's disapproval.

'No, it's OK, I'll meet you at the gym and we can go on somewhere from there. Say eight o'clock in reception?'

The same wariness stopped her from telling Sadie that she had actually arranged a date with Donovan Cooper until after the event.

A few short months later Lucy had settled into her new job and was loving every minute of the challenge that came with working for one of the up and coming public relations firms in the capital. At the same time, her relationship with Don was getting more serious. So serious that he wanted to live with her but Lucy had yet to tell Sadie. It was Lucy's flat and she dreaded suggesting to Sadie that she would have to find somewhere else to live. In the event, and to Lucy's relief, it was not the thought of having to move out that seemed to bother Sadie so much as the choice of Don as live-in partner.

'Lucy, I can see you're quite taken with him but aren't you moving ahead too quickly?' A worried expression on her face, Sadie was watching Lucy as she carefully blow-dried her hair. 'It all seems so serious. I thought we were going to have some fun and play the field once we hit the big city.'

'Sadie, I am having fun. If it was someone else you wouldn't even notice, someone from work maybe, but just because it's Don . . .'

'I can't understand what you see in him, he's so – oh, I don't know, I just think he's a big phoney with a hidden agenda.' Sadie laughed nervously. 'There, I've said it. I'm sorry but that's how I feel and you're my friend, I have to tell you.'

'You've got him all wrong, you know. Just because he's into health and fitness doesn't mean he's vain. He likes to take care of himself, that's all. You don't like him because he's not as witty and trendy as your smart-arse, deep and meaningful, Guardian-reading social worker friends from the hospital.' In the dressing-table mirror Lucy could see Sadie, stretched out on the bed behind her, looking decidedly shocked. Her deep chocolate eyes widened.

'Lucy, that is just so unfair. I would never judge anyone on their appearance or intellect, you know that. I just think he's—'

'Sadie, we have to agree to differ on this one. I don't

want your opinion, right? Now I have to finish getting ready. What do you think I should wear? It's a party but it's not a party party, if you know what I mean.'

Sadie didn't smile or respond to the subject-changing tactic; she stood up and headed for the door.

'Right. I won't say another word about Don, providing you don't keep trying to convince me that he's really a big cuddly teddy bear who loves his old mum and is kind to orphaned animals. OK?'

Lucy looked at her friend and shook her head. Their friendship had never faltered before but Sadie was really starting to irritate her.

'Fine.'

'Good.'

'All right by me.'

'And me.'

'OK then.'

Lucy got up from the stool and walked over to Sadie, her mouth twitching. Next thing they were both giggling and hugging.

'Come on,' Sadie grabbed her friend's hand and pulled her towards the kitchen, 'let's have a quick glass of vino before you go out. We can't let one of the male species come between us; after all, we're sensible, mature, working women now – allegedly!'

They were still laughing when the doorbell rang. Lucy jumped up and let Don in.

'Sadie and I are just having a girlie bonding session, I'll be ready in five.' Lucy looked from one to the other, feeling the tension building not only in Sadie but in Don as well.

Pulling Lucy to him in a gesture of ownership, he kissed her full on the lips, making sure Sadie could see him putting his tongue into her mouth. He was kissing Lucy but his eyes were on Sadie. Lucy blushed and pulled away, her embarrassment all too obvious.

'Hi, Don,' said Sadie smoothly. 'How are things at the jolly old gym? Keeping you busy, are they?'

'Why do you ask?' The smile on Don's face wasn't in the least bit genuine, it was more a curling of lips, despite Sadie's effort to be sociable.

'Just making conversation, that's all. I don't know how you do it, all that pumping iron. I can only just about manage one session before I need to eat, drink and recover.'

'I can see that.' Don's eyes flickered briefly over Sadie's round figure before focusing on her face. 'Perhaps a little less eating and drinking and you could look like Lucy instead of Mr Blobby.'

Sadie shrugged her shoulders. 'Oh, I doubt it. Horses for courses, I say, and I'm happy as a pig in a pizza palace, thank you very much. Life's too short to worry about a droopy arse.'

Lucy realised it was time to intervene. 'Come on, Don, we'll be late for the party. See you later, Sadie. Don't wait up, it might be a late one.'

That was the night Don asked her to marry him, the night he had produced a beautiful sapphire and diamond ring that fitted perfectly. Lucy had happily accepted the proposal and the ring.

It wasn't until after the wedding that Lucy found out that he hadn't actually paid for the ring. Apparently there had been a 'Buy Now Pay Later' deal on offer in the jeweller's window. Don had bought it 'now' and she had had to pay for it 'later', much later, after the summons arrived. The same as she had to pay for the 4x4 and clear all his credit cards. Lucy and her parents had ended up paying for both the engagement and wedding rings, as well as the most expensive wedding and honeymoon that Don had convinced her she really wanted.

Looking back, Lucy knew she should have taken more notice of her parents' cautious warnings. She should also have listened to Sadie. Lucy wondered if Sadie was right about Fergus too, but as quickly as the thought flashed into her mind she chased it out again. The very idea of making the same mistake twice was just too ridiculous to contemplate, and anyway she certainly wasn't planning to rush into anything with Fergus.

'I've got it! I've got the Filbrook account, the bloody enormous Filbrook account that you all said was impossible. Eat your heart out, Lucy Cooper. It's mine, all mine, and you know what that means, don't you?' Paul pulled Lucy out of her chair and danced around the office. 'I've won! I've won! I'm going to be promoted!'

'Get off me, Paul, you dumb bastard.' She tried to pull away, her irritation coupled with disappointment. The Filbrook account was so important and seemingly unattainable, Caroline couldn't fail to be impressed that Paul had wrenched it away from one of their competitors. 'Let me go! You're really starting to piss me off.'

'Wow, sniffy, sniffy.' He laughed but instantly let her go and she swirled over into the paper shredder, tearing a huge hole in her black tights. As she glared at him and rubbed her leg, Paul laughed again and moved over to Daniella, the temp receptionist. 'You'll dance with me, won't you, sweetheart? You're not jealous of my success, are you?'

The girl flicked her hair back, pulled down her micro skirt and nearly threw herself into his arms.

The crash of the reception door fiercely hitting the solid wall made everyone jump.

'Enough, for Christ's sake! Exactly what is going on here?' Caroline Pettit, her face thunderous, stood in the doorway with Luke, her husband, close behind her.

Luke Pettit really was a sleeping partner, with little interest in the day-to-day running of the firm. Although Caroline had started the agency with funds from her husband's considerable private wealth, she had since worked long and hard to make it the success it was, even to the extent of putting any idea of having children on hold. Pettit's was her baby and everything else came second, including Luke. At forty-five he looked much older than his years, with a receding hairline and a paunch that he made no attempt to disguise. Affable and eccentric, he made the occasional half-hearted attempt at exercise but on the whole he was happy staying at the house in the country and dabbling in the stock market, with just the occasional foray into London to meet up with his old public school buddies. Luke and Caroline Pettit were chalk and cheese but somehow it worked.

Standing behind Caroline, his expression was a cross between amusement and bemusement as he took in the scene in the office.

'This is a professional office not an inner city schoolyard at playtime.' Caroline's tone was frigid. 'I expected more of you, Paul, and you, Lucy. Daniella, get back to reception now and stay there if you want to continue working here.'

As Daniella scurried back to her desk, Caroline glared at the others. 'Paul and Lucy, my office. Now.'

Turning sharply on her four-inch heels which enhanced her petite five foot height, she marched into her office with Luke silently in tow. Paul pulled a face behind them but Lucy looked determinedly straight ahead, furious that she had become involved.

'Caroline, I'm sorry—'

'Oh, do please shut up, Paul. This has got nothing to do with that stupidity out there although you ought to know better, both of you. No, this is far more important. Close the door and take a seat.'

Lucy sat between Luke and Paul. The set-up was familiar. By placing three chairs in a semi-circle in front of her desk Caroline ensured that Luke knew his place in the pecking order, which was, in her eyes, alongside Lucy and Paul as opposed to beside his wife and partner. Caroline, as usual, perched delicately on the front of her desk, her hands, with perfectly manicured and colour co-ordinated nails, by her side and her feet crossed at the ankles. The pose looked casual enough, but by not sitting she stayed head and shoulders above them all and emphasised her superiority. And whereas Caroline expected her staff to be conservative in their dress, she herself went the other way. There was no way that Caroline was going to be confused with her staff, so while they were suited out in grey, black or navy, she herself was stylishly wrapped in a body-hugging, bright cerise skirt suit that broadcast a designer logo on the huge gold buttons. The tight black crew-neck sweater underneath was lightened by a delicate but obviously expensive gold chain, with a single teardrop diamond dangling loosely. Her bottle-enhanced blonde hair was carefully pulled up into a pleat, with just a couple of carefully placed loose tendrils framing her face.

'Now, I have decided, and Luke agrees with me of course, that we have to expand. The work is out there for the taking and we can't afford to let opportunities keep passing us by.' Pausing dramatically, she looked from Lucy to Paul to ensure total concentration. 'Speculate to accumulate is what it's all about. So, instead of just one of you being promoted, I have decided that both of you will be.' Looking from one to the other again, she paused for a second, just long enough for the implications to sink in but not long enough for either of them to respond.

'You will be equally senior, and equally responsible when I am out of the office or when I'm travelling. I shall be taking on more junior staff so that we can diversify. We have to grow to continue with our success. Obviously Luke will also be around to deal with any major issues and I shall always be at the other end of the phone wherever I am . . .'

Lucy could hear Caroline's voice but the words suddenly sounded a long way away. Her head was thumping and the feeling of nausea was rising once again. Panic started to set in and all she could think of was getting out of the room but when she tried to stand up, her legs turned to jelly and she slumped slowly and almost gracefully to the floor in front of Caroline.

Before anyone in the room could react, unable to control herself, she threw up all over the parquet floor, not quite managing to avoid Caroline's dainty feet.

Chapter Three

Lucy was given no choice. By the time she came round and had gathered her wits about her and the full horror of what had happened hit her, the ambulance crew was already there, summoned by a very vocal Caroline who was convinced Lucy was about to expire in her office.

'I'm fine really, it must have been something I ate, I had a prawn sandwich for lunch . . .'

'Lucy, you have to have a check-up. You were ill last week, now again today. You have to sort this out, it's just not like you.'

Caroline's lack of sympathy was obvious to everyone, including Lucy, even in her befuddled state.

She tried to sit up straight but the room started spinning again.

'You're as white as blackboard chalk, Lucy,' Paul intervened, 'you really need to go. I reckon you came back to work too soon after the virus last week. Do you want me to phone Don for you?'

'No! No, don't worry him, I'll be OK. I don't need an

ambulance, I'm fine now, it was just the prawns . . .'

The paramedics looked at each other. One shook his head.

'I really don't think this is an emergency, it certainly doesn't appear to require an ambulance. This young lady would do better to have a bit of a rest and then see how she feels. Her GP would probably be more appropriate, especially if it's not a one-off.'

Lucy felt increasingly irritated as she watched the man directing his comments at Caroline.

'I am here, you know, and I do understand what you're saying. I might have been sick but I'm not deaf or stupid and it wasn't me who called you. I know I'm not about to pop my clogs—'

One fierce, wide-eyed glance from Caroline was enough to make Lucy think better of saying any more.

More discussions continued over Lucy's head and then the paramedics turned to leave without her. Caroline was already dialling for a taxi.

'Caroline, I'm OK, really. I just need to get back to work. I'm sorry about the mess but I'm OK, I'll just go and have a wash—'

'No!' Caroline was fierce. 'You're obviously not OK and neither are my bloody best shoes. Now get off home and make sure you go and see the doctor. I'm insisting on it, Lucy. I don't want you back here until you can guarantee to me you've seen a doctor and he's given you the all-clear.'

'Leave it to me,' Luke butted in. 'I'll go with Lucy and deposit her safely at her abode. I was intending to head in that direction anyway after the meeting.' Luke's voice was soothing and sympathetic but Caroline quickly cut in.

'No, Luke, you're not going anywhere. I need you here, we still have things to sort out.'

'Not without everyone here, we can't. There's no point. We'll have to reschedule the meeting. There's nothing else that can't wait a few days. No, I'll drop Lucy off and then head off to my club. I'm stopping in town tonight so I'll see you at home later.' Without waiting for any more argument from his wife he took Lucy by her arm and led her out of the office.

Mortified, Lucy went meekly, her embarrassment complete.

'Luke, I am so sorry. I feel so stupid and unprofessional. I've never done anything like this before. Do you think Caroline will sack me? I feel mortified.'

He laughed. A huge bellowing laugh that echoed around the small, old-fashioned lift that served the four-storey building. 'You silly thing. God, if that's the worst thing that you ever do then it's not too bad. All you did was throw up, we've all done that. Usually after a few too many in my case. Even Caroline's done that but don't tell her I told you.'

'But what about her shoes? And the parquet floor? I suppose it doesn't matter if she does sack me, I'll never be able to face them all again. Paul will be laughing his socks off by now.' Lucy leaned forward and groaned as she put her head in her hands.

Luke patted her on the shoulder. 'You're too hard on yourself and also too hard on that young man, you know. He's young and ambitious and has a lot of personality. And he's popular with the clients.' He looked sideways at

Lucy. 'Just like you really. And as for Caroline, she'll be lobbing her shoes in the bin as we speak, secretly pleased that she has a good excuse for buying yet another pair. This is the woman who has more shoes and handbags than Harrods.' His smile was as gentle as his voice was soothing. 'No, don't you worry, it will all be forgotten. Caroline knows you're talented and hard-working; one thing she never does is let emotions interfere with good working practice.'

Out on the street he flagged down a taxi and helped her into it.

'You're not pregnant, are you, dear?' he asked as the taxi moved off.

Lucy couldn't believe what she heard. 'Of course I'm not,' she snapped indignantly. 'Good God, definitely not. I'm a career woman, children aren't on my agenda, or at least not for a good few years.'

'Mmmm, I've heard those words before somewhere. Caroline's exactly the same, I'm afraid, she doesn't want any either, career comes first and foremost. Still, at least you've got age on your side. It's a shame men can't give birth and then all you career wives could go to work and leave the unambitious old buggers like me to play house. I'd like that, down in the country with the kiddies, riding ponies and having picnics by the river. Still, shouldn't really be talking out of turn about the love of my life, should I?' he prattled on happily. 'Let's just get you home and then I'm off the formal business leash. It doesn't become me in the slightest. You helped me out, you know. There's nothing I detest more than boring business meetings. Now I can get off to my club with a clear conscience!'

Smiling weakly, Lucy leaned her head against the cool glass, aware of the cabbie looking at her nervously in his mirror.

'It's OK, I just don't feel well. I'm not drunk and I'm not going to throw up . . .' As soon as she spoke she locked eyes with Luke and they both started laughing.

Suddenly Lucy felt a little better. She thought Caroline was lucky to have such an easygoing and adoring husband. Even if he did insist on wearing tatty sports jackets, check shirts and shiny suede shoes, whatever the occasion.

'Well, Lucy,' the doctor leaned back in his chair and looked at his computer screen, 'nothing much wrong with you physically that I can find. Is there anything troubling you?' He paused for a second before continuing, 'Not physically but mentally. Stress at work? Something like that? Headaches and nausea can be migraine, as I said, but they can also be signs of stress. Your blood pressure is slightly low but not really outside the norm.'

Lucy heaved a sigh of relief. At least there was nothing desperately wrong with her; in the time between getting home and going to her doctor, all sorts of nightmares had passed through her mind.

'Well, I do have a stressful job but I love it, I'm sure it's not that.'

'At home then? Everything at home as you want it to be? I know you said you aren't pregnant, but is everything OK in that department?'

She hesitated and looked down.

'Come on now, I can see something is troubling you and if it's something that's making you feel physically ill then we have to deal with it, don't we?'

Lucy took a deep breath. 'I think my husband is taking steroids. I saw him with a syringe. He denied it afterwards but I know what I saw and he's been so awful lately – well, for a long time actually. He's so unpredictable now, I'm frightened of him and I don't know what to do . . .' Once the words started, Lucy burst into tears and the whole story came out.

She left the surgery with a prescription, a phone number for a helpline, an order to take it easy, and a follow-up appointment. But rather than feeling better after spilling everything out, she felt depressed and lethargic. She was nevertheless determined to be back at her desk as soon as possible and to be with Fergus at the end of the week. At least Don wouldn't expect her at the gym while she was still under the weather.

Lucy desperately wanted to ring her parents, she wanted to jump on a plane and be with them but she couldn't face the kindly disapproval she knew she deserved. They hadn't been happy about her marrying Don but they had eventually capitulated as they had throughout her life. All they wanted was for her to be happy and Lucy was insistent that by marrying Donovan Cooper she would be happy. She couldn't bring herself to tell them they had been right.

Instead she rang Fergus and arranged to meet him at the Castle on Friday.

'Cool, aren't they, girl? Jeez, I wish I was up there with them. Can you just imagine the buzz? All that noise, an audience – must be grand to be able to do that.'

'Mmmm.' Lucy hoped Fergus didn't notice her lack of enthusiasm. The pills had made her feel fractionally better but she knew that a noisy and raucous pub wasn't the best place to be; she still felt under the weather and slightly detached from her surroundings. The music was loud and, to Lucy's ear, completely lacking any comprehensible tune or lyric. It echoed all around the hot and overcrowded east London pub. Lucy hated the atmosphere, she found it almost threatening.

The pub was a bit of a backstreet boozer that seemed to attract all the local lowlife looking for some trouble to liven up the evening. Each time Lucy had been there with Fergus, a fight of some sort had broken out and the bouncers, who were all shaven-headed, broad-shouldered clones of each other, had happily waded in to drag the offenders apart. Rarely was anyone thrown out of the Castle because without the drunks and fighters the place would be empty. But at least it was a long way from her flat in Marylebone and his home in Mile End and there was no chance of bumping into anyone either of them knew. Apart, of course, from the band, but they were friends of Fergus from way back and although they took the piss out of Lucy, they were also all well aware of Margot and could well understand why he was 'playing away', as they put it.

Fergus was looking longingly at the ramshackle group of musicians crowded onto the small stage, frantically performing; his arm was casually laid across her shoulder but his attention was focused across the room.

'I wish I'd learned to play an instrument instead of wasting my time on drama. Fat chance of me getting any acting work, but a band? No one gives a toss what you look like in the music industry, the more way out the better, and you can do it in your spare time, whenever you want.' Fergus shouted to make himself heard above the monotonous beat of the music and so did Lucy.

'Oh, I don't know, I think anything is possible if you want it badly enough. We've got clients in the business and there's heaps of opportunities in television, but I think you have to do some sort of stage work first. Not many actors sail straight into TV. It's a bit like doing an apprenticeship, getting some experience.'

Fergus snorted. 'That's fine if you're single with no responsibilities and can afford to work for crap money. Don't forget, I've got good old Margot sat with her feet up all day in front of the telly doing naff all but eat and smoke, not to mention her bone idle son who I still have to support at twenty-five years old.' Despite the words his expression was one of sad acceptance rather than anger. 'And then there's India who's still at school. When she bothers to go, that is. What chance have I got of pissing about at an apprenticeship of any sort? No, I'm stuck exactly where I am, well and truly trapped, a wallet on legs, that's all I am to them.'

Lucy hated it when he talked about his family, it made her feel guilty, although Fergus had always been open about his home life and emphatically denied that she was in any way the cause of the aggravation. His relationship with Margot had apparently gone sour years before, it was only their daughter India who kept them together. He had told Lucy he had been only twenty-two when a casual fling with Margot had turned serious when she got pregnant.

Margot was ten years older and already had a son, and Fergus had left college to take up the challenge of dad and stepdad.

'Sounds like we're both in the same boat. Don only loves my salary.' Lucy's laugh was low and dry. 'But seriously, if it's what you want to do why don't you go for some auditions or get an agent? I mean I don't really know how it all works but there must be a right way to do it if that's what you really want.'

'Yeah? Like when? In between deliveries? Before breakfast? After work? No, Luce, I gave up on that idea long ago. Take no notice, I'm just fantasising.' His eyes moved from the stage to Lucy's face. 'Same as I fantasise about both of us upping and leaving and starting over somewhere away from all the shit that's happening to both of us, but deep down I know that won't happen either.' Leaning back on his rickety chair, Fergus suddenly threw up his good arm and shouted, 'But hey, let's just enjoy tonight. Live for the moment, yeah? Who knows what tomorrow will bring? Another drink?'

Lucy watched as his tall and lanky figure worked its way through the crowd to the bar. Fergus was nearly the same height as Don, though Don had the bulk of a brick wall. With his thick, wavy hair that hung nearly to his shoulders and wearing tight jeans and a loud baggy shirt outside his trousers, Fergus looked more like one of the band members than the band themselves.

He looked back at her and smiled, a gentle, genuine smile that reached all the way from the dimple in his chin to the deep smile lines around his eyes. It affected Lucy so much she wanted to cry. Suddenly she knew for certain her instincts were right about him. Fergus would never treat her the way Don did.

Sadie hadn't been impressed when Lucy had asked her to provide an alibi for her but out of loyalty to her friend, and against her better judgement, she agreed. Although she strongly disapproved and thought Lucy was being reckless, Sadie could also understand why she was looking for more out of her life than a crap marriage to Donovan Cooper.

Sadie Khan had long ago put her friend Lucy on a pedestal. She admired everything about her and jealously guarded their relationship by making herself indispensable as a friend and confidante.

The day they had first crossed paths Sadie had instantly taken to her, admiring Lucy's open and confident personality and self-assured view of life. Sadie's rather sheltered upbringing had meant that setting off to university was more of a trial than an adventure but Lucy had happily bowled up there looking for fun as well as a degree.

It was Lucy who had brought Sadie out of herself and dragged her along to all the social activities that she would never have gone to alone, and therefore ensured that her time at uni was a time to be remembered. Distraught at the thought of them going their separate ways after graduation, it had been Sadie's idea to flatshare, an idea that Lucy had happily agreed to. Despite being opposites in looks, personalities and politics it had worked well. But then along had come the dreaded Donovan Cooper and ruined everything.

Sadie had never analysed her feelings for her friend. She simply accepted Lucy's often used description that they were 'like sisters'. It had come hard for Sadie, both emotionally and financially, when Lucy had, very tactfully of course, asked her to move out. Although Lucy had lent her the deposit so that she could rent a half-decent flat nearby, and had promised her faithfully that their friendship would never change, it inevitably had. Don had never liked Sadie and he made no secret of that fact, so it wasn't long before she stopped visiting Lucy at home. Their friendship soon became limited to brief telephone conversations and the very occasional night out.

Now things weren't going well in the Cooper marriage and Lucy was slowly but surely coming back into her life. But Sadie was torn. Pleased on one hand that their friendship was returning to how it had been, Sadie was resentful that it was only because Donovan Cooper was no longer Mr Wonderful in Lucy's eyes.

A lazy night in with a glass of wine and a video for company was what Sadie had been looking forward to despite being unhappy at the thought of Lucy being out with Fergus. She had put on her big baggy pyjamas covered in marauding teddy bears and curled up on the sofa, a bag of crisps at the ready. It was her idea of a perfect evening.

Until the doorbell rang and foolishly she opened the door wide.

'Where's Lucy?' Don's bulk almost filled the doorway.

Sadie was too horrified to speak. She was supposed to be having a girlie night in with her friend, she knew that's what Lucy had told Don, her reason for not going to the gym to watch her husband strut his stuff and be self-important.

'Come on, fatso, I want to speak to my wife. Where is she? She told me she would be here so where is she?'

Sadie knew there was no point in trying to stop Don when he pushed his way past her and started flinging doors open.

'At the off-licence getting some wine.'

'Bollocks. She's not here, never has been here, and isn't likely to be here tonight. I've been outside watching. Now where is she? Tell me before I smash this poxy little shithole of a flat to smithereens. Come on, *where's Lucy?*' Don was up so close to Sadie their bodies were touching. Slowly she took a step back but found herself pressed against the wall with nowhere to go. At that moment Sadie realised for the first time exactly what Lucy had meant about him. He was terrifying.

He moved his bulk closer still and pushed before suddenly reaching both hands up inside her pyjamas and grabbing her breasts as hard as he could. Teeth bared, he twisted hard and Sadie screamed. Immediately he clamped one hand over her mouth.

'Shut the fuck up and tell me where she is, fatso.' He moved his hand from her mouth and a slight dribble of blood ran down her chin from where her teeth had pierced the inside of her mouth. 'Scream again and I'll break your head. Now tell me where my wife is.'

'I don't know.' To her dismay big fat tears rolled down her cheeks and she bit deeply into her lip in an effort to regain control of herself. 'I really don't know where she is. She was supposed to be here but I had to go out and— *oouch*.' Don squeezed and twisted her breast again.

'Don't fucking lie to me.'

'I'm not. Now get out before I call the police.'

Don let go of her and started laughing. 'And what exactly would you tell them? That you invited me into your flat? That you tried it on and I refused? That's what you'll have to tell them, because that's exactly what I'll say. The ugly fat friend who can't find her own man so has to get off with her best friend's husband. I'm sure they'll believe you!' Don swaggered through the flat from lounge to bedroom and then back again, before sinking down into her favourite armchair. 'Now I'm going to stay here until that lying cheating wife of mine turns up, unless of course you tell me where she is and then I'll just pop off and find her and leave you in peace.'

'I've told you, I don't know where she is. Why don't you just phone her?'

'What, and let her know I'm hot on her heels? No, no, I'll just wait here. Aren't you going to offer me a drink?'

Sadie couldn't remember ever having been as frightened and intimidated. Don was leaning back in her chair, his vast legs stretched out across her carpet, a sarcastic grin on his face.

The thought of what he was capable of doing to her paled at the reality of what he would do to Lucy if he found out about Fergus. Her brain went into overdrive as she wondered how to warn her friend.

'Tea or coffee? I don't have any alcohol.'

'Coffee, black and strong.' He looked her up and down, a leering smirk on his face. 'Looking at your fat arse I bet you have cream and sugar in yours.' His spiteful laugh was frightening.

Deciding the best way to deal with the situation was to be reasonable, Sadie ignored the comment and headed out into the tiny hallway. She had no shoes on her feet and no coat to hand but her bag was on the hall table so she grabbed it and ran out into the street. Despite her first instinct to scream and shout for help, Sadie knew she had to warn Lucy. Don was capable of anything.

She dug into her bag and pulled out her phone and quickly punched in Lucy's number.

'Lucy,' she screamed at the answering service, 'Don's looking for you, he's completely off his head, don't go home and don't come here, he'll kill you and probably me too . . .' She glanced at her door and saw Don. He started running in her direction.

Sadie screamed and ran straight into the little all-night corner shop. 'Help me, help! I'm being attacked – help!'

Before anyone had time to react, Don was in his jeep and roaring off down the road.

'You want me to call the police? You know him?' The woman from the shop looked quite bewildered at the sight of Sadie in her pyjamas.

'No, it's OK, he's gone now. Don't worry about it and no, I don't know him, I think he was after my handbag.' She tried to smile as the shopkeeper stared at the barefoot young woman in her pyjamas standing in front of her. 'I just popped out for some cigarettes . . .'

Sadie ran out of the shop and back to her flat. She double-locked the door and put the chain on, vowing that in future she would be more security aware.

As the full impact of what had happened hit her she started shivering and couldn't stop. She tried Lucy's mobile again and cursed as the answering service clicked in once more.

★ ★ ★

Although Lucy hadn't been comfortable with the venue, she had enjoyed just being with Fergus and feeling relaxed and at ease with him. But she knew she could not risk being late back, in case Don got in early.

The taxi dropped her off at the door and as she was jogging happily up the stairs she decided to check her calls.

As she picked up the hysterical messages from Sadie her heart started pounding so hard she could barely hear herself think. Her head started to spin and the sickness reared up in her throat once again. Terrified, she turned on her heel but before she had a chance to run back down, the door flew open. Don's arm reached out and he dragged her inside the flat by her hair.

Chapter Four

'Lucy, if you won't go to the police then you have to phone your parents, they'll help you and I'm sure your dad will sort that bastard Don out. You have to do something and if you don't then I will. I'll call your parents. I can't stand by and do nothing, in fact I'm still tempted to call the police whatever you say.'

'No!' Lucy shouted, her eyes wide with panic. 'No, please don't, it really was my fault this time, I lied to him. I'm so sorry you got caught up in all this, it was all my fault and I shouldn't have involved you. I'll deal with it, I promise. If this gets out I'll lose my job, Don would make sure of it. I know what Caroline's like about scandal. And I can't tell Mummy and Daddy, I just can't.' Lucy felt guilty and uncomfortable but Sadie was the only person she could talk to about what had happened, though she couldn't bring herself to tell even her everything.

Sadie's face was grim as she studied her friend curled up like a little girl in the armchair. 'Lucy, not only did he nearly wring your head off your shoulders, he assaulted me, sexually assaulted me to be specific, and I have the goddamned bruises to prove it. Is your job really more important than that? How are you going to explain those marks round your neck when you go to work? You simply can't let that man roam the streets torturing anyone who upsets him. Friend or no friend, *no one* does that to me. Just who the fuck does he think he is? He's off his head.'

'I know, and I am so sorry, really I am, but the thought of everyone, especially Paul and Daniella, knowing what goes on in my private life just makes me feel ill.' Lucy hesitated before continuing. 'He really is very sorry, you know,' she said, trying to defuse Sadie's anger with what she knew was completely untrue. 'It's the first time I've seen him look as if he regrets what he's done. Please, Sadie, I—'

'Sorry? Sorry?' Sadie was up from her seat and pacing the room. 'Don't try and tell me he's sorry. For God's sake, Lucy, don't you realise I listen to crap like that nearly every working day? Sorry isn't good enough for what he did to you and it certainly isn't good enough for what he did to me.'

Lucy felt trapped. 'But—'

'But nothing, Lucy. I can't stand by and watch this happen.' Sadie continued to pace back and forth in front of Lucy, angry and distracted, running her hands through her hair. 'And I bet he never said a word about what he did to me, let alone apologised, did he? The asshole! He's not only beating you up physically, he's battering you mentally, you know. You're changing and it scares me. You were the strongest, most independent person I knew, confident, happy. But now look at you. And it's all down to Donovan Cooper.'

Sadie was furious with herself for not doing what her training had instilled in her, which was to call the police last night. But this was her friend, her best friend whom she loved dearly, and it was very difficult to be objective. She had spent the night worrying about Lucy, not daring to ring her, and then this morning Lucy had phoned, sobbing her heart out.

'Look at me, Lucy. Donovan Cooper is dangerous. You said yourself you think he's pumping drugs of some description into himself. Well, if he is, then that might explain his behaviour but it's no good just knowing why he's like it. You have to do something, for his sake as well as your own. You're not the same person, Lucy, he's grinding you down, your personality is shrinking.' Sadie stopped pacing and sat down opposite Lucy.

Chameleon-like, Lucy's blue eyes became steely and hard. She jumped to her feet, almost as if Sadie's words had suddenly penetrated and woken her up. The defensive body language of before had disappeared.

'Trust me, Sadie, I'm going to deal with it. He told me last night exactly what he feels about me and I know this can't go on.'

'What are you going to do?'

'I can't tell you, I haven't decided yet, but I'm going to deal with it, I promise.'

Sadie stood in front of Lucy and took hold of both her hands. 'I'm sorry for going on at you, I really am, but I'm so worried. He scared me last night and he made me so angry because I let him get the better of me. I'm not angry with you, really I'm not.'

The guilt that Lucy had been feeling suddenly overwhelmed her. She knew she had to take hold of her life and sort out the mess she had managed to get herself into. And she also knew that she had to do it alone and that it was not going to be easy. It was at that moment that Lucy realised she would have to be much more careful about confiding in Sadie. Their friendship was putting Sadie at risk from Don.

When Don had dragged her inside, it had happened so fast that Lucy hadn't been able to react, hadn't known how to react. Don had pulled her into the bedroom and thrown her onto the bed.

'Where have you been? Have you been with that Paul? *Tell me!*'

'I swear, Don, I haven't been with Paul, I swear it.'

As Don lunged at her she dug her heels into the mattress and tried to push herself away.

'Then where were you? You said you were going to fatso's. Why weren't you there? What are you playing at?'

Lucy had tried to work out what to say but with Don's huge hands tightly gripping her throat she couldn't think, let alone speak, and then the feeling of light-headedness wafted over her once again. Don's distorted face swayed about in front of her for a few seconds before oblivion descended.

'Lucy, open your eyes, this isn't funny. Wake up.' The disembodied words swirled around in her head for a few seconds before cold water hit her face and she opened her eyes to see Don with an empty water glass in his hand.

'Shit, I thought you were dead. What the fuck is up with you lately? You're always passing out.'

Lucy tried to gather her thoughts. She wiped the water out of her eyes and massaged her neck.

'Maybe the fact that you had your hands wrapped round my windpipe had something to do with it,' she said.

She pushed herself up onto her elbows and looked at the man in front of her, the first time she had looked at him so closely for ages. The once clean-cut features were bloated and his skin tone looked almost grubby, his eyes bloodshot.

'Don, tell me the truth, what is going on with you? What are you up to? Is it steroids?'

'Steroids? Where did you get that from? Who's been talking to you?' Once again the veins bulged and his hands clenched and unclenched.

'Nobody has said anything to me.' Lucy felt her heartbeat quicken. 'I just figured it out after I saw you with the syringe, when I fainted last week. I saw you, Don, you were going to inject something and you've been acting strangely. You're always so angry now.'

Don laughed sarcastically and roughly pushed Lucy back down onto the bed. 'You really are nuts, Lucy, do you know that? You were hallucinating, you stupid bitch. I wouldn't do anything like that.' His eye movement was rapid as he looked everywhere except at Lucy. 'You're just trying to talk your way out of where you were tonight. That's why I get angry, you're so fucking annoying, you drive me crazy. *You* make me angry, nothing else.'

She sat up straight, ignoring the dizziness brought on by

the sudden movement. 'Don, I just want to help. I hate seeing you like this.'

'The only way you can help me is by getting the fuck out of my face, you interfering bitch.'

She closed her eyes in anticipation of another onslaught and then flinched as he slammed the bedroom door. In some relief, she opened her eyes – to find he was still in the room. Arms crossed, Don stood against the door, his pose almost casual.

'Now are you going to tell me where you were or am I going to have to find another way of getting answers?'

'I was with friends from work. I was going to go round to Sadie's but I changed my mind. Are you accountable for every minute of every day? Do I follow you? Do I interrogate you? No, I don't.' Lucy was trying desperately to keep the fear, and guilt, out of her voice. Silently she told herself to keep calm and keep her head. 'Don, if we're both unhappy, is there any future for us? Maybe we should take some time out from each other . . .'

'Yeah, right, you really think I'm going to walk away and leave you with this flat and everything in it? Go and sleep on a friend's floor maybe while you ponder on my future and shag around with Paul Gower? Maybe you'd like to see me kipping out in King's Cross under the arches?' His eyes were still flickering all over the place. 'Not a chance.' The venom in his voice shocked her. 'You're my golden goose, Lucy, and if you want shot of me it's going to cost you and your parents. No way am I just going to walk away with nothing, and you're not going anywhere either unless it suits me. You're my wife. I own you.'

'So what you're saying is that you don't give a toss about

me and never have, is that right? All you're interested in is money? So why are you giving me all this grief?' And why pick on Paul?'

'Because Paul Gower is just your type, the kind of man you would go for now that you're so up your own arse and a bigshot in your precious firm. He's a smooth operator, a charmer, I've seen them in the gym just like him and I know how the sleazeballs work.' His voice was getting louder and Lucy just wanted to put her fingers in her ears to shut it out. 'I've seen the way he looks at you, adding up your bank balance in his head. Well, wifey, it's not going to happen because you're mine.'

Lucy said nothing, she just looked at him, determined not to cry, not to let him see one solitary tear. But her feelings were written all over her face.

'Actually,' his voice, now a lot quieter, broke the silence, 'there is one way out of all this. Your parents can buy me off. They can buy me my own flat and donate a few extra grand, quite a few extra grand, to keep me off the streets. How about it? Not a lot to ask in exchange for all this.' He swept his hand round the flat.

Despite the simmering violence that Lucy knew was just under the surface, she almost wanted to smile. Don wasn't the brightest star in the sky, he watched too much TV and never read newspapers so he had little understanding of real life. He thought he was being clever, but he was actually being very silly laying his cards on the table like this. Lucy now knew exactly what she was dealing with.

'I'll talk to them, I doubt they'll agree, but I'll talk to them. Now can I get out of the room please? I need a drink of water, my throat is killing me.' She rubbed her sore neck and walked over to the door with a confidence she was far from feeling.

To her relief Don stood aside and let her pass.

As she stood at the sink in the kitchen, frightened and nauseous, Lucy heard the door slam. Don had gone out.

She unfolded the futon in the spare room and curled up in a ball. Shaking and crying, she pulled the duvet up over her head and prayed that he wouldn't return.

Ever.

Lucy arrived at the office bright and early on Monday morning wearing a high polo-neck, a few dabs of concealer and several heavy swipes of blusher. She had crept around the flat for the rest of the weekend, terrified of provoking Don, but bizarrely he had carried on as usual, as if nothing out of the ordinary had happened.

The meeting that she had put an end to by passing out was re-scheduled for later this morning and Lucy knew her job really would be on the line if it had to be cancelled again. She was determined to make a concerted effort to shelve her personal problems during work hours.

Paul was already at his desk with his head down.

'Morning.' Lucy smiled automatically but as he looked up she gasped. 'Whatever happened to you?' Paul was sporting a huge black eye that spread from his eyebrow down round his cheekbone. His left hand was bandaged.

'I was mugged by a couple of apes. They jumped me in the car park out the back of my flat. The bastards crept up behind me and swung me round. One punched and one kicked.'

'Bloody hell, did they get much?'

Paul frowned and then groaned. 'Shit, I forgot I can't

crack a smile or a frown without pain shooting up through the top of my head. No, that's what's so strange, one of them punched me down and the other stamped on my hand but then they just ran off.'

'Did someone spook them?'

'Don't know. One of them said something about "learning lessons and staying away from married women", with a few expletives of course. All very strange, but the police said it happens all the time, they thought I was lucky to get away with just a black eye and a bruised hand. Oh well, *c'est la vie*. Well, in London anyway. Naughty boy I may be but I've always stayed clear of the married ones, so they must have got the wrong guy.'

Lucy felt dizzy, she could feel her legs getting wobbly.

Paul was looking at her. 'Hey, it's only a black eye, for God's sake. Don't go all weak-kneed on my account.'

Lucy dug her fingernails into the palms of her hands and breathed in deeply. Slowly but surely the feeling passed but her stomach still churned at the thought that Don might have been behind the attack. Probably not, she tried to convince herself, but possibly. Quite likely in fact; Lucy didn't believe in coincidences.

'Did you recognise either of them?' Mentally Lucy crossed her fingers.

'Hardly, they came from behind and it was dark. No, just a couple of opportunists high on something or other and talking crap. Luck of the draw. At least I'm alive to tell the tale.'

Lucy couldn't help but think about Fergus. He wouldn't stand a chance if Don or any of his friends got to him or, even worse, his family.

★ ★ ★

The meeting was less formal this time as everyone already knew the outline of Caroline's plan for the company but nevertheless the thought of all the responsibility Caroline was handing over was daunting.

It was agreed that Lucy and Paul would each have their own client portfolio as well as overseeing the rest of the staff. In effect they would be joint deputies and responsible for success or failure. While Paul, who was asking all the right questions and smiling and nodding in all the right places, obviously relished the idea, Lucy was quietly panicking. She was also not concentrating as hard as she should have. There was something she had to do and she had to do it soon, much as she didn't want to. The attack on Paul had focused her mind. Even if Don wasn't behind it, Lucy knew he was capable of it and a lot more.

As soon as Caroline and Luke ended the meeting, Lucy headed out onto the roof of the building. Normally there was a small huddle of smokers from all the offices in the building tucked away behind the door, surreptitiously puffing away, but Lucy had timed it well. No one was there. Looking around furtively she pulled out her phone.

'Hi, Fergus, it's me. Can you meet me at lunchtime as usual? In the deli at one? I have to talk to you, it's really important. If you can't make it then call my mobile but I have to see you.'

Lucy was frustrated at getting the message service, she was always wary of leaving messages in case they got into the wrong hands, but she knew she had to speak to him. She had made a decision.

She didn't see Daniella come through the door and

pause on the other side, listening intently, before scurrying back inside with a smug grin on her face, her cigarette forgotten.

'You don't mean it!' Fergus looked bewildered. 'What's this all about? Lucy, tell me you don't mean it. I don't understand.'

When Lucy had approached their usual table at the back of the deli, Fergus had smiled and waved. Casual as usual, he was lolling back in his chair blowing smoke rings up at the ceiling. He didn't seem to notice the tight and determined expression on her face – not until she sat down, her back ramrod straight, and told him why she had wanted to see him.

'I'm sorry, Fergus, but I do mean it. I can't see you any more, at least not while I'm still with Don. I have things I must sort out and my relationship with you is muddying the water. I can't carry on with it. I've been lying to Don and I hate myself for it, I've never been a liar.'

Lucy knew it was the only thing to do, that Sadie had been right. She had to end her marriage to Don before diving head first into another relationship, and after seeing what had happened to Paul she also knew that she had to protect Fergus.

'But what harm are we doing? You're in a bad marriage with someone who doesn't love you, Margot wouldn't notice if I dropped off the edge of the earth tomorrow, and we're hardly out and about flaunting it. I've tried to take it slowly, so why can't we still see each other? I love you, you know that. I can wait as long as it takes but I must see you, please.'

Lucy looked down at her hands; she knew she would weaken if she so much as glimpsed his deep brown eyes gazing at her in bewilderment. Although Fergus was very tactile he had never really said much about his feelings for her. Now he was telling her exactly how he felt and it was too late. She had to protect him and to do that she had to be hard.

'How can you say that? We hardly know each other, not really. We're attracted to each other, I admit, but we shouldn't be. You're not in love with me, we're both in love with the idea of a romance, an illicit romance. That's all it is. I'm married, and so are you, to all intents and purposes. It's wrong and I can't justify it. Imagine if Don found out?'

Closing his eyes, Fergus shook his head. 'I can't take this in. Why now? What's changed so suddenly?'

Lucy didn't answer, she just carried on looking at her hands that were carefully tearing a paper napkin into tiny pieces.

'Lucy, you can't do it. I've never felt like this about anyone and I know you feel the same. I knew the first time I saw you. Leave Don, just leave him. I'll leave Margot and we'll work from there. Please, we can do it.' His voice was low but rising. 'We can move away, go abroad, whatever you like. I know I'm not good with words, maybe I should have told you this before but—'

'I'm sorry, Fergus, that's just not possible.' She hesitated, not wanting to reinforce her words and hurt him, but knowing she had to. 'I'm really sorry, but I can't see you again. I don't want to see you again, we're finished.' She jumped up so quickly she tipped the table and all its contents towards Fergus.

Her last sight of Fergus was of him sitting, mouth agape, with a lap full of hot coffee. Biting her lip hard in an effort not to cry, she pushed her way through the lunchtime crowd with her head down.

Lucy didn't spot Daniella in the corner with her hair scruffed back in a big knot and a pair of designer sunglasses on the end of her nose, listening intently, trying to hear every word.

Daniella Schwarz was a beautiful young girl with everything going for her apart from one thing: a desperate need to have what anyone else had. Clothes, make-up, money, even men. It had always been the same and now Lucy was her focus. Lucy Cooper seemed to have it all and Daniella wanted it. She didn't seem able to have her own dreams and aspirations; she wanted Lucy's job, she wanted Lucy's salary, and most of all she wanted Paul who she was convinced fancied Lucy. All of this made her dislike Lucy intensely, so intensely that she would lie awake at night plotting her downfall.

No one knew anything about Daniella and that was the way she liked it. From a ragamuffin on a London sink estate she had ambitiously transformed herself, with the aid of magazines and television programmes, into what she wanted to be visually but that still left the inflated salary she felt she deserved, and an eligible man.

Paul Gower.

Suddenly it all looked good for her. Daniella knew she had to play it clever, it was no good just barging in and handing over the information for nothing, she had to use it carefully for maximum impact and gain. She had learnt that at primary school when she had seen the school bullies, who had made her life a misery, shoplifting. By deciding to watch and wait and manipulate from afar she had been able to make sure their eventual fall was spectacular.

She planned to do exactly the same with Lucy Cooper.

Smiling, she left the deli and sauntered happily back to work.

Lucy rushed back to the office and disappeared into the toilets. Ten minutes later she came out, her face made up again and wearing a phoney smile, ready to do her job despite everything.

In the following days she tried to blot Fergus out of her mind and concentrate on how she was going to deal with all the issues surrounding her marriage, but it was difficult. Every time Don was particularly obnoxious she wanted to pick up the phone and tell Fergus she was sorry, that she hadn't meant any of it. But she managed to resist the temptation. She kept telling herself she was doing the right thing.

She threw herself into a frenzy of work to keep herself sane. She stayed late in the office, she took work home and she went in over the weekends. Her desk was the clearest it had ever been and she took on as much as she could physically handle. With it came a certain satisfaction that very slightly took the edge off of her personal situation. No way could Caroline Pettit accuse her of not pulling her weight.

A few weeks later and Lucy was still struggling with herself.

'Lucy, can we have a meeting? There are a few issues we need to address. Caroline is still away so how about her office? Ten minutes?'

'No can do, Paul.' Lucy smiled apologetically. 'Too much on. I'm waiting for a call from the States and I have to check this copy right away. I can make it later this afternoon if it's important.' She could quite easily have asked for the expected call to be put through to her in the other office but she always balked at Paul's assumption that she should drop everything to fit in with him.

'Well of course it's important!' Paul's tone was curt and demanding. He was trying to make eye contact but Lucy just looked away. 'You don't seem to give a toss about this firm,' he continued. 'I don't know why Caroline promoted you in the first place, it doesn't need two of us to keep this place running smoothly, certainly not when one of us is too preoccupied to communicate.'

Lucy continued to smile, determined not to let Paul see her irritation. 'Oh, I think it does need both of us. Caroline and Luke's thinking was that we could support each other, bounce ideas off each other, in fact work together like adults, not the Lone Ranger and his obedient sidekick.'

'I don't know what you're—'

The phone on Lucy's desk rang.

'Sorry, Paul,' Lucy shrugged her shoulders, 'I've got to take this. Two o'clock suit you?' Without waiting for an answer she snatched up the phone.

Paul was being quite difficult. Lucy knew why, but it didn't make it any easier. Their joint promotion had stolen his thunder over the big account he had hooked and he was more than ever determined to prove his superiority.

Despite Caroline spending more time out of the office trawling for contracts from abroad, Lucy felt under more pressure than she ever had with Caroline on her case. Daniella, her hair bigger and longer and her skirts even shorter, had been taken on as a permanent receptionist and her relationship with Paul had progressed until, to her obvious delight, they were generally recognised as a couple. For Lucy that meant watching her back constantly with both of them. There was no way Daniella was going to continue being just the receptionist, she was openly after a junior executive position.

Reluctantly Lucy acknowledged that they were a good-looking couple and secretly she envied them their hectic social life. The invitations that arrived at the office every day of the week were now nearly always snapped up by the couple before Lucy got a look in, and they were out networking most nights. Apart from the ones that directly involved Lucy's clients, Paul and Daniella went to all the dinners and launch parties that were part and parcel of public relations work, while Lucy was left with the odd lunchtime function no one else fancied attending.

With no one to turn to, she found herself becoming increasingly lonely and isolated. Don was getting more unpredictable by the day and Lucy felt as if she was constantly walking on eggshells as she tried to keep the peace.

Although making the right noises, Sadie was being distant and Lucy still hadn't admitted to her parents that there was anything amiss. Every week she bounced happily through their phone conversations as if she didn't have a care in the world, as if everything in the marital garden was still rosy.

Then there was Fergus. Although it was over, Lucy simply couldn't turn her feelings for him off. There had been no contact between them since Lucy had determinedly rejected all his calls, and as he wasn't delivering to the office Lucy didn't know if he was back at work. The one thing she was grateful for was her job, the job she loved. Without it Lucy knew she would have fallen to pieces. It was as if her whole life was on hold while she tried to figure out the best way to deal with Don.

Just after two, Lucy headed in the direction of Caroline's office. Paul was already settled behind the expansive desk, looking as if he belonged there. To level the playing field, Lucy took a leaf out of Caroline's book and perched on the edge of the desk beside him.

'What can I do for you, Paul?' Lucy looked down at him, all too aware of how irritating she was being.

Paul laughed. 'Get down off your perch, Mrs Cooper, and sit beside me. I come in peace! I want us to sit down, clear the air, and then get on with what we both do best – running the firm and proving to Picky Pettit that we can do just as good a job as she can.'

The cogs of suspicion in Lucy's brain went into overdrive as she silently observed Paul. This was a man who knew that appearances mattered, who always looked as if he had just stepped out of Versace's shop window. His collection of designer clothes was a standing joke in the office, the speculation being that he had more clothes than Caroline.

Today he was wearing a pinstriped charcoal-grey suit, with knife-edge creases and hand-stitched lapels, that co-ordinated perfectly with an obviously brand new navy shirt and matching tie. Paul didn't do casual; he rarely even took his jacket off in the office.

As he regularly told her, he hadn't had the advantage of a university education. He had started at the bottom as an office junior straight from school in a large advertising company and worked his way up to where he was. At twenty-nine he was in a good position but Paul Gower wanted nothing less than to be managing director of his own company and multi-millionaire status.

Lucy looked him straight in the eye but stayed resolutely on the edge of the desk.

'I'm up for that, Paul, if it's a genuine offer. I do get a bit pissed with all the nonsensical bickering. It's no good for anyone, especially if Caroline catches us at it.' Lucy nodded her head in the direction of the main office and winked. 'But what about your little friend Daniella? It's really hard for me when I feel I'm constantly batting against her as well as you. Doesn't she have a mind of her own? You seem to pull her strings and she jumps.'

Paul smiled, his small, even teeth white against the slightly swarthy complexion that gave away his Mediterranean parentage. He really was a very good-looking young man, Lucy thought as she looked at him; just a shame about the streak of ruthless ambition that soured his personality.

'Dani is OK, just a bit intense. It's not my fault she's so madly in love with me she's constantly on the lookout for any devious dealings that might hurt me!'

Lucy felt her jaw drop, she couldn't believe what he had just said.

'Are you accusing me of being devious? Me? When you're the one always looking for a short cut behind my back or over my head? Christ Almighty, Paul, you've got a nerve.'

'No, no, no.' Paul was suddenly serious. 'You've taken it the wrong way again. I said that's what Dani thinks, I didn't say I did. I think you and I could actually make a bloody good team. In fact, in time I reckon we could set up on our own and wipe the floor with Pettit's.'

Lucy continued looking at him, her expression unchanged as she tried to decide whether he was baiting her or if he really meant it.

'What? What's the matter?' Paul stared at her. 'Don't tell me the idea has never crossed your mind. You surely don't intend to spend the rest of your life as second fiddle to Caroline and her dorky husband, do you? I certainly don't, and I doubt for a second they seriously expect us to. You know what it's like in this business, even musical chairs don't move as fast. You and I are the same whether you like it or not, we could set the world alight between us.'

Lucy knew he was right but at the same time she was too unsure of him to agree – just in case he was setting her up and then went running to Caroline to score points.

'Can't say I've ever given it any thought. I'm quite happy here and Caroline's been good to us.'

'Wrong,' he interjected sharply. 'Caroline has been no more than fair and we've been cracking good workers. We owe her nothing. She would drop either of us without a second thought if it suited her. That's the nature of the business. Keeping your ear to the ground and staying one step ahead of all the other buggers.'

'And Daniella? Where does she fit into your master plan?'

Paul shrugged his shoulders, put his hands up to his head and ran his fingers through his hair. 'Daniella who?' He smiled, realised he might have gone too far. 'Sorry, I don't mean to sound callous. She's a nice girl and we're having fun together but bright she isn't. She wants marriage, two point four children and a house in the suburbs, the complete opposite of where I'm at. Now you and I are on the same wavelength, we'd make a great team if you'd only get that stick out from up your backside and loosen up. How about it?'

'You always have to be coarse, don't you?' Lucy shook her head. 'I'd have to think about it. Actually I'm quite happy here, I like what I do and the Pettit salaries are excellent. Maybe I'm not as ambitious as you think. All in all I'm content with my job.'

'And what about your home life, Lucy? Are you content with that as well? You still look pale and peaky, not the same old sparkle there.'

'Don't even go there, Paul. My private life is none of your business and severely off limits.'

With that, Lucy slid off the desk and headed to the door. As her hand pulled at the door handle, she heard him mutter, 'I thought not.'

She chose to ignore it, biting her tongue hard. She knew that there was no way she could ever confide anything to Paul.

She did allow herself a hidden smile as she wondered exactly how Paul would have reacted if she had told him the truth. That her husband thought she was having an affair with him and that Don believed he was after her so-called inheritance!

Aware of Daniella glaring, her eyes wide with dislike, Lucy suddenly smiled at the girl.

'All right, Dani? You look a mite upset. Anything wrong?'

Daniella looked away first, focusing intently on the computer screen in front of her. 'No, I'm fine, just wondered what you and Paul had to talk about that took so long. We were supposed to be going out to lunch half an hour ago.' Her expression was sullen and childlike and Lucy suddenly realised how young she actually was. In fact, Lucy almost felt sorry for her, knowing that just as soon as Paul tired of her she would be unceremoniously dumped for a newer model.

'I'm sure he'll be out in a minute. Any calls while I was in the meeting?'

'Yes, they're on your desk. One didn't leave his name, said he'd call back later, wouldn't even leave a message. He had an *Irish* accent. Ring any bells?'

Daniella's staccato responses, accompanied by an exaggerated sucking in of her cheeks, really irritated Lucy but she didn't want to show it, and she certainly wasn't going to let the sullen young girl notice how much the two words 'Irish accent' had affected her. It could only be Fergus.

'Thanks.' Lucy smiled again, trying to be friendly, but Daniella's green eyes were still focused intently on the screen. Lucy was furious.

'Dani, I know you don't like me and that's fine, I can live with that, but we all have to work together and it would be much easier if we left our differences at the door in the mornings. There are eight people working in this office now and, if all goes to plan, another four to come.

Your attitude is bad for office morale and apart from anything else, it's downright rude. I hope it won't continue because I really don't want to have to deal with it formally via the disciplinary procedures.'

The flush that rose up Daniella's neck and made its way over her whole face clashed with her red hair. Her embarrassment and anger were impossible to disguise. Daniella looked away and tried to swing her hair over her face.

Back at her desk, Lucy considered what Paul had said both about work and about Daniella. She thought how strangely love could affect people, and immediately Don and Fergus flashed into her mind, as clearly as if they were standing in front of her. Love. What stupid things it made people do.

She had thought she was in love with Don, she had been in love with Don, madly in love with him. Stupidly and blindly in love with him, or rather with the man she thought he was. And then Fergus. Fergus knew nothing about her background; he knew she had a good job but that was it. But he still liked her, was in love with her, he had said, but could she believe him? Would he wait? She doubted it; after all, she hadn't been honest with him, she'd ended the relationship harshly and abruptly, with no real explanation.

If there was one thing that Donovan Cooper had successfully achieved during their marriage it was to grind Lucy down and fill her with self-doubt about everything personal in her life and even cause confusion in her career.

As Lucy sat at her desk chewing things over, and trying hard not to pick up the phone, something was niggling away at her. Something that she knew she should take note of but it just wouldn't work its way to the front of her mind.

Later on, when she was thinking of something completely different, it suddenly jumped out at her.

Daniella! The tone of the words '*Irish* accent – ring any bells?' The sucking in of cheeks, the sly glance up through the eyelashes.

She looked over at the girl perched delicately behind the reception desk and for a moment their eyes locked and Lucy was left in no doubt. Daniella's expression didn't change but the green eyes glistened almost victoriously. And if Daniella knew something then no doubt Paul did as well, and maybe Caroline.

Lucy could feel the same old tension rising, the wobbly legs and spinning head, leaving her feeling sick with fear.

Chapter Five

When Lucy had confronted Fergus in the deli and sprung the news that she was ending the relationship, Fergus had been thunderstruck, so thunderstruck in fact that he hadn't been as agile as he would normally have been.

If Lucy had turned round as she rushed out of the deli, she would have seen Fergus scrambling to his feet, desperately trying to catch her up, to stop her, but the pool of coffee and broken crockery slowed him down. By the time he got to the door she had already disappeared round the corner towards Pettit's and he was left on the pavement with warm coffee dripping slowly down his light khaki trousers.

He found it hard to take on board what had happened and he certainly couldn't figure out why or what he had done wrong. All he knew was that the love of his life was walking away from him without a second glance and there was nothing he could do about it.

He had to go back inside to pick up his bag and he could feel all eyes on him. Looking down to avoid the looks of amusement or sympathy, Fergus snatched up his backpack and made his way out again. Home was the last place he wanted to go but it was either that or buy a new pair of trousers that he couldn't afford.

As he put his key in the lock of his house he could hear raised voices, the same raised voices that echoed around the big old East End terraced house day in and day out. He often wondered why none of them seemed capable of having a normal conversation at a normal volume. Even a fairly happy conversation was conducted at a level that echoed outside and sounded like a blazing row.

Fergus tried to get in and up the stairs without being seen but the kitchen door flew open just as he got his foot on the bottom step.

'Dad! What have you been up to?' India, his daughter, looked straight at his stained trousers and shrieked with laughter. 'Mum, quick, come and see. Dad's pissed his pants, dirty old git. He's drenched. Come and look!'

'Will you not be quite so rude, India. I spilt a cup of coffee.'

'Yeah, right, any excuse for wetting yourself. What happened? Did you come face to face with a poodle that scared the shit out of you?'

Fergus despaired of India. He had tried so hard with her, determined that his only daughter would be different to all the other kids kicking around the nearby streets, but his gentle approach to life had been constantly over-powered by Margot and her out-of-control son Simon. Now India was fifteen and he could think of no way of controlling her without Margot's support.

As he looked at her, he wanted to weep. The girl was a

stunner, sharp as a carving knife but with the manners and mouth of her uncouth stepbrother. She was tall, heading for six foot, and slender but well developed and Fergus knew for a fact that she was out and about in the nearby pubs and clubs with dubious lads, happily producing a fake ID on the rare occasions she was confronted. Her long black hair, thick and glossy, was usually pulled up on top of her head and, underneath all the cheap make-up, was a clear skin. The slightly oval dark brown eyes were framed with long dark lashes, but still she caked them in cheap cloggy mascara and outlined them in deepest black eyeliner. Despite her natural beauty, when all the make-up was in place and India was in street mode – aggressive arrogance – she appeared ugly and intimidating.

Fergus often wished he had followed his instincts and picked her up as a baby and taken her to Ireland, to his family in Dublin, who would have loved and raised her in the gentle environment he himself had been brought up in. Instead he had done what he thought was best at the time and stayed with her mother Margot to build a family life. After fifteen years, he thought, no one could accuse him of shirking his responsibilities, but it hadn't been right for either India or himself.

'India, please, mind your manners. There's no need to speak to me like that. Anyway, why aren't you at school?'

'Leave her alone, for Christ's sake.' Margot's voice bellowed down the hall. 'Straight in the door and you start. Leave the poor little cow be, she's only having a laugh.'

The smug grin that spread over India's face was quickly followed by her middle finger being stuck up in front of Fergus's face.

'That's right, Dad. Leave me be, I'm only having a laugh.' The sarcasm in her voice upset him far more than the accompanying gesture; he wanted to slap her face but couldn't quite bring himself to, knowing what the reaction from all of them would be. It was always, without fail, three to one against him in this household. So once again he said nothing.

Fergus knew his daughter could have held her own among the gorgeous models and actors that he regularly came across in the various agencies that he couriered for. But she had no ambition other than to hang around with the worst young hooligans in the area, getting drunk, picking on any unsuspecting passer-by and generally getting into trouble. It seemed to him that the future for India was either a teenage pregnancy that would effectively put a halt to her life and ruin any chance of her growing out of her problems, or prison. He hated to admit it, but his beloved daughter, the cuddly little bundle that he had fallen in love with at first sight, had grown up to be a thug and a bully.

Walking upstairs to get changed, Fergus felt painfully fed up with his life. His burgeoning relationship with Lucy had at least given him some hope for his future but now even that was gone.

He had been attracted to her the very first time he saw her but had tried hard not to think too much about it because of Margot, and then he had discovered that Lucy was married and tried backing off completely. But it didn't work, there was a spark between them. After taking a chance and asking her for an innocent lunchtime drink, which she had willingly agreed to, he really thought that he had found his soul mate and a friend.

But now he was back to square one with no idea why Lucy had suddenly changed her mind and finished with him. He could still see her in front of him, the very first time. Tall and blonde with a wide, genuine smile, she had actually noticed him as a person. Often when he dropped off packages, they were either snatched and signed for without a glance or the girls had a token flirt with 'the bit of rough delivery man', but Lucy had smiled, joked and offered him a cup of tea.

'Dad! Daaaad! Where are you?' India's voice echoed up the stairs, rudely interrupting his thoughts. 'Mum wants you! Daaaaad . . .'

'I'll be down in a minute, I'm just getting changed. And please don't shriek like that, India.' Fergus sighed and a moment later went downstairs, thoughtfully rubbing his hands down the once highly polished banister.

The big old Victorian house had belonged to Margot's mother, and she had left it to her two daughters, Margot and Lizzie. Fergus had bought Lizzie's share but as far as Margot was concerned, and as she told anyone and everyone, it was *her* house left to her by *her* mother.

The house had been in a state of disrepair, almost derelict in fact, but Fergus had spent a lot of time and money restoring it where possible and modernising where necessary and now it was worth quite a lot of money. The area where they lived in east London was no longer classed as deprived, up-and-coming young city workers were fast moving in and property prices were zooming. Yet still the family treated it with contempt. Not one of them, Margot included, appreciated all the hard work and love he had put into the place to turn it into a home for them all.

As usual Margot didn't even turn round when he walked into the kitchen. She was perched awkwardly beside the breakfast bar on a high kitchen stool with her head in her hands, gazing at the television fixed high on the wall. He walked over with his hands in his pockets and pecked her on the top of her head.

'Hi, Margi. India said you wanted me. I had an accident with a cup of coffee, had to go and change.'

'I'm gasping for a cuppa. Put the kettle on and I'll tell you.' Margot paused for a second for effect. 'Your firm rang. They wanna know when you're going back to work. Me too. Any idea? I'm getting really, really pissed off with not enough money and you under my feet. They weren't happy to know you weren't too ill to be out and about Christ knows where.' Margot didn't bother to take her eyes off the flickering screen as she spoke to him.

'You know I can't do anything until the plaster's off and so do they. What did you say to whoever it was? Did you get a name?'

'Nope. I said you'd ring when, or if, you got back.'

Fergus took the kettle over to the sink and filled it. As he plugged it in he looked over at Margot and shook his head. Mid-afternoon and she was still in the green velour dressing gown that shrouded her from top to toe. Margot had never been small but now she bordered on obese, mainly because she did nothing at all other than lounge around watching soap operas and chat shows. There were five televisions in the house and so long as she had a pack of cigarettes, a couple of bars of chocolate and a steady supply of tea, she was happy. Her hair was cropped short and bleached nearly white, she rarely wore any make-up, and when she bothered to get dressed, it was always in the same mode – tight Lycra leggings with a big baggy T-shirt or sweatshirt and clumpy trainers.

Hating himself for doing it, he couldn't help compare her to Lucy. Beautiful and stylish Lucy who talked to him, smiled at him, held his hand and appreciated his little messages and whatever time they could grab together. Bright and intelligent Lucy, who worked hard and supported both herself and her no-good husband. He smiled grimly as he thought that Margot and Don would make a fine match, providing one or other of them won the lottery!

'Why isn't India at school today? She's going to get in trouble again. We promised the head and the welfare officer . . .'

Margot swung away from the television and looked at him. It was a look that told him, without doubt, how much she despised him and how little notice she took of anything he said or did. He often wondered how she would react if he treated her the same way her ex-husband, Simon's father, had, dragging her across the floor by her hair and kicking her into submission with booted feet over any little thing that took his fancy.

Fergus had never raised a finger to anyone but instead of seeing that as a strength, Margot saw it as weakness and walked all over him.

'Oh, leave it out. I don't want to listen to all that crap again. What's school going to do for her? It never did you and me any good and it never did anything for my Simon.'

'Yeah, I noticed.' His voice was quiet.

'So what's the problem then? If she don't want to go, she don't have to. She's just a kid, let her enjoy herself.' Margot completely missed the sarcasm in Fergus's voice, she really thought he was agreeing with her.

'But Margi, she's a bright girl, she could really make something of herself, her life. I hate seeing her running round with that gang of no-goods. She'll be in real trouble before you know it if we don't do something real soon. Do you really want her in and out of the courts like Simon? Do you want coppers on the step every other day?'

For a large woman Margot could be extremely agile; she was off her chair in a flash, standing in front of him, her forefinger dabbing fiercely at his chest.

'You leave my boy out of this. You've never been interested in him, it's always India, India, India. Daddy's precious little girl. Well, it's too late now for you to start interfering with either of my kids. This is my fucking house, so if you don't like it you can just piss off, find someone else to look after you.' Her bulbous face was so screwed with fury, her eyes nearly disappeared.

Fergus allowed himself a smile. 'Look after me? Give it a rest, Margot, you've never done a jot for me in all the time we've been together. And money? How are you going to manage to pay for *your* house without me flogging myself to death on that bike? Taking my life in my hands every day while you sit on your fat arse and watch television for idiots. Jeez, you can't even manage on my sick pay for a few weeks.'

'You arrogant bastard, who the fuck do you think you are coming in here and getting on your high horse. *Bastard!*' She screamed the word at him.

He heard footsteps thundering towards the kitchen door; either India or Simon was en route to join the fray – to side with their mother. He couldn't face listening to any more so he turned quickly and went out of the back door, slamming it fiercely behind him.

'You get yourself back here, Fergus Pearson, just get back here.' Margot's voice echoed up the alleyway but he had no intention of going back. He legged it down the road, knowing it wouldn't be long before Margot was in the street in her dressing gown, shouting the odds after him for everyone to hear.

The small park a few minutes away was Fergus's favourite hideout. During the day in school term time it was usually deserted, bar a few dog-walkers and retired strollers, out looking for someone to chat to. As parks went, it wasn't exactly spacious, there were just a few bushes, a couple of trees and a rickety wooden bench with a brick under one of the broken legs but Fergus had taken to spending more and more time there since his accident. He realised he was actually getting used to a slower pace of life away from the gridlocked London streets and the haze of exhaust fumes in his face.

Sitting on the bench with his long gangly legs stretched out in front of him, he closed his eyes and turned his face to the lukewarm sun as he thought about his life. He thought about Margot, who treated him with less affection than she did the cat and she didn't like that very much. Then there was Simon, her son, whom Fergus had tried his best with but who was now a shaven and booted fascist thug just out of prison for the umpteenth time. Last but not least, and the only reason he had stayed so long, his

113

daughter India, whom he still loved but didn't like one little bit.

And then of course there was Lucy. The light at the end of the tunnel that had, without warning or reason, gone out. The story of his life, starting with Lorraine, his first love, who had only wanted friendship.

He pulled his phone out and dialled Lucy's number. It was on answering service. He didn't leave a message. Deep down he knew he should let her go, in the short term at least, but he found it so hard. He guessed something must have happened, something to do with Don that Lucy didn't want to tell him about. He wondered how he could find out. He also wondered how he would cope if, when he went back to work, he still had to make deliveries to Pettit's and come face to face with her. He wanted to see her but at the same time wasn't sure how he would react, how he would feel in the clinical reception of the agency, unable to exchange a knowing glance, a slight smile, maybe not even say hello.

He couldn't imagine it.

At last it was time for Fergus's plaster to come off. As he queued and hung around in the busy hospital waiting area, he thought about how much better it would have been if Lucy had been there with him. He had tried ringing her a few times in desperation but it was always either the message service or the phone was switched off and he didn't want to leave a message in case Don picked it up. He wanted to hang around outside Pettit's, anything just to see her, but deep down he knew that he would blow any chance he still might have if he started harassing her.

Far from getting better, it was getting worse. Absence definitely did make the heart grow fonder, he decided. The public telephone on the wall opposite his seat almost beckoned him and he did exactly what he had determined not to do. He rang her at Pettit's, but he was told she was in a meeting. He quickly put the phone down without leaving a message. No one there would know him, Lucy would never know he had phoned.

But she did, because Daniella took the call and, being a lot brighter than everyone assumed, guessed exactly who it was. Yet another piece of information for her to squirrel away until the right time.

Daniella had decided the time was right.

'Guess what, Paul? I know something you don't and for a small fee, a very small fee as it's you, I'll share my information with you.'

'Mmmm?' Paul was distracted. He was desperately trying to amend a news release that was due out the next morning and Daniella just wouldn't leave him alone. She had wheeled one of the spare chairs over to his desk and was girlishly lolling over it, trying to catch his attention. She was really starting to irritate him with her twittering and giggling. He had long decided that she was lovely to look at, good to be in bed with and great to be seen with but oh so boring to listen to. It was just a matter of getting round to doing something about it.

'Well, a few weeks ago I was up on the roof having a ciggie, I can't remember which day it was but I know it was cold, when I heard the ice maiden making a sly phone call.' She stopped and nudged him, making him lose his place. 'Are you listening to me? This is really good. As I said, I was up on the roof having a ciggie . . . Paul,' she nudged him harder, 'listen, you'll like this.'

Paul felt his nerves snap as the nudge pushed his pen over the sheet of paper. Abruptly he stood up and his chair sped across the room and banged into the wall.

'Dani, will you just go away? You're driving me nuts. I'm trying to work here.'

'Yes, I know, but listen, I'm going to tell you something really good.' Dani, too, stood up and pulled at his sleeve like a child seeking attention.

'I don't want to hear anything you have to say, in fact I don't want to listen to you ever again. Just piss off, Dani, and let me get on with my work.'

The everyday office bustle ground to a standstill as Paul's voice reverberated round the room. Everyone tried to pretend they weren't listening but the silence was deafening.

'What? What have I done? I was only trying to tell you something.' Daniella's face crumpled at the unexpected attack from Paul. 'I don't understand what I've done.'

'What you've done is irritate the hell out of me. I'm trying to work but all you can do is yak, yak, yak and tug at my bloody clothes. I'm not your father and you're not a bloody five-year-old so stop acting like one. Now leave me alone.' Paul's face was red and a thin layer of perspiration had spread over his features. Automatically straightening his tie and lapels, he looked straight ahead and walked purposefully over to the small utilitarian kitchen, firmly shutting the door behind him, leaving a weeping Daniella to be comforted by the two other young men in the office who were noticeably in lust with her.

Lucy had watched in amazement. It had irritated her to see Daniella leaning across his desk, her endless legs crossed delicately to conceal her knickers and her boobs begging for attention. It was the sort of performance that Paul usually enjoyed, but obviously not this time.

Lucy had never seen the suave Paul Gower really lose control before. With everyone busy fussing over a semi-hysterical Daniella, she slipped unnoticed across the room to the kitchen. Knocking gently, she waited only a split second before opening the door.

'Hi. Tell me to piss off if you want but I thought you might need some company. Cup of coffee? Bottle of Scotch? Something stronger?'

'Definitely something stronger. I've just made a right prat of myself, haven't I? I can't believe I just did that.' Paul was leaning back against the fridge with his arms crossed. 'I really can't believe I kicked off in front of them all. If Caroline had seen – jeez, I dread to think.' He looked at her and raised an eyebrow. 'You're not going to tell her, are you?'

'Oh, thanks a lot, Paul, now you think I'm a snitch as well as everything else!' Lucy smiled sympathetically. 'Don't forget this is me here, the one who chucked all over Caroline's Jimmy Choos. Nothing could be worse than that.' Lucy filled the kettle and got out two mugs. 'I'll make a drink, you take a few minutes to calm down, and then we'll go out. The sooner the better. Trust me, I know. The longer you stay in here, the more embarrassing it'll be.'

'Mmm.' Paul screwed his face up. 'We'll see. I suppose I

ought to go and make my peace with Dani, I can hear her sobbing from here.'

Lucy peered through the blind that hung over the glass door. 'I hate to say this, Paul, but Dani is loving every minute of the attention, they're all farting about out there like a clutch of mother hens. I'm going to have to go and call a halt before it gets out of hand. You stay here and drink your coffee, calm your nerves.'

Lucy was determined not to be seen as the villain of the piece so she fixed a caring smile on her face and went over to where Dani was holding court. She had retreated back to the reception desk and was sitting with her head in her hands, weeping prettily.

'I don't understand, I just don't understand, how could Paul do that to me? How could he speak to me like that?'

Lucy patted her on the shoulder. 'OK, Dani, I know you're upset but this isn't the right place, not in public. You go off to the ladies and I'll make you a hot drink and bring it through.'

The curtain of hair moved away from Daniella's face just long enough for Lucy to be stunned by the sheer hatred in her eyes and the nasty curl of her lips. But Daniella said nothing, she just stood up and walked gracefully across the room in the direction of the cloakrooms. Lucy followed, and as soon as they were out of sight of the office, Daniella spun round.

'Get away from me. I know what your game is, what you've done and what's coming to you.' She flicked at Lucy as if she was swatting a fly. 'You're not going to get Paul, you know, I'll make sure of it.'

'Whatever are you talking about?'

'Don't come over all innocent with me, don't *Dani* me. I know you've been shagging that courier – Fergus, isn't it? And now you've set your sights higher, on my Paul. I've been watching you. Well, you're not having him. You're married, for fuck's sake, you slut. Just how many men do you need?'

Lucy couldn't believe what she was hearing. Daniella carried on into the ladies, with a stunned Lucy behind her.

'Don't you dare talk to me like that. I'm going to have to tell Caroline.'

'You tell Caroline and I'll tell the whole office exactly what you're like. Did you know they call you the ice maiden?' She paused, waiting for a reaction, but Lucy was too stunned to even change her expression, let alone respond.

'Well, I saw and heard you in Boney's Deli and I think super slut would be more appropriate. So next time you get all uppity with me, just remember, *I know*, I've known for weeks and now I'm going to make sure everyone else knows, including your pet gorilla.' Daniella brought her hand up to her mouth, feigning shock. 'Oh, I'm sorry, didn't you know that's what they call your husband? Yep, the gorilla and the ice maiden. Flattering, isn't it?'

She turned her back on Lucy and she touched up her lipgloss, all the time looking at Lucy in the mirror.

'However, if I should get the junior exec job, and of course get to keep Paul, because I know you're going to put a good word in for me on both fronts, then I may just forget about you and your bit on the side. Think about it.' And she flounced out.

Lucy felt sick. As she stood there desperately trying to

calm herself, the door flew open.

'Are you OK, Lucy? Everyone's wondering where you've got to.' Daniella's smugly smiling face appeared in front of her. 'I said you were just taking time out, that you had a lot on your mind. That's right, isn't it? A lot to think about?'

As soon as Lucy's hand connected sharply with Daniella's left cheek, she knew she had done the very worst thing possible. She had played right into Daniella's hands. Far from looking upset, Daniella appeared distinctly victorious as she turned and left the cloakroom.

By the time Lucy surfaced with slightly calmer nerves and a bit of colour in her face, the office was back to normal and Daniella and Paul were closeted in Caroline's office. Lucy's heart sank at the sight of the pair of them together; she guessed that it would only be a matter of time before her whole life fell apart.

Chapter Six

As soon as she left the office, Lucy dialled Caroline's home number, hoping against hope that Luke would answer the phone, that Caroline wasn't back from her trip.

'Luke Pettit speaking.'

Lucy heaved a sigh of relief. She knew that, out of the two, Luke would probably be more sympathetic, more likely to listen to all the facts first and react afterwards.

'Luke, it's Lucy Cooper here. I'm really sorry to disturb you at home but I need a word with you and Caroline urgently.'

'That's going to be a little difficult, pet, Caroline's not back from the States. She decided to stay an extra week and meet with our clients in LA.'

'Can I talk to you then? It's really important. Could I possibly come and see you at home? I don't really want to discuss it in the office.'

The hesitation was brief. Lucy guessed Luke was wondering if, as a sleeping partner with very little input in the running of the company, he should be dealing with staff

121

when his wife was away. Lucy liked Luke a lot but compared to Caroline he was almost ineffectual; his motto appeared to be 'anything for a quiet life', and that applied across the board for him.

'If it's that important then of course you can. Come right on over and we'll have a chat over a wee dram or two but I can't promise to be able to help and I do have a dinner engagement later this evening.'

'Thanks, Luke, if you're sure I'm not intruding? It really won't take that long.'

'No probs, Lucy pet, none at all.'

'OK, I'll jump in a cab and be with you in about fifteen minutes, depending on traffic.'

Lucy wasn't sure what she was going to say, she wasn't even really sure why she was going but she was determined that Daniella was not going to have the pleasure of flouncing in to tell Caroline and Luke all about her personal life. She was going to pre-empt her somehow.

Lucy had only been to the Pettits' London apartment once before when Caroline hosted a company reception there. From the outside the building was quite bland, a big old box on the River Thames that in its time had been just another warehouse storing all manner of both exotic and ordinary goods from all over the world. But trading had long since ceased and the derelict building had been gutted, renovated and divided up into a series of expensive New York-style loft apartments, big empty shells of varying sizes that were bought and transformed by imaginative owners, from basic studio through to penthouse – which was where the Pettits lived.

When Lucy had visited before she had been overawed by

both the penthouse itself and also the views but this time she was too distracted to fantasise about owning one herself.

Luke answered the intercom and called her up. He opened the door and smiled a welcome, a big broad smile that genuinely gave the impression he was pleased to see her, but the invisible professional boundary was there.

'Come in, Lucy. Come in and pull up a chair, metaphorically speaking of course, and tell me what the problem is.'

When she didn't answer straight away, Luke looked at her carefully. 'I take it there's a big problem otherwise you wouldn't be here, would you? OK, time enough for that in a minute. What can I get you to drink? I'm on G and T, first of the day!' He smiled. 'Mind you, I always say that, don't I?'

Lucy sat carefully on the edge of an oversized off-white armchair, feeling distinctly uncomfortable, suddenly unsure of herself and wishing she wasn't there.

'I'll have the same, if that's OK.'

While Luke busied himself at the bar, Lucy looked around. The apartment could easily have passed for a showhouse, there was very little to indicate anyone actually lived there. All the furnishings were a careful blend of pristine but plain with expensive ornaments and fresh flowers strategically placed for maximum impact. The hand of a professional cleaner was obvious, no fine layer of daily dust coated the glass shelving, and the pile of the carpet had been vacuumed in the same direction.

Not a single thing was out of place apart from the pile of newspapers and files that were piled up in an untidy heap beside Luke's chair. She could see why Luke preferred to be at the country house with his horses and muddy dogs. Although Lucy had never been there, she could easily imagine Luke in his green wellies and well-worn Barbour jacket, with a gun under his arm and a couple of dogs running alongside him as he tramped the countryside. He just didn't fit into these chrome and glass surroundings at all.

But Caroline did, perfectly.

Chalk and cheese, Lucy thought as she vaguely wondered what made the couple tick, but the marriage seemed to work and she envied them that.

Luke handed her the drink. 'Now what can I do for you?'

Lucy took a deep breath. 'I have to hand in my notice, I have to leave Pettit's. I'm sorry, Luke, I don't want to but I have no choice . . .' Lucy was babbling, desperate to get the words out while she still had the courage to do it.

'I see.' He hesitated, looking at her closely. His almost watery eyes were fixed on her face as he spoke. 'What's brought this on so suddenly? Have you been head-hunted by one of our esteemed rivals in business?'

'Oh God no, Luke. It's nothing like that. I really don't want to leave, I love my job, but I have to go. Before it all blows and then you sack me, I have to go now—'

Luke held up his hand. 'Whoa, stop right there. I haven't got a clue what you're talking about. Now, slow down, take a hefty swig from your glass, and start at the beginning, but remember, I don't want you doing anything hasty, we value you very much at the company, you know.'

Once again Lucy was relieved that it was Luke she was

124

face to face with and not Caroline who, she was sure, would have accepted her notice with a businesslike smile and shown her the door.

'I've got myself into a bit of a fix, Luke, and I can't see any way out of it. You know my husband, Don? Well, he's about to be hit with a bombshell and I just know it's going to explode back to Pettit's.'

Lucy did as she was bid and started at the beginning, and to Luke's credit, he listened intently without interrupting or making any comment until she had finished.

'And tell me, young lady, why it is exactly that you feel you have to leave?'

Lucy looked puzzled. 'It's obvious, isn't it? Caroline hates scandal and scandal is what she'll get if Daniella goes to Don. Caroline wouldn't want that sort of thing impacting on the firm's reputation, we all know that. My severance pay would be in my hand before I could blink.'

As he took a sip of his drink, Luke's face tightened noticeably. His soft, almost effeminate features were suddenly harder and the insipid light-grey eyes shone fiercely.

'Really? Is that the way you perceive Caroline? I hadn't realised . . .' He looked at her and raised his eyebrows. 'Don't you think I'm the best judge of my wife's, and of course the company's, reactions? I think you're doing us both a disservice with unsupported guesswork like that. Now let me tell you something about my Caroline, in brief, and between you, me and the gatepost of course . . .'

By the time he had finished, Lucy had a completely different perspective on Caroline Pettit, her boss and the driving force behind what was fast becoming one of the most powerful and successful PR companies in London.

'Now, I can see that you think you're caught between the proverbial rock and a hard place, but trust me, Lucy, it can all be resolved. I will sort this out for you as far as your career is concerned. I have an idea that might help the situation but I have to discuss it with Caroline first. However,' Luke put his head on one side and wagged his index finger at her, 'your personal life is something only you can deal with and I wouldn't even presume to offer you any advice other than to follow your own instincts. You're a bright girl, you can figure out the best thing for you. So, off you go and deal with it and leave Caroline to me.'

At the door he affectionately gave Lucy a hug and kissed her on both cheeks.

'I have to be in the office in the morning, I'm under orders to check up on you all, so I'll have a word with silly Miss Daniella Schwarz at the same time and nip this nonsense of hers in the bud. Then after I've had a chat with Caroline, I'll get back to you. OK?'

'Luke, I appreciate this so much. I had visions of leaving Pettit's with no future. Are you really sure Caroline will be OK about it? Suppose Don—'

'Get ye gone, child.' Luke laughed and pushed Lucy towards the door. 'I'll see you tomorrow. It will not be a problem.'

Lucy left the apartment feeling a lot happier than she had for a long time. Her career was sort of safe, but she still had to deal with Don and her terminally ill marriage. She wondered if she dare just walk out, walk away and leave him with the flat he regarded so highly. It was easy for Luke, a millionaire in his own right, to suggest that money wasn't everything, but it was if it was all you had. No, she decided, she would see a solicitor in the morning and find out where she stood and then take it from there.

Fired by Luke's encouragement to take her life in hand, Lucy tripped out of the building in high spirits. Maybe then she could contact Fergus again, maybe they could get together again . . .

She was too wrapped up in her thoughts to notice the van careering towards the pavement, completely out of control. The squeal of brakes was the first thing Lucy heard and she looked in the direction of the sound. Frozen to the spot, she registered what was happening but her feet simply would not move. As the van headed straight towards her, with two wheels firmly wedged on the pavement, her eyes flickered in fear. The last thing she saw was the haunted face of the young driver as he wrestled with the steering wheel to turn the van away but by then it was too late for both of them.

Lucy didn't know where she was when she first came round in the ambulance to the sound of sirens, and with someone she didn't recognise leaning over her. Panic threatened to choke her when she realised there was something clamped over her mouth. She thought it was a hand, Don's hand. Had he followed her to Luke's? When her eyes finally focused and her mind started to function again she could see a concerned face and hear a voice speaking the same words over and over in an attempt to reassure her.

'You're going to be just fine, don't try and speak, we're

taking you to St Lawrence's. You'll be OK. You've had an accident but you're OK.'

Lucy tried to pull herself up, tugging at the plastic tubing.

'No!' The paramedic pulled her hand away. 'Leave it there, it's only an oxygen mask, it's to help you breathe. You were knocked unconscious.'

Lucy fell back onto the hard, narrow ambulance trolley and tried to think. By the time she was transferred into the accident centre she could just about remember what had happened. She could see again the terrified face of the driver of the van that had ploughed towards her, managing to turn just enough to avoid pinning her against the wall but not enough to avoid her altogether. She could remember being clipped by the front wing and thrown to the ground but that was all.

She tried fidgeting her arms and legs but the shooting pain that travelled up her legs into her body was so strong she was convinced she was going to lose her legs. Meanwhile her head was busy telling her she had the worst headache in the world.

She took the doctor's advice and lay still as she was pulled and pushed, examined and injected and then finally wheeled in for a battery of X-rays with an ashen-faced Sadie by her side.

By the time she was back in the A&E department she was feeling relatively pain-free and vaguely detached from the situation. Eyelids drooping, she had to really concentrate to take on board everything Sadie was saying.

Good old Sadie, she thought, always comes through in a crisis.

'I really think you should let someone call Don.'

'No.' It had been Sadie's number she had given to the staff and it was only Sadie she wanted with her. 'I don't want Don here, I just want to get out of here and get home. Caroline will have a fit if I have any more time off. Oh shit, I've just thought – can you ring Luke? That's where I was, I'd been to see him, his number's in my phone.'

'Yes, OK.' Sadie was grasping her friend's hand tightly. She was still in shock herself from the phone call. 'But I really think you should let me call Don. He is your husband and next of kin, really you should tell him, they're bound to keep you in.'

'They won't, will they?' Lucy looked at Sadie in horror, the thought hadn't occurred to her. 'I feel OK, just a bit bruised and bashed about, they don't think anything is broken.' She smiled weakly. 'A bit like as if I've gone a few rounds with Don, in fact!'

'Don't joke about things like that. It was the first thing that went through my mind when they phoned to say you had had an accident. I thought he'd beaten you up. I suppose I owe him a mental apology really.' Sadie looked intently at Lucy and half smiled. 'Although on second thoughts, not.'

Sadie left the cubicle to call Luke, promising she'd be quick. Lucy lay back against the pillow, closed her eyes, and tried to relax. As soon as her friend returned, though, the curtains whisked back and the doctor who had examined her when she was first wheeled in appeared with a folder under his arm. Slightly behind him was the familiar face of Judy, the nurse who had taken time to comfort

Lucy and give her a motherly cuddle while she was waiting for Sadie to arrive.

'Well, Mrs Cooper, good news. You were very lucky, I think you must have bounced off the bonnet. Nothing is broken although you're going to be very sore for a while with all that bruising to the pelvis and legs. It's fortunate you're so fit but we need to keep an eye on you because you took a hefty bang on the head and of course you were knocked unconscious.' He hesitated and looked first at Lucy and then at Sadie.

'Mrs Cooper, there's something else we need to talk about. Would you sooner your friend left for a few minutes or are you happy to discuss personal matters with her present?'

'It's OK. Sadie's my friend, she knows everything about me.' Lucy looked hesitantly at the doctor, suddenly anticipating something terribly wrong. 'What's happened? I thought you said I was OK.' Lucy could hear her voice rising to an unnaturally high pitch. 'Has the X-ray showed something?'

'Yes, the X-rays did show something but you are OK. Mrs Cooper, when we talked to you earlier, you didn't mention . . .' He looked directly at Lucy, obviously trying to anticipate her reaction. 'Mrs Cooper, are you aware that you are pregnant? If so, you really should have told us before the X-ray. I do understand you were in shock but we really should have been informed, unprotected X-rays are really not a good idea in your condition.'

Lucy stared at the doctor, who was clutching her notes to his chest. It took a second or two for what he had said to sink in, her still confused brain was busy thinking how young he looked, younger than her even, far too young to be a fully fledged doctor. Maybe he was just an orderly, he obviously didn't know what he was talking about.

'Don't be silly.' She laughed and looked around wide-eyed at the three other people in the cubicle. 'I'm not pregnant, you've got my notes muddled up with someone else's. Here, let me look.'

Before he had a chance to react, Lucy had snatched the folder from his arms. She carefully checked the details, and there was the name Lucy Cooper, along with all her other personal information.

She threw it on the floor. 'Sorry, wrong person. I don't know what you've done but you've got the wrong person, you've got your X-rays mixed up. I am *not* pregnant, I can't be, I don't want to be, that's why I'm on the pill.'

'Mrs Cooper, I'm sorry, but—'

'Mrs Cooper nothing. You're talking out of your backside.' Lucy looked away from him to Sadie for support but Sadie was shaking her head.

'It has to be right, Lucy. They don't get something like this wrong. Look, you've got wristbands on and that is your name, it can't be anyone else, can it? Didn't you have any idea? Hadn't you guessed?'

'Fuck off, Sadie. You're as stupid as he is.' She nodded her head in the doctor's direction. He ignored her outburst. 'Mrs Cooper, Lucy, I think we need to do a scan urgently. If you didn't know you were pregnant then I presume you've had no ante-natal checks.'

'Well of course I haven't had any bloody ante-natal checks, I'm not pregnant. It's not possible, I'm still having periods, I don't feel pregnant. Do I look pregnant?'

Throwing back the sheet, she patted her stomach through the disposable white hospital gown while at the same time remembering the three hundred and fifty pound trouser suit that she had bought only a few days before. Now it was ruined, consigned to a plastic bag under the trolley, along with the sadly scuffed Prada bag that was her pride and joy. It was strange, she thought, the things that flash through the brain in times of crisis. But even as she was protesting, doubt was building. Perhaps he was right.

The nausea, the floating head, the slight weight gain that she had put down to not going to the gym as frequently as before. Surely she couldn't have been that stupid, she thought. But even her GP, when he had raised the issue, had taken her words, 'I'm on the pill, I'm having periods,' at face value. If he hadn't guessed then why should she?

She looked at Sadie in horror as the possibility started to sink in but Sadie was unusually silent, her dark eyes unreadable as she sat holding her friend's hand but looking intently at the pale green wall behind her head.

'I can't have a baby, I can't, I have to see someone . . . do something . . .'

The doctor laid a hand on her arm. 'You must stay calm, you've just had an accident.' He looked around, almost as if seeking help. The nurse stepped forward and took control.

'Now then, dear, don't you go getting all upset, this often happens, you know. God, if I had a few quid for every unexpected pregnancy I'd witnessed I'd be a very rich woman, not working here in the middle of the night for a pittance while everyone else is out down the pub!' Smiling broadly, she continued, 'We've even had them in here nine months gone and in labour without realising what was wrong. Now, let's be practical about this for a minute and take it one step at a time.' The middle-aged woman's broad Irish accent was soothing even to the bewildered Lucy. It reminded her so much of Fergus, the gentle intonation and the smile in the voice.

'First thing is to arrange a scan. Now you lie back and chat to your friend while I fix it up. I'll be back in a short while to sort you out.' The nurse patted her on the shoulder and smiled encouragingly. 'OK, Lucy? Are you listening to me?'

'I'll look after her.' Sadie spoke quietly but her voice was positive. 'You go and sort out the tests and I'll have a chat with Lucy.'

As soon as they were alone, Sadie looked agog at her friend. 'Bloody hell, Lucy. Did you really not suspect this? How could you possibly be pregnant and not know? It's all a bit downmarket women's mag-ish, isn't it?'

'Oh, thanks a lot, Sadie, I thought you were meant to be my friend. Of course I didn't know, you daft cow. I wouldn't have let this happen if I'd known, would I?' Lucy turned away, tears of frustration in her eyes.

'I can't believe you didn't guess. It all fits.'

'Did you guess then? No you didn't and neither did I. Hindsight is wonderful, isn't it? I was on the fucking pill, for the three hundredth time!'

'Do you know whose it is?'

The question hit Lucy like a sledgehammer.

'What did you just say?'

'Oh, come on, it's a fair question. Do you reckon it's Don's or Fergus's?'

'It's none of your goddamned business and you can stop acting so fucking superior. I'm not one of your clients, you know.' Lucy paused, her anger building deep inside. She knew none of this was Sadie's fault but she was the one beside her. Lucy knew she couldn't tell the truth to anyone. If no one knew then no one could tell Don. The thought of Don knowing she was pregnant was horrendous enough but if he found out that it may not be his then everyone would be in his firing line.

'It's Don's. All right? It can't be anyone else's. Is that good enough for you? Now if this is all such a drag, why don't you just toddle off home? If you can't support me and throw off your social worker cape for a few minutes then I don't need you, I don't need anyone.'

Before Sadie could respond, the nurse came back through the curtains, dragging a wheelchair behind her.

'Right, let's get this scan over and done with and then we'll know where we are. After all, baby's had an accident as well, we have to see how he's doing. Does your friend want to come with you?'

'How should I know?' Lucy snarled. 'Why don't you ask her?'

Sadie reached over and grabbed Lucy, hugging her close. 'I'm so sorry, I'm just stunned by it all. I know I shouldn't have made light of it – engage brain before opening mouth has never been one of my strengths. Of course I'll support you and of course I'll come with you.'

As Lucy gingerly eased herself off the bed into the wheelchair, she remembered.

'Oh my God! What about work? What did Luke say?'

'He's going to pop up here to see how you are. He

sounded really upset about it.'

'Bugger, bugger. Sadie, how am I going to get out of that?'

'Lucy, you've lost me. How are you going to get out of what? You asked me to phone him and I did.'

'I know but I don't want him knowing any of this. Please stay behind, Sadie, and cut him off. The last thing I need now is for him to find out about the scan. He'll put two and two together and that'll be it.'

Sadie shook her head. 'But I don't know what he looks like.'

'Just hang around the check-in desk or whatever they call it, wait for Luke Pettit. Please?' Lucy reached out and grabbed Sadie's hand so tightly it hurt. 'Please? Just tell him I'm fine, having a few routine tests and all that, but don't let him ask anyone else anything.'

The nurse quickly intervened and pulled Sadie to one side. 'Do as she asks, please, my love. I have to get Lucy over to the scanning department right away. You just stay here, we'll be back shortly.'

Later, when everything that needed to be done was done, Lucy was admitted to the observation ward for the night. But she couldn't sleep, didn't want to sleep, all she could do was lie there and think and worry. She simply could not see a way forward.

About sixteen weeks' pregnant, they had said, and the baby appeared fine. She had seen the shadowy figure on the small screen and even had a print face down beside her bed, but no matter how much they tried to persuade her, Lucy just couldn't face looking at it, she didn't want to be confronted with the truth. In not too many months' time, she was going to have a baby. Lucy Cooper the career woman was going to be a mother.

Despite all her efforts to stay awake and try and rationalise everything, Lucy eventually did doze off but her dreams were of Don in a van running her down, Don chasing her through hospital corridors, Don trying to snatch a baby out of her arms . . .

The light touch on her arm made her jump.

'Are you OK? You were having a nightmare, I think. Here you are, a nice strong cuppa will see you all right.' The woman moved away from the bed back to the tea trolley.

Lucy got her bearings again. She heaved a sigh of relief. Don wasn't there. She was in hospital, it was the next day and she was safe. But for how long?

'Is there a phone I could use, please? I have a call I must make, I need to tell my husband what's happening.'

'There's one at the end of the corridor but you look a bit woozy. I'll wheel the trolley phone to your bed but only a quick call, please, this one is for emergencies only.'

Lucy knew she had to ring Don to pre-empt the possibility of him going to the office to look for her. After all, she hadn't been home all night and although when lying in casualty with a hefty dose of painkiller in her system she hadn't given a toss about him, in the cold light of day, and with a clear head, she realised it hadn't been such a good idea.

'Hello, Don? It's me. I'm in hospital. I had an accident last night, I was hit by a van.'

The silence at the other end made her think she had been cut off.

'Hello, Don? Are you there? Did you hear what I said?'

'Yeah, I'm here. Accident, did you say? What hospital are you at?'

'St Lawrence's. Are you going to come up here? I think I'm being discharged this morning, I was only in for observation.'

Don's sarcastic and humourless laugh echoed down the line at her. 'No way, I'm just going to phone back and check you're not lying, check that you've not been with Paul Gower all fucking night.'

The crash of the receiver going down was so loud it made her wince. Carefully testing her aching muscles and joints first, Lucy got out of bed and, with the phone trolley for support, headed towards the nurses' station where the senior nurse was busy handing over after a long night.

'Excuse me, I'm sorry to interrupt, but my husband is probably going to phone in a minute. Please don't give him any information other than that I am here and in one piece ready to go home. Nothing else, if you don't mind. I don't want him to be party to any personal details about me.' Realising she sounded quite pompous, Lucy smiled to take the edge off her words. 'I've brought your phone back.'

The severe-looking nurse, obviously one of the old school, glanced up at her, a slightly irritated expression on her shiny scrubbed face which looked decidedly weather-beaten for someone who worked indoors. The iron-grey hair, the colour and texture of a Brillo pad, was pulled back so tightly it made her eyes slant upwards.

'Mrs Cooper, we really don't need you to remind us of our duties. We never, I repeat never, hand out information over the phone without permission.'

'I'm sorry, I know that really, but my husband can be quite insistent when he wants something and I just wanted to make sure.'

'Take it from me, Mrs Cooper, bullying relatives, and we come across a lot of them on the observation ward, never get a whisper out of me or my staff. Now if you'd like to go and have a wash and brush-up and make yourself presentable for the doctor, I'm sure you'll be discharged as soon as he's seen you. Off you go and I'll deal with Mr Cooper if he rings.'

Lucy felt quite intimidated by the woman and she could see the young nurses grouped around her, eyes cast to the floor, were as well. She almost hoped that Don would ring and give her a hard time; he would soon regret it if he did.

Wash and brush-up, make yourself presentable. She smiled to herself. The last time she had been ordered off to do that had been many years before at boarding school. Lucy's natural rebellious streak suddenly kicked in and although she knew she was being childish, she determined not to do as she was told, at least not straight away. She headed instead to the public phone on the wall at the end of the ward corridor, barefoot and still clothed in a disposable paper nightie and a raggedy old towelling wrap that belonged to the hospital. Her intention was to ring Sadie but instead she found herself dialling Fergus's number, but after two rings she thought better of it. She could hear Sadie's voice telling her to deal with Don first and foremost. Quickly she replaced the receiver and turned to go back down the ward to her bed.

'Lucy . . . Lucy, hang on . . .'

Lucy stopped and turned to see Sadie almost jogging

down the corridor towards her.

'Heavens above, Lucy, you'll be the death of me. I didn't expect to have to run anywhere ever again since you stopped dragging me to the gym! Didn't you hear me calling you?'

'Sorry, I was miles away. I was just about to call you and let you know what's happening.' Lucy stopped when she saw the dragon nurse marching towards her, looking grim.

'Mrs Cooper, where have you been? Doctor's here waiting to check you over. Hurry up please, get back to your bed. We're far too busy here to run around gathering up missing patients.'

Sadie's snort caused quite a glare but Lucy intervened quickly.

'Did my husband ring?'

'No, he didn't, so far. Now please, Mrs Cooper, get back to your bed, the doctors don't have enough time for what they have to do as it is.'

Sadie walked back to the bed with her. The first thing she did was pick up the scan print and study it.

'When did you get this?'

'Last night.'

'Why didn't you show me it then?' Sadie's eyes were fixed on the grainy picture. 'You can see it quite clearly, can't you? Medical science is great, this almost looks like a photograph. You can see almost everything, it really looks like a baby.'

'Medical science isn't that great, if it was, the pill would be one hundred per cent safe and I wouldn't be pregnant.' She stopped as the doctor appeared at her bedside.

'Good morning.' He smiled wearily, his eyes heavy and

bloodshot. 'Feeling better today? You certainly look bright enough and you're moving OK.'

Lucy smiled back, she actually felt sorry for the poor man, she knew she shouldn't have blamed him for the bad news. 'Don't you ever sleep? I wasn't expecting to see you again, you should be at home tucked up with a hot water bottle. But yep, I feel fine. Still got a bit of a headache though, in more ways than one.'

The doctor reached over and took the scanshot from Sadie and studied it.

'Well, from all the tests and observations, everything appears OK both with your injuries and your pregnancy. You can go home when you're ready and we'll write to your GP. You have to arrange for ante-natal check-ups now though, it's especially important as this is a late discovery for you . . .'

Even as he was speaking Lucy was dragging the polythene bag containing her battered clothes out of the bedside cabinet and tutting over the state of them as she spread them over the bed. Sadie handed her another bag.

'It's OK, Lucy, I brought a sweatshirt and some jogging bottoms. Not that I think you'll be going jogging, but it's all I could find that would be easy to put on and wouldn't look too outrageously huge on you. Hardly Chanel, but they'll do to get you home hidden under a blanket in the back of a blacked-out van. Let's hope the fashion police aren't waiting outside, they would arrest you on sight.'

The doctor smiled at Sadie and Lucy noticed her blush furiously. He followed suit and the flush crept up over his perfectly sculptured cheekbones towards the floppy black fringe that kept falling in his deep, dark eyes. Lucy decided there was definitely something incredibly sexy about the baggy blue cotton uniform of trousers and V-necked top, enhanced only by a stethoscope and a pair of white trainers. Very George Clooney, she decided.

'Thank you, doctor . . . er, sorry, I don't know your name.' Lucy looked at Sadie knowingly.

'It's Dr Nathan. Col Nathan, shortened to make it easy for everyone.' He pointed to his name badge with two very long names on it and Lucy smiled.

'I see what you mean!'

'Well, Mrs Cooper, Lucy, take care of yourself and the baby – and your friend.' He was again looking at a red-faced Sadie.

'Her name's Sadie, Sadie Khan, and she's a social worker at St Luke's Hospital. It's not far from here.'

Sadie gasped out loud but the young doctor just smiled. 'So if I need a social worker I know just who to call. Nice to meet you, both of you.'

As soon as he was out of earshot, Lucy nudged Sadie in the ribs. 'There you are, Sadie, the perfect match for you. Isn't he just gorgeous? I bet he phones you!'

Sadie went home with Lucy in the taxi but was hesitant about going in with her.

'I'm sorry, Lucy, I really don't want to even see Don, let alone have to converse with him.'

'Please, Sadie, just come in for a second, give me a chance to see how the land lies. I'm worried how he's going to react.'

'Are you intending to tell him about the baby in front of

me? Oh Lucy, please don't, he'll be furious that I knew before he did.'

'You've got no worries, there, Sadie, because I'm not going to tell him. Not ever. I've made up my mind, as soon as I can sort everything out I'm leaving Don, leaving him for good, but I have to plan it. There's no way I'm going to end up in some dingy bedsit because I walked out on the spur of the moment. No, I'm going to do it but in my own way and on my own terms. Stuff Donovan Cooper, from now on I look out for number one.'

'And number two – don't forget the baby.'

'How could I possibly forget that?'

'And Fergus?'

'Not really an option any more with a baby in the picture, is he?'

Lucy and Sadie went in side by side but the silence spoke for itself immediately. Don had already gone out. The bedroom was a shambles with Don's clothes, both clean and dirty, strewn all over the floor and the bed.

'I wonder where he is. It looks as though he's taken one of the suitcases off the wardrobe.' Lucy was looking around in bewilderment.

'Perhaps it's your lucky day,' said Sadie quickly. 'Perhaps he's left you.'

'No, not Don, not without cleaning me out first and selling all the wedding presents. I'm going to ring the gym.'

Lucy made the call while Sadie sat on the sofa chewing her nails. Lucy hung up and then threw the phone across the room.

'You'll never guess what, he's gone to Portugal, he's gone to fucking Portugal to a body-building competition.

He'll be gone for a couple of weeks at least, they reckon. He's flying out this morning with all his equally useless mates and he never said a word to me when I phoned. He must have been ready to walk out of the door as I was talking to him. The bastard!'

'Good, be grateful for small mercies. Without him around you can start rearranging your life in peace,' was all Sadie could think of to say.

Sadie stayed with Lucy, insisting she put her feet up and rest. Cleaning, tidying and vacuuming around Lucy's raised feet, Sadie went through the whole flat like a dynamo on speed, singing and dancing and being silly in an effort to lift Lucy's mood.

'Right, it's lunchtime and I don't want to hear any crap about weight gain, you're eating for two now so I'm going to phone my favourite man in the whole wide world, Mister Pizza Delivery. Purely medicinal of course, it's a well-known cure-all, pizza can cure anything. I know, I use it all the time.'

'A cure-all did you say? Can it cure my being pregnant?'

Sadie slumped down on the sofa beside Lucy. 'Nope, I'm afraid nothing can cure that, unless of course you want a termination. It is still possible, you know.'

Tears welled up in Lucy's eyes; she had tried to keep her emotions in control but it was getting harder by the minute.

'I can't do that, how can I do that now I've actually seen it? Why did they make me look at the screen? Why did they give me that bloody awful picture? Oh Sadie, what am I going to do? This isn't how it was meant to be.'

The shrill buzz of the intercom made them both jump.

'Who's that?' Lucy looked at Sadie.

'I don't know, I can't see through walls. Shall I answer it and find out?'

Sadie pressed the button and then looked over at Lucy. 'It's Luke Pettit,' she mouthed silently. 'What shall I say?'

'Tell him to come up but you let him in while I go and get my face straight. Shit, I wonder what he wants. Why didn't he phone?'

Lucy locked herself in the bathroom and quickly whipped a flannel over her face. Luke knew she had had an accident so she figured he wouldn't be expecting full make-up and designer dress. However she did manage a wry smile as she caught sight of herself in the mirror. She was still wearing Sadie's ill-fitting clothes and looked like the orphan of the storm. Nasty red scabs were starting to form on her scraped cheek and chin and one eye was slightly blackened. The rest of her aches and pains were either internal or covered up, uncomfortable but not obvious. She didn't bother to do anything with her hair other than scrape it back behind a wide alice band.

Cautiously, aware that she looked plain and about twelve, she went back into the lounge.

'Hello, Lucy, how are you doing? You're really not the luckiest person in the world lately, are you?' Luke walked over and kissed her on both cheeks. 'Still, the good news is you're all in one piece, that's the main thing, and so apparently is the driver although the wall is going to need a bit of a touch-up. Apparently one of the pedals stuck or something. He did well not to flatten you completely.' He looked her up and down while at the same time holding both her arms.

'Anyway, enough doom and gloom, I am here as the bearer of good tidings! After a long discussion with my wife and business partner, I'm here officially on behalf of the company to make you an offer you simply can't refuse. How does the thought of a couple of months working alongside our clients in Las Vegas appeal to you? It'll get you out of the office and by the time you come back all the other nonsense will have died down. Trust me.' He smiled. A kind and caring smile that made her want to cry. 'We haven't made this up especially for you, the job was going to be on offer anyway and, to avoid any ill feeling, when you come back Paul gets to go to New York for a few weeks.'

The smile faded slightly as Luke took in the open mouths of both Lucy and Sadie.

'What's wrong? Don't you want to go to America?'

Chapter Seven

As Lucy had stood stunned in the hospital corridor staring at the unresponsive phone in her hand, Donovan Cooper had replaced the receiver and grinned. Despite being all alone he spoke out loud. 'Yes, yes, yes! Now there's a bit of luck!' He rolled his eyes upwards to look at the ceiling and leaned back in an exaggerated movement, his hands together as if in prayer. 'Thank you God, thank you!'

Ninety-nine per cent of the time Don did whatever he wanted without a thought for anyone else, least of all his wife. But even he had wondered, although only half-heartedly, if he might have gone a bit too far this time. He had drawn over two thousand pounds out of the household bank account and increased the limit on the joint credit card after secretly booking himself on the trip to Portugal arranged by the gym. There was no way he was going to travel as a pauper; after all the lies he had told, he had appearances to keep up.

It had vaguely passed through his mind that he ought to tell Lucy he intended to go; after all, he knew she couldn't actually stop him, but he had put it off and put it off again until suddenly the departure date was imminent. In fact he had exactly one hour to finish packing and get out of the flat, hopefully before Lucy got back.

He had been surprised and angry and, even though he would never admit it, concerned when Lucy stayed out all night, she had never done that before. But when she phoned and explained, he immediately saw it as a way of getting away before she found out about him going. He didn't bother to think about what would happen when he got back, he didn't even think about how injured Lucy might be. Don never thought much further ahead than the moment.

All his life Don had looked for the easy route. Despite his over-developed muscles and arrogant strutting, he actually preferred to avoid confrontation, so evasion and lying were second nature to him. As a child he had learnt that being sneaky and devious was a lot easier than getting caught out and facing the ever sad and despising face of his mother and the smug, grinning face of his brother. His father had disappeared with another woman many years before and immediately it was as if he had never existed. Don, who was only six at the time, had even forgotten what he looked like. There had been no contact from the day he left, which was exactly how Mother Cooper wanted it to be because it left her in total charge to manage, manipulate and divide her sons.

As he hurried to pack and get out of the flat before Lucy came home, his mother's face, full of shame and twisted with loathing, kept appearing in front of him. He shook his head and tried to refocus his mind but the images kept coming. He could almost hear her in the room. 'Donny, Donny, why are you such a disappointment to me? Why can't you be like your brother? He's so clever, so well behaved, he's so handsome and strong . . . one son so perfect, the other so weak and stupid . . .' The criticism was constant and never failed to make the none too bright and skinny little Donovan Cooper feel even more inadequate as each day passed. He remembered clearly how his brother, the golden boy of the family and all too aware of his superior status, would torment and tease him, both inside the home and outside. Peter Cooper also gleefully got the other boys, and sometimes girls, to join him on his campaign of terror against his slightly older but much weaker brother. Peter Cooper had been born with a spiteful streak that he joyously put into practice at every opportunity. Mother Cooper, without fail, turned a blind eye to everything her favourite son did wrong. The fact that he was handsome and clever excused him everything.

Donovan Cooper's teenage years carried on downhill until the day when he could take no more and, sneaking off to nearby Epping Forest, he slung a piece of rope from a tree and tried to hang himself.

Don forced his clothes down into the suitcase with his huge fists and slammed it shut ferociously as he tried to get rid of the memory of his lowest and most humiliating moment.

The rope had been carefully chosen by the fifteen-year-old boy, thick enough and long enough for what he wanted. He had even picked out the tree in advance and carefully chosen the branch he would use. Sturdy enough not to break under his weight but low enough for him to reach by climbing up the wide, leaning trunk.

Unhappy at school and as often as possible not there, Don was barely literate or numerate. What he hadn't worked out properly was the distance from the branch to the ground in relation to the length of the rope. Quietly determined, he had climbed up to the chosen branch and then, balanced precariously, he had looped the noose round his neck before carefully tightening the large knot. It had only taken a few seconds before he plucked up the courage to let himself fall and he could remember clearly the feeling of floating for a split second as the ground came up to meet him. But the rope was too long. Don hit the ground with a thud that stunned him just long enough for him to be found by a couple of ramblers, disorientated but without doubt very much alive.

Picking up the case and marching out of the bedroom, Don's face was red with embarrassment at just the memory of the moment.

There was no concern whatever for her son from Mother Cooper, though she had cried long and loud with the shame of it. 'How could you do that to the family? I am so ashamed to have you as my son,' she had howled, terrified that the neighbours would find out. How his brother had laughed as he had made sure that the neighbours, and everyone at school, did find out.

'Can't even fucking kill himself properly, he's completely useless, useless, useless,' Peter chanted at every opportunity.

Don had often wondered how such a tiny woman could wield such power over her sons. At barely five foot tall and less than seven stone she looked as fragile as a new sapling in spring but her gaunt, spiteful face, framed by short, thick hair, dyed black, told a very different story. Her life was ruled by appearances and worrying about what others thought of both her and her sons. Peter, big, blond and handsome, with a ready smile, was a son to be proud of; Don, with his lanky frame, mousey hair and permanent frown was not.

With the derisive laughter ringing in his ears and an intense feeling of failure and shame invading every second of his life, the teenage Don was left with two choices: to try again and risk even more humiliation, or do something to change himself. Plumping for the second option, he hoped he would be able to make his mother proud of him and stick two fingers up at his brother at the same time.

But what had started as a couple of evenings a week fitness training gradually built into a full-time preoccupation. Donovan Cooper had found a purpose in life. Body-building.

Don slammed the door of the flat and headed off on his trip to Portugal. Stuff Lucy, he thought. He was the man of the house and as such he could do whatever he liked. As a husband he was in charge for the first time in his life and there was no way he was going to let a little thing like a wife take that away from him.

Carrying his heavy case as if it was a simple carrier bag of shopping, he ran down the stairs, still thinking about his mother. He decided that, as soon as he won his first competition, achieved some obvious success, he would go back to the immaculate little house that his mother had ruled all her life. He had hated it, the permanent smell of bleach and cleaning polish that hung over every surface as she meticulously and obsessively cleaned from top to bottom every day, going on and on at him as she did so. Savouring the thought, he imagined marching in and waving his award victoriously under her nose. Then he would show his brother as well before breaking all the bones in his pretty but smug little face. Golden boy Peter's precious blood all over Mother Cooper's precious carpet – that would teach them both.

Smiling in anticipation, Don had hailed a taxi in the street and disappeared round the corner just as Lucy and Sadie had arrived from the other direction. Neither saw the other.

'Las Vegas?' Lucy looked stunned. Wide-eyed and pale as typing paper, she stared at Luke who was smiling expectantly.

'Las Vegas?' Sadie repeated robotically.

Luke looked from one to the other. 'Yes, that's right, I'm sure you know where Las Vegas is. Lucy, remember the new US hotel chain we're going to represent? Well, it was originally agreed that Caroline would spend some time there at the flagship before going on to their property in New York but she's been away so much lately I've persuaded her to delegate. Sooooo,' Luke paused dramatically and mimed a drum roll, 'you get to go to Vegas and then Paul goes to New York. Good experience for both of you and I get to spend more time with my workaholic wife.'

Lucy and Sadie looked at each other; both were thinking exactly the same thing. Lucy was sixteen weeks' pregnant.

The atmosphere in the room was taut. Luke sensed something was passing between the two of them, a secret communication, and was baffled. He had expected Lucy to whoop with joy at the news but instead both she and Sadie looked as if he had announced a death.

'Is something wrong? Lucy? Don't you want to go?'

Lucy pulled herself together. 'Sorry, Luke, it was just such a shock, not what I was expecting at all. It sounds wonderful, a couple of months in Las Vegas – yes, wonderful. I can hardly believe it. When do you want me to go?' Lucy deliberately didn't look at Sadie again, she could only imagine the expression on her face.

'Well, that's more like it.' Luke smiled and gave an exaggerated sigh. 'You had me worried there for a second, I thought all my hard work with Caroline on your behalf had been in vain. How soon? Well, just as soon as you can tie up all the loose ends in the office. But you look ready to drop right now so I'll leave you to get over your mishap and decide exactly how you're going to arrange it all. I'll see myself out.'

Lucy almost jumped in front of him. 'What about Daniella?'

'No problem there, Lucy, I'm dealing with Daniella. She just needs to be reminded of the ground rules that help keep our staff happy and smiling.' Luke raised a hand to Lucy in an almost regal wave and disappeared out of the door.

As soon as the door shut, Sadie sprang into life. 'Lucy, you can't, you're pregnant and they don't know. Supposing something goes wrong? What about ante-natal? You know what the doctor said, you can't go all that way—'

'Can't I? Just you watch me. There is nothing in this world that could stop me taking up an opportunity like this. Oh yes, I'm off to America and the sooner the better, preferably before Don gets back from his little boys' outing to Portugal!'

'But Don will look for you.'

'It's OK, Sadie, I'm not completely dumb, I'll make sure he knows where I am and why but it'll give me the breathing space I need away from it all. So long as he has enough money, it won't be a problem to him.' She smiled genuinely for the first time in days. 'And who knows? It might be fun! No Don, no Paul and no Daniella.'

Putting her head on one side Sadie looked at a point in the distance and pursed her lips thoughtfully. 'And Fergus? Doesn't he warrant a mention, good or bad?'

The smile vanished from Lucy's face. She limped painfully over to the window and looked thoughtfully out.

'If you were my social worker, what would you advise me to do?' she asked without turning round. 'Should I curl up and block out my problems or get to grips with my life and do the best I can?'

When Sadie didn't respond, Lucy turned to her friend and stared at her. 'Tell me then, what would your professional advice be?'

Sadie hesitated. 'To get on with your life I suppose, to remove yourself from the situation, but I'm not your social worker, I'm your friend.'

'It shouldn't make a blind bit of difference. So, I'm going to get on with my life as best I can. I shall ring Fergus and tell him what I'm doing, I owe him that, and then the ball will be in his court when I come back. As for Don, would you want Donovan Cooper as the father of your baby? Would you even want him in the vicinity of a helpless baby? Any baby?'

Sadie smiled sadly. 'Oh Lucy, I hope it works out for you, I really do, and you know that, whatever happens, I shall always be here for you. I'll miss you even if it is only for a couple of months. And when you come back I can look after you. You will keep me up to date with how it's all going, won't you?'

'Of course.' As Lucy replied, the corners of her mouth started to turn down and her bottom lip trembled. 'Now, how about a coffee after all your hard work?'

'*Sit*,' Sadie ordered. 'I have to go back to work this afternoon so make the most of being waited on while it lasts.'

Lucy didn't sit down. 'Sadie, can I ask you something? It's a big favour and I don't mind if you say no.'

'I'm not cleaning the toilet, I draw the line at that!'

'Would you come and stay here for a few days? Keep me company? Just a few days until I go back to work. I could really use the company right now . . .'

Much as she loved Lucy, Sadie had always found her slightly insulated from real life. She guessed it was probably a result of her cosseted upbringing when she had never wanted for anything, but in the few minutes Luke had been in the flat, Sadie had seen something different in Lucy. A new determination, or maybe it was a deeper insight into real life; whatever it was, she could see that Lucy was taking control of her life by herself.

Sadie had met Lucy's parents many times and had secretly found them a little disconcerting. They were nice people, very nice people in fact, and Sadie knew that they loved Lucy dearly but she could also see that their love for each other far outweighed what they felt for their only daughter. There was no disputing that they were an attractive and genial couple, but their obsession with each other to the exclusion of even Lucy seemed odd to Sadie. At first she had thought it quite endearing that a long-married couple in their fifties were still so close but after a while it started to irritate. The secret codes and signals that made them smile, the constant touching, the hugging and kissing in public, never seemed quite appropriate in front of their daughter. They were a conjoined pair, so instead of Lucy being the third corner of a family triangle she always seemed to be the odd one out. Like an uninvited guest at a party.

Sadie often wondered if that could be why Lucy got involved with Don so quickly. Maybe subconsciously she wanted to be one of a pair herself instead of the permanent gooseberry in her parents' marriage.

'Of course I'll come and stay,' Sadie told her. 'It'll be just like the old days. Flatmates again. I'll bring my stuff round this evening after work. Aahhh . . .' She paused. 'Supposing Don comes back? I don't want him to find me here.'

'I've thought of that. I'm going to ring Lara at the gym and pretend I know all about it and ask her to keep me up to date with how the lads are doing in the competition. That way I'll also know when I have to aim to be gone by.'

Sadie picked up her bag. 'I really have to get back to work now. I'll see you later but in the meantime put your feet up and rest, woman. You've got an exciting time ahead!'

Lucy didn't do as she was told, she was too restless and there was far too much to think about. Wandering aimlessly about the flat, she knew with certainty that her marriage was over, it had been for a long time but she had been unable fully to admit it. Nothing had ever really gone wrong in her life and she found it hard to admit failure at the one single thing she had desperately wanted. A long and happy marriage, friendship and companionship with her husband, financial security and then eventually a smiling and cuddly baby. Just like her parents, in fact.

She smiled to herself wryly. Yep, she thought, and a cottage in the country with roses round the door, a labrador by the fire and a big black Aga in the kitchen bubbling away with homemade jam . . .

That's what reading too many novels at boarding school had done for her, she decided as she looked in Don's wardrobe to get an idea of how much he had actually taken with him. Real life just wasn't like that and now she knew she had to face up to the idea of an acrimonious divorce and a very unromantic life as a single parent, maybe even an unemployed single parent when Luke and Caroline Pettit found out she had deceived them both.

Lucy went back to the office three days later, filled with trepidation at the thought of having to face both Paul and Daniella. Arriving exceptionally early, she made sure she was the first there and was safely ensconced behind her desk before anyone else arrived.

She needn't have worried, the solicitous inquiries about her accident and recovery soon eased away her concerns and within an hour it was as if the previous week had never happened.

Apart, of course, from Daniella Schwarz, who kept her head down, carefully avoiding eye contact. Lucy still felt uneasy about the girl but she knew she had to trust Luke's word that Daniella would cause no problems.

'Well, well, if it's not the bionic woman.' Paul appeared beside her with a bunch of flowers. 'Smashed into by a van, thrown up in the air, flung across the road and walks away without a single broken bone. Welcome back, even if it is only for a short while. I hear Las Vegas beckons.' He offered her the flowers with a smile. 'Give me New York any day, I say. Big Apple, here I come!'

Lucy laughed out loud. 'You just never give up, do you? I know that you know that there is diddly squat between the two. Las Vegas, New York, New York, Last Vegas, it's only work wherever it may take us. But thanks for the flowers anyway. Very kind of you.'

'My pleasure. When you've got time I'd like a word, in private. Nothing urgent, mind, but I'd be grateful.'

'I'm free now if you like. I'm just trying to tie up loose ends, as Luke put it. Give me two minutes and I'll meet you in Caroline's office.'

Lucy watched Paul walk back to his desk, his eyes not flickering even for a second over to Daniella who, despite the disinterested expression on her face, was watching everything through her eyelashes. Lucy's instincts told her that, whatever Luke said, the girl bore a grudge, a big one.

She shrugged it off and went through to meet Paul. After all, she thought, what could Daniella do to her now?

★　★　★

'I see Dani is still giving you the evil eye.' Paul wasn't smiling as she would have expected.

'Evil eye? I thought she was doing a good job of *not* looking at me. What have you done to her?'

'Well, I've finished with her and, before you ask, yes, she did pass on the little titbit about you and Fergus the courier. Lucy, Lucy,' he shook his head, 'whatever possessed you? A glorified delivery boy, of all people, when you could have had me!'

Lucy held up her hands. 'Stop right there, Paul. All you know is what silly Dani told you so don't you go making moral judgements. Who else have you imparted this great piece of gossip about the *ice maiden* to? Does everyone know?'

'Oh, thanks a lot, really, thank you.' Paul actually managed to look quite offended. 'For your information, that is why I wanted to talk to you, to tell you that it won't go any further. I told Dani her fortune over it. Wheeler-dealing in the office is one thing but that was a bit too personal even for me.'

Lucy didn't say anything, she just walked over and sat down opposite him. As she carefully crossed her still aching legs and folded her hands in her lap, she looked him straight in the eye. It was a challenge.

'Do you mean that or is this another of your little office jests?'

'Yes, really, I mean it.' He smiled his very best cheeky chappie smile. 'I would hate my personal life to be used against me at work. Jeez, I'd have been out long ago if that was a benchmark for employment. No, I'll poach your clients and sneak a look at your accounts, maybe even dob you in to Caroline if you screw up, but personal life? Not on.'

'Mmmm. Why the change of heart, Paul? What's going on?'

'Oh, come on, I'm not that bad, you know that really. So I screw around and duck and dive a bit, but that doesn't make me Satan. I'm young, free and ambitious – since when was that a crime?' Paul grabbed his lapels, lowered his thick dark eyebrows and glared at her, pretending to be villainous.

Lucy's features softened and she laughed. 'You're right, you can do whatever you like, it's not for me to judge, especially in my situation. I'm really grateful that it's not done the round of the office, although I'm still not sure of Dani. Just for the record, I'm not seeing Fergus any more and Don and I are all but over, that's why I'm pleased to be going to the States.'

Paul grinned mischievously. 'So now you're going to be young, free and ambitious as well. Great. Am I in with a chance at last?' Paul stood up and posed with his hands on his hips, 'You should see me in black biker's leather!'

Lucy laughed harder. 'I'd rather not!'

She stood and went to the door but stopped in her tracks. Daniella was staring in the direction of the office, a look of pure hatred distorting her beautiful face. She obviously still blamed her for the split with Paul, not to mention the black mark against her name with Caroline and Luke. Maybe a couple of months away from the office will help, Lucy thought as she walked purposefully back to her desk. Perhaps Dani would meet someone else in the meantime. Even better, the girl might find another job.

Lucy deliberately turned her thoughts to her forth-coming trip. She was really looking forward to it and any other problems would have to wait until she got back.

Chapter Eight

Looking around the departure lounge, Don was horrified at how many other competitors were going to Portugal. The 'Body Builders of Europe' competition wasn't one of the majors, and Don had thought he was in with a serious chance of winning but looking around he suddenly felt uneasy. From being on an exceptional high, he could feel his mood sinking as he saw his dream disappearing. The thought of winning was his justification for sneaking off, having convinced himself that if he won, then maybe the red carpet would be laid out on his return.

'Who are all these?' He turned to Jonno. 'I thought there was only four of us going?'

'Yeah, that's right, four from our gym, but there's three or four other clubs that are sending guys, as well as a couple of female teams. This comp is a good stepping stone for semi-professionals. We're all travelling together, group booking was cheaper. I think we've got about half the plane.'

'Shit, mate, why didn't you tell me? That screws my

chances. Just look at them, some of them must be bloody circuit crawlers. Look at the gear they've got on. We're the only ones without a uniform.'

Jonno looked around at the assembled passengers and then punched Don on the arm, a playful punch that would have floored an average man.

'Uniforms? Don't be such a big tart, we don't need uniforms to win.' He leaned over and put his mouth close to Don's ear. 'What we've got is better than fucking uniforms, isn't it, my friend? It's how you perform that counts, not what you wear on the fucking airplane. We'll wipe the floor with those ponces in their matching gear.' He laughed. 'Posers, the lot of them.'

Jonno McMahon was the manager of Body Beautiful Inc. and in complete charge of everything and everyone. The gym had all the high-tech equipment imaginable and a reputable franchise company behind it, but Jonno had his own profitable little sideline that made his legitimate salary look like mere pocket money. He would do anything for anyone – at a price.

'You *are* clean now, aren't you?' Jonno continued as he eyed the fidgety Don suspiciously. 'Only if you're not you'll be out on your ear for good.'

'Of course I am, do you think I'm stupid?' Don fired back but he couldn't bring himself to look Jonno in the eye. He knew he had cut it fine but, at a small competition, he had decided testing was random enough to take a chance. He thought he was clean of the muscle pumping steroids Jonno generously provided him with on a regular basis, he hoped he was clean, but he had exceeded Jonno's deadline by a week, working on the assumption that his trainer and supplier was always over-cautious.

'I hope you're not stupid, Donny boy, but if by any chance you are, and if by any chance you get caught you're on your own, don't fucking bring me into it.'

Don was well aware of Jonno's reputation for violence. This was a man who didn't need chemicals to be violent, it was inside him all the time, and he loved it. Don looked sideways at him. Physically, Don could probably have overpowered the small, older man and no doubt done a lot of damage but, unless Don actually killed him, he knew Jonno would be back with weaponry in hand and several thugs in tow.

After several years dabbling in protection and blackmail, the man who liked to think of himself as a bit of a Godfather had carved himself a niche in the lucrative drugs market and nothing worked better as a legitimate cover than managing a top-flight gym and health club. Well aware that the police would love to get under his skin and find a good reason for hauling him in, it was Jonno's proud boast that he had never been caught for anything more than a few driving offences and a touch of brawling outside a nightclub. It had been Jonno to whom Don had turned when he wanted the frighteners put on Paul Gower and the man had happily sent his henchmen out to put in a bit of practice. An ex-boxer past his prime without any success of note, Jonno had a grudge against the world and thoroughly enjoyed any opportunity to flex his muscles and hurt people, albeit secondhand. Jonno didn't often get his own hands dirty.

'Give it a rest, you know you can trust me, I'd never let you down.'

'Ladies and gentlemen, the flight to Faro is about to board, would all passengers . . .'

The announcement provided a timely interruption for Don and he sighed with relief as they gathered their hand luggage and headed slowly towards the queue forming for embarkation.

Jonno nudged Don. 'Oi, Donny boy, look over there, look at those two. Christ, I wish they were with us, we'd wipe the board. I wonder who they're with.'

Don looked over at the two women who had caught Jonno's eye. At first glance they looked like clones, both tanned deep, gravy brown with yellow-blonde hair and triangular, muscle-bound bodies that were far more male shaped than female. The matching tight black and white trousers and zipper tops emphasised the outline of their over-developed muscles. Don had seen many like them and, despite being a body builder himself, he found it singularly unattractive in women. But this was not something he would ever admit to Jonno.

'Yeah, they look cool. You'll have to find out who they are, maybe we could get a night out.' Don smiled as if he really meant it.

'What about the missus then?' Jonno looked sideways at Don, his eyebrows raised in mock surprise. 'I'm sure the Lady Lucy wouldn't be too happy if she knew you were messing around – in fact you're lucky you haven't been caught already. The stuck-up bitch can't be quite as bright as she likes to pretend, can she?'

Don really wanted to tell him to mind his own business, but, much as he hated it when his wife's name was bandied about the locker room, he could never summon up the courage for fear of antagonising Jonno. Instead he laughed and launched into his usual bravado.

'My wife knows her place. I'm the boss and she does as she's fucking told and if I want to shag around then she just has to wear it. She knows the score. She was the one who couldn't wait to get married so, tough! I can't help it if I'm some sort of sex god.' Don flexed his muscles at Jonno and winked.

'Good on you, Donny boy. Now let's get boarded and hope those two are near us. Help pass the time a bit, quickie in the bog maybe, rejoin the old mile high, it's been a while.'

Don smiled nervously. 'I dunno about that, I'm supposed to be focusing on the competition.'

'I didn't mean you, you dickhead.' Jonno laughed long and loud and marched off ahead of a red-faced and very angry Don who was left to trail behind like a lackey carrying not only his own bag but Jonno's as well. The urge to hit the man and hit him hard was rising rapidly and it took all of his willpower to hold back.

Suddenly this trip didn't seem such a good idea and he wished he wasn't going, but he had backed himself into a corner and there was no way out of it.

Lucy was, on the surface, successfully blanking out everything except her forthcoming trip. She was throwing her clothes about, aware of Sadie's quizzical gaze on her but determined to ignore it.

'So, what do you think I should take? Mostly formal? Mostly casual? Maybe I ought to take just the minimum and then go shopping once I get there. I've heard that all the designer shops are in Vegas – Chanel, Gucci, anything you like, enough malls to keep me occupied the whole time I'm there. I can shop till I drop, a shopping mall for every day of the month. I can't wait.' Lucy held up a flimsy black dress that was almost see-through, with skinny straps and a wavy hem. 'What do you reckon? How about this one for partying the night away?' She threw it back on the bed and grabbed another. 'How about this for the casino? Can't you just see me leaning seductively over the roulette wheel, thrusting my bosoms at the sexy high-rollers?'

As Lucy twirled around the room holding the dress in front of her, Sadie sighed loudly. Lucy knew that her bright-eyed, nonstop acting was starting to irritate Sadie, but then Sadie was starting to irritate her.

'It's work, for heaven's sake, not a bloody holiday. And you're pregnant and trying to keep it a secret. Just look out the things that are too big and take them. You'll soon grow into them.' Sadie's voice was flat and tired. 'I'm sure you'll get away with casual there, more so than you would here in the office. Anyway, I thought you were broke.'

Lucy threw the hangers on the bed and plonked herself down beside Sadie. 'You are such a party pooper, do you know that? You're a miserable cow and you're starting to get on my nerves bigtime. I just want to go to the States, do my job, enjoy myself and then come home. Why do you want me to be aware of my problems every waking minute? You're turning into Saint Sadie, the patron saint of facing up to reality. Well, I don't want to just at this moment, so why do you have to keep reminding me?'

It was impossible for Lucy not to notice the hurt expression that swept over Sadie's face.

'Because you're in denial, that's why, and unless you face up to it you're going to end up in an even worse mess. And then what's going to happen when you get back and Don notices you're pregnant? And he will notice because by then there'll be no hiding it. You can't run away from it for ever.'

Lucy jumped to her feet and almost screamed, 'Do you think I don't know that? Do you think I'm completely stupid? Just leave me alone! You're interfering, you're always interfering.'

Sadie stood up. 'OK, so I'm interfering but what I can't understand is why you can't be open about it all. Bloody hell, it's not against the law for a woman, married or single, to have a baby. They can't do anything about it, they can't sack you. Just think about it all, Lucy, think about it before you dig yourself into a hole you can't get out of.'

Without looking at Lucy again, Sadie left the room and firmly shut the door behind her. Lucy watched her go then threw herself onto the bed and burst into tears. She knew she was in denial but Sadie just didn't understand that that was exactly where she wanted to be.

Sadie had accepted that the baby was Don's but those in the office who knew about Fergus would all wonder, especially Dani and Paul. Lucy knew she couldn't face that and had already decided that she would have her time in the States and then, when she came back, she would leave Don, leave her job and leave London, but she wasn't planning to turn her back on Fergus. An idea was growing in her mind but she was keeping it to herself for the moment.

When Lucy had found out that Don had cleared out the bank account and was running amok with the credit cards, she had phoned her parents. As always they transferred the money without asking too many questions. Lucy had inferred she needed it because of her trip and her parents believed her. Although she hadn't told them what was going on, perversely she almost wished that some kind of sixth sense would warn them that their daughter was in trouble, that they would know without her having to actually say it. But it hadn't happened. The money, far more than she had asked for, just came winging its way along with a rather vague promise to try and visit her in Las Vegas and lots of love and kisses.

Lucy knew she was being irrational but she couldn't bring herself to deal with any of it, not until she came back from Las Vegas. She wanted the trip so much, it showed that Caroline and Luke trusted her and it was also good experience for the future. But apart from that she was really looking forward to getting away. Las Vegas. The flight was booked and she had been allocated a suite in the hotel for her whole stay. All she had to do was be ready to go in a few days.

Everything and everyone else, except Fergus, could wait.

Standing sideways, Lucy looked at herself in the mirror and decided Sadie was talking nonsense. The slight bulge of her belly was easily disguised by a pair of tight-fitting trousers topped with a sweatshirt. The majority of her clothes still fitted so no one would ever guess. Smiling to herself, Lucy said a silent prayer of thanks for her training at the gym; her muscles were well toned and she could hold herself in for as long as it took.

'Sadie,' she called through to the lounge without going in, 'I'm going for a walk to clear my head and then I'm going to the gym to find out what's going on with Don. I'll be back in a couple of hours.'

Without waiting for a reply she hot-footed it out of the door for her pre-arranged meeting with Fergus. The surprise in his voice when she had phoned had cheered her up. Maybe everything would work out one way or another.

By the time she got to the arranged spot, Fergus was already there sitting on the grass with his back against the wide bough of a tree. Although he couldn't help but see her heading towards him, he stayed where he was, his long legs pulled up to his chin and held by his arms. Lucy felt her heart palpitate at the sight of him. It hadn't been long but so much had happened, it felt like years.

'I didn't know if you'd come.' Lucy smiled as she walked up to him.

'Yes you did, you know I'd have to, you know I wouldn't be able to keep away.' Fergus stood up in front of her and put his hands in his pockets, his shoulders hunched and his body language defensive. Lucy wondered whether to kiss him on the cheek, the same as she would anyone else, but decided against it. Fergus had an invisible barrier wrapped around him and Lucy knew it wasn't the right time to try and break through it. It was as if she was standing talking to a stranger she had just met.

'How's things? Are you over the accident?' Lucy knew it sounded inane but wasn't sure what else to say. The easygoing, smiling Fergus that she knew so well was missing and in his place was someone she wasn't so sure of.

'Yeah, OK, everything's fine. Arm's OK now and I've got a new bike. Are you still under the weather? You were feeling sick and dizzy most of the time.'

'Oh yes, that's all right now,' Lucy wanted to smile, 'it was just a passing thing. I haven't seen you at Pettit's.'

'No.'

'Why's that? Aren't we on your route any more?'

Suddenly his hands were out of his pockets and his whole stance changed. 'Jeez, Lucy, why would you think I don't go to Pettit's? Hmm? I changed my job so I didn't have to bump into you. And why exactly are we standing in a frigging public park talking to each other as if we were just passing acquaintances chatting about the weather? Come on, Lucy, let's just cut to the chase. What is it you want?'

Lucy opened her eyes wide and stared at him. 'I thought you'd be pleased to see me. I wanted to talk to you but if that's how you feel then—'

His arms shot out and he took hold of her hands. 'Lucy, of course I'm pleased to see you and of course I want to talk to you but I don't know where this conversation is going and it's driving me crazy. I haven't slept a wink since you phoned and now we're standing here like strangers.'

'It's difficult, I don't know if I'm going to make things worse by being with you . . .' Her face crumbled. 'I just don't know what to do, Fergus, everything is such a mess, I've screwed up bigtime.'

'Hey, hey. Come on, let's go somewhere else. The pub . . .'

'I don't want to go to a pub, I want to talk to you! Come home with me, we can talk there.'

'You are joking, aren't you?' The disbelief in his eyes would have made Lucy laugh under any other circumstances. 'What about your crazy husband?' Fergus almost spat the words out.

'He's not there, he's in Portugal. Only Sadie is there and she knows everything.' Lucy stopped and managed a slight smile. 'Well, almost everything.'

'Lucy, don't restart something you're not going to finish, I don't want to go through all this again.'

'Let's go and talk.'

Sadie's face gave away exactly what she thought when Lucy and Fergus walked into the lounge together.

'Sadie, this is Fergus. Fergus, this is Sadie, my best friend. She's helping me sort a few things out at the moment.'

Sadie and Fergus eyed each other silently, like combatants in the ring. Fergus was the first to speak. Holding his hand out to her he smiled sheepishly.

'Hello there, Sadie, I've heard a lot about you.'

'And me you.' Straight-faced, Sadie took his hand briefly. 'What's going on, Lucy? Am I missing something here? You said you were going to the gym.'

'I lied. There are things Fergus and I need to discuss in private. Do you mind if we shut ourselves in the lounge for a while? We won't be long.'

'It's your flat, it's up to you.' Sadie went out to the kitchen and Lucy heard the door slam.

'Sorry about that, Sadie can be a bit over-protective, a bit of a mother hen. She's a social worker and finds it hard to switch off sometimes. I upset her earlier by calling her

Saint Sadie. It was a bit unfair.'

Fergus didn't answer, he just looked long and hard at Lucy. It was obvious to Lucy that he felt uncomfortable and on edge in her home, her marital home, the one she shared with Don. In unison they both sat down on the sofa, both perching on the edge, not looking at each other.

'Look, Fergus, I know I've not been fair to you. I should have given you an explanation at the time so now I'm going to be honest. What I did was for the best. Someone at Pettit's found out about us and was threatening to tell Don. I was scared he would kill you. Literally.' Turning towards him, she touched his shoulder and pulled very gently, making him turn to face her. 'So much was going through my mind at the time, I didn't feel well, I was worried about my job. I just thought it was for the best.'

Fergus still said nothing. His normally expressive eyes that Lucy loved so much were completely unreadable.

'I did it for you, Fergus. I didn't want to finish with you but I had no choice. It wasn't right what we were doing and it wasn't fair to anyone so, rightly or wrongly, I made the decision.'

Slowly he ran his hand back over his hair, pushing it away from his face, but it fell straight back again. Lucy resisted the urge to reach out and do it for him.

'Just in case it might have slipped your notice, I am a big boy now, you know. Jeez, I'm ten years older than you, do you not think I'm able to make my own decisions? Do you not think I should have been party to the decision-making? It affected both of us, not just you.'

'It's not that.' Lucy hesitated, shaken by the angry hurt in his voice. 'I know Don and it wasn't safe for you or me.

I think he had Paul Gower beaten up because he decided it was him I was seeing. He tried to throttle me, he attacked Sadie. Bloody hell, Fergus, he would have killed you. He weighs eighteen stone, he works out and injects bloody horse medicine into himself.'

Fergus jumped to his feet and started pacing like a panther in a cage. 'Then why are you still with him, Lucy? Why do you stay with him? Answer me that. I don't understand. If Don is all the things you say he is, why are you still here?'

Lucy's chin started to tremble uncontrollably, she had never heard Fergus shout before.

'Why are you still with Margot if she's all the things you say she is? What's the difference?'

'I offered to leave her . . .'

'Offering isn't the same as doing, so don't lay all this on me. Anyway, I'm not still with him. Well, not really. That's why I wanted to see you but it's no good shouting at me because I don't fucking understand it myself, in fact I don't even understand myself any more. I'm sorry . . .'

Before she could say anything else Fergus was over to her and she was in his arms sobbing. 'I'm sorry too. I'm just so frustrated with it all, I don't know what to think.' He kissed her face and whispered gently, 'Sshh, it's OK, I'm sorry too, don't cry, it'll be OK.'

Wrapping his arms round her, he kissed her gently on the forehead and then on the lips, entwining his hands in her hair and pulling her into him. Initially Lucy froze but as he held her tighter and kissed her harder, she found herself responding, but as soon as his hands moved down towards her breasts, she started to pull away.

'No! For Christ's sake, not now. I need to talk to you, anything else will just muddy the waters even more.'

'I'm sorry,' Fergus mumbled into her hair. 'I've just missed you so much.' He kissed her again very, very gently.

Lucy heard the door open and looked up to see Sadie in the doorway.

'Sorry to interrupt, I came to see if you wanted a drink but I can see you're otherwise occupied. I thought you were just going to talk.'

'Oh, Sadie, stop being so uptight about everything. Fergus and I *were* just talking.'

Sadie sniffed. 'Yeah, right. So do you want a drink, either of you? I'm making one for myself.'

Lucy was angry. Angrier than she had ever been with Sadie, her best friend. She stood up. 'Sadie, what is it with you? You're so goddamned judgemental nowadays, it's boring. You know the situation and I need to talk to Fergus, alone, without you hanging around like you're a mother keeping a watchful eye on a naughty teenager. I've got a mother, thank you very much, I don't need another one.'

Sadie looked long and hard at Lucy and then at Fergus. 'Well, perhaps if your mother and father managed to tear themselves away from each other and spend a little more time caring about you rather than just throwing money at you then you wouldn't be in this mess.'

Stunned and lost for words, Lucy just looked at her friend in silence.

Sadie was defiant. 'I'm sorry, Lucy, but that's how it seems to me. You treat me like a surrogate mother and expect me to sort out your problems all the time. What about me? I've tried, really tried to help you, but all I get is a bollocking if I disagree with you.' Nodding her head in the direction of Fergus but without looking at him she continued, 'You're always asking me what you should do about this one, about Don, but what do you care about my opinion? Unless of course it's what you want to hear.' Sadie's voice was getting higher and higher. 'It's just not fair.'

'What's not fair? I tried to set you up with the lovely Dr Col but you turned him down. I've taken you here, there and everywhere with me, but you've changed. You're no fun any more. You don't have to be here, you know. I thought you wanted to be.'

Sadie's face crumpled. She turned and ran out of the door, slamming it behind her.

Lucy looked at Fergus. 'I've never seen her like that before. Whatever's up with her?'

Fergus smiled wryly. 'Oh, Lucy, for someone so bright you can be very naïve. Can't you see? She saw us together, she was confronted by you and me in each other's arms. It's so obvious. She's jealous! It's written all over her face!'

'You're mad. That's Sadie, we've been friends for years. I've never heard such crap in all my life! She's my best friend, we've always been there for each other. God, that is such a macho thing to say, wait until I tell her.'

'Don't do that, Lucy. I'm not saying she would ever want anything more but that woman is far more attached to you than you seem to realise.' His face was suddenly serious. 'I mean it, you'll devastate her if you start making jokes about it. Just think about it, Lucy. The way she feels is written all over her face. She's in a lot of pain right now, don't make it any worse than you really have to. She probably doesn't understand it herself.'

'But that's crap, she cares about me as a friend, we're just friends.'

'OK, Lucy, if that's what you think then so be it, I'm sorry I said anything. Anyway, that's something that can wait just a short while. Now tell me what's really going on. Why did you want to talk to me? Am I to be allowed in from the cold?'

Lucy took a deep breath. 'I'm leaving Don, I'm going to work in Las Vegas for two months. I leave on Monday. And then I'm leaving Pettit's and moving away from London.' Looking down at her hands, she started picking at her nail varnish. 'And I'm pregnant, quite a lot pregnant in fact, nearly five months now.'

Fergus didn't answer. He crossed his legs and arms defensively, his gaze quizzical. The unspoken question hung in the air like a black cloud.

'Aren't you going to say anything?' Lucy prompted.

The silence and complete lack of emotion from Fergus unsettled her.

'Please say something. I need to know what you think.'

'There's not a lot to say, you've obviously made up your mind, made your decisions. What does Don think about the baby?' His voice was as expressionless as his face.

'He doesn't know and I'm not going to tell him, and before you ask, I don't know whose it is, Don's or yours, but if it is Don's then I don't want him to be part of it.'

'And us? You haven't mentioned us at all in this.' He looked at her, his eyes probing but conveying nothing.

'Well, that's up to you, Fergus. The ball is in your court.

Is there still an us or have we gone too far to go back?'

'I'm not sure, Lucy. What about the baby? If it is Don's, can you live with yourself if you keep Don away from his child? Will you be wanting to go back to him after it's born? I need time to think, we'll have to meet up again.'

'But Fergus, I'm going to Las Vegas.' She could see that he was near to tears.

'Then maybe you should have told me all this earlier, maybe we'll just have to see what happens after you get back.' Fergus was pacing the floor now, his long legs stretching back and forth, leaving footprints in the carpet. 'Oh, I don't know, I have to think about it all. It's too much to take in in one go, it's just too much. This is *déjà vu*, I've been here before.'

Before Lucy could answer him he had grabbed his coat and was out of the door. Her confusion was total. It wasn't that she had thought he would whoop with joy but she had expected some sort of reaction, positive or negative, not the in-between confusion that had sent him scurrying out like a rabbit.

After the door closed, Sadie crept back into the room apologetically, two cups of coffee in her hands.

'I'm sorry, Lucy, I was only concerned that you're going to make another mistake, you're so mixed up at the moment.'

Lucy looked at her, her mind on what Fergus had said. Although she didn't believe it for a minute, she found herself thinking back to all the times Sadie had become completely absorbed in nearly every aspect of her life, maybe more than just a friend would. No, Lucy reprimanded herself, it was just Fergus being over-sensitive.

'That's OK, Sadie, apology accepted, but please, please, in future let me make my own decisions, my own mistakes even.' Lucy looked at her friend and smiled, aware of Sadie's wary eyes. 'I can do that, you know!'

'I know.' Sadie looked like her old self again as she smiled widely. 'So have you decided what you're going to do about Fergus? He wasn't at all what I had expected, you know, he looks so ordinary and skinny compared to Don. Not your type at all, I wouldn't have thought.'

Lucy laughed. 'Going for the opposite, you mean? Maybe to begin with but not now. He's genuine and that counts for a lot to me after Donovan Cooper. But this may all be irrelevant because he's gone and I don't know if he's coming back. I've only got till Monday and then it's lift-off. Shit, shit, shit, why do I get myself into these messes?'

For the first time ever, when Sadie came over and put her arm round her, Lucy flinched and pulled away. Sadie said nothing but the look on her face and the hurt in her eyes spoke volumes.

Maybe Fergus was right, but even if he wasn't, the seed was sown and the easy relationship was gone, at least for the moment.

Donovan Cooper was not a happy man; in fact, he was finding it increasingly difficult to control his temper. The tension was building and the red mist of anger was in front of his eyes most of the time. His expectations of winning had unrealistically soared when he had scraped through the preliminary rounds but suddenly he found it all slipping away as his confidence faded and he made elementary errors. He was a no-hope outsider and he knew it, Jonno had made sure of that. The man who had encouraged him to enter, prodding him into giving it a go, was suddenly on his back telling him he was useless, and even the other competitors were eyeing him scornfully. In the small London gym, Don was top dog and he found it hard to accept that, realistically, he didn't stand a chance in a big competition, drugs or no drugs. All his cash had gone and the credit card was up to its limit. If he didn't win then it would all have been a waste of time and he would have to go home with nothing to show for it all.

'Donny boy, what are you playing at? You can't skulk in here like a two-year-old throwing a wobbler. You've blown it all on your own, there's no point in sulking about it.'

Don looked up to see Jonno with the two women from the airport, April and Pam, the clones, draped on either side of him. All three were grinning widely. Don found it hard to hide his distaste. In Don's eyes Jonno had little going for him apart from a big mouth and a lot of cash but that seemed to be enough for the two women, who had clung to him like limpets ever since they had been here.

'I'm just taking time out to compose myself, get my head in the right gear. There's still a chance. How do you know I've blown it?'

'Forget it, Donny boy, you've been all but beat already. You might just as well throw the towel in now, you don't stand a fucking chance. It's all over bar the shouting.' Jonno grinned broadly at the clones and they both laughed obediently.

Don had been sprawled along the bench when they had come in, wearing just his electric-blue Lycra trunks and an unzipped tracksuit top. It made him feel at a disadvantage so he slowly and carefully sat straight and put his hands under his vast thighs. He knew that if he didn't put his fists out of reach he would smash Jonno to a pulp.

'I'm still in the competition, I still have a chance of a place.'

'Yeah, right. As much chance as I have.' Jonno looked him up and down. The expression on his face reminded Don of his mother's when he had disappointed her. 'No, if I were you, I'd retire gracefully rather than face the humiliation. There's always next year, if you put that little bit extra in, go the extra mile, so to speak. No pain, no gain.' Jonno winked at him. 'If you know what I mean, Donny boy.'

Don tried to hide his distaste as he took in Jonno's acne-scarred face and greasy slicked-back hair. As usual, he was dressed top to toe in black; pleated-front chinos and a plain T-shirt were topped with a loose-fitting jacket with the sleeves pushed up. As he looked down at the fake crocodile patent shoes, Don thought that if Jonno MacMahon was trying to look like a villain then he was succeeding, almost to the extent of being a caricature of a television hard man.

April left Jonno's side and went over to Don, perching carefully beside him on the bench and flexing her long, muscular legs in front of her. The seductive smile and body language reminded Don of a snake waiting to pounce on a captive mouse. The tiny bikini top that she wore for the competitions looked almost pornographic on her muscular chest, which bore little resemblance to a woman's naturally soft and rounded shape. A pair of tight Lycra leggings covered the bottom half and hid the grossly distended muscles in her legs that Don had seen in action both on the stage and off.

'What are we going to do tonight, Donny?' April purred in his ear but loud enough for the others to hear. 'I'm going to give you a chance to make it up to me, if you know what I mean, after your little mishap last time. Perhaps you can prove to me that it was only a one-off deflation.'

The crimson blush that swept over Don's face was a combination of embarrassment and anger. It was bad enough that it had happened, but to know that both Jonno and Pam knew all about it was just too much.

April ran her hand up and down his thigh, each time moving her hand a little further up. Licking her lips suggestively, she gazed at him as her hand brushed across his crotch. She leaned closer, her brittle yellow hair inches from his eyes. It looked like strands of straw to Don, and the aroma of sickly body oil made him feel physically ill. He tried to smile but his facial muscles just wouldn't respond. He was a small boy again, being humiliated.

The four of them had been out for the evening after the first part of the competition and, because Jonno's hotel room was bigger and better than everyone else's, they had gone back there for a nightcap. Don just didn't want to be there, so as soon as possible he had pleaded tiredness and fled, leaving the three of them together. No sooner had he got back to his room than the phone rang.

'If you still want a job when you get home then you just get your arse back in here and collect April now! For some crazy reason she wants you so she's going to have you. Got it? You're not going to fuck up my night, Donny boy.'

The phone slammed back down before Don could answer.

What followed was Don's worst nightmare. He had gone back and taken April to his room but, despite all her best efforts, he just couldn't perform. The woman had tried every trick in the book but to no avail, Don just could not get it up.

After she had left, for the first time since he was a boy, Don had cried with shame.

'Come on, Donny boy,' Jonno said now, 'show the girls you can shag as well as the rest of us.' He paused, looking from one woman to the other. 'Well, perhaps not quite as well as the rest of us, but show 'em you can at least do it, that you're not really a great big woolly woofter with a soft little dick tucked away in your pants. I've got a little something that might just get you going where you've never been before. You'll be able to give the lovely April a night to remember.'

That night, courtesy of a lot of white powder and an inescapable fear of Jonno, Don managed to satisfy the almost insatiable April.

But it meant that the next day, with yet more chemicals – detectable ones – in his system, he had no choice but to pull out of the competition and, with no money left and Jonno not prepared to subsidise his hotel bill, he also had no choice but to go home early.

Despondently Don packed his things and got ready to leave. He had a ticket but nothing else so he would have to grovel to Jonno for some cash to get him to the airport.

Gritting his teeth, he went along the corridor to Jonno's room, but as he raised his hand to knock he realised the door was open slightly. Gently he pushed it a fraction and heard voices. The habit he had learned as a child of eavesdropping was hard to break; automatically he stopped to listen.

'Have you decided how you're going to play it with Don?' Don wasn't sure whether it was April or Pam who was speaking but he guessed it was one of them.

'Yep. I decided against letting him know anything, he's too fucking stupid, he could never carry it off.' That was Jonno's voice.

'So what are you going to do?' the female voice asked. 'We haven't got long if we're going to use him. He's leaving this afternoon.'

'Yeah, I know, but don't worry, he'll take it but he won't know. He'll do whatever I tell him and so long as he doesn't know what it is then he won't break out in a muck sweat going through customs. I'm just gonna ask him to take a few tubs of pills back for me, nothing illegal, just cheaper here than at home.'

There was a slight pause and the sound of footsteps padding across the tiled floor.

'Hang on a sec, Jonno, the door's open.'

Immediately and silently Don shot back into his own room and gently pushed the door to. His hands were shaking with rage. How dare Jonno talk about him like that to some slag he'd only just met. He was so wound up that when there was a knock on his door he physically jumped.

'Donny boy, are you in there? I just want a quick word before you leave. I've got some cash here for you, just enough to tide you over till you get home. I know you're a bit short at the moment.'

Opening the door cautiously, Don tried to smile but it ended up more as a grimace.

'What's up with you then? I come bearing gifts and you stand there with a face like a smacked arse.' Jonno dumped some notes on the bed and launched into his sparring routine, bouncing round the room with his fists in front of him, jabbing at Don. 'You're not miffed at going home, are you? You've got Lady Lucy there waiting for you. I just wish I was going back as well but I have to see it out till the end.' Jonno carried on punching at the air, a wide grin on his face. Don thought how ridiculous he looked, a middle-aged spiv pretending to be light on his feet.

'I'm grateful, mate,' Don muttered as he picked up the cash. 'I'm just trying to get packed and away.'

Jonno stopped bouncing. 'I've just remembered something, Donny boy. As you're going home before me, could you take some pills back with you for the lads? All perfectly legit. In fact I'm going to take some myself, so are the girls. By the way, did I tell you we're all going to meet up back home? That April really took a shine to you.'

Don wanted to tell Jonno exactly where to stick his pills but the words didn't come out right. His fear of Jonno overrode his brain and he heard himself agreeing. 'Whatever you want, Jonno, only I need them now so that I can stick them in the case.'

'Good on you, I'll just go and get them.' The sly smirk on the trainer's face made Don feel uncomfortable. When Jonno came back he brought with him just two tubs the size of coffee jars. Don visibly sighed with relief. They looked harmless enough. Maybe Jonno really was stocking up at source to make a few bob.

'Is that all?' he said. 'I expected something bulkier than that. What is it? Any good for me?'

Jonno laughed. 'No good for you at all, Donny boy. You're into the top-class stuff, this is for the plebs who are just starting out. No, this would be no use to you at all.' Jonno wrapped his arm round Don's shoulder affection-ately. 'When you get back, just hang on to them until I get there. I'll only be another few days and then we can get back to sorting out your training schedule. You'll do fine next time if you stick with me. It's going to cost you a bit, your gear is the best, but it'll all be worth it in the end. We're also gonna try and get a magazine shoot for the gym, with you as the star. How does that grab you? Donny Cooper, poseur extraordinaire!'

Immediately Don could see himself spread all over one of the specialist body-building publications, glossy photos that would emphasise his physique, show off his muscle tone and prove to everyone that he had made something of himself. He had already forgotten the tubs that he had pushed down into his suitcase.

Exactly as Jonno had intended.

Sitting on the plane watching sunny skies gradually give way to cloud, Don, for the first time since he had been away, gave more than a fleeting thought to Lucy and wondered how she would react when he got back.

Lucy had been his prize, a trophy that he just had to have. The cool sexy blonde that everyone at the gym had lusted after but he had won. Lucy had been the first step on the path to mending the inferiority complex that his mother and brother had instilled in him. He had never loved her, he had just wanted her in the same way that he now wanted to win a competition. He had wanted her because of what she stood for and what she had but as soon as they were married he had realised that all the things that had made him want her had actually brought all his insecurities back. The good career, the wealthy, loving parents, the ability to mix socially without being tongue-tied, he wanted them all for himself instead of second-hand. But he didn't want Lucy herself. At the same time, he wasn't prepared to give up what he did have and go back to being useless Donny. And he certainly wasn't prepared to accept the public humiliation of being dumped for someone else, especially Paul up himself Gower.

His mother's voice echoed back from his wedding day. 'It'll all end in tears, she's far too good for a useless little git like you.'

No, he would not give his mother that satisfaction. He would have to stay with Lucy until either her parents bought him out or he found someone else to support him.

'Ladies and gentlemen, we are about to begin our descent into London Gatwick Airport, please fasten your seat belts . . .'

He would soon be home. Immediately, his pulse raced. Just let Lucy say one wrong word, just one wrong word, he thought to himself as he flexed his shoulder muscles.

Chapter Nine

When Fergus left Lucy's flat, tears of frustration were pricking his eyes. Taking the stairs three at a time, he ran down into the street below. He felt stupid and desperately wanted to hide his face and his feelings from everyone until he had pulled himself together. He was worried Lucy would come after him, or even Sadie, when all he wanted was to be left alone to think. He brushed his sleeve over his face and sniffed, put his head down and started to walk quickly away.

When Lucy had phoned him it was as if a light had gone back on in his life. He hadn't been expecting miracles, far from it, but at least the lines of communication were open again and he imagined them carrying on where they had left off in the short term, with the future still undecided. He certainly wasn't expecting to have to make a decision about his whole life then and there. Lucy was pregnant and it might be his. He had been in that situation before and the past, and all his mistakes, came flooding back.

Fergus Pearson was a gentle man. He rarely lost his

temper, was kind to animals and children and worked hard, but he could also be too easygoing when it came to making decisions. That was why his daughter India was so out of control, it was why Margot and Simon both treated him with contempt, and it was also why he was still only a motorcycle courier for a second-rate company instead of an actor. Deep down he knew it, but all his life Fergus had taken the path of least resistance and avoided confrontation, so when Lucy had laid her cards on the table, he just didn't know what to do, much as he loved her.

Exactly the same as all those years ago.

For no reason at all Lorraine's face came into his mind. On the spur of the moment and without giving it too much rational thought, he turned into the underground station and took the tube to St John's Wood. As the gardens got larger and the houses grander, Fergus began to feel more and more out of place but his feet continued walking and his eyes continued checking the addresses until he reached his destination. He turned into the driveway and found a large set of electric gates barring his entry, and for the first time since the idea had come to him he hesitated.

It had been a long time. He knew the address was right because the Christmas cards continued to arrive regularly. Each year they became bigger and better until eventually Fergus had stopped reciprocating. Lorraine was firmly in his past.

Until today.

He pressed the buzzer and stood back sharply as two large and very ferocious-looking dogs threw themselves at the gates.

'Yes? Can I help you?' He recognised the voice instantly.

The deep, almost masculine voice, the carefully enunciated vowels.

'It's Fergus.'

'Fergus. Now there's a blast from the past. What the fuck are you doing here? Hang on, I'll open the side gate. Ignore the dogs, they're all noise and no bite.'

Fergus spotted a small, unobtrusive gate set back into the high brick wall that was topped with what looked like decorative wrought-iron work but was in fact sharp and dangerous. He waited impatiently, looking up and down the exclusive leafy street, thinking that at any moment he would be arrested for loitering.

The gate swung back to reveal Lorraine, who still looked exactly the same.

'Fergus, how lovely to see you. What on earth brings you here?'

'Looking up an old friend . . .'

Lorraine extended both her arms and grabbed him in a bear hug, kissing both cheeks. Then she held him at arm's length and looked him up and down.

'You've worn well, I have to say, don't look a day older. Come on in then. This is such a surprise, darling. I thought you'd forgotten all about me.'

Fergus followed her up the path through the perfectly manicured lawns and professionally tended flower beds towards the house. He noticed three cars parked haphazardly on the drive, a large Mercedes with blacked-out windows, a top-of-the range people carrier and a very flashy silver sports car. Lorraine saw him looking and laughed. 'It's OK, darling, there's no one here, they're all mine!'

The house had lots of glass and whitewashed walls that stood at unusual angles to the almost flat roof. It had obviously been ultra modern when built in the sixties or seventies but although it looked dated now, it was immaculately maintained. A triple garage that she obviously didn't use for her cars extended out to the side and was topped by a terrace edged with dozens of flower tubs that overflowed with multicoloured plants.

'You've extended, haven't you? I don't remember the house being this sprawling.'

'Husbands and kids, darling, I've got a huge study-cumhideaway in the back. I needed more room so I could run away from them all when the mood took me. I eventually got rid of the husbands but the kids all stayed with me. Aren't I the lucky one? Come on.' She stepped aside to let him in through the vast plate-glass sliding doors. 'Now follow me and we'll cut through here to the kitchen and I'll make you a cup of something.'

Fergus watched her as she walked gracefully ahead of him, her heeled velvet mules click-clacking on the polished wood floor that stretched ahead of them. She turned, aware of his eyes on her. Putting one hand on her leather-clad hip and pointing the other skywards, she posed.

'How do I look, darling? Not too bad for an old hag of nearly forty, am I? Not a single lift or tuck so far; gravity has been kind to me on the whole, don't you think? Be honest now, darling, tell me the truth, providing of course you agree with me.' She twisted and turned like a model on a photo shoot, baring her perfectly even teeth in a big fake smile.

'Lorraine, I think you look phenomenal, but then I always did, as you well know.'

Her deep laugh vibrated in the back of her throat. 'The same old Irish charm! You're about the only person who still calls me Lorraine, you know.'

'You'll always be Lorraine to me. I just can't think of you as Latisha Lowe, even when I see you on screen. It's as if you're two different people, the Lorraine that I knew so well, and Latisha, the people's favourite.'

As she tinkered with the cups and kettle, he watched her. He took in the shiny black hair that still waved over her shoulders and the figure-hugging trousers and T-shirt that emphasised the shapely body. She looked exactly the same as twenty years previously, when she had grabbed him by the arm and dragged him into her hectic life.

When Fergus had come over from Ireland to go to drama college he had felt completely lost and alone. His mother had fixed him up with lodgings at a distant relative's house and waved him off to London with tears in her eyes, thinking that he was off to make his fortune on the worldwide stage. It had been his ambition throughout childhood but he had hated it, hated being away from his family and friends, and hated being confined to one room in an obscure cousin's house where he wasn't really wanted. He was painfully homesick and ready to throw in the towel and head back to Dublin. And then he met Lorraine.

Lorraine had been the most extroverted person he had ever met in his life and she had taken him under her wing. Suddenly the young, naïve Fergus was at the centre of the 'in' group and invitations poured in. Before long he was hopelessly in love with 'Luscious Lorraine', as she was nicknamed to her amusement, and he had spent the following three years happily in her slipstream. 'We're both Irish, we have to stick together. We're siblings under the skin,' she liked to say and he could never bring himself to contradict her.

The small terraced house in Dublin of his childhood couldn't, by any stretch of the imagination, be compared to Lorraine's family's estate that bordered the western coastline of Ireland, with a country house the size of a hotel. In London she lived at the family mews house tucked away behind Oxford Street or the family country house in Wiltshire. Complete opposites and yet they clicked.

She smiled widely at him. 'Now, Fergie darling, tell me what brings you here after all this time. How long is it? God, it must be fifteen odd years. Why did you drop out of my life, you naughty boy?'

Because we inevitably grew apart, because your family had enough money for you not to have to take a job to pay your way through college, because you married an up-and-coming rock star who made a fortune to add to the one you already had, because you changed your name to Latisha and became a popular television actress who everyone loved and lusted after, because Margot trapped me into being a father when I was far too young and I had to enter the real world and give up my dream, because Margot hated you with a passion . . .

Fergus thought it but didn't say it, he just smiled wryly.

'Our lives just went in different directions,' he said. 'These things happen as you grow up. Margot had India and I had to get a job and, well, you know what Margot was like. I did try to keep in touch but she made it so difficult.'

'Silly woman. God, the abuse she threw at me. Why can't friends be friends? It shouldn't matter what sex they are, or what history they have. Still, darling, after so many years of just the odd phone call, I'm sure you haven't turned up out of the blue to reminisce. Has it all gone pear-shaped for you?'

Fergus was about to confide in her but he stopped himself. It was too soon.

'I just wanted to see you. I've been thinking about it for a while and decided on the spur of the moment and here I am. I wasn't even sure if you'd let me in, a famous person like you are!'

The dark green eyes outlined in black smiled at him. 'Oh, come on now, it was you who became too arsey to mix with me, not the other way round. Anyway, how is Margot? And the rest of the family? Your daughter must be a dreadful teenager now. For my sins I've got three daughters, from two different fathers, and they wear me out when they're all here together. Thank God two of them are away at school in Ireland half the time so it's just me, the eight-year-old and my trusty staff.' Lorraine's Irish accent was almost too slight to be noticed but Fergus could still hear it creeping through and it made him feel quite nostalgic.

He laughed. 'Your trusty staff? Jesus, that's just too much. Exactly how many staff would that be then?'

'Don't you go trying to back me into a corner, Fergie darling. I have one living in, a sort of housekeeper stroke nanny, and three living out. That's all I'm prepared to say. Darling, I earn a lot and the husbands had to cough up as well, so as far as I'm concerned, if you've got it, enjoy it. And I do.' Looking at him, she hesitated for a second. 'Am I being tactless again? I know things were hard for you but I did offer . . . you were too fucking proud. You could have had the same breaks as me, you were more than good enough, but no, you decided to change career and become a living martyr instead. No doubt the Irish ancestors would be proud of you but I think you were a little daft.'

'I did what was right.'

'Horseshit, darling. If I'd done what was right, what the family thought was right, I would either still be married to Jace and a raging addict with no inside to my nose like him, or I'd be dead. You should have done what I did and kicked off the shackles of the immoveable rights and wrongs, the stark black and white, because, darling, there is no such thing. You have to lose the guilt if you want to get on and be happy.'

Fergus smiled. 'You are just so outrageous still, do you know that? Just so outrageous. So you wouldn't be disappointed with me if I told you I was thinking about leaving Margot and running off with a married woman who might or might not be having my baby and whose husband is a gorilla-like body builder who enjoys hurting people?'

'Love it, darling, love it, but you won't do it because of your good old guilt. Margot will tweak the old conscience and you'll ping right back to her. I know you too well.' She leant over him, her cleavage too near for comfort, and kissed him on the forehead. The scent of Chanel wafted over him.

'Come on then, tell me all about it and I'll give you my valued opinion.'

After giving her a brief outline, Fergus changed the subject, which wasn't too difficult, Lorraine had always had a mind like quicksilver. They chattered about old times, good and bad, but it was always in the back of his mind how desperately he had been in love with Lorraine. He would have done absolutely anything for her and she would have done anything for him, except fall in love with him of course. And that had left him vulnerable to the predatory Margot.

To subsidise his fees, Fergus had worked evenings in a burger bar and it was there that he had met Margot. It had started out as a laugh. Lorraine had begun hanging around with Jace and his achingly trendy friends and Fergus was feeling left out and sorry for himself so when Margot had started coming in regularly and giving him the come-on, he had been flattered. After some light-hearted flirting he had eventually asked her out for a drink. They had gone on to a party, he had got drunk, they went back to her place and bingo! Margot became pregnant and Fergus had done 'the right thing', despite everyone's warnings.

'I tell you what, darling, to cheer you up I'm going to take you to a *soooooper* party tonight. It's the opening of a new club in the West End and everyone will be there. I've got a VIP ticket for two. Come with me, darling, you obviously need to get out more.'

'Jeez, I couldn't do that. I've got nothing to wear for something like that, I've got no money, and anyway it's not my sort of thing.' Fergus reacted as if Lorraine had suggested a trip to the dentist.

Lorraine pulled him up from the chair by his arm. 'Fuck off, darling, it's no good trying to pull your inverted snobbery thing on me. Come on upstairs and we'll find you something.'

The polished open staircase weaved left and right like a puzzle up three storeys to the top of the house. Lorraine flung a door open.

'OK, in you go and help yourself. There's enough stuff in here to clothe a small town. How about this?' She pulled a dinner suit from one of the rails that edged the room.

Fergus looked around in amazement. There were rails, racks, trunks and cabinets of men's clothes, women's clothes, children's clothes, shoes, handbags, and a riot of scarves and costume jewellery.

'I don't believe this, Lorraine. You've more stuff here than a large Marks and Spencer.'

'Harrods, darling, if you don't mind, Harrods. Now I'm not taking no for an answer, we're going out on the town for old time's sake so you might as well choose something. Otherwise I will.'

Fergus had to laugh. Lorraine had always been larger than life, she had also always been able to persuade him to do whatever she wanted. He knew he would go to the party with her and he also knew he would enjoy it. A one-off escape from reality.

'OK, I'll go with you, it will be an interesting experience, I'm sure. Up there with the rich and famous, imagining what might have been if I'd hung in there.'

'You'll love it, darling, you'll have a ball, and the best

part is, it's all free.' Lorraine clapped her hands and jumped up and down. Fergus suddenly remembered her other nickname from college, Bunny, after the Duracell battery rabbit that just never stopped.

Lucy had been dreading it. Her last day in the office and she couldn't tell anyone. Not for her the leaving do, the silly balloons and good luck cards. There would be no messages, no streamers over her desk and certainly no baby clothes as a leaving present. To everyone else it was just another working day, made better by being the end of the week, but for Lucy it was the end of her life as she knew it.

Although she knew she had a lot to do if she was to make sure Caroline and Paul had no reason to complain after she'd gone, it was hard to concentrate. Apart from one brief phone call from Fergus arranging to see her that evening, Lucy had heard nothing from him. She had no idea what he was thinking or planning.

There was also no news of Don; no one at the gym had a clue what was going on in Portugal, and none of them was interested in finding out, especially as Lucy had made it sound like just a passing question. With Jonno the boss away they could all relax.

'Morning, Lucy, you're early. All the excitement getting to you, is it?' Paul shouted over to her as he came in the doors. 'All set for the bright lights of the city of tack?'

Lucy looked up and smiled at him. Not so long ago her hackles would have been up and a sarcastic retort would have been exiting her mouth, but now she really didn't mind. Paul was Paul and nothing was going to change him so she just let it all wash over her. He had been kind when she needed it.

'I'm looking forward to it actually, it'll be nice to spend some time out in the big wide world with no one looking over my shoulder waiting to steal my thunder. Fancy a coffee? As this is my last day I'll make you one, a little farewell gesture.'

'Oh, thank you so much, kind lady, I'm indebted to you.'

Paul went over to her desk and bowed, Japanese fashion, in front of her. Suddenly there was a crash that made them both jump.

Daniella Schwarz had tripped over her uncomfortably high boots and fallen against the doors. Usually cool and calm in her movements, she reminded Lucy of a young foal trying to run. Her face was flushed and little tendrils of hair were hanging damply around her sweat-soaked neck.

'Good God, Dani, what's up? Is the place on fire? We're not used to seeing you this early or this fast.' Lucy smiled to take the edge off her words. There had been an uneasy truce between them since it was made public that Lucy was going away for a couple of months. Dani had calmed down as she saw the perceived obstacle to her getting back with Paul being removed and Lucy felt slightly more relaxed now that the girl knew her job depended on her discretion. But this morning it was obvious something was up. The green eyes glistened with anticipation as she hot-footed it across the office to where Lucy and Paul were sitting.

'Look, have you seen this?' She could hardly get the

words out, she was so excited. 'That's Fergus our favourite delivery boy spread all over the paper. He's gone up in the world since *we* last saw him. Look, it says at the bottom they want to know if anyone can identify him. I'm going to give them a call. That's all right with you, Lucy, isn't it? You said you weren't . . . you know . . .' Dani looked around to check no one else was in then leaned forward in best theatrical fashion and whispered loudly. 'You said you weren't seeing him any more.'

Lucy and Paul exchanged glances and then he snatched up the tabloid newspaper and spread it out over the desk in front of them.

'Page five, page five,' Dani said excitedly.

The perfectly clear full-length photograph took up half an inside page and was captioned: 'LATISHA LOWE'S NEW MYSTERY BOYFRIEND'.

The accompanying blurb followed the usual format:

Latisha Lowe, one of the most popular actresses on our television screens today, attended the opening of London's newest and most fashionable watering hole with a mystery man on her arm. She declined to name her escort, all she would say was that he was an 'old friend' . . .

Twice married . . . three children . . . previously linked with . . . starred in . . . heads together deep in conversation . . . champagne . . .

There was more, much more and Lucy read it all in fascinated horror before looking at the photograph again.

There was absolutely no question about it, the mystery

boyfriend was Fergus, done up like a dog's dinner looking decidedly furtive. Lucy read every word and then casually pushed the paper to one side.

'Good luck to him, it's up to him who he sees. I'm off to Vegas!' All Lucy wanted to do was get away so she could scream and kick furniture but the song 'Nowhere To Run' came to mind. The toilets, the roof, the deli, Daniella would follow her, of that she was certain, so she had no choice but to bite her lip, sit it out and pretend total disinterest. She didn't even bother to pick Daniella up on her facetious 'delivery boy' remark.

Daniella was reading the article carefully. 'Shit, just look who else was there. I'd have shagged him myself if I'd known he mixed in those circles.'

'Dani!' Paul's voice was fierce.

'Sorry, no really, I am sorry, I didn't mean it like that. Thinking about it, he hasn't been around here lately, do you think he's come up on the lottery or something?'

It got worse. The photograph had been syndicated and nearly every newspaper carried it, all with similar headings. Latisha Lowe was big news and the story warranted blanket coverage. Everyone in the building was talking about it because everyone knew Fergus. The general consensus was that he must have hidden talents that no one had picked up on.

'You all right, Lucy? That was a bit of bad timing, another couple of days and you wouldn't have known about it.' Paul was back at her desk. 'Did you know he was seeing her? Lucky bastard, every bloke in the country would kill to shag her.'

'Yes, well, it must be the Irish gift of the gab. I fell for it, didn't I? I just hope Dani doesn't use this as an excuse to accidentally, ha ha, spill the beans to everyone. I had hoped it was all forgotten about.'

'Leave her to me, I'll take her aside and have a chat. I don't think she would do it deliberately, not now, but she does run away at the mouth when she's excited and, boy, is she excited. A bit of celebrity mania there. See how quickly she forgets? Suddenly I'm consigned to the scrap heap of the not famous enough. It happens to the best of us.'

Lucy managed a smile. 'Thanks, but I'm OK. It was just a silly episode in my life that's over, so Las Vegas, look out.'

Lucy's mobile jumped into life. She looked at the screen and clicked it off. Fergus was out of her life, she decided. If he could do that on the day that she had told him her news then he was just as worthless as Don. Sadie had been right all along, she had no sense when it came to men.

The rest of the day passed in a blur, a meeting with Luke, several phone calls from Caroline with a long list of instructions and eventually Lucy walked out of Pettit's for the last time. Everyone thought she would be back after her trip but Lucy knew better, she just couldn't share it with anyone. She couldn't even clear her desk of all the personal bits and pieces she had accumulated over the years there because it would have looked suspect. She just took all the paperwork that Luke had given her and sauntered out at the same time as Paul.

As they walked out onto the street, Lucy caught a glimpse of Fergus loitering in one of the nearby doorways and the familiar thumping started up in her chest so strongly that she was convinced Paul would notice. Fergus must have realised that she, along with everyone else in the country, would have seen the papers. Turning her back to where she had seen him, she smiled and linked her arm with Paul's.

'Fancy a quick drink? A farewell glass of wine before I toddle off back to my packing?'

Paul couldn't disguise his surprise. 'Of course! I'd like that. I was going to suggest it but I thought you'd jump down my throat again. The Feathers over the road do you? Or do you fancy somewhere a bit more select?'

'Feathers will do just fine. We can go over any last-minute details that I may have missed.'

Paul grimaced good-humouredly. 'And there was I thinking my charming and witty personality had won you over at last.'

Lucy laughed happily as, arm in arm, they threaded their way through the traffic to the pub on the opposite side of the road. She didn't look back but she knew that Fergus was still there, watching. Good, she thought. She wanted him to understand how she felt seeing him spread all over the papers with his arm wrapped round someone else.

By the time she came out, still with her arm looped in Paul's, he had gone so she flagged down a cab and, after saying goodbye to Paul, sadly headed away from Pettit's for the last time, with her phone turned off.

Soon, she thought, I shall be up in the sky, leaving them all behind. Don, Fergus, Daniella, all the people who gave her grief would be behind her. It was a few seconds before she realised she hadn't included Paul in the list. Maybe in time he could be a friend after all. But as quickly as the thought flashed through her mind, she dismissed it again. For a split second she had forgotten that she was pregnant and in two months' time she would be starting a new life. A life that would eventually include being a single mother. The thought was singularly depressing.

By the end of the day Lucy had a phone full of missed calls and text messages. She ignored them all, hitting the delete button without listening to any of them. She didn't get on with her packing, she poured a glass of wine and fell into the armchair and put her feet up on the glass-topped coffee table, the same one she had always complained about Don putting his feet on. But she didn't care; at that moment Lucy didn't care about anything. Pleased Sadie wasn't around to disapprove, she drew deeply on her cigarette but as soon as the nicotine hit her system she felt quite sick and stubbed it out.

She heard the key in the lock and the door opening. Anticipating Sadie's comments about Fergus and the newspapers, Lucy shouted over her shoulder, 'I know, I know, I've seen it so there's no need to gloat.'

'Seen what?'

Lucy nearly passed out on the spot. Looking round, she was confronted by Don standing behind her with his suitcase still in hand.

'Don! What are you doing here?'

'I live here, remember. But if you're thinking about starting, then don't. I'm not interested.' He dumped his case on the floor, took off his jacket and threw it across the room in the direction of the sofa. 'I'm absolutely fucking starving. What's in the fridge?'

Lucy stared at him open-mouthed, she couldn't think of anything to say, her only thought was how she was going to get away.

'Why are you looking at me like that?' Don was puzzled. 'Aren't you going to say anything? You know, like, pleased to see you. I know you're not but you could pretend.'

Even the usual sarcasm went over her head, she just carried on staring at him.

'Well, fuck you then, don't speak to me.'

Don started slamming about in the kitchen and it was as if he had never been gone, as if everything that had happened since the accident had just been a dream.

Lucy had forgotten about Sadie and as soon as she heard the front door again, she began to panic.

Sadie bounded into the room. 'Hiya. God, what a day. An emergency at five o'clock, all I needed. Anyway, how did the last day go? Much weeping and wailing all round?' Sadie suddenly sensed something was wrong and looked around. She spotted the case. 'Who—'

'Since when did you have the right to walk into my flat without knocking?' Don demanded behind her.

'What are you doing here?' Sadie's response was automatic. Lucy could see the shock on her face and the anger on his and suddenly she was very scared.

Over the years Lucy had become an expert at assessing Don's moods and she could see that he was spoiling for a fight. She guessed he wanted an excuse to justify his taking off with her money without a word, and she didn't want Sadie to give it to him.

'It's OK, Don, Sadie has been staying while you were away, I wasn't feeling too well.'

'What, again? You're always sick, you should hire a live-in nurse.' Switching his gaze from Lucy to Sadie he continued, 'Well, now you just fuck off back to your hovel, you're not wanted here, you fat cow.' Don's face was twisted with loathing.

'Don't speak to my friend like that.' Lucy knew she was treading on dangerous ground but couldn't stop herself. 'Sadie is welcome in *my* home any time. She's actually helping me pack. I'm going to be working in America for a couple of months, I'm leaving on Monday.'

'Oh no you're not, you're not going anywhere unless I go with you.'

'What? Like you went off without me? Without even telling me where you were going? All you took with you was my money and my credit card. You cleaned me out.'

Don looked at her in mock sympathy. 'Oh dearie me. Never mind, Mummy and Daddy will reimburse you, I'm sure. They've got more than enough for all of us. For fuck's sake, spare me the grizzling, I'm sick of all your weeping and wailing – just *shut up!*' His face was flushed and his fists began clenching. Lucy knew she was in trouble. She looked at Sadie, who was rooted to the spot.

It took Don only two paces to reach Lucy. He dragged her out of the chair by her arms, lifted her up and slammed her against the wall. She crumpled into a heap on the floor.

Sadie started screaming. 'Stop it, stop, leave her alone!'

Don didn't even turn in her direction. He swung his leg back, preparing to kick Lucy in the stomach.

Sadie's screams got louder. 'Don't do it, you bastard, don't do it. She's pregnant.'

Don froze, his leg still raised behind him.

'Don't do it, Don, please don't do it,' Sadie continued.

Slowly he let his leg drop. He looked down at Lucy. 'Is it true?'

Lucy didn't look at him, she fixed her gaze on Sadie. 'Why?'

'Because he was going to kick the crap out of you, that's why, and if that's what it took to stop him then so be it. I'm sorry but I couldn't let him do it.'

'Er, excuse me? Am I still in the room? Now tell me what this is all about or I'll smack the pair of you.'

'I'll tell you all right,' Sadie shot back, 'so you just listen and you listen hard. You raise one more fist or foot to *either* of us and I'll have the police round here before you take your next breath. You're nothing but a foul-mouthed thug and I despise you more than you could possibly imagine. One finger, just one finger, and I'll make sure you're locked up.'

The stand-off between them was electric. Lucy watched in horrified fascination as Sadie at a mere five foot two stood her ground in front of the mountainous Don, her face a mask of contempt. Then slowly Don turned away from her and held his hand out to Lucy to help her up.

'Is it true, Lucy? Are you pregnant?'

She couldn't meet his eye. 'Yes, it's true.' Ignoring his outstretched hand she got back on to her feet and carefully brushed at her clothes, concentrating on the minute particles of carpet dust that clung to her navy blue skirt. 'Yes, I am pregnant, and yes, I am going to the States on Monday.'

'Over my dead body you are.'

'If that's what it takes.' Lucy walked out of the room with Sadie right behind her.

'I'm so sorry but I had no choice, I thought he was going to kick you to death in front of me, I thought you'd lose the baby . . .'

Lucy's voice was cold and emotionless as she looked at Sadie. 'Maybe that would have been the best thing all round. I take it you've seen the paper today?'

'No, I've been up to my neck in hassle all day. Why?'

'Well, you must be the only person in the country who hasn't seen it.'

Don appeared behind them. 'Seen what? What is all this crap about the papers, what's in the papers that's so important? Did you make an announcement about expecting my baby? Is it only me that doesn't know? That's assuming it is mine, of course, and not Paul's.'

Lucy sighed. She could feel all her strength draining from her body; she just wanted to curl up in a ball, go to sleep and forget everything.

'Don, do me a favour, just leave me alone. I'm sick of you, in fact I'm sick to the back teeth of everything. I'm going out and I don't know when I'll be back. Come on, Sadie, you can't stay here, you'll have to go home.'

'You're not going anywhere.' Don put his hand out and then thought better of it as he saw the expression on Sadie's face.

'What about my things?' Sadie said to Lucy.

'Go and gather them up, I'll wait for you.'

As Sadie scuttled off to the spare bedroom, Lucy pointedly ignored Don and put on her jacket. Then she picked up her handbag and turned to him.

'Don't even think about coming after us, Don.'

Sadie meekly followed Lucy as she ran down the stairs and out onto the street.

'Are you OK? You shouldn't be running about like this.' Sadie was breathless as she caught her up. 'Bloody hell, Lucy, that was just so scary.'

'Scary for you, do you mean? Think what I have to deal with. A kicking would be over and done with by now but now that he knows I'm pregnant, macho man is never going to let me go. He'll be out in five minutes announcing it to the world and buying drinks all round. I don't know what I'm going to do . . .' Lucy looked around as she heard her name being called.

'Lucy, wait. Lucy, I have to talk to you.' Fergus was heading down the street towards her.

'Shit, that's all I need, him as well,' Lucy muttered. 'What is it about me that attracts them?'

Sadie shook her head. 'You've lost me now, I thought he was the best thing since Coca-Cola. What's he done?'

'What's he done?' Lucy shouted loud enough for Fergus to hear. 'What he's done is get caught with someone else, the bastard, not only caught with someone else but caught with Latisha bloody Lowe in every bloody newspaper across the whole bloody country. That's what he's done. Bastard!' she screamed at him. 'I don't want to see you ever again. I hate you!' Wild-eyed, she turned to Sadie. 'And I'm really pissed at you for not keeping your mouth shut and I wish Don was stone dead and burning in hell as we speak. Is that enough for you all?'

Fergus looked as if he'd been punched in the stomach. Shaking his head, he took a deep breath. 'I can explain,

Lucy. It wasn't what it looked like, really it wasn't. Lorraine, I mean Latisha, is an old friend, she was trying to be kind.'

'I bet she was. Well, you make a lovely couple. And what about Margot? Does she know about it all?'

Fergus nearly smiled. 'She does now. Margot has always known about Latisha but she—'

'Enough.' Lucy held her hand up as if stopping traffic. 'I'm not interested. I thought you were sitting somewhere contemplating whether or not we might have a future together while all the time you were whooping the night away with the A list. Nice work if you can get it. Goodbye, Fergus, don't let me keep you.'

'I'm not going anywhere, Lucy. I'm going to follow you and keep following you until you speak to me. I'll even take you to Lorraine's and let her explain, whatever it takes, but I'm going to follow you until you give in and listen to me.'

'I'm not going to listen.'

'Yes you are, Lucy, you are.' He reached out and tried to touch her arm but she pulled away so hard she spun round.

'*Don't* touch me, Fergus. Just fuck off and leave me alone!'

While Fergus and Lucy were locked in verbal combat, with Sadie watching from the sidelines, none of them realised that Don had belatedly run down after Lucy and was standing open-mouthed and stock still, watching the scene further up the street. For once he was stunned into silence.

Chapter Ten

'Oi! What's going on? *Lucy!*'

Lucy, Fergus and Sadie all turned in unison towards the voice that was bellowing down the street.

'Shit,' Sadie spluttered. 'It's Don, what are we going to do?'

Lucy turned to Fergus. 'Get out of here, just get away. I don't know how much Don's heard . . . dear God . . .'

'I'm not going to run, I can't leave you to face him.'

'Yes you are, it'll be worse for me if you're here.' As she was speaking, she was watching Don marching towards them. 'Please go, I promise I'll phone you later if you'll just go now.'

Fergus hesitated before slowly backing away, turning and disappearing down an alleyway.

Lucy could hear the swish of fabric as Don's huge thighs rubbed the material of his trousers.

'I said, what's going on? Who was that?'

Lucy looked at him, a defiant expression on her face. 'None of your business, I don't have to explain myself to you—'

'He's my boyfriend and we've just had a row,' Sadie interrupted. 'Why? What's it to you?'

Don hesitated and Lucy could see he wasn't quite sure. She said a silent thank you to Sadie for thinking on her feet.

'He wasn't arguing with her,' he snarled, nodding his head at Sadie. 'He was arguing with you, Lucy. You must think I'm stupid.'

Making it up as she went along, Sadie carried on. 'That's right, he was arguing with Lucy but only because she stuck up for me. Anyway, he's gone now. He's just another loser, we all fall for them at some time or another.' She looked at Lucy. 'Right, I'm off now that I've got shot of him. Are you coming?'

Lucy sighed. 'No, I'm going back with Don, we have things to sort out. I'll phone you later. Don't worry, I'll be fine, won't I, Don?'

Before he could answer, Sadie was in there. 'I sincerely hope so because I won't think twice about calling the police if I don't hear from you.'

Warily Sadie walked off in the opposite direction, unhappy about leaving them together, though she knew she had no choice. Lucy was an adult and it was her decision.

'Sadie! Over here.' The disembodied voice made her freeze.

Slowly looking around, she spotted Fergus tucked just inside the alleyway, leaning casually against the wall. She glared at him and was about to carry on when he called again. 'Please, Sadie.'

She turned to face him. 'Loitering in alleyways can get

you arrested. You look like a dealer lurking in the shadows waiting for punters.'

'Thank you for those few kind words, Sadie. Do you think Lucy will be OK? I'm worried about leaving her with him, she was so angry and he seems to be so very easily antagonised.'

Sadie could just about make out Fergus's features in the dusk; he looked as if he was genuinely concerned. She softened slightly.

'I haven't got a clue, he's unpredictable and she's stubborn, a match made in hell, but it's what she wanted. Can you imagine if we'd tried to follow her? I hate Donovan Cooper with a passion but he has this hold over her. She desperately wants to break free but he always grinds her down. He's not just a bully but an emotional blackmailer as well. Bad combination.'

'Yes, I know. I still feel like a wimp for not standing my ground and having it out with him, but I've never been violent, I wouldn't know where to start.'

'Maybe you are a wimp.' Sadie smiled. 'But it's better to be a live wimp than a dead hero with a dead Lucy beside you.'

When Fergus Pearson smiled, women softened instantly. It wasn't that he did it deliberately, it was just the way he was. His naturally good-humoured face would light up and the stray wrinkles would fan out from his eyes and mouth.

He smiled at Sadie. 'Would you come for a coffee with me? I'd like to talk to you, especially as I can't get through to Lucy at the moment. I know you don't like me but I do know we are both equally concerned for her. Please? A coffee and a chat, that's all I ask.'

Sadie shrugged. 'OK, but don't expect me to tittle-tattle to you about her. I don't gossip about my friends.'

'Great. If we go down this way then we can get out the other end. There's a great coffee shop there with a lounge downstairs. More like home than home, it is. Armchairs, coffee tables – even, shock horror, ashtrays! Have you been there?'

'No, but I've been in others very similar so I'm sure I won't be too overawed.'

Sadie's sarcasm didn't go unnoticed.

'Sorry, I wasn't wanting to offend you, I was just making conversation.' Fergus shrugged his shoulders and grinned sheepishly.

They walked in silence but Sadie was very aware of his presence beside her. She barely reached his shoulder and had to take two paces to his one to keep up as he loped along with his hands in his pockets, his shoulders hunched and his head down. Sadie had been given a glimpse of exactly what Lucy saw in Fergus.

As soon as they were settled in a corner of the coffee shop, Sadie decided to bypass tact.

'What exactly did you do that sent Lucy off her head like that? She looked like she really wanted to amputate your balls, slowly and painfully.'

A look of surprise flashed over his face before he laughed. 'I know, she and several others. It's a long story, but before I tell you I have a quick call to make.'

He pulled out his phone and searched for a number.

Fergus had quite enjoyed his night out with Lorraine but he had also known that realistically it was a one-off. He was out of his league behind the velvet rope that divided off the VIP section of the club. Everyone had known everyone else and Fergus had recognised a lot of the faces from his television screen. There were TV stars, pop stars, people who were famous for being famous, and in amongst them, feeling like a fraud, there was himself. His days at drama school had at last come in useful because he had been able to act his way through the evening and carry off the pretence that this was the sort of thing he was used to. He didn't want anyone to accuse him of being star struck so he shook hands, air-kissed and made polite conversation with everyone Lorraine introduced him to. It was great fun at the time. The highlight of the evening was chatting to one of his childhood fantasies; the lowlight was at the end when they left. Although he knew Lorraine was famous he just hadn't been prepared for the photographers waiting outside at three o'clock in the morning, snapping away from all angles. Like a rabbit caught in headlights, he had frozen in his tracks and been caught full face, with Lorraine beside him, wearing her best publicity smile.

As a result of his stupidity and Lorraine's thoughtlessness in not mentioning what might happen, he had had Margot screaming death and destruction and Lucy ignoring his calls. He had taken a chance on going to Pettit's to wait for her to come out, only to be confronted by her heading into the pub with Paul Gower. All he had wanted was the chance to explain and he had even decided he would take her to meet Lorraine, if need be, so she could explain on his behalf, but it didn't look as if he was going to get the chance. Maybe Sadie could intercede for him.

'Hello, Lorraine? It's Fergus. You have got me into so much trouble you wouldn't believe . . . Yes, you have, and you know it. Listen, are you free? I'd like to pop over for five . . . That's grand. Is it OK if I bring a friend with me? . . . No, no, she's cool . . .'

After saying where they were Fergus clicked the phone and turned back to Sadie. 'Come on, we'll take our coffee back upstairs. We're going visiting if you've got time, and there's a car coming to pick us up. If Lucy doesn't want to see me any more then there's not much I can do but there is no way she's going to take off to Las Vegas without knowing the full story, and you, Sadie, are going to be the one to tell her – if you're willing, of course.'

Sadie was bemused but she had nothing else to do but go home to an empty flat. Looking at Fergus closely, she could see what the attraction was for Lucy. Not only was he very good-looking but there was an infectious enthusiasm about him that was far removed from the overbearing tension that emanated from Donovan Cooper who had made her feel uncomfortable from day one.

'So what is going on, Fergus? Lucy was just starting to tell me when Don burst in unexpectedly and started throwing his weight about. He had her on the floor, you know. He was going to kick her. I had to tell him what was going on to stop him from harming her but instead of thanking me, Lucy went ape.'

'Had to tell him what? I thought you said you didn't know what was going on?'

'Not about you, I told him about the baby. I told him she was pregnant to stop the bastard kicking her in the stomach.'

Fergus swallowed hard. He had seen Don lumbering down the street like an irate gorilla; Lucy wouldn't stand a chance if he started on her again.

'Then why did you let her go back alone with him? Why didn't you tell me straight away? I wouldn't have let her go. He'll kill her!'

'No he won't, not this time, I'm sure. He seemed quite pleased about the pregnancy but he did tell her she couldn't go to Vegas – at least, not without him. I can just imagine him doing the old macho daddy-to-be bit.'

Fergus's eyes widened. Lucy had always gone on about his eyes, Sadie recalled. If the eyes really are the gateway to the soul, she thought, then he must have a kind soul. Dark and deep and slanting very slightly at the corners, they were eyes that any girl would kill for.

'Jeez,' he said, 'I can't imagine that animal being pleased, as you put it, that his wife could be having someone else's baby. That's not a normal reaction . . . Oh, I don't know, this is all such a mess.'

Because Sadie's job was all about dealing with people in crisis, she was well trained in maintaining a neutral expression whatever the circumstances and not responding negatively to anything, no matter how shocking. That way people were more likely to open up and confide or confess. And that was exactly what she did. Putting on her social worker mask, she looked towards him but didn't make eye contact.

'Mmm, I know,' she muttered encouragingly.

'I mean, what am I supposed to do? Jump in with both feet regardless of whose baby it is? I do love Lucy, I absolutely adore her and I believe it was kismet that we met, but supposing the baby is Don's, not mine? He's going to want something to do with it. And I have a fifteen-year-old daughter to consider in all this. It wasn't a decision I could make lightly, I had to think about it.' He fell silent and disappeared off into his own thoughts, leaving Sadie to sit there inwardly steaming but looking serene. Lucy had lied to her. Her best friend, her only really good friend, had looked her in the eye and lied. Lucy had told her it was definitely Don's baby, no question. Why? she asked herself. Why would Lucy lie about it? There was no need. She idolised Lucy, loved her, and she felt unbearably betrayed.

'I don't think he knows that it might not be his. I only told him she was pregnant, he just assumed it was his. He's probably out getting pissed on the strength of it as we speak.'

'But she'll have to tell him . . .' He looked to Sadie for confirmation. 'Won't she?'

'Who knows?' Sadie shrugged.

Out of the corner of her eye she noticed a blacked-out Mercedes purr to a halt outside.

Fergus went to check it out and then called her. 'That's for us. Come on, let's go.'

'Where exactly are we going?'

'To see Lorraine, my friend who got me into all this trouble. She lives in St John's Wood, it won't take long.'

It was a rare treat for Sadie to be chauffeured across London in luxury. Leaning back against the soft, armchair-like seats, she decided she would enjoy her little jaunt but Lucy Cooper could go and take a running jump into the Serpentine. Sadie felt so hurt and betrayed that there was almost a physical pain in her chest, yet she was on her way to get the ins and outs of whatever it was Fergus was accused of, so that she could report back to Lucy and put her mind at rest. No way, she decided. She would not mediate for Lucy ever again. Right now she never wanted to see Lucy again.

'Well? I'm waiting. Tell me what's been going on, you deceitful bitch. I can't believe I had to hear it from your fat friend, and as for Las Vegas, don't you think I had the right to know?'

Lucy couldn't disguise the contempt she felt as she looked at her husband. In his usual pose of legs apart, hands on hips and shoulders pushed back to inflate his chest, he stood over her. Lucy was sitting on a ladderback chair in the kitchen and he was as close as he could get without touching her. He was being deliberately intimidating, but Lucy wasn't having it. Her days of lying down and rolling over for Don, or even Fergus for that matter, were over. It was getting late, it had been a long and emotional day and all Lucy wanted to do was go to bed but she knew she couldn't, not yet. Everything, or nearly everything, had to be resolved.

'No, Don, I don't think you have the right to know anything. I've got a better idea, you tell me what's going on. You take off without a word while I'm lying in hospital after an accident. You steal my money, load up my credit card and no doubt shag anything with a pulse. So you tell me first.'

To her surprise Don appeared to almost deflate. In that instant she knew she had caught him out by accidentally hitting the nail on the head, Don was seeing someone else. Lucy wasn't upset by the idea, in fact she felt empowered by it. For once she had the upper hand.

'Come on, Don, I know for a fact that you've been shagging around in Portugal, someone from the gym told me,' she bluffed, 'so let's hear your version.'

When he didn't answer she continued, using her most confident business tone.

'Come on then, for just once in your life be honest, but be quick about it. I've got things to do before my flight on Monday.'

Don sat on the chair opposite and looked sad. Lucy realised she was in for the 'I'm sorry I've been a naughty little boy' routine.

'I didn't want to do it but Jonno made me, I had to sleep with her.'

Lucy burst out laughing. She had just raised a cup of hot tea to her lips and it spilt all over the limed oak table. As the puddle spread and started to drip to the floor, she laughed louder. Of all the excuses Don had come up with over the years for his various tricks, she thought this was the best. Still chuckling, she fetched a cloth and began mopping the table. As she did so, she suddenly remembered buying it. They hadn't been married long and she was still oblivious to Don's true character. As soon as she spotted the table and two chairs, a honeymoon set, in a small shop in Camden she knew she had to have them. She could just imagine herself and Don in the kitchen sitting opposite each other at breakfast time. Without telling him, she had ordered it as a surprise, honestly thinking that he would be as pleased as she was. But he wasn't. After complaining virulently about the waste of money and asking over and over again what was wrong with the old one, he had emptied her purse of cash and stormed out. Next morning Lucy had found a long gouge right across the middle of the table. 'Sorry,' he had said, 'it was an accident, the knife slipped.'

Now, as she wiped the table, she could still see the mark. The damage had been repaired as far as was possible, but to someone who knew it was there, it was glaringly obvious.

With total lack of perception, Don wasn't fazed by her laughter.

'Honestly, he did,' he insisted. 'It was Jonno who made me go to Portugal in the first place, he told me I was in with a chance, and then he wanted to sleep with this girl so I had to sleep with her friend. Christ, you should have seen her, more muscles than me and a fake tan that would make your fat friend look fair-skinned.'

Lucy's amusement died. At that moment she knew with certainty there was no going back on her decision to leave him for good. Her marriage was like the table; the damage was there and always would be. The only problem was, Sadie had told him she was pregnant and he assumed it was his.

'OK, Don, I really don't want to know any more. That's the past and all I'm interested in is the future. On Monday I am leaving to work in Las Vegas for a while. When I get back, I'm selling the flat and I'll give you half, exactly half, despite the fact that you've put absolutely bugger all into it, and then I'm going to move away.'

'No way,' he protested. 'This is my home, and what about my baby?'

'I'm going to have a termination. There will be no baby. You and I will have nothing to tie us together, we can each go our separate ways.'

The fists started their familiar clenching and Lucy could hear him grinding his teeth. She rinsed out the cloth at the sink, aware of every little movement he was making.

'You can't do that, you can't do any of that, you're my wife, it's my baby, I'm entitled to more than half . . .'

Lucy could hear the desperation in his voice; for the first time he was taking her seriously.

'Don, let's get this straight. Earlier this evening, in front of Sadie, a witness, you flung me across the room and then you were going to kick me. You've admitted that you were shagging around in Portugal and you stole my money to get there, money that I had worked hard to earn, and I still have to pay off the credit card. I think you'll find I can do whatever I want.' She threw the cloth down and turned to him, her face grim. 'Now I'm going to bed, in the spare room. Just think, after I've gone you'll have free rein to do whatever you like. It might be a bit harder without any money but I'm sure you'll find a way, or maybe even a proper job. Goodnight.'

'Don't you fucking walk away from me!'

'Sorry, Don, I just have.'

Confident on the outside but terrified on the inside, Lucy walked out of the kitchen. Don didn't follow her but it was over an hour before Lucy dozed off into restless sleep, aware that he could enter the unlocked room at any time despite the bedside cabinet she had pushed against the door. Her mind was whirling. What if Don caused trouble at the airport? At Pettit's? Even in Las Vegas? She knew that when he was fired up anything was possible.

Lucy woke with a start some time later, unsure what had woken her. Her first instinct was that there was a storm and there had been a particularly loud clap of thunder but as her head cleared she knew it wasn't that. She crept out of the room and followed the noise into the lounge. Don, completely off his head, was smashing up the room and everything in it. The walls were smeared with terracotta gloss paint, the off-white carpet with paint stripper, and Don was standing in the middle of the room holding a china table lamp over his head, surrounded by broken glass and dripping blood from his battered fists. The plate-glass coffee table was in pieces.

'*Don!*' She screamed at the top of her voice. 'Stop it!'

But he didn't react, he didn't even seem to hear her. The lamp hit the floor and smashed, shards of pottery scattering amongst the glass and paint stripper.

Don's face was bright red, nearly as red as the blood dripping from his hands, and the roar that was coming from his throat was like an animal's. He looked around for something else and picked up one of the armchairs as easily as if it was made of polystyrene, and aimed it at the picture window that stretched across the room from wall to wall.

Lucy had no idea how to stop him. Frightened for her own safety as well as Don's, she crept out into the hallway. Carefully she picked up the phone and dialled 999. Then, as quietly as she could, she let herself out of the front door, pulling it to behind her but not closing it completely, and waited shivering in her skimpy nightdress at the bottom of the stairs.

The crash of the window breaking reverberated down the stairs.

Sadie was sitting on the edge of the indoor swimming pool with her feet kicking gently in the warm water. She was still trying to take it all in. She, Sadie Khan, was enjoying Latisha Lowe's swimming pool in Latisha Lowe's multimillion-pound house, drinking her drinks and eating her food after being chauffeured there. And apparently they were going to be chauffeured back home again. In the meantime, she was watching Latisha Lowe – Lorraine – and Fergus reminiscing and giggling like two teenagers.

When Lucy had been shouting about Latisha Lowe, Sadie hadn't known what she was talking about and in the coffee shop Fergus had said 'Lorraine' so it still hadn't clicked. Then the car had pulled up at a set of illuminated gates that had almost magically swished open and closed around the car like a comforting pair of arms. Slowly the car had crept up the drive, and the moment it stopped the chauffeur was round opening the door.

As they stepped out of the car, the double front doors of the house opened dramatically and in the doorway Sadie could see a woman, outlined by the lights that lit the porch, looking for all the world as if she was in the spotlight. With her arms outstretched she walked gracefully down the steps towards them.

'Darling, fancy seeing you again so soon, and is this Lucy who you've told me so much about?'

'Hi, Lorraine.' Distractedly Fergus kissed her on both

cheeks. 'No, this isn't Lucy, Lucy isn't talking to me, I'm afraid. This is her friend Sadie. I was hoping you would explain about the other night.'

Lorraine put her hand up to her mouth. 'Oops, am I in the doghouse, darling? Sorry, but it was a really flattering photograph, wasn't it? You looked so dark and mysterious, my phone hasn't stopped ringing. They all want to know if you're my new shag!' Lorraine slapped her thighs theatrically and laughed. 'Come on in, both of you, and have a drink. Don't worry, Charlie here will take you both home again afterwards. You're lucky I'm here, rehearsals ended early today, sometimes I'm there until nigh on bloody midnight.'

'This is all falling into place now,' Sadie whispered to Fergus as they followed Lorraine into the house. 'Lorraine is Latisha Lowe, right?'

'Yep, I've known her since drama school and she took me to a party to cheer me up but I forgot how famous she is and the photo of the two of us was splashed over nearly every newspaper. Needless to say Lucy saw it.'

'Oh boy, no wonder you're in trouble.' Sadie couldn't help laughing, the whole situation was so outrageous. 'I never knew you went to drama school.'

'Come on now, you two, no whispering!'

The entrance hall reminded Sadie of an ultra-modern hotel with a vast open staircase leading to a galleried landing that was almost dwarfed by a futuristic chandelier in glass and steel. It hung from the roof and lit the internal structure of the house from all angles.

Sadie tripped self-consciously along behind, only too aware of her sensible work clothes and unbrushed hair and also of the fact that she was walking behind one of the most famous faces in the country.

'Shall we sit in the kitchen? Far more cosy. I don't often use the other rooms unless it's a formal function, I prefer a good old slob-out instead.'

God, Sadie thought as she took in Lorraine's top-to-toe designer denim. Casual it may have been, slobbing out it definitely wasn't.

'Now, Sadie isn't it? I've known this silly man for more years than I could admit to without also admitting my age, and he's gorgeous. I love him to bits but I wouldn't dream of having it off with him. It would ruin a beautiful friendship. Is that what you wanted to know?'

'Not really.' Sadie smiled. She warmed to Lorraine, noticing the very slight hint of an Irish accent breaking through on certain words and inflections. 'I don't actually give a toss but Fergus seems to think I should. He thinks I should be falling for his blarney and then hurrying back to Lucy to plead his case. Reality is, I only met him a couple of days ago and I just think he's a bit of a rat, a married rat in fact!'

Fergus leaned his head back, closed his eyes and sighed deeply. 'How many times, I'm not fucking married.'

'As good as.'

'Not the same thing at all.'

'And you're messing Lucy about.'

'I am not so messing about.'

'Well, that's what it looks like to me.'

Neither of them noticed Lorraine pick up a copper-bottomed pot and a large metal spoon. Banging one against the other, she shouted, 'OK, end of round one, back to your corners! Let's have a little order here.'

Sadie bit her bottom lip in embarrassment. 'I am sorry. Fancy coming into your home and then fighting in your kitchen.' She smiled sheepishly. 'Bloody hell, this is a bit like a farce. Have you got Jeremy Beadle tucked away in the pantry?'

Lorraine laughed and then took Sadie by surprise by going up to her and giving her a big hug and a kiss on the cheek.

'Jeremy Beadle in my pantry? Love it, but no way! Jeremy Irons? Yes! Beadle? No! Now let's all have a drink and calm down. Do you know this is so much more fun than learning my lines! Come on, let's go through to the pool, I've got enough cossies for a swimming team in the cabin.'

Pleading that she couldn't swim and was water phobic, Sadie got away with sitting on the edge fully clothed, apart from her tights and shoes. There was no way she would have stripped off down to a swimsuit and displayed her voluptuous curves in front of the streamlined Lorraine in a bikini, so she watched instead.

The socialist side of Sadie felt slightly guilty about how much she was enjoying herself wallowing, albeit temporarily, in the lap of luxury. She had also taken a real shine to Lorraine; the woman was entertaining and excellent company. Sadie couldn't remember the last time she laughed so much. When she thought about it, the previous weeks with Lucy had been all doom and gloom and she hadn't realised quite how much it had affected her own mood.

And Fergus! What a dark horse he was turning out to

229

be. Guiltily, Sadie realised that she had pre-judged him on the information she had. She had known he was a motor-cycle courier in London, that he had a long-term partner he still lived with and a teenage tearaway daughter and was seeing a married woman. In her eyes all that had added up to 'conniving bastard'. Now she was discovering that he was actually a very intelligent, intellectual man with a terrific sense of humour and, apparently, friends in high places. Sadie had definitely warmed to him while at the same time chilling towards Lucy. The strength of her feelings surprised her.

While Fergus and Lorraine were larking about in the water, her phone had rung but when she saw the caller was Lucy she had switched it off. The hurt of being lied to had really upset her, not just because it meant Lucy didn't trust her but because she couldn't understand why. Did Lucy really think she would tell everyone?

'Don has gone mad, I'm waiting for the police, I don't know what to do . . .' Lucy's voice was hysterical as she left a message pleading with Sadie to call her back. For a split second Sadie hesitated but then she deleted it.

She didn't tell Fergus.

Lucy had the communal front door open so she saw the police car arrive. There were no flashing lights, no sirens and the two policemen obviously didn't think it was an emergency. Calmly getting out of the car, they put their caps on and walked up to her. Then they went up to the flat.

Almost immediately they were down again muttering into their radios and calling for back-up. They put Lucy into the squad car out of harm's way and waited until the back-up arrived, using the time to get the gist of what was going on from her. A crowd began to gather on the pavement, curious and observant, rubbernecking eagerly in the hope of seeing something exciting.

By the time the police were ready to go up, Lucy felt decidedly uncomfortable about being part of the entertainment so she got out and followed the four police officers and two Alsatians back into the building.

'Mr Cooper?' she could hear one of them shouting. 'We're coming into the flat. Now calm down and tell us what's wrong.'

'Mr Cooper,' another voice called, 'Don, I want you to think about what you're doing. Now let us in and we'll try and sort it out for you . . . Come on, be sensible, I'm sure we can talk about this.'

Lucy tried to follow them into the flat but the female officer stopped her.

'Don't go in, love, it might set him off even more. Let us deal with it. Is there a neighbour you could go to? A friend you want me to call?'

Lucy looked meaningfully at the closed doors of the other flats. 'Hardly, it's the middle of the night and they're all keeping their doors firmly bolted. Not that I blame them. No, there's no one and I'm not dressed. I have to go in, I have to know what's going on.'

'Hang on while I see if he's calmed down.' But as she spoke the crashing and banging started up again, followed by raised voices. The dogs were on the landing outside, straining at the leash and, after a few more minutes, when it became apparent Don wasn't going to stop whatever he was doing, the dog handlers went in.

Lucy took the opportunity to follow.

'Mr Cooper, this is your last chance to calm down. Put the table leg down and then lie on the floor.'

Don's responding roar was followed by barking and then Lucy heard Don's voice. 'Get those fucking dogs away from me, get the bastard animals away.'

'If you settle down, get down on the floor, then we'll put the dogs back. OK?'

Lucy looked round the door and saw Don sitting against the wall with his arms up over his face and head. Not a single thing in the room was undamaged, it looked as if someone had thrown a bomb in through the window.

She backed out quickly.

She watched as the police marched Don downstairs in handcuffs, with the dogs still close by. As he passed her he hissed at her, 'Bitch. You'll be sorry.'

He towered over the police officers, making them look young and skinny by comparison.

'Mrs Cooper – may I call you Lucy? We have to ask you a few questions. As soon as the wagon arrives, your husband will be taken to the station and charged and I'm sure kept in the cells overnight to cool off. Now, has he been drinking?'

Lucy shook her head, she couldn't bring herself to speak.

'Is he on drugs?' The police officer made direct eye contact as he asked the question.

Again she shook her head but then she looked up. 'Well, not really, but sort of . . .'

'What do you mean by sort of?'

'He's a body builder, he's been taking steroids I think.'

The two officers exchanged knowing looks.

'That might well explain it, we've seen it before. We call it roid rage. That stuff brings out the aggression. Do you know what he takes?'

Lucy shook her head.

'Do you mind if we have a look around?'

'Help yourself.'

Lucy grabbed a robe from the bedroom and then went into the kitchen where the policewoman was boiling some water in a saucepan on the cooker. 'I'm just making you a coffee. It's the only thing I could find.'

Looking round the kitchen that she had designed herself, Lucy finally started crying. The table and chairs were covered in paint stripper, as well as most of the units. She cursed herself, for she was the one who had bought all the stripper and paint to decorate the bedrooms and then forgotten about it.

'He's really gone to town, hasn't he?' the policewoman said sympathetically. 'But at least it can all be mended or replaced, more than could be said for you if you hadn't got out.'

Lucy thought about it; the woman was right, everything was replaceable.

'Mrs Cooper?' One of the men came into the kitchen. 'Are these what your husband takes?'

Lucy looked at the tub of pills that he was holding out to her in a rubber-gloved hand. 'I don't know, I don't recognise them, I've never seen them before. Where were they?'

'In a suitcase in the lounge.'

'He must have brought them back from Portugal, he's only just got back from a competition there. That's when it all started, when he got back. I'd had enough, I told him it was all over, that I wanted a divorce.'

'There are two of these tubs. We're going to have to take them with us for forensics. Check them out.'

'Yes of course, whatever you want, just please keep him locked up, until Monday if possible. I'm going to the States for two months to work and I'm leaving on Monday.'

As she was talking the policeman was unscrewing the top from the plastic pot. He looked inside and then handed it to his colleague who also looked. Then they both looked at Lucy.

'Are you sure you know nothing about this, Mrs Cooper?'

'Absolutely positive. Don's the fitness freak, not me as you can see.' She managed a watery smile.

Putting his thumb and forefinger carefully into the top of the tub, he gripped a piece of polythene and pulled. The bag that he pulled out didn't contain any pills but it did contain a lot of white powder.

'Oh shit,' said Lucy, 'that looks like coke.'

'Mrs Cooper, you're going to have to come to the station as well. Obviously the substance needs testing but you're right, it looks like cocaine in those bottles. And you know nothing about it?'

Lucy looked grimly at the policeman standing in front of her. She vaguely wondered why it was always the pompous arse who got to ask the questions while the kindly faced one lurked in the background looking sympathetic.

'I called you, remember? I dialled 999 and invited you in. Do you think I'm that stupid that if I knew there was enough coke in the flat to supply half the noses in London that I wouldn't have got rid of it first?'

He didn't smile; straight-backed and clean-cut, he reminded Lucy of a robot.

'That's as may be. We'll need a statement from you and we're going to have to carry out a thorough search of the premises. Is there anyone you want us to call? You need to get that window fixed right away as well. Anyone you know who can do it? Anyone who can come and support you?'

Her brain said 'Fergus, I want Fergus' but her mouth said, 'No, there's no one, but I can manage perfectly well now that Don isn't here.'

Chapter Eleven

To Lucy's complete surprise she made it to the airport in plenty of time for her flight to Las Vegas but she didn't indulge her usual habit of browsing the shops. Emotionally drained and battered, she grabbed a large coffee and sank gratefully into the big comfortable seats in the business lounge.

Don was in prison, charged with, among other things, drug smuggling; Fergus had been spread over all the tabloids and wasn't returning her calls; she was pregnant; her home was trashed; and she had no job to go back to. Lucy almost smiled at the thought of it all. There was really nothing else that could happen to make her life any worse at the moment.

She tried to imagine what had been going through Don's brain when he took the trip through customs with a valuable haul of pure cocaine; she wondered how much he had been paid, unless of course his protestations of a set-up by someone unknown was true. Don had always been easily led by his so-called friends but cocaine in his suitcase? Even for Don that was stupid. Despite everything, Lucy wondered how he would cope in prison. With his looks and arrogant swagger, he would find it harder than most. She almost felt sorry for him.

And Fergus? How could he have gone straight off with someone else? Unless of course he had been seeing her all the time.

The one thought that kept jumping uninvited into her head was whether, given the luxury of knowing earlier, she would have terminated the pregnancy. A part of her was excited at the prospect of having a baby, but the main emotion was one of resentment. The stupid accident had pushed her into a situation that had changed everything. Without the pregnancy she knew she could have worked things out a little better; instead, Don was off his head, Fergus was backing away, and to protect herself and the baby, she felt she had to leave the job she loved, move away and start a new life as a single mother.

Completely unaware of her action, Lucy laid her hand on her stomach.

It was still hard to comprehend that there was a small person growing inside her. Lucy had always known that she would want children one day but not so soon and she could never have imagined being pregnant without knowing it and, most importantly, not knowing who the father of her child was.

Lucy glanced at the screen that flickered silently in the corner; to her surprise it told her that her flight was about to start boarding, which meant she had been sitting in the chair for nearly two hours doing nothing but mull everything over.

Wearily she got to her feet, picked up her bag and made her way to the aircraft that was going to take her thousands of miles away from it all. As she walked down the tunnel to the airplane, she shook herself back to the present. For the next few weeks, she determined, there was little she could do to deal with the problems so she would concentrate on the job in hand and push everything else out of the way.

No doubt it would all still be there when she eventually got home.

Lucy's eyes scanned the crowd waiting in the arrivals hall until she saw the sign with her name on. Not the usual handwritten piece of card but an elaborately printed gold board with her name etched in black italics under the logo of the hotel she was going to. Knowing that she didn't look her best after a long flight, Lucy was relieved to see that the woman holding the sign was quite casually dressed. Her pale lemon slacks and pristine white blouse were not a million miles away from Lucy's own sky blue linen trouser suit. Her shoulder-length subtly highlighted hair hung straight and shiny and her make-up was carefully understated.

Lucy fixed a smile on her face and went up to her.

'Hi, I'm Lucy Cooper.'

'Lucy, hi.' The woman smiled widely, showing perfectly aligned teeth, and took Lucy's proffered hand. 'I'm Gwyneth North, we spoke on the phone. I'm so pleased to meet you. And this is John, he'll take your luggage for you. John is my assistant, we'll both be working with you throughout your stay.'

'Hi, Lucy.' John's voice was confident and friendly, his

handshake firm. 'I'm sure you're going to enjoy your time in Vegas and of course our fabulous new resort hotel, you're going to just love that. Really you are.'

With one hand lightly on her back, he ushered her forward. 'It is going to be so good working with you, we really want to promote in the UK. Is this your first time here?'

Chatting superficially, they made their way to the front of the airport and as they exited the main doors, a gleaming white stretch limo pulled up in front of them. It was more like a lounge on wheels than a car.

Lucy had done her research and knew that the hotel where she was going to work and live had a fleet of limousines for their VIP guests. The high-rollers who would gamble fifty thousand dollars or more in a session without batting an eyelid and the famous stars who visited the hotel either on vacation or to perform in the cabaret all received the same treatment. It was part of the constant striving of every hotel in Las Vegas to be the biggest and best. But Lucy hadn't anticipated the same treatment for herself.

Gwyneth and John talked fast and friendly all through the short drive to the hotel.

'Now, Lucy, we've drawn up a schedule for you including a familiarisation tour around the property this evening,' Gwyneth smiled, 'and of course we'll both be joining you for dinner, but apart from that we're going to leave you free for a couple of days to recover from your flight. However, if you need us you can just call anytime.'

'Excuse me,' John interrupted politely with a smile, 'you might want to take a look, this is the Strip. Nearly all the luxury properties are grouped in this area, including us. If you look to your right you can see the Hoopers Inn and Casino. As you know, that's where you're going to be based.' He smiled as he directed Lucy's gaze to left and right like a tour guide.

'Over here is the Venetian, and on the right the Bellagio. Our hotel is in the same class although maybe not quite so large, and we're not themed in the same way. Our target market is slightly different . . .'

The place was everything Lucy had anticipated and a small thrill ran through her as she really took in, for the first time, the fact that she would actually be working in the middle of it.

Soon they pulled up at the hotel entrance, after a quick spin round the awesome brand-new building that, to Lucy's eyes, was virtually a self-contained town. Gwyneth and John escorted Lucy to her suite twenty-three storeys up and then left her to rest. The events of the previous few days caught up with her rapidly and she fell asleep fully clothed on the day bed in her new sitting room.

After a few days in Las Vegas, Lucy had settled easily into her new environment. She hadn't realised quite how much she had missed the networking and socialising with like-minded professionals. Gwyneth and John had devised a flexible rota that gave her a complete insight into the workings of both the resort hotel she was there to help represent, and also the competition. Lucy took on everything that was available with enthusiasm and worked as many hours as she physically could. She wanted to learn everything possible and to make a good impression on her new clients, but also, by working until she dropped, she could block out the situation she knew she would have to face when she went back to England.

The working days were long and hard, and weekends off didn't exist, but she thrived on it. Sometimes, for just a short while, Lucy even forgot that she was pregnant. But then her back would ache a little, her normally slim ankles would puff up a fraction and the alien urge for an afternoon siesta would overcome her.

To her surprise she had soon adapted to the different way of living and working, and the informal working conditions also helped her ignore her expanding waist. A quick trip to a shopping mall and she had a selection of elastic-waisted trousers and skirts, and loose-fitting blouses and jackets that looked cool and efficient but not unprofessional. After topping up with shoes, handbags and several formal outfits for the many functions that were scheduled for her, Lucy felt satisfied with both her appearance and her circumstances. Offers of dates flowed in and although she always politely declined, it was good for her battered self-esteem.

If only they knew, she thought to herself with a smile, gently touching her well-disguised bump that was prone to moving quite fiercely at inappropriate moments. But no one guessed, or if they did they never let on.

Lucy had just returned to her suite for a break one afternoon when the phone rang. It was George Beacham, her elderly downstairs neighbour in London, who was overseeing the repairs and decorating of her flat in England, and had quickly become Lucy's main contact with home. She cut him short and then phoned him back, to save his phone bill.

'It's good to hear from you, George. How's it all going?'

'No problems, young lady, but I wanted to hear how you're getting on in sin city. I've always fancied a little flutter in Las Vegas, you know, even though I'm a sensible man at heart.'

Lucy smiled. Apart from a couple of conversations with the police about Don and his situation, and numerous calls from Caroline, Lucy had only heard from George. After just a few weeks in Vegas, she already felt that she was living in another world.

After a scary interrogation by the police, Lucy had been allowed home, and George had knocked on her door to check that she was all right. Lucy knew he lived alone but she had never spoken to him other than a perfunctory hello in the hall, but in a few short minutes he had taken control of the situation. He took her down to his own flat, made her a hot toddy and wrapped an old blanket round her. Tactfully he asked her what had happened and she found herself confiding in him in breathless sentences punctuated with shuddering sobs. From that moment, George Beacham MBE, a retired bank manager and a widower with no children of his own, was firmly in charge. Assuring Lucy that he hated being retired and bored, and was looking for something to do, he volunteered enthusiastically to sort out everything while she was away.

'It's wonderful here,' Lucy told him now. 'I could easily get hooked on this lifestyle. My suite is actually bigger than my flat at home, and the food! I must have put a stone on.'

As she was talking, Lucy looked out of her window at the late-afternoon traffic that was almost gridlocked below; cabs and limos vied for space on the busy street, and holidaymakers did the same on the sidewalks. The scene had become familiar but she still relished it. In fact, Lucy loved her vibrant and exciting temporary working life.

'I think I must be really shallow. A little bit of luxury and a lot of sun and I'm off in a world of my own. Shame I have to come back soon.'

'Well, I'm looking forward to seeing you. Now let me bring you up to date on your flat . . .'

In the short term, at least, Lucy could almost pretend the rest of it wasn't happening. But suddenly her departure date loomed large, she had to face reality once again.

'Do you never stop working?' Gwyneth appeared silently beside Lucy, who was helping out at the main reception desk.

'Not if I can help it,' Lucy laughed. 'I find it all so interesting. If I wasn't doing what I'm doing then I would love to work in a hotel like this. Something different every day.'

'Well, we've got something different for you tonight, that's for sure. Is nine o'clock in the conference room convenient for you? There are some people we'd like you to meet.'

'Sure, no problem. Formal or informal? Do I need my party frock?' Lucy smiled, although she had already decided to have an early night in preparation for her flight home.

'Neither, just come as you are.'

Lucy looked down at her lightweight slacks and shirt. 'Really? Like this?' she laughed.

'Just like that will be great. See you at nine.'

Lucy watched as Gwyneth marched off purposefully in the direction of the bustling casino. She didn't want to go back. She wanted to stay exactly where she was and leave all her problems in England. But she knew she couldn't.

Her initial knock on the door of the conference room wasn't answered so she knocked again.

'Come!' a deep voice bellowed from the other side. Suddenly Lucy was apprehensive. Why had she been summoned? Had she done something wrong? Was Caroline unhappy? Cautiously she opened the huge door and slid inside.

'SURPRISE! SURPRISE!'

Surprised Lucy certainly was.

About thirty people were inside, all holding helium balloons and grouped around the conference table that was edged with be-ribboned bottles of champagne and centred with a huge cake.

'Au revoir Lucy, we'll miss you,' the scarlet icing vividly declared. As the cheering started Lucy's eyes filled up.

The celebrations went on until midnight and made her impending departure even more difficult.

Lucy desperately wished she could turn back the clock. To when she wasn't pregnant. To before she had met Don.

But she couldn't and now she had to go home and face up to her mistakes.

Chapter Twelve

As the aircraft circled over Heathrow, waiting for clearance to land, Lucy looked out of the window at the familiar ground below. In some ways she felt as if she had been away for years, but at the same time it was as if it was only yesterday that she had taken off, hoping to leave everything behind her. In a way she had, but now she was back. Her mind shied away from looking ahead; instead she thought back about her time in Las Vegas.

It had all gone so well it was almost too good to be true. Lucy had been a big success with the clients and she had been wined and dined royally. She had got to know Las Vegas inside out and had acquired a mine of information about its luxury hotels. She had even been offered a substantial salary increase if she would defect to one of Pettit's rivals. Oh, not to be pregnant, she had thought as she regretfully declined a dream of a job. Still, Caroline had informed her via email that she was pleased with her performance and Lucy knew she had a large bonus waiting in the UK in her new bank account. Not only that, but with her large expense allowance, she had been able to finance all the work on the flat and still come out on top.

But now it was time to face the future.

Once through customs she looked around the waiting crowd hoping to spot a board with her name on it – Caroline had informed her that a car would pick her up and take her home. Home to what? she had mentally sighed. Hopefully all the repairs and redecorations would be completed but it would still be strange to think about going back to an empty, unwelcoming flat after so long living in a lively hotel that buzzed twenty-four hours a day.

'Lucy! Over here!'

Lucy looked and could just about see Luke Pettit's balding head at the back of the throng. Far from being pleased to see a friendly face, she was horrified. Quickly pulling in her stomach and tugging her pashmina round over her midriff, she forced a smile and pushed her trolley towards him.

'Lucy, how lovely to see you back at last. We've missed you.' Luke took her by the shoulders and kissed her on the cheek. 'You look really well. How was the flight? Did you get any sleep?'

'Hi, Luke, I didn't expect to see you here, but it's nice to see a familiar face instead of a driver. Yes, the flight was fine but I'm knackered and looking forward to sleeping in my own bed again.' Two lies in one sentence, she thought. An anonymous driver she didn't have to make conversation with would have been preferable and she was dreading going back to the flat and her own bed. But she knew it was what Luke wanted to hear.

'Oh, you know me, any excuse to get away from doing

any real work. Come on, the car's in the car park but it's not too far, here, give me that.' He took hold of the laden trolley. 'God, did this mountain of goodies get through or are you into excess baggage? You look like Elton John with that lot.'

Lucy laughed. 'Not quite, although I have to admit I did do just a teeny bit of shopping. It was all too good to resist, the shops are so tempting and everything is much cheaper, but I didn't go mad, I didn't gamble – well, only small change, and I did work my socks off as well. What's been the response?'

'The feedback we've had is first class, they really loved you, so now we're trying to figure out where to send you next after Paul gets back from New York. Looks like it might be the Caribbean for you in another few months. You and Paul seem to be turning into the hotel and travel experts.'

Lucy felt sick at the thought of what she was going to miss out on.

'How are things at the office?' she asked. She knew she ought to inquire but she didn't really want to know.

'Just great. The new execs have settled in well, and we're actually looking for new premises. We're starting to out-grow the ones we're in now. Business is booming, in fact, touch wood, chuck salt over the shoulder and all that. Still, plenty of time to talk about that later. We don't want to see you until Monday morning, give you time to get over the old jet lag and catch up on your own life.' Luke paused and looked at her. 'Any resolutions there? You can tell me to mind my own business but take this as a personal show of concern, not employer/employee.' He pushed the trolley up to his mud-splattered Volvo estate, opened the back and piled the cases in. He didn't look at her but she knew he was waiting for a response.

'Well, just before I left for Vegas, more or less the night before in fact, Don smashed up the flat. I had to call the police and he was arrested. Still in jail, hopefully – at least, the police have informed me he is.'

Luke's head shot up. 'Good God, did he hurt you? Why didn't you tell us?'

'My personal life was a bit too high-profile for my liking the couple of months before I went away. I didn't want to push my luck any further. But no, he didn't hurt me physically this time but it didn't do me a lot of good to see him so completely off his head.'

'Silly girl, you could have told us,' was all he said before driving out of the car park and heading back to London.

No, I couldn't, she thought, because then you would have stopped me going – but she didn't say anything. She knew Luke genuinely believed what he was saying.

A few minutes later, when they were stuck in a traffic jam, he looked at her.

'Come on then, tell me all about it. I'm impressed that you could go away and work as well as you did, given what you'd been through.'

'That's why I never told you at the time, you wouldn't have let me go. I do appreciate that the company has to come first, you know.'

'First, yes, but not to the detriment of our staff if we can avoid it. I've told you before, Caroline's background has made her ambitious and determined never to be hard up, but she's not uncaring, far from it.'

'The police called Don's rampage roid rage. I've never heard of it but apparently it's a common side effect of steroids, it makes users aggressive and they get so pumped out they lose control. I've found out that the stuff Don has been sticking in his body is about the strongest there is. Anyway, this time he's really in trouble because he brought some stuff in through customs and the police found it.' Lucy inferred the stuff was only steroids, she didn't want to admit that Don was also a cocaine smuggler and that he had been charged as such.

Luke was driving round a roundabout when his mobile phone filled the car with the sound of Tchaikovsky's 1812 Overture.

'Get that, will you, pet? It's Caroline, she probably didn't trust me not to forget to collect you from the airport.'

Smiling at him, Lucy picked up the phone.

'Hello, Caroline. It's Lucy, how are you?'

When Caroline Pettit had received the initial phone call from her husband about Lucy's difficulties both within the company and in her private life, her first reaction was exactly what Lucy had anticipated.

'I'm not having it, Luke. I will not have the Pettit name dragged through the mud. For heaven's sake, I turn my back for a few days and suddenly the office has turned into a den of iniquity with everyone having it off with everyone else. Lucy has to go, and so for that matter does Daniella the walking-talking Barbie doll. I'm just not having it.' Caroline was in Los Angeles, tired and stressed, with only one free day scheduled in her extended four-week business trip, and the last thing she needed was bad news from home. The flight from New York after a heavy week with clients had really knocked it out of her and she knew there was more of the same to come. Much as she loved her job and was motivated every day by the pursuit of success, she missed being in the office at the hub. She also missed her husband when she was away too long.

'Caroline, darling, I know exactly how you feel but think about it, if we start firing staff, bloody good staff at that, solely because of their personal problems, then firstly we'll end up with no one in the office and secondly we'll have lawsuits flying at us like gnats. Lucy is a good employee and the clients love her, and as for Daniella, she's just a kid, she just needs to learn that the gossip of the play-ground has no place in the work environment. A jolly good bollocking should sort her out.'

Caroline began to feel irritated. Luke was always so reasonable. Much as she loved and respected her husband, she sometimes found his typically Libran way of balancing all the facts before making a decision frustrating. She herself was much more spontaneous, she trusted her own judgement and liked to act immediately. Deep down she knew Luke was often right but this time she wasn't sure.

'I hear what you're saying, Luke, but can you imagine the fallout if Lucy's lout of a husband turned up and wrecked the office? What if he hurt someone? Now that would be a lawsuit worth worrying about. Whatever was the silly girl playing at, having an affair in the first place?'

As soon as the words were out, Caroline regretted them.

'Sorry, that was a stupid thing to say. OK, Luke, you win, as always. We'll keep her but exactly how are we going to manage the situation? You've met her husband. God only knows how someone as bright as Lucy got caught up with a piece of pond life like that.' She paused briefly and when she continued her voice was thoughtful. 'I've always thought, ever since I first met him, that Mr Cooper was Lucy's Achilles heel, that one day he would ruin her career and possibly her life. I just hope it's not going to be now, at our expense.'

Caroline could hear the smile in Luke's voice when he answered.

'I doubt it. We can't anticipate what might or might not happen but we can work to try and contain the situation. Still, at least we agree in principle. Now, I've got another idea. I think it will solve the problem and also give us a little more time together – I really miss you.'

'And I miss you too.'

After putting the phone down Caroline had grabbed a towel and headed off for a few lengths in the rooftop pool. The small independent hotel where she always stayed was not well known and its understated, old-fashioned style of luxury was at odds with many of the ostentatious properties in and around Beverley Hills. But Caroline loved it there and usually had no trouble relaxing but now, rather than savouring it, she was chewing over the proposition Luke had put to her. It would definitely mean a little more free time with her husband but she wasn't sure that she wanted to delegate any more responsibility for her beloved company, especially with the reservations she now had about Lucy.

The company was doing very well and she and Luke were both extremely wealthy, and wealth to Caroline meant security; she didn't want anything to compromise that. She thoroughly enjoyed the luxury she had worked so hard for and she was prepared to pay for it, but at the same time she expected value for her money. Although she bought expensive designer clothes, they were always classic designs that would last and she flew business class instead of first class. She stayed at quality but understated hotels instead of the more opulent establishments, and used cabs whenever she could instead of hired limos. Caroline could spend money as easily as the next wealthy woman but she could never waste it.

Despite approaching forty, Caroline never forgot her childhood, and the insecurity it caused her meant that she needed her own cushion of financial security, independent of Luke's wealth.

Caroline was the eldest of five children born to a mother and father who, despite being well educated and intelligent, had dropped out and happily embraced an easygoing, hippy lifestyle of self-sufficiency on an isolated farm in the Welsh hills. None of the children ever went to school, their education was all home-based and an airy-fairy mix of necessary curriculum and dreamy socialism. Caroline grew up knowing everything there was to know about breeding chickens and the works of Karl Marx, she could also paint beautiful landscapes, make exquisite hand-thrown pots and painstakingly turn a tatty old piece of material into something wearable. But she knew very little about the real world.

Her most enduring memory was of being permanently cold, of walking about with her skinny arms wrapped round her body and her sleeves pulled down over her hands. Rough, hand-knitted sweaters covered thin cotton frocks, and darned tights with worn-out wellington boots or inadequate plimsolls were the only protection from the seemingly never-ending slush and slurry on the hillside. Aware that it was probably an exaggerated memory, she still couldn't get rid of it, no matter how hard she tried to remember the good times as part of a close-knit family. The warm summer picnics and the lazy days spent picking flowers to press had faded; she just remembered the cold and the lack of anything remotely luxurious. 'Necessity is the mother of invention' was a phrase forever imprinted on her mind and she hated it with a passion. The same way she hated vegetable hotpot. Just the thought of it made her want to vomit.

The day she determinedly walked out of the family home at sixteen she vowed never again to wear homemade hand-me-downs or black plimsolls with the toes cut out. She also promised herself that she would make a success of herself and have all the comforts and material things that her parents had decided weren't necessary. Central heating became one of her obsessions, as did thick carpets and curtains, and huge beds covered in all-enveloping duvets.

Caroline knew that her parents loved all their children and did what they themselves had thought was right but she had always hankered after more. The occasional family trips into the local town had shown her what was on offer – the clothes, the furniture and, most of all, televisions. After gazing transfixed at the window of the TV rental shop for as long as she could get away with, Caroline had desperately wanted a television set that would help her see the world outside. A world that she knew so little of but longed to get to know.

Her determination to break away from the farm as soon as she was old enough had eventually paid off and her parents had sadly put her on a train to go and live with her maternal grandmother in Kent. At the moment of parting, the unworldly sixteen-year-old had promised she would visit, that she would keep in touch with them all, but over time the gulf between her lifestyle and her parents' became too big to breach.

Caroline had very quickly embraced the capitalist life that her parents abhorred and it wasn't long before she was living in a flatshare in London and temping around the city. Her lack of formal education was quickly overcome because the one thing that Caroline had been taught was self-confidence, and she soon discovered that the best way forward in the young and vibrant world of advertising was bluff and double bluff. Before long she was a successful executive with more job offers than she could ever have imagined.

Totally committed to her career, Caroline had had no desire for marriage. Then she had met Luke. He was older than she was, married and slightly eccentric but she was instantly hooked. Because of his marriage it was a long time before she found out that his feelings were exactly the same. A lot of heartache was suffered all round before they could be together but their marriage had turned out to be good and strong. As was her baby, Pettit's PR Consultancy, the only baby she could have. Luke thought she just didn't want children; she had never told him about her teenage pregnancy and the consequences of her decision to have it terminated.

The situation Luke had described to her over the phone had really set her nerves on edge. Could she really trust the whole Las Vegas portfolio to Lucy Cooper when she was up to her neck in personal problems? Would Donovan Cooper cause a scandal and send clients running off to competitors? And she couldn't help thinking that sending Lucy off to the States wouldn't be the end of it. She felt sure there was more to what was going on than either she or Luke was privy to.

The concerns niggled away at her all through her trip.

Caroline was at her desk in the office when she rang Luke in his car. It was really Lucy she wanted to speak to, to congratulate her on her success because she felt slightly guilty about her previous reservations. There had been no trouble at the office, nothing had been heard of Don, Paul had a new girlfriend, even Daniella appeared to have a new man in tow. In fact everything was going remarkably well. Luke had been right after all. The situation had been dealt with without any scandal, lawsuits or damage.

She had been shocked when Luke had shown her the paper with the picture of Fergus Pearson looking very sexy, dark and moody, with his arm around Latisha Lowe. For a courier he certainly moved in elevated circles. Or perhaps he just got lucky on his delivery routes. That was how he'd met Lucy, after all.

Now Lucy was back and Caroline could relax. If nothing had happened so far then it must have all blown over, she thought gratefully. Lucy had done a good job and she was hoping Paul would do the same in New York. It had been hard to hand over the reins but it was nice to spend more time at home in the country with Luke. Her feet did itch from time to time, though. Caroline knew that if she had to stay too long in one place she was inclined to go a bit stir crazy.

'Come on then. Let's get you and your baggage indoors and check the place over, make sure it's habitable,' Luke said cheerfully outside Lucy's house.

Walking apprehensively up the stairs, it felt strange to Lucy to be back here, she hadn't wanted to return to the flat ever again but she knew she had to go somewhere in the short term. There was so much to do in the next couple of weeks.

When she'd phoned from the States, the police had told her that Don would be kept in custody and reassured her that he would stay there until his trial. But standing outside the door to her flat, it all came back to her and she could again see Don, his face distorted with hatred and fury, about to throw the armchair at the window. She started shaking so much she couldn't get her key into the lock.

'Here, give that to me. Don't worry, it'll be OK, I'm sure.' Luke took the key and opened the door, then stood back to let her go in first.

Cautiously Lucy walked in, conscious of the smell of paint. The flat just didn't look like her home any more. She kept touching the replacement mail order furniture as if that would somehow make it familiar. She had chosen it, but it was impersonal and alien. She felt like an intruder, carefully pushing open each door and looking before entering.

'Well, Lucy,' said Luke, 'this all looks hunky-dory to me, so if you're happy with it all I'll leave you to get unpacked and we'll see you in the office on Monday, but not a day before. Unfortunately there will be a meeting at ten thirty for a debriefing with my good lady wife, but then I'm sure you expected that.'

I won't be there, Lucy thought sadly. She hated the thought of it but no one could know she was pregnant, no one who might sometime, somewhere, let it slip to Don. She had told him she was going to have a termination; as long as he continued to believe that, she felt sure he wouldn't try too hard to find her.

As Luke kissed her goodbye at the door, George Beacham puffed up the stairs.

'I thought I heard you, lovey. Welcome home. Is everything all right for you?'

'Oh George, it's wonderful, thank you so much. I don't know what I'd have done without you.' Lucy looked at him affectionately and thought wryly that when the going got tough her friend had disappeared but George, someone she barely knew, had stepped in.

Pulling his shoulders up and straightening his back, the elderly man positively bristled with pride.

'It was a pleasure. Now all your post is on the worktop in the kitchen and there are a few bits and bobs in the fridge for you but first, are you going to come down and have a cup of tea with me? You can tell me all about your adventure.'

Lucy and Luke exchanged amused glances. All she wanted to do was undress and get into bed; the flight and being nearly seven months pregnant were taking their toll.

But George had worked hard and been so kind, Lucy couldn't refuse him.

'I'd love to, George, then you can tell me all your news as well.'

Her post was neatly piled up in date order and all the bills and receipts were carefully filed in a folder, along with a clear and comprehensive statement of account.

'George, you're wasted doing this, you should be working for Pettit's. It's just so efficient the way you've done all this for me. I really, really can't thank you enough.'

'I've enjoyed every minute of it, young Lucy, it's made me feel useful again.'

'I'll just get changed and then I'll be right down.'

Smiling broadly, George went back to his flat.

It passed through Lucy's mind that she could speak to Caroline and see if they could offer him anything part-time, and then she remembered, she was leaving. Leaving the flat, leaving Pettit's and getting right away to where Don would never find her.

Now, back on home territory, Fergus came alive again in her mind. Fergus, whom she hadn't had any contact with since the fiasco in the street. She wondered what he was doing, whether he was still with Margot or if he had gone off with Latisha Lowe, the gorgeous, larger-than-life actress he had been wrapped around at three o'clock in the morning. Latisha, the darling of the public, who certainly wasn't fat and spotty with greasy hair like the person Lucy viewed in the mirror. So much for the bloom of pregnancy, she thought, and then wondered how many other women felt cheated when their skin erupted and their hair drooped. Even the dry summer heat of Nevada hadn't helped much on that front.

And of course Sadie, who hadn't responded to her calls and letters. Had Fergus been right about her? Lucy just couldn't understand why Sadie had turned from best friend into indifferent stranger in one evening.

On an impulse, she picked up the phone and dialled Sadie's number. She got the answering machine.

'Hi, Sadie, it's me, Lucy. I'm back. Please, please, please call me, I've got so much to tell you. I don't know what I've done or why you're ignoring me but I'd really like to see you.'

Lucy stripped off her travelling clothes and, without thinking, tried to pull on a pair of old leggings that were in the wardrobe. She could barely get them up over her expanded belly.

'Oh shit, shit, shit,' she cursed loudly. She dragged them off and threw them across the room in the general direction of the bin.

She found a pair of Don's designer joggers and a new sweatshirt that was still in the wrapping, and tried them on. Looking at herself sideways she thought she actually looked a bit waif-like. Yep, she decided, she could still get away with it. Quickly she slipped on her trainers and went down to see George.

Sadie had been about to pick up the phone when the answer service kicked in. Standing beside it, she listened to the message but didn't pick up the receiver. She was still bitter and hurt, and hearing Lucy's voice made her angry all over again. Her best friend, her only friend, couldn't trust her enough to confide in her.

But that wasn't the only reason Sadie didn't pick up the phone. She was having fun hanging around with Fergus and Lorraine and she didn't want Lucy butting in on it, and she certainly didn't want Lucy to know that Margot had kicked Fergus out after his photograph had appeared in the papers. He was now sleeping on Sadie's sofa while he looked for somewhere else to live, and that was something else she preferred to keep from Lucy. Sadie didn't fancy Fergus in the least but she liked having him as a friend, with the added bonus that it evened the score with Lucy. Lorraine, however, was a different kettle of fish. Sadie knew she had a crush on Lorraine, same as she had had with Lucy. It wasn't sexual, the time would come when she would marry a nice man who her parents approved of, and in the meantime sex with anyone, male or female, was out of the question. But throughout her life, even in junior school, friendship, for her, had meant total commitment. As soon as she had a close friend she just had to be a part of their lives, to know their secrets and to share in everything. She was adept at making herself indispensable, as she had with Lucy, and she was now successfully attaching herself to Lorraine.

Sadie glanced at the phone and purposefully deleted the message. She had left work early to get ready for another big night out that Lorraine had invited herself and Fergus to. She went into the bathroom and turned on the taps, her excitement rising at the thought of all those celebrities she would meet. She wasn't going to let Lucy Cooper spoil it for her.

The front door opened.

'Sadie? Are you in?'

'Yes,' she shouted. 'I'm just getting ready for tonight. I wanted to grab the bathroom first.'

'I'm not going, I'm completely shattered. Margot has been creating havoc at the base, I have to go and see her.'

The bathroom door flew open.

'You can't do this to me.' Sadie was panicking. 'I've been looking forward to it all week.'

Fergus's disembodied voice echoed from the kitchen. 'You can go on your own, can't you? Lorraine won't mind, I'm sure. Do you want me to phone her?'

Sadie's panic dissipated instantly. 'Would you? I so want to go but I know it's you she really wants along, Mystery Man. I'm sure she won't be too keen on just me.'

'She'll be OK about it,' he shouted through. 'I'll ring in a sec. I need a drink right now to prepare me for the wrath of Margot – again. By the way, is there still no news of Lucy? I'm sure she should be home by now.'

Sadie closed the bathroom door again and pretended she hadn't heard. It was much easier to lie by omission.

Sadie had never moved so fast as when the phone rang again. She snatched it up, her heart thumping.

'Hello?'

'Sadie! It's me Lucy. Didn't you get my message? Sadie, please let's talk, I don't want to fight with—'

'Sorry, you've got the wrong number.' She replaced the phone.

'Did I hear the phone just now?' Fergus called.

'Yes, it was a wrong number. Can you give Lorraine a ring now?'

Fergus tipped the bottle and poured himself the remaining

half-inch of vodka. He didn't want to admit it to Sadie but he was struggling financially and really didn't want to be in the position again of going out with Lorraine without any cash in his wallet, and his credit card had been refused earlier in the day at the petrol station. That was why he had to go and see Margot, it all had to be sorted out once and for all. Much as he hated dossing down at Sadie's, he was relieved to be away from Margot and didn't want to go back but he truly wished he could persuade India to leave with him. He was convinced that if he could get her away from her dangerous stomping ground he would have a chance of saving her from the life he could see she was aiming straight at.

The phone rang again and Fergus reached it just as Sadie flew out of the bathroom.

'I'll get it, I'll get it,' she shrieked.

'It's OK, I'm here.' He smiled then spoke into the phone. 'Hello?'

'Hello?'

There was a pause.

'Fergus? Is that you? What the fuck are you doing there? Why does Sadie keep hanging up on me?'

It took Fergus a few seconds to get to grips with what was going on, but then it hit him.

'Lucy? It is you, isn't it? Oh God, it's so good to hear your voice, I was just saying to Sadie—'

'It's OK, Fergus, I get the picture. That's why Sadie won't talk to me, that's why she wouldn't return my calls before I left. It's you and her, isn't it? Christ, it didn't take you long, must have been all of an evening.'

The phone went dead. Fergus looked at Sadie. She was

standing beside him, wrapped in a bath towel, with a guilty but at the same time defensive expression on her face.

'She's not right for you, you know. Lucy was supposed to be my best friend and she lied to me. You can't trust her, I don't trust her . . .' Her voice faded as she saw the look of disbelief on his face quickly change to anger.

'How could you do that to me, Sadie? You know how much she means to me, how much I desperately wanted to see her, to speak to her. You were supposed to be helping me. You were her friend.'

'I did help you. I helped you get over her. We've been having a good time, haven't we? Just you, me and Lorraine? We don't need Lucy Cooper any more, either of us.'

Chapter Thirteen

Despite being dog tired, Lucy was too restless to try and sleep. The moment that she had been trying not to think about had arrived.

The letter to Caroline and Luke was on the table, explaining how sorry she was but that she had an emergency to deal with and would not be coming back. All her notes were neat and tidy, ready to be biked over to Pettit's on Monday, along with the letter. There was nothing they could fault her for, she had made sure of that – except for running away.

In a fit of energy Lucy opened all her cupboards and drawers and started sorting everything she owned into piles. A charity shop pile, a 'don't know' pile and a keeping pile. She worked feverishly, her mind only half on what she was doing.

Fergus and Sadie? It just didn't seem right somehow but he was obviously comfortable enough at Sadie's to answer the phone. But then what about Latisha Lowe? What about Margot?

Had Fergus fooled her completely? Was he really just a two-timing, or even three-timing, bastard with a persuasive manner?

She had decided to rent the flat out when she moved. George had advised her to keep hold of her property for the short term at least. 'It's your investment,' he told her, the bank manager in him clearly evident. 'Don't do anything drastic, at least until you've taken legal advice about Don's interest in the property.'

Lucy knew he was right so she was intending to pack up and disappear off to her parents in Dubai. George had persuaded her in his kindly, fatherly manner that it was time they knew the truth. She would ring them right away, she decided, let them know she wanted to stay with them for a while, maybe even until the baby was due. She would phone them before she changed her mind.

A ring on the intercom interrupted her. Her first reaction was not to answer it but the persistence of the caller gave her no option. Pressing the speaker button she just said, 'Yes?'

'Hello, is that Lucy? This is Lorraine here, but you'll know me as Latisha Lowe. Can I come up and speak to you for a moment? It won't take long.'

'I've got nothing to say to you.'

'I know, but you should hear what I have to say to you. You'll be pleased you did, I promise.' The voice was persuasive.

Lucy pressed the entry button then opened the front door and waited.

She didn't know quite what she had expected but it wasn't the casual combat trousers and trainers that were much the same as she herself was wearing. The differences became obvious, however, when Lorraine held out a perfectly manicured hand. The solitaire diamond on her ring was the size of a frozen pea. Latisha Lowe may have been dressed casually but everything, from the sunglasses perched on top of her head down to the trainers on her feet, was new and very expensive. She certainly had style, Lucy acknowledged silently.

'Hi, Lucy. I don't know you but I've heard so much about you. You're just as Fergus described you. Is it OK if I come in?' The smile was wide and friendly and reached her eyes but Lucy didn't return it.

'If you must, but I'm really busy and still jet-lagged. I only got back from the States today.'

'OK, I'll be as quick as you like.'

Lucy showed her into the lounge. Lorraine looked at the chaotic piles of clothes and laughed.

'Good Lord, you must have had quite a shopping spree if you've got to clear out all of this to fit everything in. That's what I do, shop, shop, shop then dump the stuff that I'm pissed off with in the attic room.'

Lucy didn't react, she just looked at Lorraine and said, 'What was it you wanted to say to me?'

Lorraine moved a pile of clothes and plomped herself down on the armchair, casually crossing her legs and leaning back to get comfortable. She rummaged around in her bag. 'Do you mind if I smoke? I know you're pregnant . . .'

Lucy wouldn't look at her. 'Do whatever you like, but if you do smoke you'll have to give me one as well. I'm trying hard to give up but not getting far.'

Lorraine jumped up again. 'I know, shall I make us both a drink? Then we can sit and relax and I'll tell you why I'm here and if you don't like it then you can tell me to fuck off and I will.'

Lucy smiled; she just couldn't maintain her frosty manner in the face of Lorraine's disarming frankness.

'Go on then, tell me what this is all about.'

'Well, it's about Fergus obviously. He asked me to come and put things right.'

'Why couldn't he do it himself?'

'Because you won't talk to him of course. He's been pining away for weeks and now you're back but you still won't hear him out. Fergus and I are old, old friends from way back in drama college. I love him dearly but I would never sleep with him, never have done, never will. Sex ruins friendships, don't you think?'

'Then why was he hanging off you in those newspaper photos? Never mind the cat that got the cream, he looked more like the lion who got the impala all to himself.'

Lorraine smiled at her and shook her head. 'Come on, you're in PR, aren't you? Mountains out of molehills and all that, anything goes when there's not a lot of news and there's a photograph to fill a gap. Fergus came to me for a friendly ear and I took him out to a do that I had no way of getting out of. That's it. Finish.'

'And Sadie? Where does she fit into it now? And Margot? For Christ's sake, he's lining them up.'

'Nonsense, and you know it. You're being a bit of a hypocrite. What about your own husband? Let he who is without sin cast the first stone et cetera,' Lorraine purred, flicking her hair back and running her fingers through it.

'Fergus is one of the kindest, nicest, most loyal men I have ever met and that's something for me to say considering I've had three husbands and am currently in my "all men are bastards" mindset. And it's because he's a good man that he got caught up with the wicked witch Margot who, I hasten to add, he has finally left, praise the Lord and bang the tambourines. And as for Sadie, she's a strange one, between you and me, and please don't pass it on or back but I think she's got a bit of a crush on me.'

'Did Fergus suggest that to you?' Lucy asked suspiciously.

'No way, there's just something there, almost a school-girl crush. She's trying to get in on my life. All very odd, especially as she told me that she's a virgin and intends to stay that way until her wedding night!'

Lucy was silent. She didn't know what to say.

'So, enough chatter,' Lorraine said. 'Are you going to come with me to see the poor man? He's at my place now, not Sadie's, so you don't have to face her yet. You at least owe him a chance, don't you?'

Lucy caved in and within minutes they were in Lorraine's sports car with the roof down, inhaling all the London rush-hour exhaust fumes.

'I'm on my way, darling,' Lorraine shouted over the traffic into her phone, 'and I've got a present for you. Put the kettle on or pour yourself a stiff one, I'll be back soon!' Looking sideways at Lucy, she grinned widely. 'Oh, this is so exciting. I do love a happy ending.'

But Lucy was already dozing off in her seat. It had been a long twenty-four hours.

Donovan Cooper knew that he was in big trouble and he

could see no way out of it but that didn't stop him from spending his days in his cell plotting revenge. Revenge on Jonno for swapping relatively innocuous pills for something a whole lot more serious and on Lucy for winding him up, sending him off his head and then calling the police. He blamed Sadie too, as she had been there at the time, and Paul because Don was still convinced that he had played a part in Lucy wanting to leave him, and he blamed everyone for killing his baby. His baby, something his mother might have been proud of him for producing, instead of which he was locked up among a load of villains who were making his life a misery.

Don had never been near a prison before he arrived here two months previously and had little idea what to expect and not a clue how to behave. Initially he had been very frightened and to counteract it he had launched into his bravado routine, the one that he used on Jonno and everyone else at the gym. He thought it was effective, unaware that they laughed at him behind his back. But prison was far removed from the high-class gym.

Don was used to doing exactly what he wanted whenever he wanted and now he found himself answerable for the slightest little thing. He also came to realise too late that if he had thrown his considerable weight around at the start he might have been OK, maybe earned a bit of dubious respect. Had he just admitted to being charged with drug smuggling, he might not have been given such a hard time, but instead he boasted about giving his pregnant wife a battering, and that had upset a lot of people.

'Fucking hypocrites, the lot of them,' he moaned to his cell mate Billy. 'They'll beat the crap out of anyone they take a dislike to and try to call it justice but they're all just bloody thugs who like taking the law into their own hands.'

'I told you,' Billy sighed in exasperation, 'I told you that first day that if you wanted to get through this without too much aggro, keep your mouth shut.'

'Why? This is a prison, not a fucking torture chamber. They've got no right to threaten me, to nick my stuff and spit in my dinner.'

Billy looked up from the book he was reading. 'Get real, dickhead, it's survival of the fittest here, or rather survival of the smartest and strongest. You could have done all right with all that muscle behind you, they might just have been shit scared of you, but no, you had to shout your mouth off about beating up on the missus, the pregnant missus. You just don't do that in here.'

'But why not? It's none of their business—'

Billy slammed his book down and slid off the bunk. 'Shut the fuck up,' he snarled, jabbing at Don's chest, 'or I might have to introduce my fist to the back of your throat. You're driving me nuts.'

Billy was half Don's size, small and wiry and a good few years older, but his reputation as a hard man and the charge of manslaughter that was hanging over him made Don cautious of his cell mate. Nothing had happened to make him fearful, in fact Billy was one of the few who had stood up for him, but the underlying violence was always there.

'Sorry, Billy, it's just that—'

'Just nothing. Now lie down on your bunk, there's a good lad, and let me get on with my book.'

Don did as he was told. But his brain didn't stop

plotting the revenge he would wreak on everybody when he got out. Convinced that he would either be bailed shortly, since this was a first offence, or acquitted eventually, he hoped it wouldn't be too long before he could deal with them all. He was trying to keep fit, but he knew his muscles were starting to shrink. Not enough exercise and certainly no roids was having a negative effect and that was playing on his mind as well.

Screw them all, Don thought but didn't dare say out loud. Screw the lot of them, I'll make them pay.

Lorraine knew her way around London like the back of her hand and she drove very fast. She nipped in and out of the traffic and cut across other motorists to charge up narrow side streets that were certainly never designed for the modern motor car, until she screeched to a halt in a hail of gravel.

'Well, here we are, *chez moi*. Come on in and put poor Fergie's mind at rest.'

Alongside the hyperactive Lorraine, Lucy felt almost sloth-like but she obediently followed her through the house to the restaurant-sized kitchen where Fergus was sitting bolt upright on a stool, looking decidedly apprehensive.

He jumped up and went over to Lucy. 'Lucy. I didn't expect you to come, not really.' He reached out but she moved away.

'Don't, I'm here to talk, that's all. We can't pick up where we left off, I only came because your friend here was in danger of having a panic attack if I didn't.'

'Now, darling, don't exaggerate, I just persuaded you gently.' Lorraine looked from one to the other, a slightly victorious smile playing on her lips. 'Right. Now I have lines to learn, so I shall be in my study if anyone needs me. Help yourselves to anything you want.' Blowing a kiss in their direction she shot out of the room.

'Jeez, she makes me tired just watching her,' said Fergus. 'I don't know how she functions at that speed all the time. Did she really grind you down? Didn't you want to see me after she had explained it all?'

'Not really. You hurt me, Fergus, running off like that when I told you I was pregnant. I couldn't believe you would do something like that, I thought you were different.'

'I was confused, completely confused. I love you, I have done since the first time you smiled at me in Pettit's reception, but I also have responsibilities—'

'Oh Fergus,' Lucy interrupted. 'Do you really think that I expected you to whoop with joy and never go home again? It was me that had finished it in the first place, all I wanted was to explain to you, to be honest with you and take it from there. But no, you ran off to discuss it with someone else, someone I didn't even know.'

Not answering, Fergus walked over and put the kettle on.

'Tell me about you and Lorraine. The truth. I don't believe this psycho babble about just being good friends. I bet you fancied her rotten and she turned you down way back when. I bet that's why you went off with Margot, and I think that deep down you still fancy Lorraine rotten. That's why she's the one you ran to.'

Fergus stayed at the other side of the kitchen, clattering cups and saucers and fumbling with the cafetière.

275

'It's all history. Lorraine was a good friend to me but Margot stopped all that. Lorraine was gorgeous and had confidence by the bucketload whereas Margot was older, plainer, just out of a very abusive marriage and immediately pregnant. She didn't want me hanging around with Lorraine and I accepted that.'

'You haven't answered me.'

Fergus looked at Lucy but didn't go over to her. 'Yes, I was besotted with her all those years ago but so was half the college. No, I didn't make a play for her, so no, she didn't turn me down. If anything had happened then we couldn't have stayed friends, could we?' He smiled and, against her better judgement, Lucy could feel herself thawing.

'Do you know she was called Bunny?' he continued. 'After the bouncing battery rabbit who never stops. Being friends with Lorraine was, is, just grand, I'm truly fond of her and she makes me laugh but living with her? My worst nightmare!'

'And Sadie? Where does she fit into all this? Did you know I called her last night? God, did I need someone. Don went completely off his head, he totally wrecked the flat and when the police finally showed up and arrested him they found a mountain of cocaine that he had smuggled in from Portugal. It was awful; and I had to go away and leave everything in the hands of an old boy downstairs who I didn't know from Adam. Isn't that sad? Lucy No Mates!'

'I never knew, Lucy. I swear Sadie never said a word and she was with me here, I'd brought her so that she could explain to you. What happened between you two?'

'I don't have a clue. I wish I did but I don't and fond though I may have been of her, she's not too high on my list of priorities right now.'

'Yeah, I can see that.' He looked at her stomach and smiled. 'How are things with the baby? Have you told Caroline yet?'

'No. I haven't, and I'm not going to. I couldn't face the gossip, I've heard it before about other people. Thanks to Daniella they know about you so you can just imagine the speculation. And how could I leave Don and stay at the firm? He'd be in there smashing the place up.'

'Not if he's in jail he won't.'

'He won't be in for ever. If he's free and goes looking for me at Pettit's, I'll be fired; if he's jailed and it's in the papers, I'll be fired. Image matters and PR is cut-throat, it goes with the territory. And like I said, a spell in prison won't stop him coming after me. Whatever happens, I have to leave and make sure he can't find me.'

'And me?'

'You had your chance and you blew it, didn't you?' The words were damning but the hesitation was there.

Before he could respond, his mobile started ringing.

'Oh shit,' he gasped as he looked at the screen. 'It's Margot. I was supposed to be going round there to sort things out. I forgot! I'll put her off.'

'No you won't.' Lucy went over to him and gently touched his face. 'You go and do what you have to do. I'm completely bushed so I'm going now anyway. You can ring me at the flat tomorrow and we'll see where we're at. Go on, you go and talk with Margot.'

En route, Fergus made up his mind. No longer was he going to put up with Margot's bullying, India's total lack of respect or Simon's threatening. That wasn't a normal life, it wasn't how other people he knew lived. No, he decided. He was going to stand up for himself and tell them how things were going to be in the future.

Cool and calm but determined, his resolve was strong as he put his key in the lock. But all his good intentions disappeared when it didn't work. He wiggled the key, pushed and pulled, to no avail. Margot had changed the locks.

Turning on his heel, he walked back up the path to leave but the door flew open.

'Oi, you. Where do you think you're going?'

Slowly he turned to see Margot in her going-out uniform of tight leggings and baggy T-shirt standing in the doorway, one hand on her hip.

'You changed the locks.'

'Ten out of ten for observation,' Margot sneered. 'You think you're entitled to wander in and out of my house whenever the mood takes you?' She widened her eyes at him. 'What's the matter? You look gobsmacked.'

Fergus went back to calm. 'OK, Margot, if that's the way you want to play it then fine, I'm off.'

'Not until you've given me some money you're not. Now get your arse in here and say hello to your daughter, you cheating bastard.'

By then the woman next door was out on the step listening to every word. Fergus knew that Margot would happily cause a scene in the street so he went inside. Margot slammed the door and pushed past him into the kitchen.

'Am I going to get to talk to you with the television off for a change?' he asked quietly.

'I don't want to fucking talk to you, I just want my money.'

'Margot, I don't have any money and if I did, I don't have to give you a penny. I have to support my daughter, I want to support my daughter, but not you. I've taken legal advice and I know exactly where I stand. You want the house? Fine, you can keep it but you pay the bills. I will provide for India until she leaves school next month and then she gets herself a job, you get a job and Simple Simon gets a job. My role in all of this is finished. Understand?'

'Oh no you don't.' She put her head into the hall. 'India, Simon,' she yelled, 'get down here now!'

It took another three screeches before there was any movement and then both of them meandered down, pushing and pulling at each other on the way.

Fergus was losing patience. 'Jeez, you two, how old are you both? You look like a couple of toddlers fighting for attention.'

Simon made it into the room first. Three long paces and he stood nose to nose with Fergus. Although Fergus was aware of the possibility of a full head butt, he knew he couldn't be seen to back down.

'Just shut it, you. It's got fuck all to do with you what I do,' Simon snarled.

The hatred in his face was familiar to Fergus. He had seen it many times and, try as he may, he had never been able to deal with it, or even understand it. The first few years of Simon's life with Margot and her husband, his father, had no doubt not been a barrel of laughs but after that, his life had been very good. Better than a lot of his contemporaries. But the chip on his shoulder remained and slowly but surely he had turned into the thug now standing threateningly close to Fergus. Simon was wearing just his jeans and displaying the tattoos that covered his arms, back and neck, extending up and over his shaven head and culminating in a swastika at the top of his forehead. He epitomised the neo-Nazis of the East End of London and his racism found an easy target in Fergus's West Indian antecedents. Several run-ins with the law had done nothing to tame him; if anything he was worse each time he came out.

Fergus sighed. 'This is nothing to do with you, Simon. This is between me and your mother.'

'It so is to do with us, we haven't got any money,' India interrupted. 'I couldn't even go out tonight, so come on, splash the cash.' She flopped full length onto the sofa and put her feet up.

'Move it, slag, I wanna sit down as well.' Simon leant forward and pulled India's feet off, but with a move worthy of an ace footballer her foot shot out and kicked him viciously in the thigh.

Simon hurled himself on top of her and India screamed as he started pulling her hair to drag her off the sofa.

'That is *enough*, from all of you!' Fergus shouted. 'Now sit down and listen to what I have to say.' Three pairs of startled eyes shot in his direction. 'I am not a walking wallet and I don't intend to carry on being trampled all over by you all. Simon, you can get off your backside and get a job if you want money and you, India, will do exactly the same when you leave school. No more handouts.'

Margot, who had been uncharacteristically silent, suddenly turned on him again.

'You damned well will support us—'

'I will not and that is an end to it. Support for India until she leaves school, and that is all. Now I'm off.'

'Back to that whore Latisha whatsername, no doubt. Well, I'll make sure every single fucking newspaper knows about her breaking up families. I'll tell 'em all that you're shagging her. They'll love that.'

Despite being horrified by the threat, which he had no doubt she would try to carry out, Fergus just smiled. 'Whatever, Margot. I'm done here, I should have left years ago. You did me a favour by chucking me out. Now I know what life on the outside is like I'm not coming back.'

'Dad,' India's tone had changed, 'if you're with Latisha Lowe now, can I come with you? I don't want to stay here, I hate it here with Simon, he's a bully. I want to be with you.'

For a moment, just a moment, Fergus's hopes soared. Then he looked at her closely and realised that all she wanted was the kudos of Latisha Lowe and her money.

'If you really want to live with me, India, of course you can, but I'm not with Lorraine, not at all. I shall be renting a small flat.'

'Forget it then!' India turned away.

Fergus wanted to weep at the realisation that he had lost his daughter so completely. Although deep down he had always known she was more Margot's daughter than she was his, it still hurt.

India put her feet back up and clicked on the TV and within a few seconds was absorbed and oblivious to the furore going on around her. Margot was crying and threatening to take him to court, Simon was swearing and threatening to kill him, but India was off in her own world. An instant switch-off.

On the way out he palmed his daughter a twenty-pound note. 'Don't say a word.' He winked at her. He knew she wouldn't because they both knew that Margot would have it straight off her.

Taking as many of his clothes as he could fit into one suitcase, Fergus left the house and everything in it. He looked down at the battered old case and pursed his lips sadly. Not a lot to show for fifteen years of hard work, he thought despondently.

He strapped the case onto the back of his bike and looked up at the house. Automatically he noticed that it would need a new coat of paint soon. He wondered what other fool Margot would find to do it.

He put his helmet on, fired up the bike and without looking back rode out of the street.

Chapter Fourteen

Despite a good night's sleep brought on by complete exhaustion, Lucy woke up the next morning still feeling restless. Pottering about the flat shifting and moving things from place to place she didn't actually achieve very much but at least she felt she was doing something constructive. The confrontation with Fergus had unsettled her and made her doubt all the plans she had been making. For over an hour she debated whether or not to phone her parents. She kept walking to and from the phone, desperately wanting to speak to her mother one second then horrified at the thought the next.

Don't be so stupid, it's now or never, she thought, and without any further procrastination dialled the number on the phone she had been juggling in her hand.

'Hello, Mummy, it's me.'

'Darling. How are you? I've been meaning to ring you but you know how it is, the days just fly by out here. Daddy and I have been so busy. Are you still in Vegas?' Her mother's gentle feminine voice tinkled down the line.

'No, Mummy, I told you last week I was due to leave. I'm back in London now.'

'Yes of course you are, silly me. And how is everything? How's Don? Did he miss you? I couldn't bear to be parted from Daddy for that long, you should have taken him with you.'

Lucy smiled, her parents were still completely besotted with each other, even after thirty years.

'Actually, I've got a few problems. I wondered if I could come and stay with you for a while.' Lucy waited for her mother to ask her what was wrong.

'Oh, honey, the timing isn't good right now. I know you'll understand. Daddy and I are going to be back and forth almost commuting between here and the Dallas office. Did I tell you? Three times so far in the past couple of months. It's tiring but you know how it is in Daddy's world and at least we have the company jet for comfort.'

Lucy felt the hairs on the back of her neck stand to attention. 'No, you never told me you were in the States. You could have flown to Vegas or I could have come to you. It's not far, and it's been so long . . .'

'Oh, you silly thing, we had to entertain clients, I didn't have a spare minute. We were at a function nearly every single night. Texas was lovely though, we're hoping to move there . . .'

Her mother chattered on about everything they'd been doing while Lucy grew more and more despondent at the thought that her parents were too busy for her.

'Mummy, I only wanted to come and see you, to talk to you. I wasn't going to up sticks and live with you!'

'I know that, you're far too old for that. But we do miss you lots, you know.'

Lucy decided to take the bull by the horns, she knew if she didn't say anything now, she never would.

'I wanted to tell you I'm leaving Don, I have to get away from here and I have nowhere to go. Mummy, I'm—'

'That's a shame but you don't have to come all this way. I know just what you can do, darling. Daddy and I recently bought a lovely little cottage in Sussex. You could go there. We were thinking about renting it out, but you know we'd do anything for you so you can go and live there for as long as you need. I'll get Daddy to email you all the details right away. I'll even ring him at the office for you and then you can just run away to the country for a while, hmmm? I knew it would never last with you two. So, problem solved, off to Sussex you go. You'll love it there.'

'But—'

'No buts, I insist, and so will Daddy when I tell him. Anyway, it's lovely to hear from you but I must dash, I'll be late for my boring old charity luncheon. Lots and lots of love and kisses, Lucy my angel. Enjoy the cottage!'

The sound of kisses echoed down the line and then her mother was gone and Lucy was left, as she always was, completely confused. She hadn't known they had bought a cottage, or that they had been in the States at the same time as she was there. The comments Sadie had made about her parents flashed back into her mind. Oh well, her parents always came up trumps for her in the end and now a big part of her problem was solved in the short term. A rent-free cottage and income from letting the London flat would tide her over until after the baby was born, and Don would never find her there.

As she carried on with her big clear-out, she thought it over and the more she thought, the more she liked the idea.

Within an hour an email sending lots of love and detailing the property was posted on her computer, and Fergus was on her doorstep.

'I wasn't expecting you to show up, Fergus. I don't know if it's a good idea.'

Lucy was still in her dressing gown, her hair was standing out at all angles and she had not a scrap of make-up on her face. She looked a mess and she was all too aware of it. It occurred to her that she and Fergus hadn't really spent much time together at all. At the tentative beginning of the relationship it had been mostly lunch hours in cafés and pubs, then as it had progressed the odd evening here and there. Several times they had booked a hotel room just for the luxury of a few hours alone. But they had never spent the whole night together. They had never woken up together and certainly never seen each other at their 'first thing in the morning' worst. In fact, she thought, their relationship had been conducted mostly by sneaked phone calls and text messages. Was that a relationship? she asked herself, or was it just a mad fling that had got out of hand?

'Well, I think it is a good idea. It is a very good idea that we get together and talk. I mean really talk, not crap, superficial things, but how we both really feel, what we both want and expect from all this. We've got issues to resolve and now we can resolve them.'

'Why, Fergus? What's changed?'

'Everything has changed. I've left Margot for good, I've got my things at Lorraine's and I'm free to be with you, for ever. Guilt-free as well, thanks to Lorraine and her amateur counselling. A conscience can be a good thing but it can also be very inhibiting.'

'But . . .' Lucy looked at him helplessly.

'No buts.' Fergus smiled. 'I've made my mind up and now I'm going to help you make up yours.'

Taking her hand he pulled her to him and kissed her hard, his hand on the back of her head. At first she tried to draw away but he didn't let her go. Her head told her to throw him out but her body told her otherwise. And, hard as she tried, she couldn't help but respond.

'Oh, jeez, it's been so long. I really should be in therapy for letting this take so long,' Fergus moaned as they fell to the floor and stretched out on the new carpet.

'Fergus, I'm pregnant, I'm fat,' Lucy protested as he pulled her robe apart. 'We shouldn't, we haven't talked, and I'm wearing fat knickers.'

'Yes we should. I think you're beautiful and I think your bump is beautiful too.' Gently he pulled her knickers down just a little and then sat up and stared silently at her body. Running his finger round her swollen stomach, he kept murmuring, 'You are beautiful exactly as you are. Just imagine, there's a baby growing there, right under the skin. I can feel it there, I can see it, our baby . . .'

Lucy froze and then sat up sharply. 'You don't know that. It could be Don's.'

'No, Lucy, our baby.' Gently pushing her back down again, he carried on stroking and talking softly while at the same time removing all his clothes. 'A baby that we will share and bring up together, that's what matters. It will be your baby and that's what will make it our baby. Nobody else's. Regardless.'

A warm glow spread through Lucy as she absorbed his words. Maybe everything would be OK after all. Relaxing, she wiped her brain free of everything except the moment.

Although they heard the phone ringing in the background, neither acknowledged it, and Lucy had no intention of answering it. Nothing was going to spoil this, not after so long apart.

Lucy had turned over and Fergus was on his knees ready to enter her when the answerphone picked up and Don's voice intruded loudly.

'I know you're back, Jonno told me, now pick up the phone, Lucy, pick up the fucking phone.' There was a silence as he waited. 'OK, but remember you're being watched. You're going to pay for what you did to me, I promise you. *Bitch*.'

In unison Fergus and Lucy stopped and rolled back over. The moment had gone.

'Well, you have to give him credit for good timing.' Fergus wrinkled his forehead. 'Couldn't have been better if he'd been watching over our shoulders. Don't they monitor calls from prison? Is he allowed to do that, for Christ's sake? That's threatening, it's intimidation, he can't be allowed to do that, surely.'

'Fergus, I think he just did. How did Jonno know I was home? Why would he or any of his cohorts be watching me? What am I likely to be doing, for fuck's sake?'

'Who's Jonno?' Fergus asked, leaning on one elbow and looking down at her. 'I've never heard you mention him.'

'He's the manager at the gym. I didn't think he even liked Don, no one else there does. I know he was behind the little jaunt to Portugal and Don said everything was his fault but then Don always blames someone else, he'll never accept responsibility for anything. Do you know, once, when we were first married, he had this silly great off-road jeep thing that he used to cruise in. Anyway, he was driving and then he started an argument, and he was so busy shouting and cursing at me he ran into the car in front that had stopped. But apparently it was my fault for not telling him it had stopped.' Lucy opened her eyes wide, determined not to cry.

Fergus kissed her gently. 'Come on then, you'd best get dressed before you catch your death. I don't know, I've anticipated this moment for so long and now this. What are we going to do? You can't stay here, I can see that now, but where will you go?'

'I know exactly what we're going to do and where we're going to go. How do you fancy living in a small Sussex village? In a cottage. It's not exactly roses round the door and white picket fence but it looks good in the photo, and it's furnished. It's been used as a holiday cottage.' Jumping up, she grabbed her dressing gown and handed him the printout.

'Where did this come from?' Fergus looked at the paper suspiciously.

'Mummy and Daddy have bought it and said I can live there. It was supposed to be an investment or something, they own other properties all over the home counties, but they're all rented out.'

'Did you tell them you were pregnant?'

'No, I didn't get a chance – you don't know my mother – but as soon as I said I was leaving Don, they offered me this. Aren't they just great?'

Fergus said nothing. He stood up and started to put his clothes back on, his back to her.

'What's the matter?'

'I was just wondering how they'll react to me, a lowly courier who spends his day whizzing around London on a motorbike and letting his brain ferment under a helmet. Hardly a good prospect, am I?'

'Oh, they'll love you, don't worry,' she said. What she thought was, they won't actually give a toss so long as I leave them alone with each other. But to say it out loud would mean admitting it herself, admitting that Sadie was right.

He picked up the piece of paper again and read it. Although he knew he had to read between the lines of the classic estate agent speak, he could still see that it was a fantastic property and way out of his price range. Detached, three bedrooms, two receptions, conservatory, large garden, small village, within commuting distance of London – even an Aga.

'Lucy, we could never afford the rent on this, it has to be a couple of grand a month. I don't earn anywhere near enough and you won't even be working.'

'Oh, don't worry about that, we won't have to pay any rent, only the bills and of course maintain it. Sorry, I should have told you that.'

'It's not going to do my self-esteem much good, Lucy, to be subsidised by your parents.'

'I hadn't realised you were into dominant male behaviour,

Fergus.' Lucy looked at him, her expression puzzled. 'What is the problem? I need a bolt-hole, my parents have provided me with one and they can easily afford it. I'm sure it's tax deductible for them somehow and if I rent out this place, we'll be OK for a good few months.'

When he didn't respond, she looked him directly in the eye, putting him in the position of either looking away or continuing eye contact. A lesson Lucy had learnt in business. 'If it's not what you want, if you're changing your mind again then that's fine by me, but please tell me. I'm going there. It's up to you whether you come with me or not.'

'It's not that.'

'What is it then, Fergus? Do you need to talk it over with Latisha fucking Lowe first? Have you got to seek wonder woman's approval yet again?' She snatched up his crash helmet and lobbed it at him. 'Get out, Fergus, and go and make your decision in the cold light of day rather than when I'm on my back and you fancy a quick shag.'

Lucy ran and locked herself in the bathroom, staying there until she heard the front door open and close.

Right back to square one, she thought angrily.

Wrapping her arms tightly round her bump, she went into the lounge and wandered over to the window. She looked down just in time to see Fergus waving his arms about as he stood arguing with a traffic warden who was standing over the motorbike, pen poised.

Serves him right, she thought as she watched the silent exchange through the glass. But then her eyes wandered and she saw another figure standing and watching. She saw the man's eyes flicker upwards towards her. Because of the angle she knew he couldn't see her but there was no doubt he was looking at her window. He looked away, back to Fergus again, and Lucy tried to focus on him, on his face, his features, his stance. It definitely wasn't Jonno but she knew she recognised him, she just couldn't place him. The realisation that Don had been telling the truth, that someone was watching her, sent a chill through her body. Had the man seen her going in and out? Had he noticed she was still pregnant? Would he tell Don? Had he seen Fergus?

She had to get out and away, with or without Fergus, and the sooner the better.

She went to her computer and sent an email to her father thanking him for the offer of the cottage and accepting. She told him she would move in straight away.

Fergus tried hard to push them away, but the doubts had started the moment Lucy had handed him the piece of paper. The past came flooding back to him. Lucy was right, suddenly he wasn't as sure as he had been when they were both rolling around the carpet.

It was *déjà vu*. Him and Margot all over again. The abusive husband, the unplanned pregnancy, the house that was nothing to do with him. The only difference was that he had never been in love with Margot and he certainly was with Lucy.

But would it be enough? The doubts he had felt when Lucy had first told him she was pregnant came flooding back. Lucy Cooper was in a different league to him. Financially, he'd always known that, and it hadn't mattered, to either of them. But when she was eagerly telling him about the cottage, her parents' cottage, he'd immediately felt uneasy. Once again any decisions about the future had been taken away from him, his life was again being planned for him. And all because, as Margot said, his brains were in his pants.

Fifteen years of working every hour that he could both in and out of his home and now all he was left with were the clothes that he stood up in and one lousy battered old suitcase. Did he want to take that chance again? he asked himself.

Not too many days before, he and Lorraine had sat up all night talking and she had tried hard to persuade him to go for broke and give acting another try. She had offered to help him, introduce him to 'people' and give his long-hidden dreams and aspirations a jump start. Apart from India, he now had no responsibilities, he could go back to college on a grant and freshen up his skills, he could do what he wanted to do while he was still young enough. But he knew he couldn't do it if he was with Lucy. He had made the wrong decision once; could he afford to make another one at the age of thirty-seven?

Could he really take on another man's child when he wasn't even sure he wanted another of his own? And of course there was Donovan Cooper, gorilla man. Whether Don took any action or not, they would always be looking over their shoulders, waiting for him to step out of the shadows and stake a claim on the child. Waiting for him to beat the pair of them to a pulp if he ever found them.

Lucy was right. He did want to speak to Lorraine, whose dippy exterior was just a persona cultivated alongside her career. He hadn't listened to her about Margot and she had been right. Maybe he should listen to her this time.

Caroline and Luke Pettit were closeted in her office.

'Who do you think was responsible? This is just appalling.' Caroline banged her hand on the desk.

'I don't know. I'd be inclined towards straightforward mindless vandalism. This is London, it happens here. They'd break into a cardboard box if they thought there were kicks inside.'

'I'm not so sure. A few months ago I'd have agreed without a second thought, but now, with all this Lucy business,' Caroline shook her head. 'I've had a bad feeling about this all the way through. I know you're right, we can't get rid of people because of my bad vibes,' looking at him, she smiled, 'but there's something about this . . .'

After the police had checked out the echoing burglar alarm and called Caroline and Luke, they had rushed across London in the early hours to investigate. The scene that had confronted them was one of complete and total devastation. Someone had broken in and vandalised the office. No other offices in the building were affected, only Pettit's, and, as far as they could tell, nothing had been actually taken.

Computers had been thrown off the desks and the switchboard was jammed, not with calls but with orange juice, thick sticky orange juice taken from the fridge. It had also been poured over the pile of papers and files in the middle of the floor. All client data, both paper and computer, were in unbelievable chaos.

'I really don't know.' Luke sounded perplexed. 'I suppose I hope in a way that it was just drunken louts looking for a cheap thrill but who knows? Maybe a competitor? All I can think of at the moment is how we're going to clear this lot up and unscramble the chaos. It will mean a lot of extra hours for the staff, we'll have to offer a financial incentive for twenty-four-hour working!'

The rattling of the doors that Luke had bolted from the inside stopped them mid-conversation. They both froze and looked over to the entrance. Paul was peering through the glass porthole of the door.

'We're getting jumpy.' Luke laughed drily. 'I forgot to unbolt the door.' He went to let Paul in.

'Come in, Paul, welcome to Beirut.'

'Wow!' Paul exclaimed. 'What's been happening in here? It looks like a scene from *King Kong*. Who did this?'

'That's what Caroline and I would like to know.' Luke smiled grimly. 'The police think it's vandalism. They're coming back in a couple of hours to take statements. How are you fixed for a bit of manual labour?'

Paul held up his hands in mock horror. 'Oh my God, not manual work. Look at these manicured and nurtured tools of my trade. I couldn't face my public with rough hands.'

'I'll fish out the Marigolds for you then.'

Paul laughed. 'Was anything stolen?'

'No, not that we can see. Looks like they did it for fun.'

'For fun? Don't you just love that expression? That's what the police told me when I was beaten up a few months back. Nothing was stolen then, they just jumped me, muttered a load of crap, gave me a kicking and ran off, but not to worry, it was just for fun.'

Although Luke often looked like a bit of a bumbling

eccentric, his IQ was exceptionally high and his analytical mind often picked up on obscure things.

'So what exactly did the thugs who jumped you say, Paul?' he asked.

'Something about teaching me a lesson, not to mess with married women. But that's something I've never done, even I'm not that desperate. Why?'

'Nothing, just making conversation. Do you fancy a trip down to get us some coffee and sandwiches? The kitchen isn't useable and we've been here since four a.m.'

'No probs. Back in five.'

Luke decided to reserve judgement for a while, he didn't want to give Caroline any more cause for concern, but he was going to check things out for himself. Just in case, as he suspected, Donovan Cooper was somehow connected to the two incidents. Three if he included the wrecking of Lucy's flat.

He went back into Caroline's office.

'Caroline darling, I've sent Paul out for coffee and sandwiches. After that, as soon as the others get in, I'm going to pop out for an hour, get some quotes for repairing the damage. I'll leave you to mobilise the troops, you're better at it than I am.'

Luke had a lot to do when he left the building. There was the insurance company, the police, all the inconveniences that carry on long after the actual event. But that wasn't where he was going right now. He flagged down a black cab and gave the driver Lucy's address.

'Lucy, it's Luke, I need to speak to you.' Luke had his mouth pressed tight against the intercom.

'It's not really convenient, can't it wait until Monday?'

'No, Lucy, it can't. Let me in please, this is important.'

Lucy panicked. She knew that as soon as Luke walked in he would see that she was packing but there was no time to do anything about it. In the time it took Luke to climb the stairs, all she could do was grab the baggy sweatshirt again and pull it over her head.

She opened the door and stood back to let him in.

'I'm in a bit of a mess, Luke. I'm making the most of my time off and having a clear-out, getting rid of Don's things. I'm going to pack them up and send them to his mother, she's welcome to them.'

'Looks like more than Don's things, Lucy, unless he's lost a lot of weight and transformed himself into a transvestite. Looks to me like you're going somewhere. Come on, Lucy, what's going on?'

Looking at her feet, Lucy pulled at the neck of her top. 'I should be asking you that, Luke. What's so urgent that it couldn't wait until Monday?'

Luke tried to catch her eye. 'I'm afraid we're going to have to drag you back to the office before then. We've had a break-in and the place is in a mess. All the computers are down and files and paperwork ruined.'

Lucy felt a surge of relief. 'That's awful, what happened?'

'Do you mind if I sit down? We've been up all night.'

Lucy waved in the direction of the chairs.

'As I was saying, the office is a mess but there's something strange about it, something I can't quite figure out. Nothing was stolen, there was just mindless damage, but only in our office. None of the other offices in the building were touched. It's almost as if Pettit's has been targeted specifically. I suppose in a way it's like when Paul got beaten up, there was no reason for that either.' Luke looked thoughtful. 'And of course there was your flat. But then you knew who did that, didn't you?'

Lucy felt as if Luke had poured a bucket of cold water over her. Luke had been her ally, he had stuck up for her and done everything to help her. Now, she knew, he was looking at her differently.

When Paul had been attacked, Lucy had thought Don was behind it; it couldn't have actually been him or Paul would have recognised him, but he could easily have found someone else to do it. She thought about the phone call from Don, the man on the street opposite her home. If Luke really did suspect Don then he was probably justified but she wasn't going to support his theory. She had her own problems.

'Anyway, Lucy, that's all by the by.' Luke shrugged his shoulders nonchalantly. 'Can you spare a few hours? I'm afraid it's going to be all hands on deck. You can take the time back, of course, plus an extra couple of days to compensate for the inconvenience.'

'Luke, can I ask you a question?' For the first time Lucy looked him directly in the eye.

'Of course.'

'Are you going to see everyone at home or only me? I mean, you could have asked me over the phone.' Lucy already knew the answer. Luke had wanted to tell her face to face so that he could watch her reactions. Typical PR ploy. She had used it herself many times.

'I could have, yes, but as you are actually on leave it's a little different. Everyone else will be in the office today anyway. Caroline is waiting there to tell them what's going on. So, can we count on you?'

Lucy's hesitation was brief. 'Of course you can, Luke, but I can't get there until this afternoon, I've got an important appointment that I really can't cancel.'

'That's great, we'll see you later then.' Luke's innocent wide smile looked genuine but Lucy wasn't convinced he was being completely open with her.

But then neither was she. She had no intention of going into Pettit's. She had already determined that all her essentials would be packed up and ready to pile into a taxi by the end of the day. She didn't intend to spend another night in the flat and she certainly wasn't going to let anyone know where she was going.

After Luke had gone, she looked out of the window again. The man was still there, conspicuously leaning against the wall of the newsagent's opposite, reading a magazine. Not a very impressive private eye, Lucy thought to herself; he stood out like a sore thumb, an amateur sleuth who wasn't sure what to do.

But then it hit her. The man wanted to be noticed. He wasn't there to follow her or to check up on her. He was there to frighten her. And he was succeeding.

Lucy tried to figure out a way of moving out without being seen. The main entrance was out of the question but the rear fire escape led down to a side alleyway. The entrance to it wasn't far along from the main doors to the building, but if she could get her stuff down to the bottom and then have someone with a car to load it up, she herself could walk in the opposite direction and distract him.

But who?

Not Fergus, he'd wimped out again.

Not Sadie, obviously.

Not Lorraine, she didn't know her well enough and anyway she would tell Fergus.

No one from Pettit's, again obviously.

Still looking out of the window, she saw someone turn into the flats, two carrier bags in his hands.

George!

Lucy smiled to herself; the old man and the pregnant woman sneaking about up the back alley trying to avoid the surveillance over the road. It was just too farcical. But it could just work.

She went down to see George. She knew he would help and she also knew he would enjoy it.

Don felt pleased with himself. He hoped Lucy was feeling really frightened. As frightened as he had been when he had been locked in a white prison van and taken off to jail.

When Jonno had come to visit him, Don had put on a good performance, so good that even the ever suspicious Jonno wasn't completely sure of the truth.

'I'm telling you, she did it on purpose. Lucy knew what was in that case, she knows more people who snort that stuff than you could supply. She knew, so she trashed the flat, and then called the police. They would never have found it if she hadn't told them where it was. It was a set-up, I'm telling you.'

Jonno pushed himself back in the chair, forcing the front legs off the floor. 'Why?'

'What do you mean, why?'

'I mean, Donny boy, tell me why she would do that, it doesn't make sense.'

'Because she's been seeing someone else. This gets me out of the way and gives her the opportunity to shag around with Paul fucking Gower, the arsehole she works with.'

The chair crashed down, making Don jump. Jonno started drumming his fingers on the Formica table that separated the two men.

'Go on.'

'I'm sorry, Jonno, but if you'd told me what was going on I'd have been able to deal with it better, but I thought it was just roids so left it in my case. Lucy must have nosed around through my stuff like she always does, had a look and then bingo. We played right into her hands.'

'Even if this is true, it doesn't help you and me. I'm seriously out of pocket and you have to wear some of that. What are you going to do?'

Don's confidence was increasing by the second. Jonno believed him.

'Screw her parents for it. They're so fucking rich it's obscene, they can afford it. As soon as I get out.'

Jonno's raucous laugh echoed around the room, causing heads to turn angrily in his direction.

'As soon as you get out? I'll be old and grey by then, Donny boy. I'll need something on account before then, long before then.'

'You'll have to deal with it then. I'm locked up in here, in case you've forgotten.'

'True. But I'm sure we can sort something out that will suit both of us. Now I have an idea, you tell me what you think of it and then I'll tell you exactly what you have to do.'

'Better make it quick, they'll be turfing you out any minute now.'

Chapter Fifteen

George Beacham loved the idea of getting involved in a bit of subterfuge and the excitement, tempered with concern for Lucy, shone in his face as they decided the best way to do it.

'No, Lucy, I simply cannot let an expectant mother carry anything. I'll bring your cases down, all you have to do is stand at the bottom – out of sight, mind, you don't want to be seen.' George wagged his finger at her and in that moment Lucy could just imagine him as a bank manager remonstrating with an overdrawn customer. She wanted to smile but didn't.

'And of course you need to keep an eye on your belongings at the bottom, they'd be gone in the blink of an eye round here. Then,' he paused for effect, 'I'll come out of the front door and wait for the taxi which will of course be pre-booked. You will then come out of the front doors and, not acknowledging me, walk over the road and start looking in the shops. While that villain is watching you, I shall load up the taxi and we will drive round the block.

You will then follow. I shall get out and you shall get in.' George dropped his hands and took a deep breath. 'How does that sound?'

'Perfect, George.' She smiled affectionately at him. 'But are you sure you don't mind? I feel as if I'm imposing on you.'

'Oh dear, you don't know me very well, do you? This is the best thing that's happened to me in weeks. Even better than watching the cricket! What time do you want to go?'

'Can I let you know in a while? I've now got to whittle down my stuff to what I need to take for the short term instead of what I want to take for good. When I feel a bit safer I can send someone round for the rest.'

'Done. Let the countdown begin!' The old man's eyes twinkled. Short and round with a head of white hair carefully groomed, he reminded Lucy of a toby jug.

The squeal of tyres and screech of brakes told Fergus that Lorraine was on her way down the road. Her housekeeper had invited him in but he had felt uncomfortable. He had wandered off to find a café and now, over two hours later he was back outside the gates as she turned up, spot on time. One o'clock exactly, just like the housekeeper had said.

'Hello, Fergie my darling,' she shouted as she pulled up beside him. 'Jump in, it'll save playing about with the gates.'

'Is my bike safe up the road? Should I go and get it?'

'Depends on how long you're stopping. Oh dear. Wet weekend face. What's up?'

'I need some advice, I want you to tell me what to do.'

Lorraine laughed loudly and shook her head theatrically. 'Oh no, no, not a chance, darling, I presume this is relationship-related and when it comes to that sort of thing, I score low. For example, I met the most beautiful man last night. Handsome, charming. I mean, he had the manners of a prince and he was young and frisky but, unfortunately, he also had the bank balance of a pauper. I don't keep men any more, I've at least learnt that one. But I digress. You were saying?'

Pleased of a pause from Lorraine, he got in quickly.

'I want to know what to do about Lucy. I think I've just done it again.'

'Done what again?' Lorraine sighed deeply.

'Got in too deep, got myself caught up like I did with Margot all those years ago.'

'Oh, for fuck's sake, darling, there's no comparison. I mean, far be it from me to be a snob but Margot was just so uncouth and patently unsuitable. She set you up, took you for a fool and you duly obliged by proving that you actually were a fool. Then she spent the next fifteen years treating you like one big soft touch.'

'Thanks a lot.'

Lorraine laughed and smacked him gently on the thigh. 'Sorry, darling. The truth hurts, does it? Now don't you go getting all self-righteous with me. Was I right or was I right? But Lucy, now that's a whole different ball game. She loves you to bits, she supports herself and she's got character. Not to mention the fact that she's gorgeous, young and, horror of horrors, a natural blonde to boot. What's the big problem?'

Inside the house, Fergus told her exactly how he was

feeling. But every objection he came up with, Lorraine had a reasonable way of overcoming it.

'Look, Fergie, I'm just a teensy bit tired of saying the same thing and you not listening. If you love her then go for it, but if you're thinking of doing it out of one of your silly misguided ideas of duty then forget it. That's what was wrong with you and Margot and that's why you blew a big chunk of your life. She was *the wrong person!* And now . . .' The emphasis was very dramatic, as was the pause. 'Now you have to decide if Lucy is *the right person.* I'm going to get changed and you're going to make us both a nice fresh coffee. Beans are in the tin.' Lorraine blew him an exaggerated kiss and disappeared, leaving behind a hint of perfume that again took Fergus back to the past.

Lorraine had been everything to him, his adulation of her was total and he would happily have died for her if she had asked. But she hadn't. Lorraine had never asked anything of him apart from friendship and he had obliged but it had hurt, for years it had really hurt and the whiff of perfume brought all that pain back to him. He loved Lucy, loved her deeply, but it wasn't the same as the feelings he had had all those years ago for Lorraine. It didn't physically hurt when he was away from Lucy, he didn't lose his appetite if he was away from her, and he could function like a normal human being if she didn't phone when she was supposed to.

If what he had felt for Lorraine was love, then what was it he felt for Lucy?

Fergus ground the coffee beans and put them in the machine. He loved the smell of fresh coffee and leaned over to savour it.

'Boo!' Lorraine crept up behind him and squeezed his waist. 'What are you thinking about? You were miles away.'

'You, Lorraine. I was thinking about you and how I was so madly in love with you all those years ago.'

Lorraine smiled. 'You were never in love with me.'

'I was. Desperately. You know I was.'

'No, no, no! You were not. You might have been infatuated with me, I'll give you that, but you were never in love with me. Good God, man, haven't you learnt the difference yet?' She looked at him closely, as if seeing him for the first time. 'Is that what all this is about?'

'Yes, partly. I don't feel the same about Lucy.'

'Good, because if you did I'd be worried, you stupid boy. Infatuation is great, I've been there, remember? But it doesn't last, especially when the object of it doesn't live up to expectations. If, by any chance, you and I had got together, it wouldn't have lasted five minutes. I'd have driven you crazy and, I'm afraid, you would have done the same to me. No, if that's your benchmark then you're way off beam, sweetie.'

'But—'

'Pour the coffee instead of sniffing it and tell me what you're going to do about Lucy. You haven't got a lot of time before she kicks you into touch and runs off with a young, rich and handsome man. Baby or no baby, young Lucy is quite gorgeous, I hate her.' Laughing, she hugged Fergus tight. 'Joking apart, this is do it or forget it time. Lucy isn't going to hang around while you faff about being deep and meaningful.'

Fergus lapsed into silence. Lorraine was right of course, he knew that, but had he blown it already?

Suddenly reaching out, he took Lorraine's face in both his hands and kissed her firmly on the lips.

'I have to go. I'll ring you.'

'They all say that.' Lorraine sighed loudly.

Lucy was nearly ready to go. Luke had already rung and left a message and Paul had left two, but there was nothing from Fergus. Again, she thought. What chance was there for them if he ran off every time the going got tough? Mentally she pulled herself up. She had to concentrate on thinking about her safety and also the safety of her baby.

Her baby. She said it out loud. Not too many months ago the most important thing on her agenda was putting one over on Paul Gower and trying to snatch accounts from under his nose. Now suddenly she was facing the prospect of single motherhood in a house she hadn't even seen. The tears welled up as she said out loud, 'It's not fair, it's just not bloody fair.'

Looking sadly out of the window, she was horrified to see that the man wasn't there. It would be impossible to mount George's military operation if she didn't know where he was or when he might come back.

Panic sent her running down the stairs.

'He's not there, George. What are we going to do?'

'Not panic for a start, lovey. He can't be there all the time, he must have to go off and deal with personal matters now and again, and if he doesn't come back then you're safe and you won't have to rush off.'

'Personal matters? Oh, right, I see what you mean. OK, I'll go and finish packing and then if he comes back I'll order the cab.'

'Good girl. We don't want you and your baby getting all upset, do we?'

'Oh George, why can't I meet a nice man like you?'

'Oh Lucy, why aren't I fifty years younger?'

They both laughed.

Lucy went back upstairs and carried on packing her life away. She wasn't taking a lot. It was more as if she was going on holiday for a couple of weeks. Determined not to be morose, she cleaned and tidied, glancing out of the window at regular intervals.

After the longest hour of her life she phoned down to George.

'He's back, he's over the road again and I'm ready to go.'

'Jolly good, operation Move Lucy Cooper begins. You book the taxi for exactly thirty minutes' time and I'll get shifting.'

Lucy put the phone down and looked around at the flat that she had first shared with Sadie and then with Don. Her father had chosen it for her on one of his property-buying sprees and then handed her the keys with a flourish. 'A present for my princess,' he had said with a smile before jetting off back to the Middle East, tempering her delight at the flat with the uncomfortable feeling that she had been bought out of her parents' lives.

Don had always said everything was her own fault. Maybe he was right. Maybe that's why Sadie was no longer part of her life, why Fergus kept getting cold feet, why her parents weren't interested in her life.

Oh well, she thought as she locked the windows. Too late to change any of it now.

The ringing of the phone made her jump. She went over

to it and watched cautiously as the ringing stopped and the machine clicked into life.

'Lucy? Come on, I know you're there, pick up the phone, bitch.' There was a short pause before Don's voice started again. 'You can't hide away, you know, we're on your fucking tail and someone will get you. Are you scared? You should be, you'd be terrified if you knew what was coming to you. No one crosses Jonno and gets away with it. You're really going to regret this, you know, really fucking regret it.'

Listening intently, she hadn't realised that George had come in and was behind her.

'Whoever was that, Lucy?' His voice was calm but Lucy could hear the shock in his tone.

'It was Don, my husband. Now you can see why I have to go. He's behind all this, the man out there, it's to do with him, I know it is. Oh George, I'm really scared.'

'I know, Lucy, I know. Let's get going, the sooner we get you away, the better.'

Lucy crossed the road, deliberately not looking at the man who was just standing there, hands in pockets, watching her with a slightly curious expression on his face. Lucy frowned and looked intently at the postcards in the news-agent's window. Although she appeared to be reading the cards, she was watching the doors to the building opposite out of the corner of her eye. She saw the taxi pull up and then George putting her cases inside.

Still ignoring the figure that she knew was monitoring her every move, she put her head round the door of the shop and called the woman behind the counter.

'Sorry to be a nuisance, Mrs Patel, but have you got change of a fiver? My car's parked round the corner and I need to feed the meter.' She put her hands in her pocket and made a big show of fumbling around. 'No, it's OK, I've found some. I'll just nip round and do that and then I'll be back for some cigarettes. See you in a tick.'

The taxi and George pulled away and turned into a side street.

Lucy put her head down and fumbled with change, walking in the direction the taxi had taken. As she got round the corner, she saw George standing on the pavement.

'Go on, lovey, off you go. Quickly. Ring me later.'

She hugged him hard. 'George, I don't know what I'd have done without you.'

'Go on, go now, but you will keep in touch, won't you?'

'Of course I will. I'll ring you when I get there.' She got into the taxi and the driver pulled away from the kerb. Lucy looked out of the back window and saw George waving, but there was no sign of the man. They had done it. She settled back in her seat and relaxed.

Fergus had ridden like a bat out of hell to get to Lucy. Lorraine had clarified everything for him, she was right, there was a huge difference between infatuation and love and he did love Lucy. But he also knew that what he had felt for Lorraine way back then wasn't just infatuation; he had been in love with her and probably always would be just a little, but it was in the past. Lucy was his future, he was sure of it.

But as he approached her flat he saw her disappearing

round the corner. His helmet stopped him from shouting so he rode after her but the traffic signals turned to red just as he got there and he had to stop. Impatiently revving the engine hard, he was away the instant the amber went to green but by the time he saw her again she was getting into a taxi up the far end of the street, and an elderly man was standing waving.

He pulled up sharply and lifted his visor. 'Where's she going? Where's Lucy going? I need to speak to her.'

George looked at him vacantly. 'Where's who going?'

'Lucy. You were waving to her.'

'I don't know what you're talking about, lad. I was waving at my friend over the road.' George turned and walked away.

Fergus roared off in the same direction as the cab. He guessed she was going to Pettit's and decided to follow her and catch her when she got there. He had to talk to her.

Two hours later after a long and bewildering drive, his petrol gauge was registering empty and he started to panic. Not only was he supposed to be at work but he was miles away from London with no cash, no credit card and no petrol.

Just as he was about to stop and ring Lorraine, the taxi turned into a narrow lane, pulled up at a gate and Lucy got out. The driver offloaded her luggage and, as George had requested, took them all up to the front door.

Fergus inched his bike forward and looked at the building. He recognised it – it was the cottage Lucy had shown him a photo of. It was set back slightly from the road. It wasn't a chocolate-box cottage, in fact when it was built it had probably been a workman's home, but it had been extended up and out, keeping with the original design. The short and wide front garden was bordered by an old gnarled fence that really needed replacing but was edged with trees and shrubs that probably held it up.

He waited until the taxi moved off then got off his bike and walked slowly up to the front door which was still open. There were a couple of boxes on the step. He picked them up and walked straight in.

'Hello, girl, did you really think you could get away from me that easily?'

Lucy dropped the box she was holding. 'Christ Almighty, you just scared the crap out of me. What are you doing here? How did you find me?'

'Easy, I followed you. Did you not notice me?'

'Can't say I did. Why are you here?'

'Because I realised what a complete and utter dork I was being, I realised that I love you more than anything else in the world. I was being incredibly stupid and my brain was befuddled but now I know. Please, Lucy can you forgive me? All I want is to be with you, whatever.'

Lucy took a step towards him and slapped his face sharply. 'Don't give me all that old blarney again, Fergus Pearson. It doesn't work. I am so pissed off with you and your scared-rabbit trick. So no, I don't forgive you. Just fuck off back to London and leave me to get on with my life.'

'I can't do that.'

'Yes you can. Now just get on that bike and disappear. I never want to see you again.'

'Lucy, I really can't, I don't have any petrol!'

She tried not to look at him, she tried not to be

persuaded by the charm that she had first fallen for but it was impossible.

'Oh, for heaven's sake, Fergus. This has got to stop, I just haven't got the energy for it.'

'In that case you go and have a lie-down and I'll sort this place out for you. It smells a bit musty to me.'

Lucy looked at him and felt her shoulders sag. She sighed deeply. 'OK, but don't think this is the end of it. I've still got to explain the true meaning of the word "commitment" to you.'

Chapter Sixteen

Jonno McMahon was once again sitting opposite Donovan Cooper in the visiting area. And once again he was very angry.

'I'm telling you that wife of yours has done a bunk, flitted, gone. She is definitely not there. Not at the flat, not at work, nowhere to be seen.'

'Since when?'

'Last seen three weeks ago. I went to the flat and rang the wrong buzzer deliberately and someone said she'd moved. They wouldn't let me past the fucking security door though. Come on then, she's your wife, where would she be?'

'At her parents? She might have gone there, Mummy and Daddy would no doubt provide her with a bolt-holt. Might be worth a try.'

'And where do they live?'

'Dubai.'

'You're having me on, aren't you? The fucking Middle East? How are we going to get to her there, you dickhead?'

Don went on the offensive. 'Don't you have a go at me, buster. You got me into all this mess and then, when all you had to do was snatch the bitch and hang on to her for a few days, what do you do? You fucking lose her, let her move away right under your nose. It's not me that's the dickhead, it's you for pulling the stunt with the stuff in the first place. Billy says I should—'

'You what?' Jonno was on his feet so quickly all eyes in the hot and sweaty visitor's room turned to him, anticipating a brawl.

The woman at the next table glared at him. 'Some of us want some privacy.'

Jonno sat down again and lowered his voice. 'Have you been blabbing off to your cell mate? Have you? Christ, I was right, you don't have any brains. Billy, whoever he might be, can say whatever he likes but it's me you listen to, Donny boy. Me, understand? Now where can I get some keys to your gaff? At least I can go in and have a nose around, look for something, anything. A pointer to where she's gone.'

'There's a spare set in my locker at the gym.'

'Good. Give me a ring when you can and I'll let you know if anything's changed.'

'If you get really stuck there's always Lucy's fat friend Sadie Khan. You know her? The fat bitch who was always hanging around her.'

'Now I thought that one was a bit of all right, had a spark about her, you know what I mean? *Asian Babes* an' all that.'

Don shook his head. 'You're kidding.'

'Yeah, well, that's by the by. What about her?'

'Lucy would do anything for her. Not worth as much to the parents, but Lucy would go for it and anything is better than nothing.'

'I'll bear it in mind. Give us her address and we'll keep her for first reserve.'

'Do me a favour, Jonno?'

'Such as?'

'Arrange for super smoothie Paul Gower to have another seeing-to. A really good kicking this time. Make sure he never fucks my wife again.'

Jonno marched confidently up to the flats and let himself in the main doors. He didn't want anyone who might notice him to think he was acting suspiciously so he braved it out with a swagger and once inside headed straight up the stairs, trying to look as if he knew where he was going. A few moments later, his heart pounding nervously, he was inside the flat with the door closed behind him.

'Nice gaff,' he muttered to himself as he looked around, just a cursory glance before he settled down to a proper search. Straight away it was obvious nobody was living there. Lucy Cooper had most definitely done a bunk. The bed was stripped and the duvet carefully folded at the end but there were a few discarded clothes on top. He looked in the rubbish sacks that were stacked in the corner and saw they were full of men's clothing. Don's. He smiled to himself at the thought of all Don's belongings being carted away with the rubbish. The dishwasher and washing machine were both empty, with the doors left open, and the waste bin had been emptied.

Jonno turned the place inside out, cupboards, wardrobes,

everything was tipped out as he searched for some clue as to where Lucy had gone. Frustrated, he was just about to leave when he noticed the corner of a piece of paper poking out from under the sofa. Carefully he slid it out with the toe of his shoe.

Bingo! It was an email from her father and, lo and behold, all the information he could possibly need to find Lucy Cooper. No need to mess with Sadie Khan, which was just as well; the whole cock-up was already doing his head in. As for sorting out Paul Gower, Don could forget it, Jonno thought. He didn't need that dickhead any more and doing favours wasn't his style.

He carefully folded the email, put it in his pocket and sauntered out, gently closing the door behind himself. No one would ever know that Jonno McMahon had ever been there.

Except, of course, George who had been watching warily through the gap in his front door and mentally making a note about everything to do with Jonno so that he could offer up a perfect description of him to Lucy.

Sadie was disappointed with herself. By her own stupidity she had lost Lucy as a friend and now she was being cold-shouldered by Lorraine and even Fergus.

'Shit,' she mumbled crossly under her breath as she gazed at the computer screen in her office without seeing it. Her mind was elsewhere. She couldn't understand herself sometimes. All her working week was spent solving problems both with clients and her own staff and she was good at it, she knew that. But when it came to her own life she always screwed up. It had happened at primary school with Mary, at senior school with Sophie, at University with Lucy and now with Lorraine. All she wanted was one really close friend, someone who needed her as much as she needed them, but as soon as she found it, she blew it every time by getting too involved in their lives. Now she had no close friend, no confidante and no one whose life she could emulate. Sadie tried to detach herself from her situation and look at herself from a different perspective, to see herself as others saw her.

She guessed her parents were proud of her but they never actually said so. Her academic and career success was expected and failure something that couldn't be considered. The family focus now was on getting her married but although there had been several attempts to arrange a suitable marriage for her, Sadie had so far resisted. At some point she would have to give in, before she got too old and nobody would want her, and that would upset her parents too much, but she couldn't really imagine being married. The thought of sharing her life and her bed with a man she didn't know appalled her. She loved men as friends but nothing else.

Could she be a lesbian? She asked herself the forbidden question and tried to analyse her response. No, she thought, she wasn't. She couldn't imagine having sex with a woman any more than she could imagine it with a man.

Sadie decided she was emotionally stunted. All she wanted was a really close friendship, almost a teenage friendship, like she had enjoyed with Lucy when they had shared the flat before Don came along.

Was that rational behaviour for a woman of twenty-seven? She knew it wasn't but at the same time she couldn't really see what was wrong with it. Until, of course, it became obsessive and therefore self-destructive.

She had even messed up with Lorraine, the woman she would most love to be. Attractive and effervescent, needing no man in her life and enjoying a terrific social life. But because of the way she, Sadie, had treated Lucy, the friendship with Lorraine had been decidedly brief. She had screwed up once again.

A knock on her door interrupted her thoughts.

'Yes?' She didn't mean to be abrupt but she really didn't want to be disturbed.

'Sadie, I've got a problem, have you got five minutes?'

'Sorry, David, but I haven't, I've got a meeting. Can it wait until tomorrow?'

The young man backed out. 'OK, but can we pencil in a time? I really need some advice.'

'Four o'clock. Now I have to go.' Decisively Sadie stood up and grabbed her briefcase. Signing out, she filled in the imaginary meeting and left the office.

She just couldn't deal with any more problems. She would have to have some time off. She might even go and see Lucy, try and put things right. As Lorraine had said, she really didn't have a God-given right to be party to all Lucy's secrets.

Lucy was still giving Fergus a hard time and refusing to let him move in, although he stayed at the weekends.

'I don't want you, or me for that matter, to rush into anything, Fergus. We've got all the time in the world and I need to adjust to my new life. I'm a lady of leisure now and I have to get used to it.'

'Why can't we adjust together?'

'Maybe we can eventually but for the moment it's just nice to get to know each other properly.' Lucy smiled affectionately at him to take the edge off of her words. 'I mean, I didn't know which side of the bed you preferred, which toothpaste you liked. It's all the little things. I mean, do you like the furnishings here? Is this your taste? It's not really mine, I don't do chintz, but it might be yours, and what about the village? Could you live in a village or do you prefer the city? See? We don't know each other at all, do we?'

'No we don't, but we can learn, can't we?'

The phone rang.

'Jeez, Lucy, that phone is going to drive me crazy, it always rings at the wrong moment. Leave it.'

'Oh, come on, it hardly ever rings here. Anyway, it can only be George, my surrogate granddad. He's taken me under his wing.'

By the time she got to it, the answerphone had cut in.

'Hello, lovey, George here. I just wondered if you'd arranged to let your flat, only there was a man there, he had a key and let himself in, he was there for—'

Lucy snatched up the phone. 'Hello, George. What was that about someone in the flat? No, I haven't done anything about letting it yet and nobody, except you, has a key. What did he look like?'

There was a pause. 'Just getting my notebook. I wrote it all down just in case.'

Lucy looked at Fergus and frowned. Putting her hand over the receiver, she whispered, 'Someone has been in the flat – sorry, George, I'm listening.'

'He was approximately five foot ten and about fifty. Dressed all in black. His hair was dark brown and slicked back with a little grey in the sideboards. Oh, and he was wearing snakeskin shoes but I think they were fake, and a chunky gold bracelet on one arm and a gold Rolex, may have been fake, on the other. He had keys to both doors and was in there for nearly an hour. Does that help?'

'Yes, George, it does. It sounds like Jonno McMahon from the gym. He must have got the keys from Don. I wonder what he was looking for.'

'You, I think, Lucy. He's been round before, I think, spoke to that young lad in number three, asked if he knew where you were.'

'What did he say?' Lucy was starting to sweat and she felt quite faint.

'Just that you had moved. He didn't let him inside the building.'

'Thanks, George. What would I do without you? And when are you coming to see me?' Lucy chatted for a while, despite just wanting to put the phone down and scream.

'What was that all about?' The concern on Fergus's face completely belied his casual tone of voice.

'Jonno McMahon has been into my flat, he had keys. The thought of that slimy bastard nosing through all my things makes me feel sick.'

'Was there anything there that would help him find you?'

'No, nothing, but it still makes me feel ill. How dare they? What do you think they're up to, him and Don?'

'I don't know, but what I do know is you're not going to stay here alone. Like it or not, I'm staying. There's more going on here than just Don being a pain in the arse, this

322

smells really dodgy. I think you should call the police.'

'But what about your job? It's too far—'

'I'm going to go off sick. I'm not leaving you here on your own.'

'I don't understand it, it's just not like her. Something must have happened, something to do with Don maybe. Do you think we ought to call the police?' Luke threw the question out generally.

Caroline, Luke and Paul were having a crisis meeting. When Lucy had failed to either turn up or respond to their messages, both Luke and Paul had been to her flat, but with no success.

Caroline's first reaction had been to rant and rave, sack her in her absence, curse her to hell and back and then just get on with the job of clearing up. The contractors were called in to deal with the superficial clearing up but it was down to the staff and the IT experts to get to grips with everything else, but three weeks on the office still wasn't functioning properly.

'I imagine she's just done a bunk away from that pseudo-human husband of hers,' Caroline said. 'I can't believe she would leave us in the lurch like this. For God's sake, fifty per cent of the relevant information on the Vegas account is in her head, we haven't even had her write-up on it yet. I told you it wasn't on, Luke. I told you but you knew best. Now look where we are.' Caroline was pacing the floor and Luke and Paul had to keep moving their feet out of her way. Back and forth she went.

'Hey, calm down. This isn't helping. Lucy wouldn't do this for no reason.'

Caroline spun round. 'Luke, stop defending her. Good God, without all this nonsense Paul would be in New York keeping our clients happy and we would be continuing our successful expansion. This has set us all back.' Caroline paced even faster. 'What she has done is unforgivable. I just hope she doesn't expect a reference from us because all I would say is that when the going gets tough, Lucy Cooper bales out.'

Tentatively Paul spoke for the first time. He had never seen Caroline lose it before. 'I agree with Luke, this isn't like Lucy. I know we had our differences but she was strong on loyalty and she always went the extra mile when it was required.'

Caroline laughed humourlessly. 'You couldn't stand the sight of her, Paul. Why the sudden support for your arch rival?'

'Sorry, Caroline, but that's really not true. We might have had the odd falling out but that was it. I admire her tremendously for working through all the shit she had to put up with. No, Luke is right, something must have happened to her and I'd also lay a penny to a pound it's to do with Don.'

Luke looked at Paul, wondering if he should put his concerns into words.

'Paul,' he said tentatively, 'did you know that Don Cooper thought that you and Lucy had something going together? That he was convinced you and Lucy were having an affair?'

'I wish.' Paul started to laugh, but remembering where he was he stopped abruptly. 'Whatever makes you think that?'

'Lucy told me herself. Bearing that in mind, do you think it's possible that Don had something to do with your so-called mugging that wasn't really a mugging, just a battering for no apparent reason? You said your attackers warned you to stay away from married women.'

'No way, Luke.'

'Oh, for heaven's sake, Luke,' Caroline cut in. 'You're just clutching at straws now to excuse the girl's behaviour.'

'No I'm not. I think Donovan Cooper is only one step removed from being a certifiable psychopath. He thinks Lucy is having an affair with Paul; Paul gets beaten up. Paul and Lucy both work at Pettit's, we get vandalised and again nothing is stolen. Lucy tells Don she's leaving him, Don smashes their apartment to smithereens. The common denominator is?'

'Don.' Paul's voice was expressionless. 'It's all possible so, to move it on a step, what's next for him? It has to be Lucy. I bet she's in hiding somewhere and doesn't want us to know where she is in case he comes rampaging in here looking for her.'

'I said all along it would end up back here.' Caroline sat down sharply. 'If, and I say this with reservations, you are right, Luke, then I suggest we are all very careful because Don Cooper isn't doing this alone.'

'I'll see what I can find out,' Paul offered, 'maybe I can charm some information out of someone, somewhere.'

Paul and Sadie both turned up at Lucy's door at the same time.

'You're Paul, aren't you? You work with Lucy.'

'Yes, that's right, and you are? Sorry, I'm not good at

names,' Paul lied easily. He couldn't remember if he had ever met the woman standing beside him or not.

'Sadie, Sadie Khan. I'm a friend of Lucy's – well, I was until a few months ago when we had a big falling out. I've come with a peace offering.' The bunch of cellophane-wrapped carnations that Sadie was holding looked a bit sad but Paul smiled encouragingly.

'Nice thought. Does she know you're coming?'

'No, there's been a bit of a stand-off so I thought I'd just turn up. These things are easier sorted face to face. Why do you ask?'

'Well, I'm hoping that we're wrong but it seems that Lucy has disappeared off the face of the earth and we're worried sick about her at Pettit's. I know there have been problems with the apeman, Don. Do you know her husband?'

Sadie's face tightened. 'Too right I know him, and I know what he's capable of. I hate him with a passion. Are you sure she's just not answering the phone or the door? Maybe she doesn't want to see anyone if Don has been giving her a hard time again. He won't have been impressed with her going off to the States without him.'

'Well then, let's see if she'll answer the door to you. After you with the buzzer.'

As Sadie put her finger up to the intercom, the door opened and an elderly gentleman looked them up and down.

'Can I help you?'

'We're here to see Lucy Cooper, she lives on the top floor.'

'Not any more she doesn't, I'm afraid. She's moved.'

326

'Since when?' Sadie shot back at him.

'About three weeks ago, and no, she didn't leave a forwarding address but I'm more than happy to collect names and numbers just in case she returns for anything.' With that George put on his favourite vacant expression, the one that ensured he was quickly dismissed as a vague old man who knew nothing. It worked a treat with canvassers and door-to-door salesmen.

'Yeah, OK, but it's really important we get in touch with her, we're very worried. If you do see her then I'm Paul Gower and this is Sadie . . .' Paul paused and looked at her.

'Khan, I'm Sadie Khan. Paul works with her and I'm an old friend. I'm sure you've seen me before, I stayed here for a while with Lucy. We're both a little worried so it would be nice if she could call us.'

'OK. I'll tell her if by any chance I do see her, but as I've said, she's moved.'

Paul and Sadie walked away together.

'Tea break?' Paul suggested.

'Good idea,' Sadie responded. 'Maybe we can pool some information. There must be some way to find her. I could phone Lorraine, she might know or, if push comes to shove, I'm sure I've got her parents' address somewhere.' Sadie was almost talking to herself.

Paul shook his head. 'Maybe we ought to go to the police. There's something wrong here, I'm sure of it. Lucy thinks too much of her career to do this without a damned good reason.'

Chapter Seventeen

After talking it through and sharing everything they knew, Paul and Sadie took the bull by the horns and went together to the local police station with what little information they had. Predictably, they didn't get much of a response, so Paul was surprised when soon afterwards two plain-clothed police officers visited each of them separately. They were the same two detectives who had been involved in the original arrest of Donovan Cooper.

They hadn't believed Don's cock-and-bull story. In their experienced eyes, the big lump of a man was nothing more than a mule, maybe unknowingly, for someone else, and a born bully whose use of steroids made him prone to fits of uncontrollable rage. No one who had just successfully, and knowingly, brought a large consignment of class A drugs through customs at an international airport would then leave them carelessly lying around in a suitcase. Despite the raging bull behaviour, it would surely have filtered through even his confused brain that police plus a large amount of cocaine in his bag equalled big trouble and he would have at least made some attempt to hide it.

Paul told them about the possible connection between his assault and the break-in at Pettit's and they didn't dismiss the theory out of hand. In fact they found it a distinct possibility.

Once they started to piece together everything they had and found out where Don worked and who he had been in Portugal with, alarm bells started ringing straight away.

Jonno McMahon. The one who always got away.

It didn't take them long to track down Lucy.

They knocked on George Beacham's door and he opened it cautiously, with the chain on.

'Hello, sir. We're investigating the whereabouts of a neighbour of yours, Mrs Lucy Cooper. She owns one of the top floor flats. Do you know anything about where she might be? When did you last see her?'

George wanted to say he knew nothing but he couldn't bring himself to lie to the police. 'Come in, officers. I have a phone call to make and then I will talk to you.'

Leaving the officers in the front room, he picked up the phone in the hall and dialled Lucy's number.

'Lucy, I'm sorry, but the police are here and they're looking for you. What do you want me to say to them?'

'Put them on the phone, George. It's OK, you've done more than enough for me. I'll take it from here, and if they want to have a look round the flat then let them. This is all getting a bit too complicated.'

Reluctantly Lucy revealed her whereabouts and agreed to be interviewed at the cottage. She also gave George the go-ahead to tell the detectives anything they wanted to know.

George did precisely that, leaving them agog at his meticulous note-taking and memory for detail. His notebook would have put many a lackadaisical police officer to shame.

The detectives retrieved the answerphone tape of Don's last threatening phone call, in which he had mentioned Jonno. Lucy hadn't wiped it and Jonno had missed it. They dusted the flat for fingerprints but Jonno had been too clever to leave any. For the moment all they had was the tape, George's description of Jonno and the details of the man who had hung around watching the flat. Donovan Cooper himself was zip-lipped; his fear of Jonno McMahon was stronger than the thought of a long prison sentence surrounded by acquaintances of Jonno.

'I don't really understand how this has all come about.' Lucy looked at the detectives. 'I told you everything I knew about Don and the drugs and all the other stuff that went on. Why has this come up again? Has someone said something?'

'Actually yes, two friends of yours who were concerned about your alleged disappearance.' The officer flicked his notebook open. 'Paul Gower and Sadie Khan.'

'Ah.' Lucy sighed. 'Now I feel mean. I should have – oh shit, shit, shit, I've just realised, with everything that was going on I forgot to send the letter and the files to work.' Lucy's face was a picture of pure horror. She couldn't believe what she had done. 'No wonder they're looking for me.'

'Perhaps you ought to get in touch with them then, they've done you a favour by bringing all this into the open. There are concerns that your husband was behind both the mugging of Mr Gower and the vandalising at Pettit's. Add that to Mr Cooper's behaviour and the information we received from your neighbour Mr Beacham and we need to look a lot further into all this.'

The other detective spoke almost aggressively. 'Why didn't you get in touch with us about the man watching your flat? You could have put a lot of people in danger. We're dealing with serious crime and serious criminals here. It certainly wasn't very helpful, to say the least.'

Lucy flushed angrily. Angry at them talking to her as if she was a criminal herself, but also angry because she knew they were right.

Everyone she had any connection with was affected by the whole affair. According to the detectives, Luke and Caroline went everywhere together now and security both at their home and at the office had been tightened considerably. They were also both staying in London all the time because the apartment was easier to secure than the rambling country house in acres of grounds.

Paul had grudgingly accepted police advice and moved into a friend's house for the moment. Sadie was with her parents on the pretext of needing some time off from work. Lorraine had her dogs and a top-of-the-range security system but the television company had also provided her with a bodyguard. Latisha Lowe was an expensive investment and they had to protect her. Wily old George had only his instincts and his old cricket bat by the door but that was all he wanted.

And of course Fergus didn't leave the very pregnant Lucy's side, but that actually suited him very nicely, it was the only place he wanted to be anyway.

Lucy hated having her privacy invaded, albeit officially. But at the same time she felt a tiny element of relief that it was all in the hands of the police. The threat of danger was wearing her down and making her paranoid. If she had been living somewhere familiar, she thought, she could have handled it a bit better but because she didn't know a soul in the village, any passing stranger walking his dog or making his way to the local pub could just as easily be connected to Jonno McMahon and Don. She treated every ring of the telephone and every knock on the door with suspicion.

Before the detectives left, they promised not to tell anyone about the imminent baby, and to keep her whereabouts secret. Then they went off to interview Don again in the hope of nailing Jonno McMahon once and for all. The operation to finally catch the sleazeball and see him imprisoned had become their challenge.

'Oh Fergus, what a great big can of worms we've opened. What started out as a few flirty glances exchanged over the reception desk at Pettit's has caused all this chaos. It just goes to prove there's substance in the theory that a solitary butterfly gently flapping its wings in the middle of the ocean can eventually cause a tidal wave thousands of miles away.'

'Butterflies don't live in the ocean and if they ever did decide to fly that way, their lifespan isn't long enough for them to get past Dover.'

'Ha ha, very funny. But just think about it, think how many people have been affected. Margot and India, Caroline and Luke, Paul, in fact nearly everyone I can think of. Even Sadie, who is obviously worried about me. This has impacted on them all and just because we couldn't keep our hands off each other.'

'I don't think so, Lucy. Margot and India I will take responsibility for, but everyone else? No way. Don would have done what he's done without us. Don't forget, he still doesn't even know about us, does he? He thinks you're having an affair with Paul. No, lay the blame where it belongs, squarely at Donovan Cooper's door. Now, fat woman, what are we going to do for the rest of the day?'

Lucy was stretched out full length on the sofa. She picked up a cushion and threw it across the room at him. There was no way of disguising the bump now. When she twisted and turned in front of the mirror, it never failed to surprise her that she looked absolutely normal from the front and the back. But sideways on she looked as if someone had stuffed a football up her jumper. She would often stand close up to the mirror, watching her bare belly take on a life of its own as the baby kicked and elbowed its way around inside her, looking as if it was trying to break out. The friendly village midwife regularly popped in and exchanged a check-up for a cup of tea and a chat. Living in the cottage was never meant to be a permanent thing; Lucy was a city girl and she knew she would go back to London sooner or later, but for the time being she was enjoying the slower pace of life.

Despite anticipating that something might happen, the day that it did, and the way that it did, caught everyone by surprise.

The knock on the door sent Fergus cautiously to the

spyhole and Lucy to the window in the sitting room.

'It's OK,' she called to him as she saw the delivery van parked by the kerb and a man with a box in his hands and a clipboard under his arm. 'I think it's the baby stuff I ordered.'

Fergus opened the door and a smiling driver, his face shielded by a baseball cap and a lowered head, handed over the package. 'Sign here, sir, please.'

Fergus picked up the large box and put it down inside the hall before taking the clipboard. It was then that he saw the gun lying almost innocently in the hand of the delivery man.

'Not a word now, just back away a little and let me in.' The man had stopped smiling.

Involuntarily, Fergus looked towards the sitting room and Lucy.

'Don't even think about it,' the man muttered quietly. He pulled a scarf up over his face, tugged his baseball cap lower over his forehead and pushed the gun into Fergus's stomach.

Fergus backed into the hall, and as the man closed the door behind him, he saw the van drive off slowly. The gunman had an accomplice.

'What have we got, Fergus?' Lucy's voice carried out into the small square hall.

Fergus and the man looked at each other.

'Go on then, in you go, don't keep the lady waiting.'

The expectation on her face changed rapidly to one of undisguised fear when Lucy saw the masked man with a gun firmly clasped in his hand. A gun that was pointing directly at Fergus's back.

'Who are you?' Lucy whispered. 'What do you want?'

'You, Mrs Cooper. You are what I want and it looks like I've got what I want, haven't I?'

There was a gentle tap on the window and for a moment Fergus hoped against hope that someone had seen something.

The man waved the gun in the direction of the front door. 'Go and let my mate in, will you? And don't bother trying anything because I've got the girlfriend and the gun.'

The second man also pulled a scarf up over his face as Fergus let him in. In a strange way the movement reassured him because if they didn't want to be identified then maybe he and Lucy might get out alive.

'Right, both of you, no fucking about now, just hand over your mobiles.'

'It's upstairs.' Lucy trembled as she spoke.

'Go and get it then. My mate will go with you.' He looked at Fergus. 'And where's yours?'

'I haven't got one.'

The barrel of the gun whipped across his face so fast he barely saw it. He felt it, however.

'Bollocks,' the man snarled. 'Go and get it.'

Lucy started to cry, she couldn't help it, but she wasn't making any noise. Eyes wide, the tears rolled down her face and dripped onto her T-shirt.

Fergus felt his eye swelling up and closing. 'I promise you, I really don't have one. We have one between us, that's all we need, we're always together.'

'How sweet,' the man sneered, and then looked at Lucy. 'Go on then, go and get it.'

Lucy stood up slowly and the second man gasped.

'Fucking hell, man, she's pregnant. Look at the size of her, we can't do this, she's about to pop.'

A chink of light appeared in Lucy's brain, an awareness of sympathy from the man, so she deliberately stood with her back arched and her stomach pushed out as far as it would go.

'Then pop she will. Don't be such a prick,' the first man replied. 'She's not the first woman to carry a sprog and she won't be the last. Fact of life. Go on, take her up to find the phone.' He looked at Lucy. 'And don't even bother to think about the landline, it's cut.'

Playing on the second man's reluctance, Lucy slowly plodded up the stairs, pulling on the banister with one hand while the other massaged the small of her back.

'You OK there? Do you need a hand? Just tell me where the phone is and I'll get it for you.'

'Oh, would you? Thanks.' Lucy looked at him and smiled despite the tears. 'It's beside the bed, I keep it there for emergencies, I haven't got a phone upstairs yet.' Lucy frantically tried to think how she could take advantage of the man's sympathy.

'Come on, get a move on and get back down. We've got business to attend to.' The voice that shouted from downstairs was aggressive and impatient. Lucy was concerned for Fergus.

She waited for the second man and they went back into the lounge together.

'Got it.'

'Give it here then. All clear upstairs?' The first man held his hand out and the second man handed over the phone.

'Yep, as far as I could see.'

'Good, now we can get down to business.'

Fergus's eyes were all over the place, on the gun, on the two men and on Lucy. If only he could communicate with her somehow.

'What's all this about?' he asked.

'What it's about, not that it's any of your business, is that Mrs Cooper here got Mr Cooper arrested and she gave the old bill something that wasn't hers to give away. Now my job is to recoup the lost cash as per the retail value to us of the goods involved. As soon as we've got that, plus a bit extra for the inconvenience you've caused us, we'll just toddle off back to where we came from. Nobody gets hurt and everybody's happy. A couple of hundred grand should just about cover it.'

Lucy was listening carefully; the first man's voice was familiar but she couldn't place it.

'Two hundred thousand pounds?' she said. 'In your dreams. I'm overdrawn.'

'Maybe, maybe not, but if you can't find it yourself then we know a man who can.'

'Who's that?'

'Your father. I hear you're daddy's little princess and money is no object so just one phone call and all your problems will be solved.'

'Did Don send you? Is this his way of getting back at me?'

'Sweetheart, no one *sends* me anywhere, least of all that plank Don Cooper. Now enough chatter. Phone the old man and get the cash or the latest in your long line of boyfriends here is going to have to, very slowly, end up in

338

considerable pain. Quite the little slag on the sly, aren't you?'

'What do you mean?' Lucy burst out. 'You don't even know me.'

He laughed. 'Oh, I know everything about you, absolutely fucking everything. Who do you think it was that sorted out your last boyfriend? You've upset a lot of people, little lady. Now talk to the old folks and get our money.'

'But I don't even know where my parents are, they're travelling between Dubai in the Middle East and Texas in America all the time.'

'I don't need a geography lesson, I just need you to find them and I'm sure you can if you really try.'

Fergus was trying to send Lucy a silent message. 'Don't argue with him,' he wanted to say. 'Do as he says and buy some time, enough time for me to think.' At that moment Lucy looked at him, the terror in her eyes undisguised. Imperceptibly he nodded his head. Just the tiniest movement but Lucy saw it.

'OK, OK, I'll try, but I may have to leave a message.'

'Good girl, now you're getting the idea. It's quite easy really.'

Remembering George's detailed description of Jonno, Fergus decided to concentrate and try to do the same.

Man One. Six foot. Twelve stone. Darkish hair. Eyes brown. Blue stonewashed jeans. Cheap. Black trainers. Cheap. Black tracksuit zipper top. Black baseball cap. No logo. Man Two. Five foot eight. Ten stone. Ginger hair. Eyes blue. Clothes ditto. All new, probably bought for the occasion.

'Oi! Paddywack, I'm talking to you.'

Fergus jumped.

'Not boring you, are we?'

'I was looking at Lucy, can't you see she's going into labour? She's expecting a baby, for Christ's sake.'

Quickly Lucy grabbed her stomach. 'It's all right, Fergus, just a twinge, I'll be OK.'

'Holy shit, man, we've got to go, we can't carry on with this now. I'm not going to be responsible for anything going wrong.' The second man seemed genuinely disturbed so Lucy focused her attention on him.

'I'll be OK, I just need to breathe. Do you mind if I open the window a little?'

The second man had already taken two steps before he was stopped in his tracks.

'Touch that window, asshole, and you'll be the one in pain. Can't you see she's putting it on? This is turning into a pantomime. Now you,' he pointed at Lucy, 'I'm going to give you your phone and you're going to ring Daddy and tell him what we want, and you can tell him that I have absolutely no qualms about maiming either you or your boyfriend here . . .' He hesitated as Lucy gasped again.

Lucy desperately wanted to go to the loo, the baby was pressing down on her bladder and it was uncomfortable. She had a flash of inspiration although she still found it hard to overcome her natural modesty.

She let her muscles relax and as she stood up she emptied her bladder.

'Oh, my waters have broken, oh God, what am I going to do?'

True or not? wondered Fergus desperately.

'Can I go and get some towels?' he said urgently. 'Please? You can't leave her like that.'

'I'll go with him,' the second man blurted out. 'You've got to let him help her.'

'Go on then, but remember, I've got your woman and a gun.'

Fergus went up the stairs three paces ahead of the second man. He ran into the bedroom where the airing cupboard was and flung the door open wide. So wide that it shielded his jacket which was hooked on the back of a chair.

'Help me grab some towels, will you? I don't know what we need, I've never done this before. I'm just shit scared. The baby's not due yet and she's already had problems.'

The man leaned in and started pulling towels out, leaving Fergus just enough manoeuvrability to reach into his jacket pocket and grab his mobile, which by pure chance was on silent mode.

'I'll just get a wet flannel. Have you got kids?'

'Yeah, I've got three. I started young.'

'And were you there at the births?'

'Yeah, but in hospital, not in the middle of my fucking lounge!'

'I know, nightmare, isn't it?'

A voice shouted up the stairs. 'Come on, what are you up to?'

'We're coming, just getting some gear.'

Fergus took a deep breath, and while rummaging in the bathroom cupboard with one hand, he felt the digits on the phone and pressed 999.

'Right, let's go before your mate gets trigger-happy. You

take those and I'll take these.'

The man ran down the stairs, leaving Fergus just enough time to speak. 'Police, help. Hostage. They've got guns. Begonia Lodge, Camersley.'

Clicking off the phone he stuffed it between the towels and ran as fast as he could down the stairs. He went straight over to Lucy whose eye fluttered just enough for him to recognise a wink.

'Here, Lucy, grab these and sit on them.' As he handed them to her, he looked down and lifted the corner of the bundle. Fergus was standing between her and the first man as Lucy palmed the phone and stuffed it down her waistband of her very damp trousers, then he moved to the side so that they were both in full view of both the men. 'It's OK, sweetheart, we'll manage, we'll manage if we have to.'

He turned to the first man. 'Look, I know what you're here for but this baby isn't due for another few weeks, what's going to happen if something goes wrong? Please let me call an ambulance.'

'No fucking way, I'm seeing this through regardless. I've got an interest in that cash myself.'

The second man protested. 'What if the baby dies? What if she dies? No way, man, I'm out of here.'

He turned towards the door and Fergus saw the gun start to rise. Jeez, he thought, he's going to shoot him in the back. Fergus jumped forward and tried to push the gun towards the ceiling. There was a scuffle, Lucy screamed and the second man was on the floor, trying to crawl to the door.

Lucy physically jumped when the gun went off. The

second man was still moving but Fergus was lying on the floor clutching his shoulder. Blood seeped through his fingers.

'You bastard, you've shot him, you've shot him.' Forgetting about the gun the man was still holding Lucy went over to Fergus and knelt down beside him. He was as white as a sheet and the blood was spreading. Lucy didn't register the police sirens in the distance.

The two men did. The second man sat up and put his head despondently in his hands, but the first man pointed the gun at Lucy.

'Get up, you're coming with me. I need you to get me out of here.'

Lucy stood up slowly, terrified, torn between helping Fergus and protecting herself and the baby. As she straightened, her head spun and she slumped back to the floor, out cold.

'Look what you've done to her, you fucking maniac!' The second man rose from the floor like a cat jumping onto a fence. He landed smack on top of the other one and they both fell to the ground. This time Fergus got his hand to the dropped gun and pointed it at them.

Despite the pain and blood loss, he struggled to his feet and backed into the hall. He opened the front door and called out. 'Police ... help ... it was me that called you ... I've got the gun and my pregnant wife has collapsed ... please help.'

'EVERYBODY COME OUT OF THE HOUSE WITH YOUR HANDS ABOVE YOUR HEADS AND LIE DOWN ON THE GROUND WITH YOUR ARMS AND LEGS SPREAD ...'

Fergus kept the gun trained on the two men until they got to the door, then he tossed it out and the three of them went out and lay down.

'Lucy is still inside, she's pregnant and has collapsed, somebody help her.'

By the time Lucy came round, Fergus had been taken off in an ambulance and the two men, now without their scarves, were being led away. Now Lucy could put a face and name to the voice.

'Tony?' She looked at him in disbelief. 'Tony, how could you do that to me? How could you?'

He grinned at her, a familiar almost friendly grin that belied the events of the last couple of hours. 'These things happen, sweetheart. No hard feelings, eh?'

'You bastard, you were Don's friend.'

He laughed. 'Me? Friends with dickhead Don Cooper? In your dreams, lady!'

The second, unfamiliar man looked at her, his face a mask of misery. 'I'm sorry, I didn't know what was going to happen, I never would have gone if I'd known. How do you know Tony?'

'He's been in my home, eaten my food and drunk my drink. He's Don's drinking buddy.' She looked over at him again. '*Bastard.*'

The second man was still looking at her. 'I'm sorry.'

'I know, but at this moment that's no consolation.'

Lucy didn't look at either of them again as she climbed into the back of the waiting ambulance to be taken to hospital. All she could think of was that surely it was all over now. There was no way Don could get away with this one, or Jonno for that matter.

She lay on the stretcher and relaxed as blankets were wrapped round her. Everything seemed far away and disjointed, and she wondered briefly if she would wake up and discover that none of it was real.

Then she became aware of a strong smell of urine.

It was real. It had happened.

The tears started slowly but, once they started, there was no stopping them.

Chapter Eighteen

Lucy sat beside Fergus's hospital bed, unharmed but feeling exhausted and tearful after a night in the hospital under observation. After she was discharged she had gone home to wash and change but then had made her way back almost immediately to see Fergus and reassure herself that it was all over.

She tried to smile and unconsciously rubbed her stomach. 'Well, Fergus, you're a bit of a celebrity again. The world and his mother have been wanting to know the story, according to the nurse. I suppose it's big news for a small village. If we were still in London no one would even have noticed, let alone been interested. A bit of a gun siege there is on a par with a whiff of puff!' Her hand continued to rotate. 'The local rag have left messages and they've been trying to get in to see you for a photo and a quote but the staff aren't having any of it. My hero!' Lucy kissed her hands, pressed them to her forehead and then, palms up, held them out to him and bowed her head.

Fergus reached out weakly and touched her knee. 'Enough already, you! I'm certainly not a hero round here. I reckon they all think we've besmirched their little village by bringing a touch of London gangsterism with us, but it'll die down soon, as soon as they find Mrs Dalton's missing cat or catch the milkman spending too long in number thirty.' He attempted a smile but it was fairly half-hearted – his shoulder throbbed and his head was still muggy from sedatives and painkillers.

'But never mind London gangsters,' he raised his eyes to the ceiling, 'far worse than that, Margot is coming this afternoon with India. I told them not to but there you go, Margot always was a law unto herself. I just hope she doesn't get hold of what really happened, she would probably string both of us up, and I'm sure you don't want to meet her in here.'

Lucy's heart sank. 'How did they find out?' Then it dawned on her. 'You phoned her, didn't you?'

'I had to, I couldn't have India finding out about it from the papers or a reporter,' Fergus pleaded. 'India is my daughter, don't forget, she had to know what had happened to me. I wanted to tell her and she's too young to get here by herself. Simon is driving them down.'

'Why all of them? Why the whole family?' Lucy was more than a little scared at the thought of a confrontation with the notorious Margot and her family. 'Why does Margot have to come? I suppose I can understand India, but Margot? And Simon? Come on, Fergus, that's pushing it a bit. Next thing all your old friends will be thrashing down here. And what about the family from Ireland? Or Jamaica even?'

Fergus winced. 'Ouch, that was a bit mean for someone in my fragile condition. I'm supposed to be having peace and quiet.'

'Oh, quit the jokes just for once. You won't get much peace and quiet with Margot in here shouting the odds. Why did you phone? What exactly has all this got to do with Margot now?'

Looking completely bewildered, as if he was unable to comprehend Lucy's irritation, Fergus tried to calm her down. 'India is entitled to know, she has a right. Anyway, it's too late now to change it. I never expected them all to hot-foot it down here but Margot is India's mother and I thought as I've been shot, they're bound to be a tad concerned, although maybe they're just enjoying it and are coming to gloat.' Smiling, Fergus tried to diffuse the situation.

'Who else have you told? Is Lorraine due here any moment with a celebrity photographer in tow? Oh yes, I can just see it in *Hello!* magazine. "Compassionate actress rushes to shooting victim's bedside." That'll make sure everyone knows the ins and outs of the whole bloody fiasco.'

'You're being a touch over-dramatic, aren't you? It wasn't exactly my fault all this happened. And yes, I did call Lorraine actually, but she won't say anything, as you well know.' He paused. 'You don't really mind, do you?'

Lucy could feel her irritation fading away. 'I'm sorry, you're right, I'm being a thoughtless bitch. Of course you were right to tell them, they're your family and friends, after all.' Leaning forward, Lucy was about to plant a kiss on his forehead when the crack of the door against the wall made her jump back.

A troop of doctors and nurses swept in. The small side ward was suddenly so crowded, Lucy ended up pressed against the metal bedhead.

'Well, Mr Pearson, how do you feel today without that piece of ammunition lodged in your body?' Before Fergus had a chance to reply, the doctor continued, 'You really are a very lucky man. The bullet missed all your organs, it even bypassed most of the bones. You should be up and about shortly, all being well. A couple of days and you can go home. A fortunate escape, I think.' Tall and thin, almost to the point of emaciation, the consultant smiled gauntly as he looked around at the white-coated students who were with him. 'Any questions?' He passed a cursory glance over Fergus. 'No? OK, let's take a look then. It's not often we get gunshot wounds in this hospital. If you'll excuse us for a minute or two, Mrs Pearson.'

'My name is Cooper, Ms Cooper.' As soon as she said it Lucy realised how pompous it sounded but it annoyed her that everyone made assumptions on the strength of her pregnancy.

'Apologies, Ms Cooper—'

A loud and angry voice at the nurses' station just outside interrupted him.

'I don't give a stuff who's with him, I'm going to see him. Now tell me where Fergus Pearson is before I go and search for myself. I know this is the right ward – just look at this poor child, she has the right to see her father, and if that bleeding Lorraine is in there I'm really going to kick off, I'm telling you. So tell me where he is.'

As everyone turned towards the door, Fergus looked at

Lucy, an expression of sheer panic on his face.

'It's Margot, she'll go mad if she sees you, if she finds out who you are. What are you going to do? Now's not the time for a confrontation, not if India is with her.'

Lucy's irritation returned. 'I'm not going to do anything apart from leave. I don't want to be part of this, thank you very much. You phoned her, you can deal with it.'

Looking down to avoid all the curious eyes in the room, Lucy slid out of the door and, turning into the corridor, walked in the opposite direction to where Margot and her family were standing. She stopped at a noticeboard, pretending complete absorption, and listened. She desperately wanted to look, to see the harridan Margot and the family she had heard so much about, but was too nervous of a public scene.

'I'm telling you, I want to see my husband.'

'Your husband? But I thought . . .' The nurse pulled herself up, tactfully trying to avoid putting her foot in it.

'Thought what? I've already told you, Fergus Pearson is my husband and this is his daughter and stepson, and we want to see him *now*.'

'If you could hold on just a moment then, Mrs Pearson, I'll be right back. As I said, the doctors are with him at the moment.'

Lucy watched out of the corner of her eye as the nurse, unaware that Margot was hot on her heels, hurried into Fergus's room. As she opened the door, Margot pushed past, closely followed by India and then Simon.

'What's all this crap about you getting shot up, you stupid dumb bastard?'

Despite everything Fergus had told her, Lucy was still

horrified at Margot's relentless aggression.

'It was an accident, just one of those things. I'll tell you all about it later. Can you give us five minutes? The doctors are just checking me out.'

'I just wanna know what's going on.' India's shrill tone made Lucy wince. 'Come on, Dad, fess up. Jeez, my dad in a shoot-out. See, Si? He's not such a boring old git after all.'

'Not now, India, and keep your voice down, there are some really sick people here, you know.' Fergus's voice had a disheartened edge to it and Lucy could imagine him looking at the daughter whom she knew he loved dearly but disliked intensely.

'That's right, and you, Mr Pearson, are one of them.' The consultant's voice was commanding. 'Now if you'll all excuse me, I have to examine my patient, *in private*. After that you are welcome to come back in but quietly, if you please.'

Lucy turned and quickly left, before Margot and her tribe appeared back in the corridor. Her intention had been to go to the canteen, have something to eat and then go back when the coast was clear, but instead she went outside into the grounds. She suddenly felt unbearably lonely and, almost on auto-pilot, went home.

Back at the cottage, Lucy went straight up to the small bedroom that she had temporarily designated as the nursery. Fergus had given the walls a quick lick of lemon paint, and a pair of bright yellow, teddy bear-edged gingham curtains hung at the windows. All the paraphernalia that seemed to come with a tiny baby was in place. Pride of place went to the frilled and canopied Moses basket on an elaborately carved stand. It contained an unassembled mobile and a plush brown teddy with a yellow satin bow round his neck. Propped up in the corner was a top-of-the-range car seat that had cost a small fortune, even though Lucy hadn't yet got round to buying a car. Every time she looked at it, the silliness made her laugh. A car seat bought on the spur of the moment with no car to put it in. She also smiled at the mountain of babywear, mostly still in their packets, more clothes than one newborn baby could ever get through.

Lucy picked up a small, pristine white sleepsuit and held it to her face with one hand while gently holding her distended stomach with the other. It was hard for her to imagine that the small being kicking inside her would soon be wearing it. Boy or girl? she wondered. Adamant that she didn't want to know at the time of the last scan, she now wished she had found out; that way she would have been able to stop calling the baby 'it'.

Lucy thought back to when the doctor had first told her she was pregnant, how horrified she had been at the thought. Termination and adoption had both gone through her mind but now, as it kicked and squirmed, she was relieved that she had dismissed both options. At some point soon she knew she would have to tell her parents as well as Caroline and Luke. It was hard enough having to face up to everything herself and to go over and over it with anonymous policemen, but the thought of telling family and work colleagues was both daunting and embarrassing. But Lucy knew she had to face up to it. Now the danger had passed, now that Don was hopefully going to stay locked up, maybe she could get some semblance of her life back.

But with or without Fergus?

Feeling alone and dejected, Lucy tried to contemplate her future. Much as she loved Fergus, she wasn't sure if she would be able to trust him completely. And yet there was a baby involved. Don's? Fergus's? Did it really matter? Lucy hoped that it wouldn't, but how could she be sure? It wouldn't be long before word got back to Don that his wife was due to give birth – Tony would see to that. And then? Would Don try and claim the baby as his own? She thought about India, Fergus's daughter, and wondered how she would cope with a difficult adolescent like that.

When the doorbell rang, she gasped with terror and hunched, quivering, on the landing.

The letterbox rattled loudly. 'Ms Cooper? Are you in there? It's the police, Ms Cooper. Are you OK?'

Lucy slid cautiously down the stairs with her back to the wall and silently crept over to the spyhole before carefully opening the door, with the chain in place.

'Are you OK? We've just come to have a chat with you, see if you're up to making a formal statement yet and to update you on the case.'

Relief washed over Lucy as she recognised two of the police officers from the day before. Throwing the door wide, it took all of her willpower not to fall straight into their arms.

'Hey, you're shaking. It's OK, calm down. Would you sooner we came back another time? You don't look too good.'

'No, I'm OK. I'm still jumpy, the doorbell scared the life out of me. I need to know what's going on, whether this really is all over. I don't think I can take much more of it, the last few months have been like a nightmare I haven't been able to wake up from.'

Taking her gently by the shoulder the older of the two men led her into the lounge and to the sofa.

'OK then, we'll talk about it, but first point this young man in the direction of your kitchen and he'll make you a hot drink. I take it you don't want anything stronger?'

'No, it's OK, I don't want anything at all, just information. Have you got Jonno McMahon? What about Don? I have to know if I'm safe, if my baby is safe.'

The detectives looked at each other cautiously.

'Well, it's a bit complex. We have Mr McMahon in custody at the moment but we still have nothing concrete to link him to it all, no one is saying anything and that includes your husband. As it stands, we may well have to bail McMahon but your husband is still locked up and likely to stay there for quite a few years. Still, we're hopeful we'll get them all in the end.'

Lucy frowned. Was she safe or wasn't she?

A sudden sharp contraction made her moan and double up.

'What's wrong? Are you all right?'

'I think the baby is coming, I think I'm going into labour.'

Under normal circumstances it would have made Lucy smile to see two grown men, and policemen at that, exchange worried, wide-eyed glances.

'I'm . . . not . . . expecting . . . you to deliver it . . . Just get me to hospital.'

'You just sit there, Ms Cooper, Lucy, and we'll call an ambulance. Now relax and breathe like they taught you.'

'I never went to any classes, I've been too busy.'

'Well, I have, so trust me. I'm a father of two so I know what I'm talking about. So first things first, *relax . . .*'

'Relax? Are you off your head? How can I relax when I'm about to give birth? And prematurely at that.'

'I'm sure you're not about to deliver on the spot, Lucy, it'll be a while yet. Just don't panic, I'm sure there's no mad rush but we'll get you to hospital as soon as possible.'

When he patted her hand, Lucy wasn't sure whether she felt reassured or not, all she knew was that now the labour had started, she was dreading it and wanted Fergus beside her. But he was in hospital himself and the family from hell was with him.

'You were telling me what's been happening . . .'

'Everything is under control there, we'll talk about it another time. All that matters for now is you and your baby. By the way, I nearly forgot, I've got a letter here for you. We were asked to pass it on but obviously we had to read it first, I hope you don't mind.'

Lucy took the sheet of paper out of the envelope. It was from Sadie.

'I need to make a phone call before I go anywhere.' Lucy smiled.

Fergus would never have believed that it was possible to achieve the high level of embarrassment that completely enveloped him when Margot, India and Simon barged into the room. The respite when the doctor ordered them out didn't last long. They soon came crowding back in.

'Has the stuck-up old bastard gone for good? What a dickhead.' Margot grinned at Fergus and then started mimicking. 'It was all "If you'll excuse me", da de da de da, "in private", da de da de da. Just who the fuck does he think he is?'

Fergus couldn't bring himself to even look at Margot as he answered as forcefully as his aching body allowed. 'He's the surgeon who operated on me, that's who he is, a skilled and intelligent man who probably couldn't believe what he was hearing. Jesus, Margot have you no manners at all?' Fergus was incensed. 'And you, India, how dare you come in here behaving like a guttersnipe. I wish I'd never told any of you what was going on.'

Simon and India both laughed.

'Oooohh, hark at you, you big tart,' Simon sneered. 'Shame the bullet wasn't a bit higher. Like straight through your brain.' He glanced at Margot before carrying on. 'Oops, I forgot, you haven't got a brain apart from the one in your pants that comes to life for Latisha Lowe.'

'Margot, get him out of here, just get him out of here.'

'If it wasn't for him we wouldn't be here, he brought us.'

'That doesn't give him the right to behave like that . . .' Fergus's voice trailed off. His shoulder hurt like crazy, his head echoed as if it was being used as a drum, and he was feeling sick. 'India, can you call the nurse for me? I don't feel too good . . .'

India's face suddenly straightened and she ran from the room.

The nurse arrived, surveyed the situation and promptly started ushering the family out. 'That really is enough for one day. He's not too well and needs rest. I think you all ought to go home and keep in touch by phone.'

'But we've come all the way from London.'

The nurse smiled sympathetically. 'I know and I'm sorry, but first and foremost we have to consider Mr Pearson and his wellbeing, don't we? I'm sure you only want what's best for him and at the moment that's plenty of rest and recuperation.' And she firmly herded them all out.

Fergus suddenly opened his eyes wide. 'Hang on, I'd like India to stay, just India – if she wants to, that is. I need to talk to her alone. I'll send her home in a taxi later.'

'You can't do that,' Margot started, then decided against it. 'Oh, bollocks to you, I can't be arsed with all this. Come on, Si, let's get out of here. You too, India, out!'

The fifteen-year-old looked from one to the other. Fergus said nothing, not wanting to force her to choose between her parents but at the same time not wanting her to walk out on him. He knew that it was a defining moment in their relationship.

'I'm staying with Dad.'

Margot's eyes widened. 'In that case, don't bother coming back at all, you stupid little cow. You'll regret this, this pathetic little shit doesn't want you, never has, never will, he's just after the sympathy vote. You'll end up on the streets.'

'Whatever. Bye, Mum.' India's tone was one of disinterest but Fergus knew better.

Margot turned on her heel and, with a smug Simon in tow, left the room.

'She doesn't mean it, you know, your mum just flies off the handle and doesn't think about what she's saying.'

Trying to keep his voice light was difficult but he didn't want her to know how much he despised Margot for talking to her like that.

'I don't give a toss. She's always threatening to chuck me out but she never has – yet. Anyway, why did you want to talk to me? Got yourself a new girlfriend, have you?'

Fergus smiled sadly. 'I'd forgotten just how perceptive you can be, sweetheart. There's a good brain tucked away in there, it's a shame you don't let everyone know.'

'Yeah, right. Don't change the subject.'

Fergus looked hard at his daughter. The make-up was thick and the hair a mess but underneath it all was his daughter. India, the little girl he loved so much. She was sitting in the chair beside his bed with her knees pulled up. With a start Fergus realised that this was the closest he had been to his daughter both physically and emotionally for years. India hated any form of affection and would back off whenever Fergus reached out. Eventually he had just given up trying.

'You're right, India, I do have something to tell you but I want you to hear me out before you say anything at all, then after that you can ask whatever you like. Deal?'

'I suppose,' she muttered. 'But I don't want any crap about what a waste of space I am and what a mess I look.' India glared at him. 'You're always saying I'm clever and I'm pretty but I'm not, I'm thick as shit with a face like a pig and a huge arse but I'm quite good at covering it all up.'

'Whatever makes you say that? Where has this idea come from?' Genuinely bewildered, Fergus frowned at her.

'Because it's true. Mum and Simon are always telling me.'

Fergus needed time to think. The painkillers were wearing off and his shoulder throbbed so fiercely he could feel his concentration slipping.

'Darling, can you get the nurse for me again? The pain is coming back . . .'

Once more the nurse hurried in and then out again, to return with a small tray and a hypodermic syringe.

'I've sent your daughter up to the cafeteria for a while. Now let's see what we can do about this pain. Roll over for me, will you? Onto your good side.'

Fergus didn't feel a thing. As the nurse left the room he closed his eyes, and then opened them again when he felt a gentle tap on his hand, unaware that several hours had passed.

'Well, you needed that, didn't you?' The nurse was smiling down at him. 'I wanted to have a word with you before your daughter comes back in. I've been asked to tell you that Lucy Cooper has been taken to the maternity ward, she's in labour.'

Fergus tried to sit up but his body didn't want to function properly. 'I have to see her, I have to be with her.'

'Not a good idea at the moment, but if you leave it with me I'll see if I can sort out a wheelchair or something. I'm not sure but leave it with me. Also there was a phone call from a lady called Lorraine. She's on her way to see you.'

Fergus slumped into his pillows, it was all getting too complicated.

'When she gets here, can you send her straight to see Lucy? I have things to sort out with my daughter first.'

At that moment the door was pushed back.

'What have you got to sort out with me, Dad?'

'Your dad is worn out, dear,' the nurse said. 'It's been a long couple of days for him so it might be good if he didn't tire himself out any more than necessary. I can't be with him all the time so I'm going to have to trust you to keep an eye on him. Be patient with him and don't let him overdo it.'

Fergus waited until the nurse left.

'India, sweetheart, there's something I have to tell you.'

Lucy was frightened, really frightened, and her eyes were glued to the monitor beside the bed. Everything that had happened over the past months and days paled into insignificance compared to her fear of something happening to her baby. She wanted it safe and well and delivered only when it was due, not several weeks early.

The midwife had tried to reassure her that her situation was far from unusual. 'We've got a good strong heartbeat, no sign of distress and baby is quite a good size.' She took Lucy's hand and rubbed it gently. 'Chin up and we'll help you through it. Now I have to disappear for about an hour, my other mum is going to deliver any minute, but I'll be back.' Handing Lucy the buzzer, she smiled. 'There's always someone at hand if you ring the bell, so you're not on your own. Oh look, you've got a visitor.'

Lucy looked at the figure standing at the end of the bed holding a bunch of flowers and wearing a sheepish smile.

'Sadie!'

'Sorry, I know you said not to but I had to come, you

sounded so upset. I won't stop long. You don't mind, do you? I'll go if—'

'No. Please stay. Oh God, this is all going wrong, everything is going wrong. The baby's not due, it's going to die, I just know it, this is my punishment for not wanting it.' Lucy didn't want to cry but it was hard to stop her bottom lip and chin from trembling.

'Don't do that,' Sadie frowned, 'you look like a goldfish with indigestion. You have to relax and be happy and then you'll have a happy baby. If you're stressed you'll get a little sod who will pay you back by screaming for six months.'

'If it's OK I won't mind if it screams for ever.'

'Oh, I think you will, Lucy, I really think you may regret that comment.'

Lucy tried to smile. 'I've missed you.'

Sadie pulled a chair up to the bed. 'And I've missed you but now isn't the time for delving into anything deep and meaningful about anything. Let's just sit here and have a good old gossip to pass the time, just like we used to. Now, who shall we rip to shreds first?'

'Let's try Paul Gower.' Lucy looked sideways at Sadie. 'Your names have been linked, so I want to know how you hooked up with him and what's going on.'

'I wish, Lucy, I really wish but your Paul Gower doesn't go for the likes of me. He prefers tall, scrawny fashion plates who earn a bloody sight more than I'm ever likely to.' Sadie pulled a face. 'I think he's gorgeous and I don't understand how you let him slip through your fingers.'

'Paul didn't slip through my fingers, he was never there

in the first place. He's not my type at all. I agree he's not as bad as I thought he was but that's about it, and anyway—' Lucy stopped mid-sentence. 'Oh God, that was a big one! Sadie, what am I going to do if this all goes wrong? I'm so scared, I really want Fergus here with me.'

Sadie wasn't looking at her. 'You may not have Fergus but it looks as if you're going to have a girlie birthing session. Just look who else is here.'

Dressed down in faded jeans and totally clear of make-up, Lorraine was barely recognisable.

'Hi, everyone, have I missed much? Fergus has been unavoidably detained so he's sent me instead.'

Fergus and India were both in tears. He couldn't recall the last time he had seen his daughter cry and all he wanted to do was hug her close and make it all go away. But he couldn't.

'India, I'm sorry that you've found out like this but you had to know. I'm going to have to go and see her. So much has happened and the baby is coming early. Do you want to come as well?'

India looked up at him and Fergus could see that behind the façade was one very scared little girl who had just realised that her father really wasn't coming back to the family home.

'I hate you so much, I really hate you . . .' The venom was still there as she sobbed the words.

'I know that's how you feel at the moment and I don't blame you but I just want you to remember that whatever happens, I love you more than anything in the world and you'll always be my girl.'

'Supposing the new one is a girl, how will you feel then?' India challenged him.

'No different, I swear, no different at all. Now the nurse is going to wheel me over to the maternity ward. Do you want to go home now or wait for me to get back? I'd prefer you to stay a bit longer but it's your choice.'

'I'm going. I don't want to be here, I want to go back home even if you don't. You can go and visit your new family, you bastard!' India raised her arm and fisted her hand. For a split second Fergus thought she really was going to hit him and he automatically covered his bad shoulder with his other arm and closed his eyes.

The blow never came and as he opened his eyes he saw India disappearing out of the door.

'India,' he shouted, 'India, don't go, please.'

Footsteps headed in his direction, but it wasn't India, it was the nurse, pushing a wheelchair in front of her.

'Right, Mr Pearson, are you ready? I'm going to wheel you down and leave you there. When you want to come back, get them to call me, but do not get out of the chair and do not get over-excited. If you take a turn for the worse I shall be in big trouble!'

The rough white cotton blankets wrapped round his shoulders and over his legs made Fergus feel like an old man being taken out for a stroll in his bath-chair. He could just imagine the comments if Margot or Simon saw him, let alone India.

Fergus arrived just as Lucy was being taken into the delivery room, too confused to acknowledge him properly.

'You're in the nick of time,' said the nurse. 'Now don't forget to come back to the ward, will you, Mr Pearson? No jumping into the spare bed in here, it's strictly mums and babies only.'

Sadie and Lorraine beat a tactful retreat as both Lucy and Fergus were wheeled into the delivery suite.

Chapter Nineteen

'So, let me get this straight. What you're telling us, Paul, is that Lucy Cooper has had a baby. That she was pregnant when she went to Las Vegas and then disappeared to suburbia with Fergus the courier without a word to anyone.' For once it was Luke who was speaking and Caroline who was completely speechless.

'That's right.' Paul Gower smiled. 'Not only that, Don sent a couple of hired thugs round for a touch of armed blackmail and Fergus got shot. Lucy went into premature labour and is now in hospital on one ward with Fergus on another. Good story, huh?'

'How do you know all this, might I ask?' Luke's voice was disbelieving.

'Her best friend – you know we bumped into each other at Lucy's front door. Well, we've sort of kept in touch and she phoned me today with an update.'

Luke frowned. 'So everything was down to Donovan Cooper. Lucy was right about him. I'm not surprised she went on the run, I'm just hurt that she felt she couldn't confide in us, be honest, in fact.'

Caroline nodded. 'I told you what would happen so don't look all dejected and betrayed now. We should have sacked her way back when, that way we wouldn't have had all this disruption to cope with. I wonder if Lucy Cooper has any idea of the problems she's caused this firm, and as for you, Luke Pettit, you collected her from the airport and even went round there afterwards, how can you not have noticed a bloody great pregnancy?'

'I think you'll find that Lucy is well aware of everything that has happened to both her and us,' Paul interjected politely. 'Apparently she's mortified about the whole thing. She knows she's blown it for herself in the business. She had all the files ready to send to you but the little problem of a kidnapper with a gun got in the way. Sadie reckons they'll move well away and start afresh.'

'Good!' Caroline looked down at her desk and pretended to be engrossed in a piece of paper.

'Come on now, my darling, you know you don't mean that. The poor girl has been through a real trauma. I think we ought to go and visit her and still the waters of guilt.'

'You're mad!'

'I know.'

Paul looked from one to the other. 'Well, I'm off down there as soon as I finish. Apparently Latisha Lowe is there with her. A new friend of Lucy's. Sounds just up my street, a trendy and wealthy older woman, I've not had one of them yet.'

'Paul!' Caroline glared at him.

Luke grinned widely. 'Give her our love and tell her that we'll be in touch, firstly to see the baby and secondly for the belated feedback on the Vegas trip. Tell her there's no hard feelings and that we understand perfectly.'

'Huh,' Caroline grunted. 'By the way, what did she have?'

'A boy, five and a half pounds, very small but OK. They've called him Finbar. He's the spit of Fergus apparently, lots of thick dark hair.'

Neither of the men noticed as Caroline flicked a finger under her glistening eyes. She had thought that talk of pregnancies and babies didn't upset her any more, but suddenly it all came back to her.

'Excuse me, I have to go to the cloakroom.'

Pressing cool, damp tissue to her eyes, she remembered her own pregnancy. She wondered what would have happened if she had gone ahead with it. Would she have still met and married Luke or would she, at a very naïve seventeen, have struggled hopelessly with single mother-hood? She would never know; she had made her decision and had had to live with the consequences ever since.

Caroline knew that she could never penalise Lucy for deciding to go ahead with having her baby regardless of her situation or her career. She thought she might even offer her her old job back in time, after she had been seen to be hard as nails of course.

She wiped her eyes, adjusted her already immaculate clothing and marched back into the office with a purpose-ful expression pasted on her face. She had learned to live with the past a long time ago, but just occasionally it jumped up and bit her sharply.

'Isn't he beautiful?' Lucy gazed at her baby. There was no

doubt of his parentage. Finbar John was the son of Fergus.

'Yes he is, but now I really have to get Mr Pearson back to his own ward. They'll be thinking I've run off with him! He can visit again tomorrow.'

Fergus looked at Lucy and his son. The tiny baby reminded him so much of his daughter when she was born, the thick dark hair and soulful eyes that didn't look as if they belonged with a newborn.

He kissed them both and reluctantly let himself be taken back. His mind was on the baby, his son, so he didn't immediately notice the figure sitting cross-legged in the corridor.

'India?' he said when he saw her. 'I thought you'd gone home.'

'I couldn't go,' she mumbled. 'I had to stay. You didn't give me any money to get back.'

Although he knew that wasn't the reason, Fergus allowed his daughter the explanation. 'I'm pleased you're still here. Come back in with me and we'll sort something out.'

'Has the baby been born yet?'

'Yes it has. You have a little brother, his name is Finbar, after your granddad. He looks just like you did when you were born.'

'Poor little git!'

Lucy sank back against her pillows and let the conversation going on around her wash over her. Sadie and Lorraine were making cooing noises and getting positively clucky but Lucy felt removed from it all. The relief that all was well with the baby was tempered with the picture of the rest of her life stretching ahead of her, no career, no money, and still her parents didn't know any of it. Their first grandchild was lying in a cot beside her and they had no idea.

'I have to ring Mummy and Daddy, I have to tell them, it's not fair that they're not here to share it.'

Sadie looked surprised. 'Haven't you told them yet? Lucy, you are so bad. Do you want me to call them? Ask them to ring you here? I don't need to tell them what's happened. Just ask them to call.'

'It's difficult, they know nothing about Fergus, the baby, all the hoo-ha with Don and his henchmen. There's so much I haven't told them.'

'Well, now's your chance. Take my mobile out into the grounds and give them a call,' Lorraine joined in.

'Later, I'll do it later. I have to think of the right words.'

'OK, sweetie. Well, we're off and then you can get some sleep. Make the most of it while you have the chance. Sadie is coming back with me. Ring us tomorrow, or rather later today.' Lorraine air-kissed Lucy from a distance.

Sadie settled for a good old-fashioned bear hug. 'All forgiven?'

'Everything. The past is past, we've been friends for too long to bear grudges, either of us. Mind you, the future is a total shambles.' Lucy smiled. 'A shambles with a baby and no job or money between us.'

Lucy waited for the jibe about her parents' money but to her relief Sadie said nothing at all.

Sometime later, Lucy awoke with a start. She remembered Finbar and wondered vaguely why he had been silent.

Pulling herself up, she looked into the empty crib.

Don!

But then she spotted Fergus over by the window, a contented Finbar nestling in the crook of his good arm. Lucy heaved a sigh of relief and watched for a few seconds.

'One day, my son, all this will be yours.'

Lucy crept up behind him. 'Oh, that is such a cliché! All what?'

'Everything, anything, whatever he wants he can have.'

'If you get everything you want then it's not worth having.'

'If I didn't have a gammy arm I'd pull you towards me for a family bonding moment.' Fergus paused and looked down at her. 'We are a family, aren't we?'

Lucy smiled. 'Of course we are. Whatever happens I think we'll survive now, don't you?'

'Oh, I do. I do.'

Epilogue

The christening of Finbar John Pearson turned out to be a lavish affair with lots of big hats, enough champagne and smoked salmon for far more people than were present and much celebration.

Lorraine had pushed the boat out and insisted on holding the reception in her garden, which was decked out in blue balloons with huge blue overhead lights casting an eerie glow over the guests. In a figure-hugging white suit that emphasised her tan, and her hair swept up and held in place with white feathers, Lorraine looked just like the star she was.

The parents of the small guest of honour, Fergus and Lucy, were a little overshadowed by her but they didn't mind in the least because with his designer christening outfit and toothless smile, young Finbar was certainly in the spotlight.

Sadie, looking like the cat that had got the cream, had turned up with an immaculately dressed Paul Gower. Despite half-heartedly protesting about being 'just good friends', she stuck to him like glue. For his part, Paul looked surprisingly content with Sadie beside him but no one could quite take it seriously – apart from Lucy who thought they would be good for each other, providing, of course, Paul could curb his wandering eye.

Caroline Pettit, with a hat the size of a serving dish on her head, could have passed for a walking advertisement for Ralph Lauren and Jimmy Choo. She was happy at the prospect of Lucy returning to Pettit's but she continued to pretend to disapprove of Luke's decision. Lucy's apologies had further weakened her already wavering resolve to be unforgiving and she had agreed to a meeting. She had surprised herself by feeling almost maternal towards Lucy, and as for baby Finbar, she was silently besotted.

Luke, too, had brushed up quite well after Caroline had forcibly ripped his favourite old jacket off his back and persuaded him into a lounge suit. He pretended to accept responsibility for the decision to take Lucy back while fully aware that it was down to his wife really. He truly understood her.

India, trying hard to maintain an air of aloof boredom, looked almost conservative in black and white striped trousers and a white top, although the bare midriff and pierced belly button were on full display as a protest. She was wearing far less make-up than usual and her long dark hair was hanging free halfway down her back. Fergus, who had instigated his daughter's new appearance, had to be restrained from warning off the assorted young men from the world of public relations who were grouped around her.

George, meanwhile, brushed and polished to perfection,

was happily entertaining all the young women.

The rain had stayed away, the caterers had turned up on time and the gardener had done his work well the day before.

Far, far away from the celebrations, Don was still on remand and awaiting trial, as were Tony and his fellow gunman.

Jonno McMahon was believed to be in the Mediterranean after being released on bail, having decided against staying around while the police tried to pull together a case. Always brilliant at getting others to do his dirty work, it was proving very difficult to tie him into any of it.

Lucy's parents hadn't been able to get to the christening, in fact they hadn't been able to get over at all so their one and only grandchild was still a stranger to them. They were very apologetic and offered to put the cottage in Lucy's name as an investment and set up a trust fund for Finbar. Lucy accepted graciously and told everyone what kind and loving parents she had. No one, not even Sadie, contradicted her.

'That went well. Didn't it?'

'Mmmm. It was surprisingly intimate considering Lorraine had a hand in it. It worked really well. Do you know, India was almost civil to me? She seems quite taken with her baby brother.'

'She's been looking at old photographs and the likeness to her when she was a baby is amazing. It's going to take a while but I think the downward spiral has been halted, thank God.'

Fergus and Lucy and baby Finbar were back in Lucy's London flat.

'So what are we going to do next?' Fergus looked at Lucy, his face shadowed. 'There's still a lot to be resolved.'

'In the short term, Fergus? Nothing. We'll just bumble along as we are and enjoy Finbar. In the long term? We're going to be happy. I've decided.'

'You've decided, have you?'

'Yep. I've decided.'

'It seems I have no choice then. Happy it is.'